AMY LYNN

By Jack July

Dedication

Jennifer
My beautiful Wife
Thank you for allowing me to chase yet another crazy dream
I LOVE YOU!

Patrice Jones (PJ)
When the rest of the world was not interested,
You read my writings, chapter after chapter.
Thank You so much.

Stacy Robnolt and Annie Jackson.
Your inputs were as priceless as your friendship.

Ace of Spades HQ.Com
Thank you ron and ronnettes

Authors Note

My decision to write this book was motivated by watching President Obama hang the Congressional Medal of Honor around the neck of Staff Sergeant Salvatore Giunta. As the president read what he had done, I sat back and wondered., where do we get these kids? These wonderful, brave young men and women that put on a uniform and decide that their life is worth less than a brother or sister in arms or even the greater good?

I once heard the expression, "You are the sum of your experiences." OK, I can buy that. But I believe there is so much more. It isn't just the sum of your experiences but the experiences of those who have influenced you. What makes them who they are? I lived with my father for 18 years, never knowing much about him. He was not a good man and I never knew why. His actions and examples taught me to be less than honorable.

Throughout the years I have met people, wonderful people that stood by me when I was at my worst, when my life was at it's lowest. I often wondered who mentored them? Who made them who they are? Why would they waste time with me? But they did and I am a better man for it. I wanted to write all of these peoples' names down in a list. I'm sure, however, that they already know who they are. If I have shaken your hand and called you friend, you are one of them. Thank you, I love you.

This book is about a girl named Amy Lynn and those who loved her. She was exposed to both the best and worst of humanity. Her trials and travails are somewhat autobiographical in nature, though I will never disclose what is real and what is fiction. The charactors in this book are either real people or compilations of people from my life. I hope while reading this book you will think about those that love you, those that put themselves out for you. Then take the time to find out who and what shaped them because it will be worth your effort.

I am a math major. You will not need a thesaurus to read this, so just sit back and enjoy the story of Amy Lynn.

Chapter 1

Amy opened her eyes as Granny Patches' ole rooster woke her up like it did every morning. As she lay in bed she felt the warm breeze coming through the window; another hot August day had begun in Black Oak, Alabama. The house was eerily quiet. It had been six days since she heard her brother's closet door slide open, his chair squeak as he sat down to put on his socks and boots, his gentle steps as he walked to the side of her bed, and his whisper, "Amy, get up, let's go." She would never hear those words again.

Amy gently climbed out of bed. When she stood up she noticed her gown sticking to her back. *Sweat,* she thought. Nope, her little brother Joseph had peed the bed. She blamed herself. She knew she should have made him pee before he went to bed but there were so many visitors and so much going on, she forgot. She would add washing bed sheets to the day's chores.

Her boots, shirt, and bib overalls were left beside the bed. There was no sense in waking her little brother, so she carried her clothes to the bathroom to change. She thought about a bath but there was no point. She would just be getting dirty and sweaty, anyway. She would take a shower after her chores. She wiped herself down with a washcloth, got dressed, and went into the kitchen. The light switch was being stubborn again; she wiggled it around a little and...on.

What she saw was more proof that it all wasn't some bad dream. Stacks of pies, cakes, corn bread, and pans of biscuits covered the table and counter like it was the Braxton family reunion. She wanted to cry, but the tears were all gone, only a hollow, empty ache. She didn't feel like eating but she was thirsty. Orange Kool-Aid; Amy and her big brother Kerry drank it by the gallon and laughed at each other's orange mustaches. She opened the refrigerator but couldn't find it. The pitcher was somewhere behind the fried chickens, hams, bowls of mac and cheese, and collards. In the South, food is love and they all loved Kerry. A glass of water would have to do.

Ten steps down the back stairs. She counted them every day. The stars were disappearing in the glow of the rising sun. She never noticed that before as she was always too busy talking to Kerry. It was a long walk to the barn. It seemed much longer alone. For the past two years, Amy got up with him and helped the best she could. Kerry taught her how to throw chicken scratch, how to collect and wash the eggs, mix the milk for the calf, and shovel the manure. The work never bothered her, just as long as she could be close to him. He was her world and whether she knew it or not, she was his.

She flipped up the wooden latch and went inside the dark, old barn. The milk crate was right where she left it. It made a good stool so she could reach the pull string for the light. She would have to remember to ask her daddy to make the string longer. Something moved in the corner. It was Blackie. She walked to the corner, reached down, and picked up the four-footlong black snake. It didn't seem to mind. With her right hand holding his body and her left behind its head, she kissed it on the nose. "Hi Blackie," she sighed. Her hand slid down his belly and she noticed that he was pretty fat. Blackie ate the bad snakes and Amy appreciated it. She gently set the snake back down in the corner and it crawled behind the hay bales.

4

Amy thought she would start with the pigs. She pulled the lid up on the thirty gallon feed can to find it empty. *I should have asked Daddy to fill this up for me yesterday*, she thought. *Now I have to find another way.* She looked over at the pallet where the bags of feed were stacked. She tried to move one but at one hundred pounds it didn't move easy. A shadow in the doorway got her attention, then a voice.

"I figured I'd find you down here."

Amy knew that deep baritone voice. It was her uncle Jack. Jack pulled up the milk crate and took seat; he wanted to look at Amy eye to eye.

"Hi, Uncle Jack, whatcha doin' up already?" Jack was famous for sleeping late, his "job" kept him up most nights.

"Well, I ain't been to bed yet and I come to see what you were doin'. What *are* you doin'?" He laced his fingers together and stretched his arms out between his knees as he waited for an answer.

"Chores," she said proudly. "Animals to be fed and cleaned up after, eggs to be collected; just, chores."

Leon raises some good kids, he thought. "Amy, honey, I think me and your daddy can handle it," said Jack

Amy stood up straight with her chin raised and shoulders back. She spoke slowly and annunciated every word, "These were Kerry's chores, now they are my chores."

Uh oh, Jack thought, *she's stubborn like her momma.* "Amy, you are twelve years old. Nobody expects you to do all of this. Don't be in such a hurry to grow up. Be a little girl, at least for just awhile." He could not have expected what came next.

Amy cocked her head and crossed her arms not believing what she just heard. Anger began to well up inside and her words began soft.

"Little girl?" she whispered, "Little girl? Well, sir, let me tell you about this little girl."

She stepped to within a foot of his face, "When my momma died, Joseph was eighteen months old. This little girl took care of him, dressed him, changed his diapers, and wiped his little butt. I washed all of our clothes, cooked dinner, cleaned the house, and helped Kerry on the farm. I've been doin' it since I was seven years old. You want to show up now and tell me to be a little girl?"

Amy started to pace back and forth in the barn and began to get louder, "Daddy works seventy hours a week in that mine tryin' to pay off Momma's medical bills. Me and Kerry did it on our own. We didn't ask nobody for nothin' and I'm sure not askin' for it now. Go on, Uncle Jack," she pointed toward the door. "Git."

Amy pulled hard and slid the bag of feed off the pallet.

Jack tried to speak, "Amy, I..."

Amy turned it up another notch, "And another thing, I am sick and tired of that lazy Aunt Gloria and that busybody Aunt Sharon showin' up at the house at least once a week talking trash about my daddy." Amy changed her voice to a nasally mocking tone. "'It's a shame you kids have to live like this. Why can't Leon find a wife to take care of you kids?' Next time they show up here I'm runnin' 'em off. Aunt Gloria sits at our table stuffin' her fat face with food that I made for Daddy and the boys. They are starlings, Uncle Jack, starlings. They fly in, eat our food, crap all over everything, and leave. Yes, sir, next time they show up, I'm runnin' 'em off."

Jack was staring at the ground, his massive shoulders hunched. It had been awhile since he felt shame like this. He lived less than a mile away and never thought about these kids, what their lives were like without their momma and what all they were going through. He spent time with Kerry, but everybody wanted to spend time with Kerry. *I can fix that*, he thought.

Jack stood up straight, took a deep breath, and said, "I hear ya', Amy Lynn. Lock up the barn and let's go back to the house. We'll get your daddy up and talk about it."

Amy slowly stood up straight and faced Jack, her fists balled up to her side, and there they were—those big emerald green eyes and they were on fire. Jack hadn't seen eyes lit up like that in near fifteen years. They were her momma's. Then that voice again, like the low growl of a little dog that decided not to take any more beatings.

"You ain't listened to a word I said. No, sir, I will not."

Jack took a step back and for a moment he was silent. Then he smiled, or at least the parts of his face that still worked smiled. He looked down and thought, *Oh shit, another Braxton.* Jack walked over to the pallet and picked up the bag of feed. Reaching into his pocket he pulled out his knife, cut the top off of the bag, and dumped it in the bin. In a soft voice he said, "You reckon I could help?'"

Her rage began to slowly drain away. She looked up at Jack and with a stern voice said, "Yes, sir, but just help."

An hour later they left the barn, walked down the short side of the hollow, and began the climb toward the house. Amy stopped, looked up at her uncle Jack, and said, "I'm sorry I yelled at you like that. I hurt inside. I hurt real bad."

Jack stared at her for a few seconds then reached down, picked her up, and, surprised by how heavy she was, he let out a little grunt. He kissed her on the cheek and said, "We all get to the other side of enough, honey. I understand, I miss him, too."

He set her down and they continued up the hill. Jack looked at her and said, "That starling thing. Kerry said that, didn't he?" She looked up sheepishly and said, "Yeah." Jack laughed and replied, "Well, honey, he wasn't wrong."

Chapter 2

$\mathcal{A}$my walked through the back door followed by her uncle Jack. Joseph was already up. Amy could hear the cartoons in the living room. She thought about what to feed him for breakfast, and then she saw the spoon sitting in the pecan pie plate. The boy was up to no good already. Daddy would want to eat, he liked little ham and biscuit sandwiches and she had plenty of both. She put on a pot of coffee and in the distance heard, "LEEONNN, GET UP. Amy's got coffee for us."

Leon answered back, "Alright, Cuz, I'll be up in a minute."

Leon put on a t-shirt and some bibs and walked into the living room. He tussled Joseph's hair and said, "Good morning."

Joseph answered back, "Good morning, Daddy," without taking his eyes off Scooby-Doo.

Leon walked in the kitchen rubbing his forehead. Jack chuckled and said, "Boy, your head looks like it wore out three bodies." Leon bent down and gave Amy a hug and kissed her on the head, looked at Jack, and said, "Well, I guess that's what I get for passin' the jar with you."

Amy, standing amongst the stacks of food, looked up at her daddy and said, "Daddy, what do I do with all this food?"

"Well, Amy, what would Jesus do? Granny Patches would probably appreciate somethin', your uncle Jack and Carla Jo would probably take a little, too."

"Mmmph," Uncle Jack grunted while nodding his head and shoving ham and biscuit sandwich number three in his mouth. "Don't forget those Hatfield boys. No tellin' the last time they had a decent meal."

Amy scrunched up her face, "Daddy, them boys are strange."

"Maybe," her daddy replied, "but you'd be strange too if you lived their life."

Jack motioned his head to the front door. Leon nodded and told Amy they were going to sit out on the front porch. Leon opened the front door and felt the breeze that was coming from the south right through Granny Patches' lilacs. Leon tilted his head back and took a deep breath. Then he looked over at Jack and said, "They won't be able to put anything in a can that smells like that. Katherine helped her plant all them bushes."

They sat on the rockers across from each other. Jack, Leon's cousin and best friend, slid to the edge of the seat and said, "I'm sorry, Leon."

"Bout what, Cuz?"

"You and the kids are the only family that I have. I should have done more to help after Katherine died. Now Kerry? I can't imagine how you feel. Just know I'm here for ya'."

Amy bumped the door open and handed a cup of coffee to Jack and her daddy. She then ran back inside only to return moments later with a plate of ham and biscuit sandwiches for her daddy. "Daddy, I'm gonna divide up that food. Uncle Jack, do you want anything special?"

"Whatever you do is fine with me, just make sure I get one of those pecan pies," Jack smiled and winked as Amy walked back inside. He took a sip of coffee, sighed, and said, "Look, I'm not telling you your business. you got some good kids, so you're doin' somethin right. It's Amy, ya' know, she's a girl. She needs a woman to talk to. Someone to teach her about, ya' know, women things."

Leon nodded, let out a deep sigh, and said, "Yeah, I know."

"I was thinkin' that maybe she could spend some time at the house with me and Carla Jo. Carla Jo's a classy woman; she could teach her some girl things. Free ya' up for time with Joseph, whatever."

Leon knew Jack was trying to help. Problem was, Leon had spent the last six days barraged by friends and family with friendly advice, all wanting to help. He'd about had enough. "Jack, I've just lost my son and I'm not feeling too good about my ability to be a daddy. Do you think we can have this conversation another time?"

Jack bowed his head and said, "I'm sorry, Cuz. I'm no good at this."

"Yeah, ya' are," Leon assured him. "You're here."

Both men looked up as they heard the sound of gravel crunching under tires and watched as a police cruiser parked in front of the house. It was Sheriff Gene Carter.

Leon got up and stuck his head in the door of the house and hollered, "Amy, would you bring Sheriff Carter a cup of coffee, and wrap up one of them pies and stick it in his car?"

"Yes, sir," Amy yelled back.

Like his daddy and his granddaddy, Gene Carter was the much-loved Sheriff of Jackson County. Locals referred to him as Sheriff Teddy Bear. At six-foot-seven and three hundred pounds, he was an imposing figure. He played offensive tackle for Auburn while earning his criminal justice degree. "Southern gentleman" would describe him best: polite, mild mannered, and kind. it was said he could charm the rattles from a snake. He grew up in Black Oak and had great respect for the culture of the community. Because of that he turned a blind eye to the moonshine stills a couple of the families still operated. He never carried a gun, at least that anyone could see. In the trunk of his car, however, was an arsenal that would make a third world dictator jealous. There were two things that Sheriff Carter took particular umbrage to: harming a child and dealing drugs. Participating in either of these activities would place you in the company of the unfortunate few that watched Sheriff Teddy Bear turn into Sheriff Grizzly Bear.

Sheriff Carter walked a slow walk to the porch. This part of his job was never easy and he dreaded it. He stopped at the bottom step and looked up at Leon and Jack. "Gentlemen," he said in a forceful, business like tone.

Jack and Leon politely replied, "Sheriff."

"I'm here on business, Leon. I have Kerry's autopsy report,"

Leon took a sip of coffee and said, "He drowned in that damned old river, what else is there to know?"

The door swung open and Amy appeared with a cup of coffee, "Milk and two sugars right, Sheriff Teddy Bear?"

Sheriff Carter smiled, took the coffee, and set it on the porch rail. He bent down and scooped up Amy, giving her a big hug and a little peck on the cheek, and said, "Yes, ma'am, that's exactly right." Sheriff Carter adored children, especially the Braxton children.

After gently setting Amy down, he spoke seriously to Leon. "That's not all there is to it," he said. "You can read about it or I can just tell you."

"So, tell me," Leon spoke with a heavy sigh.

The sheriff motioned his head toward Amy as if to say, "Are you sure you want her to hear this?"

"Go ahead Sheriff, it's fine," said Leon.

The sheriff pulled the report out of the envelope and began to read, "Numerous bite marks on the victim suggests that he came in contact with a nest of *Agkistrodon piscivorus*. The victim went into shock and then drowned."

"Aga what?" asked Leon.

"Cottonmouths," the sheriff clarified.

"Oh shit," whispered Jack under his breath.

"I knew it!" exclaimed Amy. "I knew it was something else. My brother could have swam the length of that river!"

Sheriff Carter sat down on the porch swing and leaned back. Amy sat down beside him. Gene could see the pain on Leon's face.

Sheriff Carter had brought news of tragedy to several families during his career. He couldn't remember being this personally affected.

Jack looked over at Sheriff Carter and watched his features soften and his body slouch. The sheriff changed into Gene. Gene took his job seriously, almost as seriously as he took his friends, and the three men had been friends since childhood. Gene Carter lifted the radio from his belt and called, "Dispatch, this is Sheriff Carter."

"Go ahead, Sheriff."

"I'll be out until this afternoon. Please send my calls to Deputy Nolan," requested Gene.

"Yes, sir, Sheriff."

Chapter 3

$\mathcal{A}$my leaned back in the swing behind Gene, hidden from her dad and Uncle Jack. She hoped that they would forget she was there. She loved listening to the men talk.

Gene looked over at Leon and said, "You know, I've been helping Coach Ramsey for quite a few years now. I really think Kerry had a shot to play college ball. He had great instincts; it was like he knew what was coming before the ball was snapped."

Jack nodded in agreement and said, "I was at the homecoming game when they played Castle Rock. Three sacks, two interceptions, and eleven solo tackles. The boy just took over the game. I never stood up to cheer about anything before, but watching him play I just couldn't help it."

Leon looked away wistfully and spoke quietly, "You know, I missed that game. I had to work. Coach Ramsey invited me to the schoolhouse the following Monday to watch the film with him. It was something else. I was so proud of him."

"You know there were scouts from several college programs that were interested in him. Scouts throughout the SEC saw the film of that game," said Gene.

"How do you know that?" Leon asked.

"Cause I sent it to 'em," Gene replied.

They all laughed. It was the first time Jack had seen Leon smile in a long time.

Jack looked at Leon and said, "You know that boy could hunt, too. Him and that friend of his, Rob. Every year they brought back some of the biggest bucks in the county. Last year he come up the driveway with a ten pointer; drug my ass out of bed to show me. I told him, 'Damn boy, save some for the rest of us.'"

Leon smiled and said, "He wasn't really my son, he was his granddaddy's boy. When Kerry was three years old, Daddy showed up on the front porch, told Katherine he was takin' him for a walk in the woods, and for the next six years we hardly saw him. Pissed Katherine off something terrible. When Kerry was about six, Katherine put her foot down and said Kerry was going to stay home with the family. Kerry started screamin' and didn't stop for two days. We tried bribin' him, whoopin' his ass, and everything else we could think of. After a broken table, a broken lamp, and cuts and bruises from throwin' himself on the floor, Katherine gave up. She was in tears when she called Daddy to come get him. Daddy ended up talkin' to Kerry about how important his momma and family were. We actually saw him a little more after that. I never much minded. I kinda liked him spendin' time with his grandaddy. I was workin' so damn much back then. I know if she would have just talked to Daddy instead of being a hard ass about it, I'm sure they could have worked it out. But Katherine had her way and that was that."

Leon looked around Gene to Amy and said, "Would you bring the coffee pot out here?"

"Yes, sir," Amy said as she disappeared into the house.

Jack chuckled and said, "Sounds like another green-eyed girl I knew."

Leon smiled and nodded his head.

Jack looked at Leon and said, "You know, Hillbilly Jesus had that effect on more than just Kerry."

Leon narrowed his eyes at Jack and said, "You know I don't like it when you call Daddy that."

Gene spoke up and said, "Well hell, Leon, he damn near was. Where he walked, men wanted to follow. When he spoke, men listened and if you messed with him, he would smite you."

Leon shook his head and scoffed, "Smite? I don't think so."

Gene's eyes got serious and he replied, "Yeah, smite. Ask the Gossets and those McCutcheons."

"Wives' tales," Leon muttered.

Gene, in a serious tone, said, "When my daddy had to cut down dead bodies hangin' in a tree, that's not a wives' tale. You were a little boy, that was all kept from you."

Jack nodded and said, "My daddy told me some stories about his brother-in-law, Marcel. He wasn't to be crossed."

The screen door slowly swung open and Amy came out with the coffee pot in one hand and a bag in the other. She sat the coffee by her daddy and put the bag in the front seat of the sherrif's car.

Gene said, "What's in the bag, Amy?"

Amy smiled and said, "Sweet potato pie."

Gene looked at Leon and said, "Can I keep her?"

Amy sat back down next to Gene on the swing and said, "Kerry taught me how to hunt."

"He did?" replied Leon.

"Yes, sir," Amy replied. "Joseph stayed with Granny Patches and he took me with him. He taught me how to shoot a rifle. His friend Rob said I was a natural. You wanna see, Daddy?"

Jack said, "Sure, show us what you got."

Then Amy stared at her daddy and waited for final approval. He nodded. Amy jumped off the swing excitedly and said, "Be right back."

Amy ran to the kitchen and grabbed a pie plate. She went out the back door and ran to the fence line east of the house. She slipped the edge of the pie plate into a split on top of a fence post and ran back into the house. She then went into Kerry's room and pulled a fifteen round clip out of his desk drawer. After taking three rounds out of the ammo box, she snapped them in the clip and shoved the clip into her pocket. Lastly, she went into the closet and pulled out Kerry's .30 Caliber Carbine.

Amy told Joseph to go stand by Daddy and headed out the front door.

"Now that's a rifle!" said Gene.

"Ah, Amy, where is the twenty-two?" Leon asked.

"In Kerry's room," Amy replied matter-of-factly.

"Why don't you use that instead?"

"Cause I learned to shoot with this. Besides, a twenty-two is a varmint gun. Can't kill a deer with it."

"This should be good," whispered Jack to Leon.

They all got up, walked into the front yard, and stood behind Amy.

"Where's your brother?" asked Leon.

"Right behind you, Daddy," said Joseph.

Amy reached in her pocket and pulled out earplugs. While putting them in her ears, she said, "Kerry said you should know where everyone is, you should know what's behind your target, and you should protect your ears."

Amy walked past the edge of the house, licked her finger, and stuck it in the air. Then she walked back to the front of the house, reached in her pocket, and pulled out the clip. She turned the rifle to its side, stuck in the clip and slapped it hard.

"What are you shooting at?" asked Jack.

"That pie plate over on the fence post," Amy replied.

"Where?" asked Gene.

Jack pointed toward the fence line, "Way over there."

Gene arched his eyebrows skeptically as Amy jacked a round into the chamber and sat down on the grass. She tucked her right leg under her butt and stuck her left knee up in front of her. She rested the forestock on her knee, reached up to the rear sight, and gave the windage a click. She looked through the sights and then, with her index finger, clicked off the safety. Jack watched her chest expand as she took a deep breath and then began to let it out. The rifle let out a loud crack and they all watched as the pie plate fell off the fencepost.

Amy clicked the safety on, removed the clip, and jacked the live round out of the chamber. She stood up, handed the rifle to her daddy, picked up the live round, and stuck it and the clip in her pocket before running off across the field to get the pie plate.

"I had no idea she could do that,"said Leon, astonished.

"One shot? I'm not sure I could that," Gene marveled.

"Looks like you got yourself a little sniper. That's about 130 yards with iron sights into a nine-inch target. That's not easy," Jack said to Leon.

"Well, Leon, looks like you got yourself a huntin' buddy," said Gene.

They all walked back to the porch except for Joseph, who ran down to the barn to get his bicycle. Leon set the rifle in the corner against the rail and sat down.

"It looks like Kerry was a good teacher, too. That was a military shootin' position. Kerry must have got that from Marcel," said Jack.

Amy climbed back on the porch holding the pie plate. She looked a little disappointed. "I missed, Daddy. I hit the top of the post right below it and that's what knocked it off."

"So you were six inches off center from one hundred and thirty yards? If it was a deer, you wouldn't have had to chase it far, Amy," Jack replied.

"Honey, that was a fine shot. This fall I'll take you huntin' and we'll get you your first deer," Leon assured her.

"I got that last year huntin' with Kerry and Rob, a six pointer," Amy said proudly.

Leon thought to himself, *My God, I don't know anything about this girl.*

Jack noticed Leon's bewilderment and changed the subject, "Which one of those girls here yesterday was Kerry's girlfriend?"

"I'm not sure," Leon admitted. "He brought that Cole girl around here, Marilyn, I think was her name. Kerry said she was just his friend. It's sad he will never know true love, never get married or have kids. He would have been a great Daddy."

They sat on the porch and talked for a few more hours about Kerry. Lunch time rolled around and the men raided the leftovers. When they finished eating, Leon told Gene and Jack that he had to go back to work tonight and needed some sleep. Leon thanked the sheriff for his visit and walked him to his car. Amy went back inside to get the food she packed for Jack.

Leon walked back to the porch as the sheriff drove away. Jack looked at Leon and said, "She's Marcel."

"What?" asked Leon.

"She's just like Marcel. Daddy used to talk about Marcel all the time. How they were when they were kids. Even growin' up with that mean ass Daddy, Marcel was always a good person, smart and not scared of shit."

Leon shrugged and said, "Well, that's her momma, too."

Jack said, "Yeah, I suppose. My offer still stands. I'd bet Carla Jo would enjoy time with her."

Leon looked at the ground and said, "Yep, I think we will have to make that happen. Thank you, Jack, for everything."

In an extremely rare moment, Jack hugged Leon. Jack didn't hug other men, but it just seemed right. He turned to walk toward his truck when Amy came bursting through the door.

"Wait, your stuff!" yelled Amy.

"Thanks, hon, I almost forgot," Jack said. He set the bags in his truck and hugged Amy. "I'll see you tomorrow morning," he said with a smile.

"Bright and early, Uncle Jack," Amy reminded him.

"Yes, ma'am," Jack replied. He fired up his truck and drove away.

Amy looked at her daddy and asked, "What did he mean when he said I was like Granddaddy?"

"That's just Uncle Jack talkin', don't mind him," said her daddy.

"What was Grandaddy like?"

"That would take a long time to explain. I'll tell you what, next time we go fishin', and I mean soon, I'll tell you all about your granddaddy. For now, I have to get some sleep. Wake me up at nine," her daddy told her.

"I love you, Daddy,"

"I love you too, Amy."

The Story of Marcel Braxton

In June of 1932, Marcel Braxton was born. He was the youngest of three brothers that were born to Lethal and Gertrude Braxton. Lethal was King of the River Rats, a moonshiner and outlaw. He was a hard and dangerous man. He didn't mind killing people that got in his way, but he preferred to torture them. His reputation as a violent man kept him safe from challenges to his authority. He was good with a knife and many who crossed him wore the scars. He ran his business with an iron fist, and his wife and children were not immune to his violence.

As a child, Marcel stayed around the house with his momma. He helped her in the garden, learned to cook and sew, and went to the little schoolhouse for his lessons. He was a nice kid, a happy kid, and a joy to his mother until he was eight years old. That was when he was supposed to help his older brothers and they used him as a pack mule, hauling bags of corn and sugar to the stills. He was not mean by nature, but during that time he learned to call it up when he needed it. While dealing with his abusive brothers, there were times when he needed it. His middle brother Jimbo was particularly hard on him both verbally and physically. On day Marcel had enough. When they returned to the house, Marcel went into the kitchen and retrieved a rolling pin. He stood on a chair inside the entrance to the kitchen and waited for Jimbo to walk through. When he did, Marcel hit him on the top of his head so hard that blood shot up to the ceiling. He knew his daddy was gonna beat him but much to his surprise, he did not. Marcel's daddy told Jimbo he deserved what he got and that he had better never lay another hand on Marcel.

When Marcel was seventeen, the feds arrested him while he was tending one of his daddy's stills. The judge gave Marcel a choice: the military or prison. Marcel chose the US Marines. The Marine Corps loved those southern boys fresh out of the woods. They were easy to train, not afraid of spiders and snakes, rarely got lost, and they could knock a pimple off a gnat's ass at one hundred yards with most any weapon you gave them. They made Marcel a sniper and one year later he was fighting for his life in the Chosin Reservoir. Marcel earned a silver star, two bronze stars, and a purple heart. Marcel never spoke of the war to anyone. He came home a very different man. On the battlefield he promised Jesus he would live a godly life if he survived. He did his best to keep that bargain.

Marcel took the money he had saved while in the marines and built a house up on String Hill Road. He married his sweetheart, Jennie Lee Murphy, when she was 16 and he was 21. Old Man Murphy did not approve of the marriage. The Braxton family name was not a good one. They were known as outlaws and moonshiners. He didn't want his daughter in that family. Jennie's daddy sent his oldest son to bring her home. When Jennie's brother Bobby showed up and demanded she come home with him, Marcel walked out on to the front porch with a shotgun. As Bobby turned to run, Marcel filled his ass with birdshot. The message was sent. Marcel Braxton, like his daddy, was not to be trifled with.

Lethal Braxton drove up to Marcel's house about a week later. He told Marcel he needed to "get his ass back to the river" and help his family with the business. Marcel refused, things got heated, and they got into a fight. Marcel started to get the best of him when Lethal pulled a knife. Jennie knew Lethal's reputation and had already retrieved a rifle to protect Marcel. Jennie Lee sent a rifle shot past Lethal's head and told him the next one was going in his eye. Marcel told Lethal if he ever saw him on that hill again he would kill him. Lethal laughed and said, "I guess I raised you right."

Marcel never saw his daddy again.

A hard man not afraid of hard work, Marcel took a job in the coal mines. He worked every day except Sunday. On Sunday morning you would find him in the front row of the Black Oak Baptist Church. He didn't touch alcohol and he didn't smoke, but he did enjoy a chaw of Red Man chewing tobacco. If he wasn't working, he was farming, and if he wasn't farming, he was hunting or fishing. It was not unusual for Marcel to drop off a bag of groceries to a struggling family, help tend a farm when a family member was sick, or show up with tools to repair a home, car, or tractor. There was no need to ask; folks just looked up and there he was.

Jennie Lee gave birth to four children. The first, Gerald Wayne, died of pneumonia when he was a baby. Then came Gloria Jean, Leon James, and Sharon Marie. Marcel was hard on his kids; he expected much of them. Marcel left school in the third grade. He couldn't read or write and regretted it every day, so he demanded his children get the education he couldn't have. When they got home from school they worked the farm. On Sundays the kids were in a church pew and dressed in their finest clothes.

They did have their fun. Marcel took them to the river to fish and camp, and they got to spend the rest of their lazy Sundays at the swimming hole out behind their Uncle Herman's house. As strict as he was, he still let his kids be kids. Marcel's teachings to his children had one over riding theme: the survival of the family. He understood that evil showed it's ugly face when and where you least expected it.

In 1960, Lethal and his wife mysteriously died in a house fire. Marcel's two brothers also turned up missing, never to be heard from again. Overnight, Hank Gosset became the head River Rat. He took over the entire liquor manufacturing and distribution network along with gambling and prostitution. Sheriff Franklin Carter went to see Marcel as it was rumored that Marcel would seek vengeance against the Gosset clan. Much to Sheriff Carter's surprise, Marcel said, "I ain't seen them people in years. They brought it all on themselves; it ain't nothing to me."

Sheriff Carter was relieved; the last time a war broke out over moonshine distribution, twelve people were killed, one of them being Sheriff Eugene Carter, Franklin's daddy. Hank Gosset did not see Marcel's lack of need for revenge for what it was, however. He mocked him behind his back and called him a coward. When word got back to Marcel he just smiled and shrugged his shoulders, which was just his way.

When Lethal Braxton ran his operation, he kept it down by the river and in the camps, away from the good people of the surrounding counties. Hank Gosset didn't see it that way. He didn't care about the community, he cared about money. He opened several "private clubs" throughout Jackson, Sibly, and Shelby counties. Crime began to infect some of the peaceful family communities. The people complained to the county sheriffs but on the surface they were just clubs; nothing illegal was happening. The local Baptist Ministers Association had several discussions about the increasing crime and corruption of the children. Drugs and alcohol began to show up in the high schools. They all agreed something had to be done, but no one could agree on what that something was. They must have prayed real hard, though, because something happened that would shake much of central Alabama for decades to come.

Jennie Lee went to the grocery store in Lewistown every Friday when Marcel got off work. On this day her car wasn't running right, so she took Marcel's old truck. While backing out of a parking space at the grocery store, Jennie's foot slipped off the clutch and she rammed into a pretty red Thunderbird driven by Stevie Gosset. Stevie was his daddy Hanks favorite, a sadistic, spoiled little bastard that had a reputation for hurting people. Despite the early hour, Stevie and his friend Joe McCutcheon had already been drinking and as Jennie got out of the car, apologizing profusely and promising to fix his car, Stevie looked at the damage and screamed, "LOOK WHAT YOU DID!" He grabbed Jennie by the hair, dragged her to the back of the car, and pushed her face against the damage. Before Jennie could speak or defend herself, he slammed her head against the car. He let go of her hair, slammed her to the ground, and began to kick her. A couple of men tried to come to her aid, but Joe pulled a pistol and fired a shot into the air. Stevie kicked her 'til she stopped moving, and then he jumped in his car and backed out, running over Jennie's leg and breaking it. It was said that they were laughing as they left the parking lot.

Marcel looked up from under the hood of Jennie's car as Sheriff Carter and Brother Taylor pulled into the driveway. He stared at Sheriff Carter in disbelief while he told Marcel exactly what happened. After he finished, Marcel asked him, "Did you call the Murphys?"

The Sheriff said that Jennie's parents, the Murphys, had been contacted and were on their way to the hospital.

"Good," Marcel said. "Thank you, Sheriff."

Brother Taylor offered to pray with Marcel, but Marcel stoically turned away and walked back toward the house. Sheriff Carter felt a cold chill. Something bad was coming, real bad.

Sheriff Carter rounded up his deputies and spent the rest of the day and into the night looking for Stevie and Joe with no success. What he didn't know was that Marcel had gotten to them first. He had burned the car and left their cut up bodies hanging in the tree next to it.

Word spread like wildfire about the attack on Jennie Lee and the heinous deaths of Stevie and Joe. As predicted, Hank Gosset and Old Man Joe McCutcheon swore vengeance on Marcel and his family. Gosset spent Saturday calling up some of the most violent men in central Alabama. He was offering two hundred dollars a man. Gosset got his crew together, about forty men. On the other side of the county another gathering was taking place, an impromptu meeting of the Baptist Ministers Association.

Sheriff Carter didn't bother asking Marcel what happened, he already knew, and in so far as Sheriff Carter was concerned, he was well within his rights. Sheriff Carter got wind of what Gosset had planned. He went up to Marcel's house to offer him protection. Marcel turned it down; he would stand alone. As Sheriff Carter drove away from Marcel's, he was still trying to figure out a way to help him. Driving down the hill he saw a line of cars coming toward him that stretched over a quarter mile and was led by Brother Taylor, president of the Baptist Ministers Association. In less than an hour, over a hundred armed men and four preachers converged on the hill.

Across town, Hank Gosset stood on the back of a truck and told his men what he had planned. What Hank failed to recognize was that many of those men knew and liked Marcel and hated Stevie. After learning of Hank's plan and the intended victim, over a dozen men handed Hank back his money, got in their cars, and drove to Marcel's to stand with him. One by one the crew Gosset put together walked away until it was just Hank and Old Man Joe. The truth about Hank and Joe is the truth about most men of their ilk: they were badasses as long as they had the advantage. They were not about to face Marcel alone.

When word got out that there would be no retribution, the ministers took the opportunity to go one step farther. On Sunday morning, twenty-two congregations did not meet in their sanctuaries. The ministers led them to sixteen "private clubs" and honkey tonks, most owned by Gosset but some not. Voices were raised and hymns sung to Jesus as they burned those places to the ground. After the services, the crowds reached a fever pitch as they demanded to go to the river and burn the camps. The ministers quelled that impulse. They had purged their communities of the dens of iniquities without firing a shot; going to the river would not have the same result.

On Monday morning Brother Taylor drove, by himself, to the river to see Hank Gosset. He let him know in the flowery terms of an old southern minister that if there was any retribution against Marcel, the camps would burn. Hank Gosset believed him.

Marcel was seen as the man that single-handedly brought the criminals to their knees in central Alabama. One of the River

Rats referred to him as "Hillbilly Jesus" and it stuck. Marcel was offered jobs, local political office, and the presidency of his Miners Union Local, among other things. He wanted none of it. He nursed his wife back to health and returned to the simple life he loved. He didn't agree with nor embrace his notoriety. In reality, all he had done was kill two men that almost beat his wife to death, but in the end, legend crushes reality and the legend of Marcel Braxton was born.

In 1988, Marcel and his best friend Larry Tilly were killed in a mining accident. Over two thousand came to the funeral including several politicians, not because they knew him but because they knew the legend. Hank Gosset paid for the headstone. Over time, Marcel and Hank made peace and even went fishing together a few times. Hank mourned the loss of his son, but he had sense enough to know that Stevie was responsible for his own death. Old Man Joe McCutcheon, on the other hand, never let it go. On his deathbed he made his children swear revenge on the Braxton name.

Six months after Marcel was buried, Jennie Lee died in her sleep. Doctors could not find a cause. It was suggested to be grief. It was rare, but she wasn't the first person to die of a broken heart.

Before he died, Marcel had helped his son, Leon, build a small house across the road from his. When Jennie died, Leon paid his sisters for their share of the land and moved his family into Marcel's house. Larry Tilly and his wife Deloris had no children and after Larry died, she couldn't maintain the farm. She sold it and Leon moved her into his old house. Deloris helped Katherine with the kids. When needed, she sewed patches on to their old worn play clothes. Kerry called her Granny Patches.

Chapter 4

Uncle Jack kept his word to Amy. Every morning at 5:30 he was at the barn to help her. Even though it was clear within a few days that she could handle all the chores on her own, he continued to come because he enjoyed her company. They talked about hunting, fishing, the family, and whatever else came up. After awhile Jack began to forget she was twelve as she had a mature manner and common sense. Some would say she was smart and yes, she was, but it was more; it was the speed at which she learned.

Jack asked Carla Jo if she would spend some time with Amy. It had been a long while since she had spent any time with her at all. Haunting memories of Katherine's death kept her away from the Braxton home. Carla Jo was hesitant at first. She never had children of her own and besides that, her life was full. Her job was demanding and had brought her high visability and respect in the community. But more important to her was nurturing the strong, loving relationship she had with Jack. Because of that, respecting Jack's wishes was also important to her. Carla Jo understood that being the woman in a adolescent girl's life was a big responsibility. Escorting a young girl through the pitfalls of her teen years was challenging and at times, emotionally draining. It was clear that

Jack did not understand what he was asking of her. Establishing a relationship with a child was a full time responsibilty. Carla Jo gave it much thought, but in the end it wouldn't matter. It was what Jack wanted, so she would do her best.

Carla Jo didn't think Amy had ever traveled past Lewistown and she was right. There was really no need. Everything she needed was in Black Oak. Her family, friends, church, and school were all right there. She was extremely sheltered. Other than the little things she picked up from her friends at school, Amy was ignorant of pop culture. There was a television in her house, but Amy didn't watch it. There really was no time. She would play the radio as she worked in the house and she listened to what she remembered her momma listening to, old country music. It gave her good memories of her momma singing along with Patsy Cline, Dolly Parton, and Loretta Lynn.

Where to begin, Carla Jo thought to herself. In a few weeks school would start. Junior high would be far different than anything Amy was used to. Carla Jo would start there. Sunday after church Cala Jo invited Amy for lunch. They walked into a bedroom that she had converted into a library. Hundreds of books lined the walls. There were two big chairs in the room and she invited Amy to sit down in one of them so they could talk.

"Did you read all of these?" asked Amy.

"Yes, some two or three times," Carla Jo replied.

Wow, that's a lot of readin', Amy thought.

Carla Jo continued, "I love to read. Books let you meet people you have never met, take you to places you have never been, and teach you things you might never have learned. My favorite thing is that you can read people's thoughts. You learn the why. Why did this person do that?"

"I read in school. I liked *Treasure Island.* I really like books about animals. Most of the time they tell you what to read. It's read this, write about it, who, what, when, where…it's just borin'," Amy admitted.

Carla Jo walked around the room looking for something. "I think you would like this," she said as she pulled a book from the shelf and handed it to Amy.

"*Rikki-Tikki-Tavi* by Rudyard Kipling," Amy read. She opened the inside cover, which read, "To Annette, Love Daddy."

"Who's Annette?" Amy asked.

"Annette is someone I used to know. Read it and bring it back. We'll talk about it. If you like this book, if you really enjoy reading it, I'll find you another," Carla Jo offered.

They walked back to the kitchen and sat down to eat. Amy started to notice things about Carla Jo. First of all, she had an accent. The way she spoke was like the woman on the TV news. She used words that Amy had never heard before. But it was more than that. The way she moved was like a cat. When she picked something up she didn't grab it, she reached out to touch it and it sort of floated. When she sat down she was gentle, like a butterfly landing on a flower. Amy had never seen another woman that looked like her. She had long, straight, coal black hair and her eyes looked like the Chinese people she had seen in movies at school. Her skin was caramel colored, not like most black women. Her lips were full and her teeth were perfect and white.

She's beautiful, Amy thought.

"How old are you, Aunt Carla Jo?"

"That's not something that should be asked of a woman, or answered by a woman," Carla Jo replied with a slight smile.

"I'm sorry, I didn't mean nothin' by it," said Amy.

"Don't be sorry Amy, that's not what our relationship is about," she said. Then she replied, "I am forty-four."

Amy grinned and, holding her spoon like a shovel, slurped down some soup. Carla Jo smiled and shook her head.

Carla Jo studied Amy for a few moments and then asked, "Do you like being a girl?"

"I never gave it much thought. They don't treat me any different at home. Well, there is one thing. I wish I could stand up and pee."

That one caught Carla Jo in mid-drink. Tea shot out of her nose as she laughed.

"What?" asked Amy.

"Oh Amy, you and every other woman," Carla Jo said through a chuckle. Then Carla Jo sat up straight in her chair, folded her hands in her lap, and said, "In two weeks you start junior high. It will be very different than what you are used to. Did you ever think about changing your style?"

Amy cocked her head and with confusion in her voice asked, "My style? What do you mean?"

"You know, hair style, clothes, shoes, maybe a watch or a piece of jewelry," Carla explained.

"I like the way I am," Amy insisted. "Don't you like me the way I am?"

Carla Jo watched Amy's eyes, hoping her feelings weren't hurt. Maybe she went a bit too far.

"No, no, no, honey, I love the way you are. You are smart and honest, and hidden somewhere under those bib overalls, t-shirt, work boots, and ponytail, you are beautiful."

"So you're sayin' I dress like a boy?" Amy clarified.

"No, you dress like you work on a farm because you do. Don't you have a birthday in a week or so?"

"Yep, I'll be thirteen," Amy said. For a moment she thought about what Carlas Jo had said, and then said, "Aunt Carla Jo?"

"Yes, Amy?"

"Where do we find style?"

Carla sat back in her chair, clapped her hands together, and with a self-satisfied grin said, "The city."

Amy got up early the next Saturday morning. She finished her chores with Jack then went inside to take a bath. She scrubbed under her nails with a brush like Carla Jo had asked. She went into her closet and got a dress; not the one she wore to church, it was too special, but the other one. After all, she had two.

Amy's daddy drove her to Uncle Jack's. Jack was in the garage when they pulled up and when he saw them he yelled for Carla Jo to come out. Carla Jo stepped out onto the porch and Amy's eyes went wide. She was wearing a floral print sundress that draped lightly over her body. In the morning sun Amy could make out the outline of her body beneath the dress. Her lips were painted red like cherries and she wore a pearl necklace that matched her earrings. She floated down the front steps in high heeled, low top boots with laces and little bows on the heels. Reaching in her purse she pulled out a pair of gold-rimmed sunglasses and put them on. Amy thought she looked like a movie star.

Then Amy heard a rumble from the little garage next to the big one that Uncle Jack had been working in. Uncle Jack was backing out Carla Jo's shiny red Camaro.

"That's your car?" Amy asked, amazed.

"Well, a beautiful princess like you needs a beautiful carriage," Carla Jo replied.

"Carla Jo," Leon spoke in a serious tone, "easy."

Carla Jo knew what he meant. She had a reputation for trying to straighten the curves on the back roads. Carla Jo looked at Leon, gave him a little smile, and nodded her head. Amy climbed into the car and waved goodbye to her daddy. Her daddy smiled and waved back. Carla Jo got to the end of the gravel driveway and turned onto the asphalt, and then promptly smoked the tires all the way past Ed Gwinn's conveniance store.

Leon looked at Jack and exclaimed, "DAMMIT, JACK!" As the Camaro disappeared into the distance.

Jack shook his head and said, "I'll yell at her when she gets back."

"No, you won't," snapped Leon.

Jack laughed and said, "You're right, I won't."

Carla Jo kept her word and almost ran the speed limit. Amy watched the people as Carla Jo drove by. The pretty girl in the fast car got a lot of looks and attention. They drove through Lewistown and hit the state highway. It was a good forty minutes to the city.

"I read that book," Amy told her.

"What did you think?" replied Carla Jo.

"It was great!" Amy went on to give Carla Jo the condensed version of the evil cobras and the faithful, brave mongoose as she remembered it.

"What did the story mean to you?"

Amy thought for a moment and said, "Rikki fought for the people he cared about. I guess it means you should protect the people you love?"

Carla smiled, reached over, grabbed her hand, and said, "That's good enough. Would you like to read more?"

"Yes, ma'am, I think I would," Amy replied.

"Great," said Carla Jo. She reached into a little case and pulled out a CD, slid it into a slot in the dash and hit a button. Carla smiled, glanced at Amy, and said, "This is one of my favorite songs and I think you'll like it."

It was not the kind of music Amy listened to, but the beat felt strangely good. It made her feel like moving. Carla Jo *really* liked it. Amy watched her tapping on the steering wheel and dancing in the seat. Amy mused to herself, *I think my Aunt has a wild streak.*

The skyline off in the distance began to come into view. She had only been past Lewistown once that she could remember. The city looked much different in person than it did on TV. It was bigger; way, way bigger. They got off the highway and drove down a busy street. There were so many cars and people. The buildings were ten times bigger than her school. Carla Jo stopped the car and a handsome man in a red jacket opened the door. He offered his hand to Amy, but she jumped and backed away. Carla Jo touched Amy's arm and said, "It's OK, you can get out. He wants to help you out of the car."

"I can get out on my own just fine, thank you," Amy said.

The man in the red jacket smiled warmly and stepped aside. Amy got out and looked around. It was so noisy and what was that smell? The city smelled like she was standing next to the exhaust pipe on her daddy's tractor. Carla Jo walked around to Amy's side of the car and held her hand as they walked toward the nearest building. It had two huge white pillars and the whole front of the building was made of glass. The doors were as big as barn doors and above them a name was written in big gold letters. Carla Jo looked down at Amy and said, "Welcome to Francois."

The doors seemed to open by magic. They walked in and the smell was very different. It smelled wonderful, like the smell of every flower she had ever known combined with the sweetest perfumes. The ceiling was high and the room was huge. The white marble floor seemed to go on and on. Around the edge of the room were shiny chrome chairs and mirrors. There were beautiful women and handsome men everywhere. The walls were trimmed with gold and hung with bright, colorful paintings. Music played in the background. Amy's eyes kept going from one thing to the next. The closest thing she could compare it to was how Brother Taylor described heaven.

From across the room Amy heard, "Carla Jo! Carla Jo!"

A man started walking toward them. Amy thought he walked liked the women at church only faster. He had white hair with a pink stripe down the side. He was wearing a pink shirt with white pants, white sandals, and gold earrings.

"Carla Jo, how are you? Kiss, kiss!" The man said as he took Carla Jo's hands and kissed both her cheeks.

"Fabulous, Jean Paul, and you?" Carla Jo replied.

Amy thought he sounded like Cruella Deville.

"And this must be Amy!" Jean Paul said. He bent down and looked into Amy's eyes. "Oh my!" Jean Paul gazed with wonder. "You told me, but I was just not prepared. Those eyes!" He kept staring, Amy thought for a little to long. He reached out to touched her hair and Amy flinched and backed up. Carla Jo put her hand in the center of Amy's back to stop her.

Jean Paul smiled an understanding smile and said, "Do not fear Jean Paul, Jean Paul is your newest friend." Jean Paul looked adoringly at her hair and said, "So thick, so long, and the color! Is that its natural color?"

Amy looked confused and Carla Jo answered, "Yes, it is."

"Such a beautiful, light strawberry blonde; I have never seen anything this lovely. Jean Paul will make it even better," said Jean Paul, then he looked at Amy and asked, "Who cuts your hair, darling?"

"Granny Patches," Amy replied timidly.

"Well, let's just see if we can help," Jean Paul said, then paused. "Granny Patches."

He stood up quickly, turned around, clapped his hands, and loudly announced to his assistant, "Ralphie, wash on one and two!" He look back at them and said, "I will see you two lovely ladies a little later, *ciao*."

The next three hours were a whirlwind. A beautiful woman washed her hair with shampoo that smelled wonderful. The shampoo tingled her head and the woman was so gentle and friendly. Lotions and creams were rubbed on her face, hands, arms, legs, and feet. Her fingernails and toenails were trimmed, buffed, and painted with a beautiful pink color. They brought her hot, sweet tea with honey and lemon along with a funny shaped cookie. A little later, a woman brought Amy a fizzy cherry drink with a real cherry on top in the most fancy glass she had ever seen. Another man brought her a small plate with the most delicious creamy chocolates. And everyone kept telling her how pretty, gorgeous, or lovely she was. It was like a dream, except for when the woman trimmed and waxed her eyebrows; that kind of hurt. Carla Jo said a little pain is the price of beauty.

Amy and Carla Jo sat in comfortable chairs next to each other. There was aluminum foil folded up in Amy's hair and she was told that she had to sit for a while. Aunt Carla Jo said it was highlights. As they were waiting, someone brought her another cherry drink.

"So, what do you think of all this so far?" Carla Jo asked.

"This is so much fun!" said Amy.

"Yes, it is," replied Carla Jo. She looked at Amy and waved her hand as if she was gently casting a spell and asked, "What do you see?"

Amy thought for a moment and said, "Beauty. It's all so beautiful; the people, the tables and chairs, every little thing."

"What else do you see?" Carla Jo asked.

Amy thought for a moment and asked, "What do you mean?"

"Tell me what else you see," Carla Jo replied.

"Well, uh, nothin'," Amy admitted.

Carla smiled and said, "Very good Amy, you are exactly right, nothing. You see, Amy, none of this is real. This is all about making you look and feel good. They're good at it, aren't they?"

"Well, yes, I suppose," said Amy, sounding a little confused.

"You see, Amy, Francois focuses on changing the outside of people. They don't care about what's on the inside. Many of these people live their entire lives worrying about how other people see them. When we were having lunch the other day you were worried that I didn't like you the way you are. I want you to listen carefully; you have a big heart and a soul that is full of life. Most of these people would kill to have what you have. They sold their hearts and souls a long time ago. You are probably the only real thing in this room. Do you understand?" Carla Jo asked.

"I think so," Amy said, still a little confused.

Carla Jo thought she might have to slow down. This was all a bit much for a twelve year old.

"Aunt Carla Jo!" Amy said suddenly, excitement in her voice, "That's Melissa Bean, the TV news lady! She's so smart and so beautiful!"

Carla smiled mischievously, waved across the room, and called out "Melissa!"

Melissa Bean waved and began to walk over to Carla Jo. To Carla Joe it seemed that she and Melissa always had appointments on the same day. More than once Carla Jo was exposed to the vapid babblings of the former beauty queen.

"Do you know her?" asked Amy.

"We've met," said Carla Jo.

"She comin' over here!" Amy whispered excitedly to Carla Jo.

"Well, hello, Carla Jo, you look lovely as usual," Melissa said.

"It's so good to see you," Carla Jo replied. "I would like you to meet my niece, Amy."

"Well, hello, my dear," said Melissa while offering a handshake.

Amy was a bit star struck and froze, so Carla nudged her.

"Hi, nice to meet you," Amy said and shook her hand.

Melissa turned her attention back to Carla and quipped, "I wonder what the poor people are doing today?" she asked, then chuckled.

The smile began to leave Amy's face.

Carla Jo, with a serious look, said, "That was a really frightening report you did on the possibility of Iraq getting nuclear weapons."

"What?" Melissa asked, looking confused. "I don't pay attention to all that."

"What about the report of the Congress passing a bill to raise income taxes? You must have an opinion?" Carla Jo asked.

"Yeah, well, I don't concern myself with those things," Melissa said, starting to appear agitated.

"I love your hair," commented Carla Jo.

Melissa perked up and said, "Isn't Jean Paul a magician? Just look at these highlights. They'll be spectacular on camera!"

"Yes, they will. It was so nice to see you again," said Carla Jo.

"You too, Carla Jo, it was nice to meet you, Angie," said Melissa.

"Amy, my name is, Amy," Amy pointed out.

"OK, bye," Melissa said and walked away.

Carla Jo studied Amy as she watched Melissa walk away and wondered how she would react to being disappointed by someone she had thought was talented and special. She looked at Amy and said, "Sooo, Amy." Amy turned and looked at Carla Jo. "What do you think about Melissa?"

"She's not what you see on TV; she ain't smart at all. She's not even nice. She's not real is she?"

Now she's getting it, thought Carla Jo. Then Carla Jo said, "No, she's not, she's not real. She's a fraud, a fake; she's dumb as a brick. When you start junior high you will meet people like this. Do not be drawn into their fake world. Stay true to yourself and be who you are. You wanna know something else?" Carla whispered.

"What?" asked Amy

"She's got fake eyelashes and nails," whispered Carla Jo.

"Those ain't even real?" asked Amy, a little bit too loudly.

"Shhhh, not so loud," said Carla Jo and they both giggled.

Ralphie came over then and escorted Carla Jo and Amy to the salon chair where Jean Paul was waiting. Amy sat down in the chair and Carla Jo motioned Jean Paul to her side. Carla Jo whispered, "Jean Paul, she is straight out of the woods. This is her first style and she has to take care of it herself. Keep it simple."

Jean Paul's chin fell to his chest, and then he whispered back, "You put limitations on Jean Paul, you bring Jean Paul a perfect blank canvas on which to practice his art, and then you take away his favorite colors? You are killing Jean Paul."

"I knew you would understand," Carla Jo replied.

Jean Paul went to work, almost dancing around the chair as he cut and trimmed. Thirty minutes later he turned Amy back toward the mirror. Amy stared at herself and barely recognized what she saw. For the first time in her life she saw a girl, a girly girl, and she liked it.

Jean Paul brought Amy a bag with shampoo, conditioner, and a new hairbrush. He spoke to Amy about the importance of hair care and how she could keep it looking "Jean Paul fabulous." Jean Paul kissed her on both cheeks like he had Carla Jo and said goodbye. Carla Jo and Amy walked out the big front doors to Carla Jo's waiting car. The man in the red jacket opened her door and put out his hand. This time, Amy took it.

Carla Jo looked over at Amy as she put the car in drive and said, "Before we go to the mall, how about some lunch?" Amy smiled and, mimicking Jean Paul said, "that would be fabulous." Carla Jo had to force a smile.

Chapter 5

Carla Jo tried not to show any of the emotions she was feeling. There was a dull ache in her chest. Carla Jo had been having a conversation with Cindy Peterson; her daughter would also be attending Lewistown Jr High. When Jean Paul turned Amy toward the mirror, the shock of Amy's new look made her freeze. It was Katherine, only prettier. Emotions flooded through her like they hadn't in a long time. Katherine had been her best friend. Guilt fell over Carla Jo like a wet blanket. Katherine had never asked Carla Jo to look after Amy. She shouldn't have had to. Katherine was the only person in the world that Carla Jo had trusted with her past. All Katherine had ever said to Carla Jo was, "It's never too late to do the right thing." *You're right, Katherine*, Carla Jo thought. *It's never too late.*

"Aunt Carla Jo, what's wrong?" Amy asked.

"I was thinking about how much you look like your mom," Carla Jo replied.

"Momma liked you a lot. It was never just Carla Jo; it was always, *my best friend Carla Jo*," Amy said with a singsong animated voice.

Carla Jo thought to herself, *Thanks, Amy, that didn't help.*

After pulling into the valet parking spot at the restaurant, another man opened Amy's door. This time he was wearing a blue jacket and Amy knew exactly what to do.

They walked in the front door of the restaurant and Amy could smell the food. *Smells good,* she thought. A pretty girl greeted them at the door.

"Welcome to Chez Geraud, two for lunch?"

"Yes, please," Carla Jo replied.

As they followed her through the restaurant, Amy looked around at all the people. The men were wearing suits and the women were dressed like Carla Jo. Amy saw white tablecloths with candles and flowers on every table. Big chandeliers hung from the ceiling. The walls were polished wood with big paintings of flowers. As she walked by the people at the tables, they looked at her and smiled. For the first time she began to feel self conscious about her faded dress and worn shoes, even though she had no reason to feel that way; anyone that looked at her in the past never got past her eyes.

When they arrived at their table, a handsome young man pulled out Amy's chair. Amy stopped and looked at Carla Jo. Carla Jo said, "It's OK, sit."

Amy sat down and the man pushed in her chair. He went around to the other side of the table and did the same thing for Carla Jo. A waiter came and took their drink order. Carla Jo ordered them two iced teas.

"So Amy, what do you think?" Carla Jo asked.

"It's a lot nicer than the Bluebird Café," Amy replied.

Carla Jo laughed and said, "Yes, it is."

"Look around and tell me what you see," Carla Jo instructed.

"Don't tell me, these people ain't real, either," Amy sighed.

"No, no, no, not that, not that at all. This is different," Carla Jo assured her through a stifled laugh.

"They're eating?" Amy guessed.

"Look closer; how are they eating?" Carla Jo hinted.

"They eat like you."

OK, this is not working, thought Carla Jo.

Carla Jo leaned across the table and whispered, "Does your daddy fart in the house?"

"What?" Amy asked, surprised.

"You heard me," Carla Jo replied.

"Oh yeah, Daddy and my brothers are awful. That's OK, I give it right back to 'em."

Carla Jo laughed and said, "Did your daddy ever do that at a restaurant?"

"No, never; that would be rude," Amy said.

"Exactly," said Carla Jo. "That is called manners."

"I know what that is," said Amy. "My mom would always say, 'Amy, sit up straight. Amy, don't talk with your mouth full. Amy, don't slurp,' and on and on."

Carla Jo nodded and said, "Yes, your mother was very much a lady. That's what she expected from you. I would like to help you finish what your mother started."

Amy looked around the room and began to feel a little overwhelmed by all the attention. All the new places and faces were beginning to wear on her. Carla Jo noticed her growing discomfort and said, "Are you OK, honey?"

Amy wasn't sure what to say. She was grateful for the attention, but she wasn't used to any of it. She didn't want to hurt Carla Jo's feelings, but she thought it important to be honest. "It's just that, well, this is all so new. I don't feel like I fit here. Like I shouldn't be here," said Amy nervously.

Carla Jo understood what it was like to feel out of place and nodded, saying, "If you want to go home, I'll understand. Just know this; you are my family. Any place I am welcome, you are welcome. I just want to show you how other people live. It's not good or bad, it's just different. What do you say we have lunch, talk a little about manners, and when we are done, if you still want to go home, we'll go.

Amy nodded appreciatively and said, "OK."

Carla Jo was pleasantly surprised by how quickly Amy picked up on her gentle promptings. By the time lunch was over, Amy seemed almost stately. *This is almost too good to be true*, Carla Jo thought. The waiter brought the check and Carla Jo handed him the money. Just then, Amy let out a loud "BUUURRRRRRP."

The waiter chuckled and Carla Jo shook her head. Amy looked a little embarrassed and mumbled, "Excuse me." Carla Jo smiled and let out a little sigh.

They walked out of the restaurant to where the car was waiting by the curb. They climbed in, buckled up, and Carla Jo looked at Amy and said, "Do you still want to go home?"

"Well, where do you want to go now?" Amy asked curiously.

"I was thinking we should go have some fun."

"I thought we were havin' fun, sorta," said Amy.

"Oh no," Carla Jo said. "Now the fun begins. What do you say we do a little shopping?"

Carla Jo pulled into the parking lot of the mall and found a parking space. Amy had never seen so many cars. The buildings just seemed to go on forever. Once inside the building Amy looked around, her eyes widening as she said, "Whoa."

Carla Jo looked at her and said, "So what do you think?"

"Wow," Amy said. "Kerry came here with some friends once. He told me about it, but I never imagined this."

Amy walked up to the giant fountain in the center of the entrance. She looked into the water and asked, "Why is there money in here?"

"It's a wishing fountain," Carla Jo explained. She reached into her purse and pulled out a nickel, handing it to Amy as she said, "Go ahead, make a wish and toss it in. But if you tell anybody what you wish for, it won't come true."

Amy thought for a second and then threw the nickel in the water. She was sure her momma and Kerry were watching over her but adding the wish made her doubly sure.

"Where shall we start?" Carla Jo asked rhetorically. "I know, at the beginning."

She took Amy's hand and said, "Let's go."

The first store they walked into was full of girls Amy's age. They walked past dresses, jeans, and tops to the back of the store.

"Underwear," said Carla Jo. There were racks and racks of colors and styles; some with hearts, some with stars, some with pictures of kitties, and some with little bows.

"These are fancy," Amy remarked.

"What do you see that you like?"

When Amy only picked out two pairs Carla explained, "You will need at least six pairs, unless you want to do laundry every day."

Amy carefully searched the rack for something that was a little like her; not quite so fancy but a little cute. She picked out four more and went with Carla Jo to the dressing room so they could make sure she had the right size.

When Amy left the dressing room she saw Carla Jo standing by a rack. When she turned around, Amy saw something dangling from her finger.

What's that?" asked Amy.

"A training bra. Those bumps on your chest won't be getting any smaller."

Amy reflexively put her arms over her chest and scrunched her face. Carla Jo smiled, leaned down, and whispered, "Look around, all of these girls are going through the same thing. It's all part of becoming a woman. There's nothing to be scared of and nothing to be ashamed of. Come on, let's go try it on."

They made their way back to the dressing room. Amy unbuttoned her dress and slid it off of her shoulders. Carla Jo looked at her back and arms and said, "Wow, are you muscular."

"What do you mean?" Amy said, feeling a little self-conscious.

"It's not bad. It's just that I've never seen muscles like this on a girl." *It must be all the work she does on the farm,* thought Carla Jo.

It was hard to find a training bra that would fit because of her build, but eventually they found a style that worked and left the store. "I know a dress shop," said Carla Jo. "Let's go."

They spent a couple of hours trying on dresses, jeans, and tops. It was difficult to find jeans for her because of her thigh and calf muscles. When they found something they liked, Carla Jo bought it. They went to three different shoe shops. Tennis shoes for gym class and pink tennis shoes for "stylin'," as Carla Jo put it, as well as two pairs of boots, one black and one tan. They looked a lot like Carla Jo's only without the high heels. Then something occurred to Amy, something she hadn't thought of.

"Did my daddy give you the money for this?" she asked.

"No, he didn't. This is on me," she smiled a understanding smile and added, "I know it seems like a lot to you, but really, it's not a lot to me."

"We can't...I can't take this from you. My daddy always said you can't take somethin' for nothin'. It never turns out good. We have to take this stuff back."

Carla Jo had wondered if this would come up. She knew Amy was honest, had a big heart, and an unbelievable work ethic. Apparently, Amy also had a sense of pride. Carla Jo thought to herself, *It's easy to love this girl.*

"Come over here and let's sit down. I need to tell you a few things."

Carla Jo and Amy sat all of their bags down and took a seat on a bench. Carla Jo turned to Amy, held her hands, and said, "Amy, when I came to Alabama I had nothing; no clothes, no money, no family, and no friends. Your momma invited me into her home and treated me like the most special person in the world. Remember when we talked about being a real person, keeping your heart and soul above all else?" Amy nodded. "Well, I had lost mine. Your momma and your uncle Jack gave them back to me. I want to do for you the things that I think your momma would have wanted. Please, let me do this for you."

"So you're doin' this for my momma?" Amy asked.

"Yes, and I'm also doing it for you. I was hoping we could be friends. Spending time together like this is a good start."

"I thought we were friends," said Amy.

"I think we could be. Friendships take time and trust. I'm willing to work on that with you."

Amy thought about it for a few moments and said, "OK, Aunt Carla Jo. Thank you for today."

Carla Jo gave her a hug and said, "Let's go home."

They were nearly to the mall exit when a dress in a window display caught Amy's eye. "Whoa, look at that dress," she said.

"You like that?" asked Carla Jo.

"It looks almost like yours."

Carla Jo was almost giddy as she replied, "Well, let's take a look."

They walked quickly into the store and when Amy stepped out of the dressing room, Carla Jo's eyes lit up.

"Yes, very nice," she said, and turning to the sales lady she said, "We'll take it."

"Aunt Carla Jo, do you think I could wear this home?" Amy said with a little excitement.

Carla Jo looked into one of the shopping bags and, pulling out a shoebox, said, "Not without these shoes."

Once again they started for the exit. Carla Jo got to a kiosk and stopped, "One more thing, Amy."

Carla Jo scanned the rack of sunglasses, found a pair, and slipped them on Amy. Stepping back to examine her work, she smiled and said, "OK, now we're done."

They got to the exit where two teenage boys were talking. When the boys saw Amy they quickly opened the door while smiling big smiles at her. Amy kept looking over her shoulder while she and Carla Jo walked and marveled at the fact that the boys just kept on staring. Amy looked at Carla Jo and said, "Aunt Carla Jo, are those boys...?"

Carla Jo interrupted, "Yes, honey, they're looking at you. Get used to it."

When they reached the curb, Amy stopped. Carla Jo spun around when she realized her niece was no longer at her side and questioned her hesitation.

Amy, puzzled, asked, "Where's our car? It's usually sittin' out front waitin' for us."

Carla Jo laughed and said, "You are spoiled already. They don't do that here, so start walking."

Carla Jo had a plan and the first part of her plan was complete. She had two weeks to prepare Amy to face some of the most evil, ruthless creatures ever to walk the face of the earth: roving packs of materialistic, judgmental, and socially conscious junior high school girls.

Chapter 6

*A*my felt her body being pushed back in the seat as Carla Jo sped down the on-ramp and onto the highway. It had been an exciting day and she felt a little tired. She had been to the city before, but she barely remembered it. They had gone to the big hospital the day her granddaddy died. That was a sad day, she recalled.

Carla Jo glanced at Amy as she stared out the window. She looked deep in thought, so Carla Jo figured it would be best to stay quiet and let Amy process her day. Carla Jo set the radio to Amy's favorite country and western station, but Amy didn't even seem to notice.

Playing with her newly styled hair, Amy thought about the kindness of Jean Paul and the people at the salon. Those little chocolates—she had never tasted anything like that. Then she chuckled to herself when she thought about Melissa's fake lashes and nails. Her hand fell from the ends of her hair and touched the seam of her training bra. Another thought crossed her mind, *how big are these things gonna get*? Her hand fell to her lap and she gently stroked the material of her dress. It was so soft against her legs. It was a great feeling. Her toes wiggled in her boots. The leather was so soft. It felt like her feet were being gently hugged.

Peeking out of the tops of her boots was lace from her socks. She studied the pattern. *How pretty*, she thought.

Amy looked out the window as landscapes sped by and she began to wonder about people. They seemed so different in the city. Were they this different everywhere else? Then she noticed the big apartment buildings; then the neighborhoods with the houses so close together with perfect little streets. *What's it like living that close to other people?* she wondered. Then she saw big houses with their own swimming pools. They dotted what looked like a giant green carpet. Who lived there? Then it was as if she blinked and the landscape changed again to the rows of crops in the farm fields. Way out in a field on the top of a hill she saw the outline of three deer. A little buzz, like electricity, shot through her body. It would be hunting season soon.

"Aunt Carla Jo?" Amy asked slowly with some hesitation.

Carla Jo almost jumped in her seat because Amy had been so quiet. "Yes, Amy?" she replied.

"Do ladies hunt?"

"Ladies can do anything anyone else can do. Why do you ask?"

"I don't think guttin' a deer is very ladylike,"

"No, it's not; it's hunter–like," Carla Jo said, struggling with a way to explain this one. "Being a lady isn't about acting one way all of the time. It's about knowing the proper way to act in any situation. You will always want to be kind and polite and use manners when possible, but I don't think saying please, thank you, and excuse me will work well when you are in the woods."

Amy looked relieved and said, "I thought you wanted me to be this way all of the time."

Carla Jo smiled at Amy and said, "No, I don't want you to change your life completely. I just want to help you add a little something to it."

As they drove through Lewistown, Amy felt a little older and more sophisticated. She thought about how big the town used to feel to her and how small it looked now. When Carla Jo turned on to Indian River Road at the edge of town, she hit the gas. Glancing at the speedometer, Amy saw that the needle was at 80. "You promised my daddy you would slow down."

Carla Jo lifted her foot off the gas and said, "You caught that did you? It's a bad habit, one I need to break."

When Amy saw the big steeple of the Black Oak Baptist Church, she knew she was almost home. Carla Jo slowed the car down further at Ed Gwinn's store. Amy looked at the bench by the front door where she and Kerry used to sit and eat their favorite treats. Kerry always had a Grapico and a little Bama Pecan Pie. Amy liked Dr. Pepper and Moon Pies. Since Amy left Carla Jo's house that morning, she had hardly thought about Kerry at all. She wondered what he would think about her hair and dress. She felt the grief of his death starting to flow back into her body, but it wasn't as strong as before. A dull ache had replaced the constant pain in her chest. Turning up String Hill Road, Carla Jo gunned the engine for the climb to the top.

Leon and Jack were sitting on the front porch when they heard the deep rumble of Carla Jo's car coming up the hill.

"Here they come," Jack said.

When Carla Jo pulled onto the gravel drive she saw Gloria's car. *That's just great*, she thought. Carla Jo and Gloria had an uncomfortable past. Jack met Carla Jo halfway across the front yard and gave her a kiss on the cheek. Amy got out and joined them in the grass.

Looking at Amy, Jack smiled and said, "Wow, you look beautiful." He then whispered in Carla Jo's ear, "Nice job."

"Seems I have my own little Eliza Doolittle," Carla Jo said with a sense of pride.

"Eliza who?" asked Jack.

"Nevermind," she sighed.

Leon stood up and stared. He saw what Carla Jo saw in the mirror at Francois. He saw Katherine's hair, eyes, and even the little button nose. Leon felt himself beginning to choke up.

"So daddy, what do ya' think?" Amy asked as she twirled left then right.

"You are the prettiest thing I think I have ever seen," he said.

Amy smiled. Suddenly, the front door opened and her Aunt Gloria walked out onto the porch carrying two grocery bags. Gloria had a dated bufont hairdo dyed black and she weighed somewhere north of two hundred and fifty pounds. She was wearing a polyester pantsuit and when she took a step, her rubbing thighs made a swishing noise.

Gloria looked at Amy and then turned toward Leon. With a disgusted look on her face she said, "So Leon, I guess you're gonna let Carla Jo turn Amy into a slut."

"A what?" asked Amy innocently.

"That's it," growled Carla Jo. She took a step toward Gloria with visions of kicking her ass.

Jack grabbed Carla Jo's arm and whispered, "Don't do it. Stop, Carla Jo, you're better than that. Please don't."

Leon looked at the ground and shook his head, saying, "Gloria, I think it's time for you to leave. Thanks for stopping by." Gloria started to say something, but Leon gave her a hard stare and said, "It's time to leave, NOW."

Gloria walked to her car, sneering at Carla Jo. Jack had to keep a tight hold as Carla Jo mumbled something about a white trash polyester princess. After Gloria pulled down the driveway and disappeared from sight, Amy looked at Carla Jo and said, "Not very ladylike, Aunt Carla Jo."

Jack chuckled. Carla Jo took a deep breath and then said to Amy, "Well, Amy, despite our best efforts, we all fall short of perfection. That's why we shouldn't be too hard on ourselves."

Amy smiled and said, "I understand. She aggravates me, too."

After unloading the car, Carla Jo and Amy took Amy's new clothes into her room, where Carla Jo took the time to show Amy the proper way to hang everything. They also talked about the proper way to wash certain materials. Amy decided it would be a good idea to change clothes and hang up her new dress. She wanted to save it for the first day of school.

Back out on the porch, Leon looked at Carla Jo and said, "Thank you. I haven't seen her smile like that in a long time."

"It was my pleasure, she's an amazing child. I was wondering if it would be OK to take her with me to the city once a month? We'll get our hair done, have lunch, you know, girl stuff," Carla Jo asked.

"That's fine," Leon replied while reaching for his wallet. "How much did you spend today?"

"Not enough. Keep your money, Leon, I have an old debt to pay."

"I can't let you do that."

Carla Jo looked at Leon and in a serious tone told him, "You can and you will."

Jack piped up, "I've seen that look before, let it go."

"Alright then, thank you again. Tomorrow after church I'm gonna have a small party for Amy's birthday. I would like you both to come."

"We'll be there," Carla Jo assured him.

Just then Amy came back outside, gave Carla Jo a big hug, and thanked her again. Jack walked Carla Jo to her car and opened the door. "Just how much money did you spend today?" Jack asked.

"None of your damn business," Carla Jo replied.

"What color underwear are you wearin'?" Jack asked with a mischievous look.

Carla Jo smiled her best sultry smile, "Hurry home, big fella, and I promise I'll make that your business."

Chapter 7

*I*t was Sunday morning and Amy was up early again, doing her chores. It was the first day her uncle Jack didn't show up. He said he couldn't come because he had to work, but her chores seemed to go faster without him. This was probably because they talked more than they worked. After her chores, Amy took a bath and used the shampoo that Jean Paul gave her. She loved the way it made her hair smell. Ever since her adventure with Carla Jo, she was becoming more concerned with how she looked. She fussed with her hair until her daddy knocked on the bathroom door.

"Amy, you still have to get your brother ready for church and we have to leave soon," her daddy said.

"OK, Daddy," she said. She looked at the clock and couldn't believe she let that much time go by.

After piling in the truck they headed to church. Looking at her daddy, Amy noticed he seemed a little happier. He never really showed much emotion but today he just looked...better. Once at church, Amy had only taken about two steps through the parking lot when one of the older ladies stopped her and said, "Leon, looks like you got yourself a little Katherine."

Leon smiled and said, "Yep, she's growin' up, isn't she?"

Amy must have been called little Katherine a couple of dozen times that day. She didn't mind. Amy remembered her mother as a beautiful women so she took it as a compliment. Brother Taylor III's sermon was about the trials and tribulations of Job. Amy looked at her daddy and thought about how much he was like Job. He lost his wife, his son, and yet here he was, keeping his faith and thanking Jesus for his good blessings. Amy said a little prayer thanking Jesus for her daddy.

When church was over they headed back out to the truck, but before they got there Miss Francis stopped Amy and told her Brother Taylor wanted to see her. Amy's daddy had stopped to talk to a couple of friends, so he told her to go ahead without him. She walked back into the sanctuary and Brother Taylor waved her over. Before giving her a gift, he gave her a big hug and told her Happy Birthday. It was a little piece of flat metal with an angel stamped into it, just like the one Kerry had had kept in his pocket.

Then Brother Taylor took a seat on the first pew and said, "Amy, I would like to know if you would be interested in teaching Sunday school with Miss Francis. You would have to come early and help her set up the classroom, and then stay a little late to help her clean up."

Amy's eyes got big. *That was a high honor*, she thought. "Yes, sir, Brother Taylor, I would love to, but I have to ask my daddy first."

"Miss Francis already asked him for you. He said it would be fine with him if it was fine with you," Brother Taylor said.

"Thank you, Brother Taylor, I would love to!"

Amy walked tall with a little pep in her step back to the truck where her daddy was waiting and hugged him.

"You gonna help Miss Francis teach Sunday school?" he asked.

"Yes, sir!"

"Good. I have another surprise for you and your brother. How 'bout lunch at the Bluebird?"

Amy nodded her head and Joseph exclaimed, "Heck, yeah!"

Once at the Bluebird and after drinks were served, Amy's daddy looked across the table and said, "I got a new job at the mine. I won't be working nights anymore. I'll be getting up with you and I should be home not long after you get home from school."

"This day just keeps gettin' better and better!" Amy said.

"That means we can go fishin' in the evenin' at the dam, right Daddy?" Joseph asked.

"We will be able to do a lot of things we haven't done before. There is somethin' else, too. The new job came with a raise. We won't be farming anymore. I want you two to give your full attentions to school."

There was something else their Daddy didn't say. After almost six years he had finally paid off Katherine's medical bills. The monthly reminder of her painful death would finally stop showing up in the mailbox.

Amy wasn't sure how she felt about not farming anymore. She took pride in helping the family. When Amy's daddy noticed the look on her face he asked, "What's wrong, honey?"

"No chickens, nothin'?"

Hmm, maybe she liked farming a little more than I knew, her Daddy thought. "I'm givin' the chickens to Granny Patches and she'll still be doin' a little farming. I expect you both to help her out," he said.

"Yes, sir," said Amy and Joseph.

They finished up with lunch and headed home. As they turned the corner at the top of the hill, Amy saw cars in front of the house. "What's goin' on, Daddy?" she asked.

"It's somebody's birthday, ain't it?" her daddy asked with a playful smile.

Everyone that Amy loved was there: Aunt Carla Jo and Uncle Jack, Granny Patches, Sheriff Carter, and her best friend from school, Mary Beth. Granny Patches made her a chocolate cake with coconut and pecan icing, Amy's favorite. They sang "Happy Birthday" and blew out the candles, and then sat on the porch where they talked and ate cake.

Mary Beth was the first to give Amy a gift. It was a homemade card with a little picture that Mary Beth had kept of the both of them. Amy's mom took it when they were in kindergarten. Amy began to tear up. She remembered that day and she remembered her mother taking the picture. It was also one of the last pictures taken of Mary Beth before she was burned by the explosion of her daddy's still. Mary Beth still wore the scars on her face and arms.

"Thank you, Mary Beth. This will always be one of my most special treasures," said Amy.

"You're welcome, Amy," Mary Beth replied.

"My turn," said Sheriff Carter, handing her his gift.

Amy tore off the wrapping. It was a teddy bear in a policeman's uniform. Amy giggled and, giving Sheriff Carter a hug, said, "Thank you, Sheriff Teddy Bear."

Jack handed Amy a small box and said, "This is from me and your aunt." Amy opened it to find a small gold cross on a chain.

"It's beautiful," said Amy. She gave her uncle Jack a hug and said, "Thank you, Uncle Jack." She then gave her Aunt Carla Jo a hug and said, "Thank you, Aunt Carla Jo." Amy paused before whispering in Carla Jo's ear, "For everything." Carla Jo smiled and nodded.

Joseph brought a wrapped box out of the house and said, "This is from me and Daddy."

Amy opened the box and pulled out two sets of camouflage pants and jackets along with two packs of thermal underwear.

"Oh! My very own camos, thank you!" she said and then hugged her brother.

Then her daddy walked out of the house and handed her his gift. Amy stared at it for a second and then read the inscription: "I love you Amy, Daddy."

"This is mine, Daddy?" Amy asked.

"Yep, I thought it was time you had your own," her Daddy explained.

Amy pulled it to her chest and said, "A Winchester Model Seventy Featherweight with a scope...I AM GONNA KILL ME A BIG OLE BUCK!"

Everyone laughed except Carla Jo. She leaned over to Jack and whispered, "She's a little girl, that's not normal."

"Oh yeah, it is," Jack whispered back. "I told Leon already; she's Marcel, she's a pure Braxton and she's a stone killer."

Carla Jo just shook her head and thought, *Making little Annie Oakley into a lady may be tougher than I thought.*

After awhile the party broke up, hugs and thank-yous were shared, and everyone went home. Mary Beth got in the truck with Jack. Amy had wondered how Mary Beth got to the house. Very few people knew where Mary Beth's house was. Amy walked over to her daddy and gave him a long hug.

"I miss him, Daddy," she said.

"Yeah honey, me too," said Leon. He thought about Brother Taylor's sermon, the story of Job. While Leon sat in that pew he said his own prayer to Jesus: *I have had enough and I cannot take any more. I have been a good man when it was not easy. Please protect what I have left.*

Leon bent down and gave Amy a kiss and said, "Why don't you go inside, change your clothes, and we'll warm up that Model 70."

"Right now? OK, I'll be right back." said Amy.

Leon followed her into the house to grab a box of shells and the .22 for Joseph. As the family walked past the barn to the old road, they all seemed to realize that this was the first time they had done anything together in a long time. There was an unspoken happiness. This was their family. It was a good family and a strong family, and everything was gonna be OK.

Chapter 8

*I*t was the last Sunday before the first day of school. Amy was rubbing her thumb while walking down String Hill Road toward her uncle Jack's. After church her daddy had sent her to Granny Patches' so she could help pick and shell peas. They must have shelled two five-gallon buckets. Shelling peas required using a thumbnail to split the hull and sometimes this caused the skin to tear away from under the nail. Granny Patches gave her a dollar for her help, though, so she figured she would stop by Ed Gwinn's store. No doubt it would feel better to rest her thumb against a cold Dr. Pepper.

When Amy got to the bend before the hill she saw Timmy and Tommy Hatfield working on an old bicycle at the end of their driveway. Timmy and Tommy Hatfield were twins and a year older than Amy. They both suffered from Fetal Alcohol Syndrome and a myriad of developmental problems as a result of it. Because of this, the thirteen year olds functioned at about the level of eight or nine year olds. Not helping matters was the fact that their mother died from alcohol poisoning a year after they were born and their father was a neglectful and abusive drunk. Their lives were hell. Amy knew they were in the special class at school, but she never treated them that way.

"Hi Timmy, hi Tommy," Amy called.

"Hey Amy," Tommy said. Timmy never spoke so he just waved.

"Y'all ready for school tomorrow?" asked Amy.

"Yeah, I suppose," said Tommy. Timmy shook his head no.

"The bus to Lewistown is gonna pick us up at my end of the road, not at the bottom of the hill like last year," she said.

"Didn't know that. Thanks, Amy," said Tommy.

"I gotta go, I'll see y'all in the morning."

"OK, bye, Amy," Tommy said. Timmy just waved. The boys stood and watched her walk away until she was out of sight around the corner. Tommy looked at Timmy and said, "She sure is pretty."

Once at Ed Gwinn's store, Amy grabbed a Dr. Pepper out of the cooler and paid for it. On her way out the door, Ed called to her, "Wait!"

She stopped and turned around. "No Moon Pie?" he asked.

"Ain't got the money for one, Mr. Gwinn," she said.

"Take one, I won't tell the owner," he smiled.

"Well, only if you tell him I'll pay him back," she said, smiling back.

Ed laughed, "I'll let him know. See you later, honey."

"Bye, Mr. Gwinn, thank you!"

Ed Gwinn lived in a little house on the hill above the store. It used to be a company store that was built to serve the coal miners when they were strip mining in the thirties. In reality, it sold more moonshine than anything else. Ed bought it in the fifties and expanded it to include more groceries, gasoline, and fishing tackle. When the locals would run out of money, Ed just let them buy things on credit until they could pay him. He had known Leon, Jack, and Gene since they were kids. He would always toss them some free candy now and then. Now that Ed was older, the men of the community always looked out for him.

Amy crossed Indian River Road and walked the long driveway to Uncle Jack's. She saw that the little garage was open and Aunt Carla Jo's car was gone. Seeing Uncle Jack working on his old car again, she gave Bubba, Jack's dog, her last bite of Moon Pie, scratched his ear, and greeted her uncle.

"Hi, Uncle Jack, where's Aunt Carla Jo?"

"Hi, Amy, she had to leave and do somethin' for work. She told me to tell you she'd be back in awhile, so wait for her," Jack replied.

Amy took a seat on a stool by the workbench in the garage.

"Uncle Jack, I have always been curious about somethin'. Why don't you go to church?" Amy asked.

Jack had to think about that one. He didn't want to disparage the church but he didn't want to lie, either. "I did for a long time, Amy. I guess I just got out of the habit. But I still have a Bible and I know how to read it. I know Jesus and he knows me." It wasn't the truth. In reality, Brother Taylor II refused to marry him and Carla Jo because she was "a negro girl." Jack never got over that.

"Uncle Jack, do you haul moonshine?"

"What? OW!" she'd caught Jack off guard, and he'd stood up too fast, banging his head under the hood of his car.

"That's illegal, Uncle Jack, you could go to jail," she said.

"What makes you think that I haul moonshine?" Jack asked while rubbing the bump on his head.

"Well, you are always workin' on a car that I rarely see you drive. You say you have a job, but you won't tell me what it is. When you do work, it's crazy hours, mostly at night. You brought Mary Beth to my party and Mary Beth's house ain't on any map. Mary Beth said you come to visit her daddy three or four times during the fall. We both know what Mary Beth's daddy does. If you're tryin' to keep it a secret you ain't doin' very good," Amy replied.

Jack leaned against the car and wiped his hands with an old shop rag. His car was built for one thing: hauling moonshine. It had a high performance engine and a chassis capable of handling 800 lbs of extra weight. It was not a daily driver. He smiled a nervous smile and said, "Got it all figured out, do ya'?"

"I don't want to see you go to jail, Uncle Jack."

Sighing, Jack walked over and sat down beside Amy. "I appreciate that, I really do," he said. He thought for a few minutes and added, "Amy, I'm gonna tell you some things I think you need to know. I would never ask you to keep secrets from your daddy, though, so if you need to tell him I told you these things go ahead, but I'd rather you didn't. More important, don't talk about these things with anyone outside the family."

"OK, Uncle Jack," Amy said with excitement in her voice.

"Your family has been in the corn whiskey business for almost a century. Every member of your family at one time or another has made, hauled, or sold whiskey. Whiskey money fed your grandparents and great grandparents during the Great Depression. That land you hunt on was bought with whiskey money. This land you are standin' on right now was bought with whiskey money. The place where you bought that Dr. Pepper you are holdin' in your hand was built with whiskey money. The whiskey business is as much a part of your family as the Baptist church. Now that I think about it, that big beautiful church you prayed in this morning was built with whiskey money."

"My granddaddy wasn't in the whiskey business, my daddy told me that." Amy said. She knew more about the business than she let on. She was, after all, a Braxton.

"Not directly, he wasn't. Your daddy told the truth. But Marcel Braxton grew some of the finest corn in the area for making whiskey. He'd sell his crop and add to his land every year. Did 'ja ever wonder how you got three hundred acres to hunt on when your granddaddy was a coal miner? All I'm sayin' is that things are not as simple as they appear."

"But it's still against the law," she replied.

Jack sighed and said, "And that is where the line between right and wrong gets blurred. Much of moonshinin' is just family tradition. What you have is a bunch of men hundreds of miles away deciding how we are supposed to live our lives. They say their laws are more important than our traditions, and our allegiances to them is more important than our allegiances to our own families. They come up with laws and folks find ways around 'em. I'm having a hard time explaining this to you, so I want you to promise me something."

"Anything, Uncle Jack."

"Wait 'til you are much older to pass any judgments. Just because something is legal doesn't make it right, and just because it is illegal, that doesn't make it wrong. Understand?"

"I think so. But do you haul moonshine or don't cha'?" she asked.

"Hey, I think your aunt just got here," said Jack as the squeal of tires turning hard off of asphalt echoed up the drive.

"You're not gonna answer, are ya'?"

"Nope, but someday, when you're grown, I'll tell you everything. And Amy, there is a lot to tell."

The Story of Jack Brown

Jack Brown, son of Hermann and Martha Brown, was born in Black Oak, Alabama, in 1949. Jack was the oldest of four with three sisters. His youngest sister died at three years of age after an allergic reaction to a bee sting. His father, Hermann, worked for Lethal Braxton making moonshine. It was said that Hermann's recipe was one of the best in the south. Martha, Jack's mother and sister of Jennie Lee Braxton, stayed home, raised the kids, and tended a small garden. Life was rather idyllic from the outside. They never went hungry. They had a little money and a decent home. When Hermann decided to drink what he made, however, it was another story.

Hermann was an extremely violent drunk. Most of the time Martha would see it coming, take the kids, and hide at Marcel's until Hermann sobered up. When they didn't make it out, Jack watched his momma take severe beatings. When Jack turned twelve, he had enough and got in between them. He figured there was nothing his daddy could do to him that was worse than watching his momma get beat. He was right, but just barely.

Jack took after Martha's side of the family— the men were all around six-foot-two and strong as bulls. When Jack was sixteeen he was already bigger than his daddy. One hot summer day, Hermann, in one of his violent rages, hit Jack, but this time Jack didn't cower or back away. He didn't move. Jack's own rage came out in a fury that almost killed Hermann. Afraid of his father's vengence, Jack hid out at Marcel's house until Hermann showed up with intentions to hurt him bad. Marcel chased Hermann off, but Jack knew he could never go home.

A few days later, Marcel took Jack down to the river and introduced him to a tug boat captain, Captain Wally. Marcel sat Jack down and told him that this was his chance to get out and live his own life. Working the barges was rough work for rough men and Marcel figured if Jack could survive Hermann, he could survive anything. Marcel was right. Jack worked hard, listened to the older men, and learned the necessary skills. Within a couple of years he had become one of Captain Wally's favorites. Then came the draft for Vietnam.

Jack had a low selective service number and figured he would get drafted. Captain Wally talked Jack into enlisting in the Navy so that he wouldn't end up in the jungle carrying a rifle. That and some of the skills he acquired on the river would be useful. Jack listened and a few weeks later he found himself in boot camp.

Unfortunately, Jack didn't take well to being picked on for his southern roots. After a fight with another recruit, a company commander that was a little more impressed with his own pugilistic skills than he should have been, decided to teach Jack a lesson. The company commander wound up in the dispensary (military hospital) and Jack ended up in the brig (military jail).

In defense of Jack, several recruits stepped forward to say that the company commander had initiated the attack. He was only defending himself. The master chief petty officer of the command (MCPOC) saw something in Jack; an iron will combined with a modesty that made him easy to train. Giving him the benefit of the doubt, the MCPOC had the charges dropped. Upon graduation from boot camp, the master chief pulled Jack aside and drove him to a little base on Coronado. There the master chief introduced Jack to men the likes of which Jack had never met before. These men were intense, strong, and confident. Jack felt a strange feeling wash over him. This was a place he had never been, yet it felt like home. The men, however, didn't feel the same way about Jack. Another quick-tempered backwoods hillbilly was not something the SEAL Team was looking for, so they gave Jack a list of physical requirements and sent him on his way.

To fulfill the SEAL Team's requirements, Jack had to go to school to earn a job rating first. The master chief was honest with Jack about his odds and they weren't good. Jack needed to do two things: graduate near the top of his class in Boatswain's Mates School and get in shape. Jack, however, had an edge on the other sailors in his class because of his work on the river barges. Every day after class Jack would go to the gym and work out for two hours, and then he ran to the base pool and swam laps until he was exhausted. After the ten week school, Jack ended up graduating second in his class and six weeks later, found himself at that same little base in Coronado with fifty-two other men.

Seaman Brown was not the strongest, fastest, or the smartest in his class. During hell week, however, the SEAL Team instructors began to see what the old master chief saw. Jack had a fire in his soul that would not be extinguished. The tougher things got, the more Jack responded. By the time Basic Underwater Demolition School had ended, there were only eight sailors left.— and Jack was one of them. Intensive training in various combat skills continued for eight more months, and then it was time for Petty Officer Brown— he had received a meritorious promotion— to be assigned to his first unit.

Petty Officer Brown was deployed to a team in the Rung Sat Special Zone. His team was tasked with supply and troop movement disruption, and carrying out river operations on the

Mekong Delta. They conducted mostly face-to-face and hand-to-hand combat. Accordingly, the killing was very personal and Petty Officer Brown, to the amazement of his team, learned his role quickly. He was good at killing; extremely good at it. In 1969, when the war began to wind down, the number of missions for Jack's team increased.

In early '71, Petty Officer Brown went out on his last mission. It was a snatch/grab operation in a village so small that it wasn't on any map. When they snuck into the village, they were immediately ambushed. Jack was stitched with machine gun fire from his waist to his face. The bullets tore away part of his jaw and shattered a cheekbone. When he fell, he reached for what was left of his face with one hand and returned fire with the other. The next thing he knew was that he was being dragged through the jungle by his shoulders. Then everything went fuzzy.

Jack awoke in an army field hospital. As his eyes refocused he could hear a soft voice singing "Amazing Grace." A face with Asian features made him jump. Was he a POW? Then he saw the name on the uniform, Watkins, followed by the collar insignias for a US army lieutenant. He heard another voice in the distance.

"Watkins, get your ass in here," yelled the major.

"Major, this man isn't dead!" marveled Lt. Watkins.

"Well, this one will be if you don't get your ass in here!" the major replied.

Jack felt his gurney move and heard arguing going on around him. He felt IVs going into his arm. Before blacking out again, the last thing he heard was the soft voice that had been singing to him say, "Well, Petty Officer Brown, looks like you won't be dying today."

After being transferred back to the US, the navy surgeons at Balboa Hospital in San Diego did everything they could to put Jack's face back together. The bullets had hit Jack from the side and shredded his chest and stomach muscles. Those injuries could heal, but it would require Jack to do exercises that were both difficult and painful. They fixed his jaw to the point where he could talk, but his face was a scarred mess. He was finally discharged in '73 and returned to Black Oak. Being that the war was controversial, he came home to little support and fanfare. He received a small monthly disability check from the military and it was just enough to feed him and pay a few utility bills.

While he was deployed, Jack's daddy had died of a heart attack and his mother, suffering from dementia, was put into a home. His sisters had married, moved away, and never looked back. Jack had inherited the family home, but it was run down. Not long after his return to Black Oak, his uncle Marcel and cousin Leon showed up with some tools. Ashamed of his injuries and current living conditions, Jack tried to hide from them. When that proved unsuccessful, he pulled out a gun and ran them off. That was a mistake because fifteen minutes later he was introduced, for the first time, to the force they called Katherine. When he tried slamming the door in her face, she kicked it off the hinges. Standing face-to-face with Katherine and staring at those blazing, green, determined eyes made him think twice. She was not happy with Jack's attitude and explained there would be some changes from here on out. There *were* changes.

Over a period of three months the Braxtons repaired Jack's home. Katherine dug through his medical records and found the exercises he was supposed to be doing to get his strength back. Jack would later joke that Katherine was harder on him than his instructors at Coronado.

As his health improved, so did his attitude. He felt a need to get out and do something so he got his daddy's old car running and drove to the river to talk to Junior Gosset. Junior was Hank Gosset's oldest son. When Hank died he took over the family business. He was every bit the outlaw his father had been, but he was also a savy businessman with a likeable personality. He put the profits of his ill-gotten gains into legitimate businesses. He owned three car dealerships and a couple of fast food restaurants in Lewistown.

Junior offered Jack a job running one of his clubs along the river but Jack refused. He was still too self-conscious about his face to go out in public. Besides, he didn't really like dealing with people. Then Junior told him that what he really needed was bootleggers. When Jack told Junior he didn't have a car set up for that, Junior reached in his pocket, pulled out a wad of money, and asked him, "How much do you need?" He found an old '68 Chevelle and went to work on it. For the first time in a long time, Jack was excited about something.

The thrill of his newfound occupation gave Jack a renewed sense of self. He got some of the spark back that he had in the SEAL Team. He built a small cinder block building behind his house and filled it with work out equipment. He decided to get his SEAL Team body back and through extreme exercise, he refreshed his soul. There was, however, a downside. The healthier he got, the lonelier he became. He wanted a relationship like Leon and Katherine's, but in the meantime he found female companionship in Junior's clubs by the river. Three rum and cokes and $50 usually did the trick, but it wasn't the same and he still could not get over being self-conscious about his face. He stayed away from town and decent people, which further lessened his chances of finding someone to love. One of the most fearsome warriors ever to walk the face of the earth was held prisoner by his wounds. It would take the will of a plucky five-year-old boy to break him free.

Jack had just finished lunch when he heard a car coming up the driveway. As it parked, Little Kerry jumped out and Jack met him on the porch.

"Whatcha doin', Uncle Jack?"

"Nothin'," Jack shrugged. Jack figured he would be watching Kerry while his momma went to town. Instead, Kerry invited Jack to Lewistown to go to the movies with him and Katherine.

"No, no thank you," he replied.

"Why not?" Kerry asked, and then explained, "It's the new *Star Wars* movie."

"No, you and your momma go ahead," Jack said as he turned to go back in the house.

"Is it because of your face, Uncle Jack?" Kerry blurted out, and Jack froze in his tracks. "My friend Kenny has one leg shorter than the other and he wears a funny shoe. I don't let anyone make fun of him." He reached up and grabbed two of Jacks fingers, "C'mon Uncle Jack, I won't let them laugh at you!"

Jack looked at Katherine who was waiting patiently in the car. She slowly raised her hands and shook her head as if to say, I had nothing to do with that.

Looking back at Kerry, Jack took a deep breath and said, "OK."

Hatchet Jack, the Terror of the Mekong, a CIA-sanctioned assassin, and the man known as the Devil with the Green Face, was terrified as he opened the door of the movie theater's lobby. Then, to Jack's surprise, nothing happened. Nothing. No one stared, no one laughed, and no one really seemed to care. People looked, but just for a second longer than usual. Jack purchased his ticket without incident, made his way into the theater, and sat down next to Kerry and Katherine. The theater was packed so another little boy sat down on the other side of him. He looked at Jack for a moment and asked, "What happened to your face?" The little boy's mother, sitting on the other side, recoiled in horror when she heard her child's comment.

Jack smiled, looked at his mom, and said "It's OK." He then turned his attention toward the little boy and said, "I got shot during the war."

"Did it hurt?" asked the little boy, in awe.

"Yes, it did."

"Does it hurt now?"

"Nope," Jack assured him.

The little boy paused and stared for a moment, "My name's Frank," he said introducing himself.

"My name is Jack, nice to meet ya," Jack said, and they shook hands.

Jack really enjoyed the movie. He had not been to one in years. Afterward, he offered to take Katherine and Kerry to the Dairy Freeze for ice cream and Kerry accepted with a resounding, "Heck, yeah!" As they were sitting on a bench eating their ice cream, an old man with a cane approached Jack. He had a Korea Veterans VFW hat on his head and introduced himself as Colonel Anderson, President of the Lewistown VFW. He gave Jack a card and invited him to come to a meeting. Jack said he would think about it.

The Colonel replied with, "I know who you are, I know what you are. We were really hopin' you would come."

Jack looked at the old man suspiciously and asked, "What do you think you know?"

"Hatchet Jack, Terror of the Mekong? Yes, we know."

"Thank you, sir," Jack said. "I'll think about it."

"Hatchet Jack, Terror of the Mekong? What's that about?" Katherine asked after they climbed back into the car for the ride home.

Jack just stared at the floorboard of the car. Marcel was the only one who knew all about Jack's military service, or so he thought. "I'd rather not talk about it, Katherine. Thanks for the movie, I had a good time."

Kerry sat in the back seat with a big grin. *Now Uncle Jack can take me to the movies,* he thought to himself.

One evening, after dropping off a load of shine on the other side of town, a combination of loneliness and curiosity got the better of Jack so he decided to stop by the VFW. He walked in and found, sitting at the bar, his old supply chief. *I'll be damned,* he thought. After giant smiles and handshakes, they talked for hours. Jack met several other men that were "in country" at the same time as him. It brought back a lot of good feelings as well as some bad ones. By the end of the night, he was glad he came. Before he left, the old chief asked him if there was anyone from back in the day he wanted to find. The chief informed Jack they had a network where they could locate most anyone. Jack thought for a moment and said, "Yes, Lt. Watkins, Army nurse."

"Old flame?" asked the chief.

"Nope, she saved my life."

The old chief called Jack about a week later and told him what they had found out about Lt. Watkins. Discharged in '74, Annette Wilamena Watkins' last know location was Philadelphia, no address. *Not much help,* Jack thought, but he had an idea. He called Miss Kitty Carter, Gene's wife, who ran the sheriff's office. Her real name was Susan, but everybody called her Miss Kitty. Miss Kitty said she wasn't sure what she would be able to find out, but if Lt. Watkins had any contact with the law, a traffic ticket, whatever, maybe she could get an address. She also reminded Jack that what she was doing was not exactly legal and to keep it to himself.

Two days later, Miss Kitty was knocking on Jack's door. Jack invited her in and asked what she had found.

"You might want to sit down, Jack," she said.

They both took a seat at the kitchen table and then Miss Kitty said, "How well did you know this woman?"

"I haven't seen her in years," said Jack. "What's wrong?"

Miss Kitty opened a manila envelope and pulled out a mug shot. "Is this her?" she asked.

Jack just stared for a moment. It was Lt. Watkins, but her eyes were dead. She looked terrible. "Yeah, that's her," Jack sighed.

"OK," said Miss Kitty, "here goes. Annette W. Watkins, street name Raven; six arrests in the Tioga section of North Philadelphia for prostitution, three arrests for possession of drugs, and two years of prison time served for possession with the intent to distribute heroin. Jack, this is a very bad person."

Jack just sat there, stunned. Finally he raised his eyes to Miss Kitty and said, "Thank you, Susan, I am grateful. If there is anything I can do for you, let me know. Can I keep this?"

"Yep, just don't tell Gene I did this. He'd be pissed," Miss Kitty said. She gave Jack a hug and left. Jack sat alone, staring at the picture.

For the next week Jack could not reconcile the picture in his mind of the young nurse and the picture in front of him. Jack never had bad dreams about combat, but he did have dreams about Lt. Watkins standing over his gurney. That smile, those bright eyes, and that soothing voice. *Something is wrong*, Jack thought, *I need to talk to her. I need to find out what happened.* Jack slid the big green wooden box from under his bed. He had one more mission. Folks in North Philly would thereafter refer to it as the Night of the Tioga Monster.

Chapter 9

When Carla Jo got out of her car she was dressed in green scrubs.

"Are you a nurse?" Amy asked.

"Sort of," she replied. "Come on in, I'm hungry. Did you eat yet?"

"Yep, I'm not really hungry," Amy said as they walked into the kitchen.

Opening the refrigerator and browsing the shelves, Carla Jo asked, "So, tomorrow is your first day. Are you ready?"

"I think so," said Amy, a little hesitant. "It's all new so I guess I'm a little nervous."

"Good, I'd be worried about you if you weren't." Carla Jo took a deep breath and asked, "What do you know about sex?"

"Sex? What do you mean?"

"Sex...you know, how babies are made."

"Oh, yeah, well, we bred cows before. The bull sticks his penis into the cow's vagina and fertilizes the egg with his sperm. I reckon it works the same way with people," Amy said matter-of-factly.

Whew, thought Carla Jo, *that was easy*. "Yep, it does. What do you know about menstrual cycles?"

"What?" asked Amy curiously.

OK, here we go, thought Carla Jo. As she began to explain about the special monthly visitor, Amy looked horrified. "It could happen any time, any place, and I want you to be prepared. You need to keep one of these," Carla Jo showed her a pad she had removed from the bathroom drawer, "and a clean pair of underwear with you or close by."

"That's just gross," said Amy, wrinkling her nose.

"It can be, but it's important that you learn how to care for yourself and keep yourself clean," Carla Jo said. "Now let's talk about boys."

"Boys?" Amy asked quizzically.

"Boys are like those bulls you saw. Once a boy reaches a certain age he has but one thought: getting his penis into your vagina. He will tell you anything you want to hear, he will lie, he will do things for you, he will give you presents and any other thing he can think of. You should know this for what it is and know what they are doing. Accept no gifts and take no favors. Once you do, that boy will think you owe him something and I have already explained what that something is."

"I don't know any boys like that," said Amy dismissively.

"Trust me you will," said Carla Jo, then she narrowed her eyes and spoke with an intensity that Amy had never heard. "There is one more thing. Never, ever go anywhere with any boy or man that you do not know, never. Do you understand?"

"Yes, but why? I'm with Uncle Jack all the time and nothin' bad ever happens."

"That's family," said Carla Jo. "I'm talking about strangers or people you just barely know. Some men and boys think that if they want sex, they can just take it. They will hurt you to get it. Do not put yourself in that position. Stay with your friends; stay around people you trust."

"You are scarin' me a littl,e Aunt Carla Jo," Amy said.

"Good. You don't have to be afraid of everything and everyone, you just have to pay attention. Do you understand?"

"Yes, ma'am, I think I do."

Carla Jo's demeanor changed. She smiled at Amy and said, "I know this is all a bit much, but these are things you need to know and understand. Have you ever been in a fight?"

"A fight, like a fist fight?" Amy asked.

"Yes."

"A boy hit me in school once, but Mary Beth picked him up and slammed him into the ground. He didn't hit me after that."

"Your uncle Jack wants to spend a couple of hours with you. He's going to show you a few things about defending yourself," said Carla Jo.

"Fightin' and crazy sex people? What is this school like? I'm thinkin' I don't really want to go," Amy said seriously.

Carla Jo laughed and said, "No, honey, it's not going to be that much different than your old school. You will meet a lot of new people. Growing up around here you know everybody and everybody knows you. Your world is getting bigger. But the bigger your world gets, the more complicated it becomes. The better you understand what goes on around you, the less likely you will run into any problems. You are going to love your new school. It will be fun, I promise."

"OK, if you say so. Thanks…I think."

Carla Jo leaned her head toward the window and yelled, "JACK!"

"Is she ready?" Jack yelled back.

Carla Jo ushered Amy outside to where Jack was sitting on the back steps.

"You ever been in a fight?" Uncle Jack asked.

"Aunt Carla Jo just asked me that and no, not really," Amy said, a little impatiently.

"Good," said Jack. "The goal is not to ever have to fight. If you can walk away or talk your way out of it, that's what you do. Do whatever you can to avoid fightin'."

"OK, Uncle Jack," Amy exasperated.

"You have never seen me fight, have you? I'll answer that. No, you haven't. You have never seen your daddy fight, have you? No, you…"

Amy interrupted, "Yes, I have."

"When?" said Jack, surprised.

"One day Daddy pulled into the Quick Stop, the one in Black Oak, and saw this man yellin' at Aunt Carla Jo. He called her a nigger. Daddy pulled his gun out of the truck and beat him with it. Then Daddy made him get on his knees and apologize. That man was bleeding a lot. Then Sheriff Carter pulled in and the man started yellin' and pointin' at Daddy, and then Sheriff Carter hit the man, too. Daddy was so mad he forgot I was in the truck. He apologized to me all the way home, but I never could figure out why he felt sorry."

"I forgot about that," said Jack. "I think your daddy might have gotten a little carried away."

"What would you have done?"

Jack thought for a moment, then another moment, and then he said, "Honey, that's just not important. What's important is to avoid fighting when possible."

Carla Jo was standing by the back door listening, She chuckled and said, "Smooth, Jack, real smooth."

Jack looked back over his shoulder at Carla Jo and said, "Ain't you got somethin' to do?"

She laughed again and Jack continued, "I want to teach you some things to help you defend yourself. If anyone tries to hurt you, defend yourself. If they call you names or anything else, ignore it and walk away. If someone puts their hands on you, make them wish they hadn't."

Jack spent a few hours teaching Amy how to develop power through a solid stance, four basic punches, and some defensive moves; nothing complicated, nothing she could use to seriously injure another student, just a few basics. They practiced on the heavy bag Jack had hanging next to his little cinder block workout shed. Jack shouted out combinations of punches and she delivered. She was powerful for her size as well as fast. *Damn fast*, Jack thought.

Amy worked up a little sweat during her training so Carla Jo brought her a sweet tea. It was getting close to dinner time by then and Amy said it was time for her to go home. Jack offered her a ride home but she said she would rather run, it would get her in shape for deer hunting. Carla Jo and Jack wished her well on her first day of school and after scratching Bubba behind his ear, she headed off across the yard.

Eight minutes later Amy was standing on her front porch. She could smell fish frying in the kitchen. Her daddy and Joseph were cooking what they caught that day.

"Smells good, Daddy," Amy said, famished from her workout.

"I hope you're hungry. Me and Joseph caught a mess of blue gill. How was your day?"

"Oh, it was all right. I helped Granny Patches, talked to the Hatfield boys about school, got a Dr. Pepper and Moon Pie from Mr. Gwinn's—I owe him twenty two cents. Then I hung out with Carla Jo and Uncle Jack. Carla Jo wanted to talk about sex and boys," Amy said.

"Did 'ja learn anything?" her daddy asked.

"Boys are scummy," she said.

Her daddy laughed and said, "Hey, I'm a boy!"

"Yeah, but you don't count," Amy explained. "Then Uncle Jack taught me how to fight...No, I mean self-defense," Amy said, correcting herself. "What does he know about that stuff?"

Leon thought to himself, *if you only knew.* "If you want to learn about self-defense or..." *assassinating foreign political leaders*, he thought but didn't say, "or stuff like that, you can do worse than Uncle Jack."

When they sat down to eat, her daddy had his own advice to give about school. He didn't seem as concerned about things as Jack and Carla Jo. He basically said that she was smart, had a good family name, and if she worked hard she could do anything she wanted. He also said that if she brought home any bad grades, she could forget about hunting. Amy had done well in school so far, so she was sure it wouldn't be a problem.

They did the dishes and cleaned up the kitchen after supper. Her daddy wanted to watch the news and when Amy saw that the news lady was Melissa Bean, she laughed out loud.

"What's so funny?" asked her daddy.

"Her, Melissa. She's a phony and she's dumb as a brick," Amy said.

"How do you know that?"

"Aunt Carla Jo introduced me to her. I met her," she explained.

"What? Where?" asked her daddy in disbelief.

"In the city. Aunt Carla Jo has some interesting friends."

Chapter 10

Amy stood in Kerry's room looking into his dresser mirror. She looked good, she thought. She reached down and picked up the tote bag that Carla Jo gave her. Carla Jo said it was called a Parade something or other. It must be special, she thought, because Carla Jo was proud of it. Then she yelled for her little brother and told him she would walk him to Granny Patches' for breakfast, but that he would have to walk down the hill to the bus by himself. She locked the door to the house and started walking across the road with Joseph. He stopped, looked up at her and said, "I think I know where Granny Patches lives."

Amy looked at him and thought, *Someone else is getting older, too*. She put him in a headlock and kissed him on his head about a dozen times. He pretended to struggle and complain, but he loved the attention. He hadn't gotten much lately; not as much as she thought he needed, anyway.

As she reached the end of the road, she saw that Tommy and Timmy were already there. They stared at her as she approached.

"Hi, y'all ready for school?" Amy asked, but they just kept staring at her.

"HEY, can you hear me?" Amy yelled.

"Sorry, Amy," Tommy said. "You just look so different, like you should be on TV or somethin'."

"It's just new clothes Tommy, it's still me," Amy said.

Just then they heard the air breaks on the bus as it pulled to a stop and Amy climbed aboard, said hello to the new bus driver, and started looking for Mary Beth. She didn't have to look long because there she was, same seat as usual. Mary Beth was the first one on the bus, so she got to pick her seat and she always picked the same one. Amy slid down next to her and gave her a hug. Then she noticed that Mary Beth smelled a little sweaty. She must have been up since 5 a.m. helping her daddy haul sugar to the still, she thought. He was trying to get one more run on a pot of mash from the day before.

"Did 'ja have chores this morning?" Amy asked.

"Yep, workin' with my daddy. I almost didn't make the bus."

"Me too. My chores should be ending in about a week. Daddy's takin' the animals to slaughter and he's givin' the chickens to Granny Patches."

"For doin' chores, you sure smell wonderful," noted Mary Beth.

"It's this shampoo I got when I went to the city with my Aunt Carla Jo," Amy explained. Amy went on to tell her of the adventures in the city and shared some of the things that she and her aunt had talked about. Time flew quickly and soon the thirty minute bus ride was over

Off the bus and walking up to school, Mary Beth and Amy were walking past a group of girls when one said, "Look, the garbage truck just got here." Amy looked around for a garbage truck, but she didn't see one. Suddenly she heard a voice coming from the opposite direction.

"Amy! Amy!" She heard a woman calling. The woman got out of her parked car and said, "Remember me? Cindy Peterson? I saw you at Francois."

The four girls said in disbelieving unison, "Francois?"

"Yes, ma'am, nice to see you again," Amy said.

"I love your tote. Prada, very nice," Mrs. Peterson complimented her.

"Thank you, ma'am," replied Amy. "It was sure nice seein' you again, but I better get to class."

Amy continued to walk toward the front entrance with Mary Beth, who looked at her and asked, "What's she talkin' about?"

"I saw Mrs. Peterson at my aunt's beauty shop," said Amy.

Inside, the seventh graders were herded into the gymnasium where Principal Nolan gave an orientation speech. *She seemed nice enough*, Amy thought after the orientation. Then they found the table with their schedules and were told to report to their first class. The day went pretty fast and before she knew it, it was time for lunch.

Amy got her tray and began to look at the food selections. Her Aunt Carla Jo warned her against anything with a lot of sauce. One little mistake would ruin your look for the whole day. She chose a mixed fruit plate, some french fries, and chocolate milk. She paid for her lunch, turned, and looked out over the vastness that was the junior high lunchroom for a familiar face. Then she saw a girl waving at her. It was Candice Peterson.

"Come sit with us," called Candice.

Amy took a seat next to Candice and the other three girls she had seen by Mrs. Peterson when she got off the bus. After introductions were made all around, Amy saw Mary Beth off in the distance. She stood up and waved to her friend until Mary Beth saw her and began to walk over. Noticing this, Allison, one of the girls said, "No, Amy, I don't think so."

"You don't think so? What do you mean?" asked Amy.

"This table is reserved for us. We really don't want any freaks," said Allison.

Amy felt a heat slowly growing inside her. She was getting mad, and then she said, "She's not a freak. Don't call her that, don't *ever* call her that. She's my best friend."

Then suddenly it hit Amy, everything that Carla Jo had tried to explain to her at Francois. Amy might be dressed like them, but she didn't act like them. Never could she imagine treating people like that. She decided that she could sit with the fake, phony, stylish kids or she could go have lunch with Mary Beth. Amy stood up, picked up her tray, and said, "She means more to me than all the pretty things in the world."

"Don't ask to come back," said Candice in a snotty tone.

"Bye, Candice."

As Amy walked over to where Mary Beth was standing, Mary Beth looked at her quizzically.

"What was that about?" asked Mary Beth.

"Fake people," said Amy.

"What?"

"Do you know who Melissa Bean is?" Amy asked.

"The news lady?" replied Mary Beth.

"Yep, have I got a story for you."

Chapter 11

*A*my was a watcher. She didn't speak much, but she saw and heard everything that went on around her. She had spent most of her life surrounded by adults or by Kerry and his friends. The petty gossip, the whining about schoolwork and certain teachers, and talking about cute boys, movie stars, or musicians had no appeal to her. She found herself isolated by her own choice. With the exception of Mary Beth, Amy was a loner and as a result, she immersed herself in books.

As the first month went by, she began to understand what was expected of her. She would sit and listen to the lectures until she figured out what the teachers wanted from her. She would do her homework in class and then she would take out one of the books that Carla Jo had given her her and read. She was getting bored.

Carla Jo was right about the boys. They would stop her in the hall and want to talk. She was polite and listened, but then she dismissed them and went on her way. She would occasionally find a note stuck in her locker professing love from an unknown admirer. That made her laugh, but rumors were starting about the very pretty, quiet girl. One was that she had a boyfriend in high school and the other was that she didn't like boys at all but girls, instead. Then there was an incident that would give them something else to talk about.

Amy was on her way to class when she saw Mary Beth backed up against the lockers, her books clasped close to her chest, and her head down. Candice and her friends surrounded her. Amy forced her way through the group and asked Mary Beth what was wrong.

Candice spoke up instead, "I don't like the way this bitch looked at me."

Amy turned her attention toward Candice, smiled, and said, "I'm sure she meant nothin' by it. Let's go, Mary Beth."

"She's not going anywhere 'til she apologizes," snarled Candice.

"Come on, Mary Beth," Amy said as she grabbed her arm and started to walk away. Then Candice shoved Amy and Amy's books hit the floor. Amy spun around and hit Candice in the sternum with a palm strike, causing Candice to fly backward and land flat on her ass. The other girls backed up as Candice sat on the floor, gasping for air. Amy's big green eyes flashed as she looked at Candice and in a low growl she said, "Don't you ever put your hands on me, Candice Peterson, ever."

Picking up her books, Amy and Mary Beth walked away without looking back.

Once out of earshot, Amy looked at Mary Beth and asked, "Why didn't you fight back? You are way stronger than her. You could break her in half like the plastic Barbie Doll she is."

"I know that, but my daddy said if I get in trouble he would whoop my ass."

Amy understood. "I'll tell you what, the next time they try that with you, defend yourself, come tell me, and I will have my uncle Jack on your front porch before you get home tellin' your daddy how they were treatin' you. No matter what he said, your daddy wouldn't want people treatin' you like that."

"You think so?" Mary Beth asked.

"I know so."

"OK, thanks for stickin' up for me."

An hour later Amy was sitting in Principal Nolan's office with Carla Jo. Carla Jo was Amy's emergency contact. Leon worked in the mines and was not available during the day. Amy explained what happened. Then Candice Peterson's mom showed up a little later demanding that Amy be removed from school. Amy sat outside the office while those conversations were taking place.

"I'm going to call the sheriff and have her arrested for assault!" threatened Cindy.

When Carla Jo started laughing, Cindy Peterson snapped, "What's so funny?"

"Sheriff Carter? You want to call Sheriff Carter? Go ahead, Cindy, I'll give you his phone number. Then next weekend when Amy, her daddy, and Sheriff Carter are walking through the woods deer hunting, they can have a big laugh about how Amy sat a bully on her ass."

"Candice is not a bully," Cindy protested.

"Yes, she is, she's the worst kind," said Carla Jo.

"OK ladies, I've heard enough," interrupted an irritated principal. "I will bring the girls into my office and we will discuss the matter, exchange apologies, and move on. If there is any repeat of this I will have them both removed from school."

"Sounds fair. Thank you, Principal Nolan," said Carla Jo.

"This is a travesty," Mrs. Peterson grumped.

"Well, I can do it this way or suspend them both. Candice did start it," the principal explained.

"Fine," said Cindy as she stormed out of the office.

Amy saw Mrs. Peterson walk out of the office followed by Carla Jo.

"Am I in trouble?" she asked.

"No, but we do need to work on your diplomacy skills."

Amy hugged her Aunt Carla Jo and said, "Thank you."

"I'll talk to your daddy tonight. He won't be happy, but he'll understand. Don't worry about it, go back to class," instructed Carla Jo.

Carla Jo was right. Amy's daddy was not happy, but he did understand. Uncle Jack, on the other hand, was proud as a peacock, but he knew better than to show it.

Amy and Mary Beth didn't eat lunch alone anymore. The next day they were joined by two other girls, then six, and by the end of the week their table was packed. Amy didn't ask for it and certainly didn't want it, but the nerdy and awkward kids looked to Amy as the Pied Piper of the Lewistown Junior High social underclass.

Chapter 12

*I*t was 5 a.m. on a brisk November morning, the first Saturday of deer season. Leon and Gene were sitting in Leon's kitchen, dressed in their camouflage hunting clothes and having a cup of coffee. Amy had just walked out of her room after getting dressed when a knock came at the door. Amy answered it.

"Good mornin', Uncle Jack. Are you ready?"

Jack reached down to give her a hug and said, "Good mornin', slugger."

"JACK!" yelled Leon from the kitchen, "It's not somethin' to be proud of!"

"Yeah it is," whispered Jack to Amy.

Gene smiled at Leon and said, "I heard about that. Deputy Nolan's wife came by the office and told us that Amy put that spoiled brat Peterson girl on her ass. From what I understand, she needed it."

"Yeah, well, this family has had enough violence in it. I'm tryin' to teach her another way. We should be settin' a good example and that means you too, Jack," said Leon, loud enough so Jack could hear him.

Amy and the men grabbed their rifles and walked down to the old road behind the barn. Leon knew that Amy had been walking those woods with Kerry for years. He looked at Amy and asked, "Well, you know more about these woods than most. Where should we go?" Amy, of course, had an opinion.

Amy looked out at the woods then back to the men, cocked her head to the side, and in a confident, direct tone said, "Here's what I'm thinkin'. The wind is coming from the northeast, which is just about perfect. At the bend on the old road I found three dear trails. I'm gonna run down there and see which one has any fresh tracks or sign. Since all the trails end up at the same place, I'm gonna follow the trail and push them into the holler by Whiskey Creek. When they come out of the brush at the end of the trail they will go one of two places: either along the north side of the creek through the brush, or up and across the north side of the holler. If y'all set up on the south side of the holler about halfway down, you should get a shot no matter where they come out. Don't go straight across the holler or they'll smell ya'. Walk east a good half mile before you start down into the holler. It should take me around twenty minutes to start down the trail, so y'all better get a move on."

Gene looked at Jack and asked, "Did 'ja get all that?"

Jack laughed and replied with, "I was hopin' you did."

Leon was impressed. He stared at Amy for a moment, nodded his head, and said, "OK, sounds good to me. But first I want you to put this on." Leon handed Amy a bright orange stocking cap and added, "I would like to be able to see ya'."

"OK Daddy," Amy said as she slung her rifle on her back and took off jogging down the road.

"Well, I think I know why Kerry and Rob took her with 'em," said Leon.

"Yeah, they used her as a damn huntin' dog," said Jack.

"Cutest huntin' dog I've ever seen," said Gene.

"Well, you heard her. We best get a move on," Leon decided.

The men found their way to the holler above Whiskey Creek. They crept down the side and set up their positions. After about five minutes they heard a rustling from down below and saw a doe trotting next to the creek. They shook their heads at each other. They didn't want to shoot a doe.

Minutes later, Jack saw something in the brush across the creek. He signaled to the other men and they watched patiently. Slowly and deliberately a large buck began to creep from the brush toward the creek. Leon signaled at Gene to take the shot. While lifting his rifle slowly, the sling got hooked on a branch. The buck moved farther out toward the creek. Gene gingerly cleared the branch and began to lift his rifle. Then the buck froze and looked back over his shoulder. Steadying the rifle, Gene got the buck in his sights, moved his thumb to click off the safety, and then CRACK, a shot echoed through the holler.

The buck hopped straight up, took a couple of steps, then fell over. They looked back and forth at each other, finally realizing that none of them had shot. Off in the distance they could see a little orange dot. Slowly Amy came into view, running along the creek. Climbing down through the brush they heard a "WHOO HOO!" Amy sat down her rifle, unsheathed her buck knife, and leapt onto the deer, plunging her knife into his throat.

Amy stood up. She was sprayed with blood and held the buck knife over her head. With an expression of unbridled joy on her face she said, "This ain't a zoo. How long were y'all gonna look at it?"

Jack walked up next to Leon and whispered, "See, I told ya'. She's Marcel, she's a stone killer."

"I see what you mean," said Leon.

They dressed the deer by the creek and then carried it back to the barn. Amy's daddy asked her if she wanted it mounted.

"Nope, too small," she said. "There is only one mount I want: Old Red."

"Old Red?" asked Jack curiously.

Leon smiled, shook his head, and said, "Yeah, there's a tall tale about a deer as big as a bull with oak trees for antlers. I ain't never seen it."

"Kerry saw him," Amy said as she turned to stare longingly at the woods, "He's out there gettin' bigger and bigger. I'm gonna get him!"

Amy didn't get another deer that year. She never even saw one. Her daddy explained to her that she wasn't going to get one every time she went out. Amy had a hard time with that concept. She was supposed to get one every time she picked up a rifle. Amy got frustrated, but she was no quitter. By the end of the season, she had learned the most important thing about hunting: the time she got to spend with her Daddy, Uncle Jack, and Gene.

Chapter 13

$\mathcal{A}$my finished junior high as an honor student. She struggled a little with math, but her Aunt Carla Jo helped her through it. She was also popular with the other students, which was hard for Amy to figure out because she really didn't talk to anybody or makes close friendships. Mary Beth was Amy's best friend and that was that.

Mary Beth, like Amy's uncle Jack had once been, was extremely self-conscious about her face. As Mary Beth got older the scars on her face faded, but they were still visible. Amy took Mary Beth to her uncle Jack and Aunt Carla Jo's house to spend time with them. Uncle Jack even had a couple heart-to-heart talks with Mary Beth about how he dealt with his disfigurement. Amy enjoyed watching Mary Beth come out of her shell. She was happier and more relaxed.

Reading became a big part of Amy's life. Time spent with Aunt Carla Jo talking about books and authors began to change her in ways not even Carla Jo could have expected. Amy improved her vocabulary and she no longer sounded like a backwoods country girl. In conversations with her daddy, he would have to stop her and say, "in English, Amy." Leon was far from illiterate, but he was not as well read as Amy. Life outside Alabama also intrested

Amy. After reading about these places she wanted to see them for herself.

When Amy graduated from eighth grade, Carla Jo took her on a long weekend to New York City. Amy flew for the first time. Sitting by the window she was in awe of the sheer size of her country. They went sightseeing, took a carriage ride through Central Park, and had lunch at the top of the World Trade Center. The highlight of the trip was when they went to see a play. It was called *Les Miserables*. The actors were so incredibly talented. They made her laugh, cry, and think. On the airplane ride home she made a vow to herself: when she got old enough, she would travel as much as she could. She would see the world. At the time she had no idea how prescient her vow was.

Leon's life was changing, too. He bought a new truck, a fishing boat, and he had a girlfriend. He had always dated women but nothing that was long term. Now he felt like he had found the one. It was Miss Francis, the Sunday school teacher. She was ten years younger than him but that didn't seem to matter.

Amy really liked Miss Francis, but she didn't like the idea of sharing her daddy. Amy didn't want to be selfish or jealous, but she couldn't help it. Carla Jo and Amy had several long talks about the properties of love and how it didn't divide it, it only added up. Amy had also become very independent. She didn't need another parent or someone telling her what to do. At the end of all of their conversations, Carla Jo concluded their talk with the same advice, "If you love your daddy, you will make it work." Amy decided she would do her best.

Amy's brother, Joseph, had been spending a little time with Jack learning about cars. Joseph was a typical nine-year-old boy with a lot of energy and curiosity, and as Jack and Joseph worked on the Chevelle, it slowly morphed into something that more resembled a racecar. Jack had thought about taking it to the local stock car track and running it in the street stock division, but he couldn't have his car tore up and still do his job. His time with Joseph was making him rethink that. Maybe he could build another car just for racing. Joseph loved stock car racing. His favorite driver was Dale Earnhardt. Joseph didn't have many shirts that didn't have the number three on it.

Granny Patches was getting older and her garden was getting smaller. Still, she insisted on having one. She was a child of the Depression and having a garden was a must, even though the cost of planting, fertilizing, and canning became more expensive than if she would have just gone to the grocery store. Amy didn't mind helping her.

On the first day of summer vacation after eighth grade, Amy spent the morning in Granny Patches' garden, weeding. It was pretty hot so afterward she threw on her swimsuit,pulled on an old sundress as a cover up, grabbed her brother, and headed for the swimming hole behind her Aunt Carla Jo's.

On the way down String Hill Road Amy saw Tommy, Timmy, and another boy who looked to be a little older.

"Hi Tommy, hi Timmy," said Amy.

"Hey," said Tommy. Timmy waved.

The other boy nudged Tommy, and Tommy said, "Amy, this is my cousin Ed. He's from Saint Louis. He's staying with us for awhile."

The reason Ed was staying with them was because his father was in prison charged with sexual assault against Ed's eight-year-old sister. Mr. Hatfield agreed to take him because he came with a monthly check from the state.

Ed stepped forward and put out his hand. Amy stuck out her hand in a friendly manner to shake it. That wasn't what he had in mind, however, and he tried to pulled her hand up and kiss it. She jerked it away.

"I'm sorry, did I scare you?" he asked as he let his eyes take a long walk all over Amy's body. Ed caused the hairs to stand up on the back of Amy's neck.

"No, I...I have to go. Nice meeting you, Ed," said Amy politely.

"Why don't you come back another time? I'd really like to get to know you," said Ed in a seductive tone.

"No, I don't think so," said Amy in a resolute tone. "Bye Tommy, bye Timmy," she said.

"Bye Amy," Tommy said. Timmy just waved.

As Amy walked away with her brother, Ed looked at Tommy and said, "I'm gonna fuck her."

Chapter 14

Amy could see the storm clouds gathering to the west, but she didn't care. It was the third Saturday in the month of July. This was Carla Jo and Amy's Francois day. Joseph and her daddy went fishing early that morning so she figured she would spend the day with Carla Jo. Carla Jo had promised her crepes for lunch so they would eat first and then go to their appointment.

She packed her tote bag with her nice clothes so she could change at Carla Jo's. It was already hot and humid, and the sweaty look wasn't something she was going for. After locking the house she started down the road. Thoughts of high school occupied her mind. She was sure Carla Jo would have some advice for that, too. She was letting her mind wander when Tommy came running to the end of the driveway.

"Amy, Amy," Tommy said excitedly, "we got a new hound dog puppy. Wanna see it?"

"Oh, well, that's great, but I have to go," said Amy.

"He's really cute, come see, Amy!" said Tommy.

"OK," Amy said, giving in. The boys didn't have much to get excited about so she would humor them and take a look. Besides, she did like puppies. Joseph had been bugging her daddy to get him one, so maybe she could bring him by to take a look at this one later on.

They walked up the driveway and turned the corner to the other side of the barn. Ed was standing there with a twisted smile on his face.

"Hi Amy," said Ed with that same, sick-sounding seductive voice he used last time they spoke.

"Yeah, hi," said Amy, unimpressed. She turned to look at Tommy and said, "OK, where's the puppy?" While looking at Tommy she noticed his demeanor had changed. He had a serious, dark look on his face.

"Right here," said Ed. "I'm the puppy, pet me."

"This isn't funny, Tommy, I have to go," said Amy nervously. She turned to discover that she was surrounded. She tried to walk past Timmy, but he stood in her way. Then the boys began to close in around her.

"Show us your titties," Ed demanded. He reach out to touch her, but she pushed his hand away and backed up, though she only managed to back into Tommy. When she turned around and tried to push her way past him, she quickly discovered that he was too big to shove. He pushed her back toward Ed who reached for her again.

"Stop this, stop this now," pleaded Amy. "I have to go." Amy saw an opening between Ed and Timmy so she made a break for it. Ed tripped her as she ran by and she went down hard.

"Get her, hold her down," said Ed. Tommy and Timmy landed on her, grabbed her arms, and pinned her to the ground.

"NO, STOP, NO, GET OFF ME!" shouted Amy repeatedly. She began to panic as it became clear what was happening.

"Now, let's see those titties," said Ed.

He straddled her and reached for her shirt. Amy ripped her arm free from Tommy and punched Ed in the face. Ed fell to the side of Amy, holding his nose. She took a big swing at Tommy's face and missed, and in response they put their entire weight on her arms and shoulders.When Ed jumped back on top of her, she could see the rage in his eyes.

"You fucking little bitch!" Ed growled. "If that's the way you want it...." He punched Amy in the side of the face. Stars swirled around her head. Buttons popped off her dress as Ed ripped it open. She could feel her back being lifted off the ground as he grabbed her bra and pulled it. Amy let out a bloodcurdling scream and kicked her legs. Ed fell off of her to the side. He started to climb on her again when Amy saw a target. She kicked him in the crotch as hard as she could. She heard the air leave his lungs as he fell to the side and rolled over. Tommy looked a little confused, like he didn't know what to do. Ed began to scream, "YOU FUCKING BITCH! YOU'RE DEAD, YOU FUCKING BITCH!" over and over while rolling on the ground, holding his crotch.

Amy caught Tommy's eye. She begged, "Please, Tommy, it's me, it's Amy. Please Tommy, stop. Let me go, please." She saw something in Tommy's eyes, like he was coming out of a trance. Locked in Amy's gaze, Tommy's eyes began to soften. "Please Tommy, please Tommy," Amy said over and over. She could feel Tommy's tight grip on her arm begin to loosen.

At that point, Ed had gotten up and was beginning to stagger around, like he was looking for something. With a renewed sense of urgency, Amy tried to pull away from Tommy's grip, but it tightened again. In one last attempt to get away she arched her back, craned her neck in a violent spasm, and screamed as loud as she could. That's when she saw Mr. Hatfield standing at the window of the trailer, watching. Out of the corner of her eye, Amy saw a shadow and turned in time to see Ed in midair . His knees landed on her chest and she felt the air rush out of her lungs. In Ed's hand she saw a rock. The rock went up, the rock came down, and then everything went black.

Carla Jo looked up at the clock. Amy was running a little late. *That's unusual*, she thought. She needed milk anyway, so she decided to walk down to Ed Gwinn's and pick some up. She left the door unlocked in case Amy showed up while she was out. As Carla Jo walked out the front door she could see Bubba pacing, whining, and staring at the hill. Carla Jo stopped and watched him. *It's unusual for that damn dog to even move*, she thought. Scanning the yard for what might be upsetting him she felt that something wasn't right. She didn't see anything, but for some reason she had an uneasy feeling. She eventually decided to shake it off and continue to the store.

The Story of Bubba the Dog

Rory Chapman was one of the best machinists in the state. His shop was located south of the city and he had been there for almost forty years. Unfortunately, his area was deteriorating. Gangs, drugs, and assorted lawlessness were the rule, not the exception, but he couldn't leave. The machines were far too big and heavy, and the cost to relocate would put him out of business, so every year he made the block wall around his business a little higher and the razor wire on top a little sharper. Despite the dangerous area, auto racers and bootleggers still brought him engine parts to machine. Old Man Chapman was the best and everyone knew it.

Jack pulled his truck up to the gate at Rory's and waited for him to open it. Jack was building a new engine and he wanted the crank shaft balanced and polished. Looking out the window of his truck absentmindedly, he saw a dog sitting ten feet down the sidewalk. His head was caked in blood, from where his left ear had somehow been torn off, and a large flap of skin was hanging off of his side. He looked as though he had been ripped open like an envelope. He had what appeared to be numerous puncture marks on his chest and legs. Drips of blood formed small pools under him. He looked skinny, like he hadn't eaten in awhile, and he still had that puppy look with his big feet and a head that was just a little too big for his body. He was wobbling a bit. When he made eye contact with Jack, he stopped wobbling and lifted his head. Jack thought the gesture looked like he was trying to keep his dignity. The gate opened and Jack pulled in.

When Jack greeted Old Man Chapman, the first thing he asked was about "that dog out front." Old Man Chapman had no idea, but he did say that dog fighting was big in the neighborhood and that the dog was probably a practice dog or a loser. Jack thought to himself, *That dog isn't a loser.*

Jack took care of his business, drove out the gate, and parked by the curb. The dog was still there and so were two local thugs. After getting out of his truck, Jack walked to the passenger side, opened the door, and then kneeled next to the dog.

"Bubba, you look like a Bubba. You're coming home with me," said Jack as he picked up the dog and set him in the front seat.

"YO, MOTHA' FUCKA'," the biggest of the two thugs shouted. "THAT AIN'T YO' DOG."

Jack was spreading out an old blanket he kept on the floorboard to make the dog more comfortable as the thugs approached Jack's truck, continuing to yell.

"I'M TALKIN' TO YOU MUTHA' FUCKA'."

Jack calmly reached between the seats, grabbed his .45, and as quick as a cat he spun around and placed the barrel of the .45 on the thug's forehead and asked, "Whose dog is this?"

The combination of Jack's appearance and the gun froze the thug in his tracks. "Yo man, I...." the thug stuttered.

Jack pulled the hammer back on the .45 and asked again, "Whose dog is this?"

"That's yo' dog," the thug quickly replied.

"Run," Jack growled.

On the way back to Black Oak Jack talked to the dog. He told the dog it would be OK and that he was hurt in battle, too. He spoke of dealing with the mental and physical pain of his injuries. He spoke about the loneliness and isolation while he was in the hospital and in rehab. His fears, angers, and disappointments all came spilling out. Everything Jack had never said out loud he told Bubba on the forty-five minute ride home. An emotional dam in Jack had burst. Something about that dog had blown the dam up.

When Jack got home he laid the dog on the dining room table and called out for Carla Jo.

Carla Jo walked into the kitchen to see a battered and bloody dog on the table and a panic in Jack's eyes. "What the hell...," said Carla Jo, looking a bit shocked.

"You gotta help him, I think he's dying," said Jack

Carla Jo was struggling to understand exactly what was happening. She looked at the dog and it's numerous injuries and said, "Jack, I'm not a vet."

"Just try, please, try to help him," pleaded Jack.

Carla Jo looked at the dog again, then at Jack, and said, "This dog is all but dead. I can't do anything for him."

"DAMMIT, CARLA JO, TRY," Jack roared.

Carla Jo's mouth fell open and her eyes got big. Jack had never raised his voice to her before. Then she noticed his lip starting to quiver as a lone tear rolled down his cheek. She shook her head and said, "I wouldn't know where to start, he needs a vet or he's probably gonna die, Jack."

"I remember a time when you wouldn't give up," Jack said.

Right then Carla Jo understood. With a soft and gentle voice, Carla Jo said, "Oh my god, you think this dog is you. You never did deal with anything that happened to you in Nam, did you?" Jack didn't answer. "Alright, I'll make some phone calls and see if I can find the vet."

Carla Jo located Doc Langer at Cloward Farm just across the border in Sibley County. Doc Langer didn't usually care for pets. His specialty was cattle and farm animals. He told Carla Jo he was busy and he was sorry he couldn't help. Jack showed up at the farm and convinced him otherwise.

Doc Langer worked on Bubba for two hours, rehydrating him with IV fluids and injecting him with antibiotics. Then the doctor cleaned and sewed up his wounds. When he finished, Doc Langer looked at Jack and said, "If he makes it the next twenty-four hours, he has a shot, but I wouldn't hold out much hope."

Jack apologized to the doctor for bringing him to the house under duress. Jack's exact words had been, "You get your shit and get to my house or I will cut your fucking head off." He promised the doctor if he could do anything for him, he would, and paid the doctor a hundred dollars more than his fee.

Jack sat on the couch with Bubba's head in his lap the rest of the day and into the night. Jack and Carla Jo had long conversations about the war. It was the first time Jack had discussed it in detail. Bubba went into convulsions a couple of times and Jack was sure that Bubba was done. Each time, however, he calmed down and continued to breathe.

That night, Jack fell asleep on the couch sitting up with Bubba. Around 5 a.m. the next morning, Bubba woke him up with a whine. Figuring he was thirsty, Jack got a turkey baster, filled it with water, and gave Bubba a drink. The dog tried to sit up, but he was in too much pain. The next afternoon, he sat up. To celebrate, Jack made him a couple of scrambled eggs, which would become a daily event.

Bubba came with a couple of issues, the first being that he couldn't bark. He could whine or growl, but not bark. The second, and most troublesome, was that he was mean. He hated people. He loved Jack and tolerated Carla Jo, but everyone else needed to beware. Jack put up signs in the driveway warning people and kept Bubba in the house unless Jack was outside with him.

Bubba was also the cause of Jack and Carla Jo's biggest disagreements. Carla Jo said Bubba wasn't staying in the house, but he stayed in the house, anyway. Carla Jo said Bubba wasn't sleeping in their bedroom. He slept in their bedroom, anyway. Carla Jo said Bubba wasn't sleeping in their bed and it cost Jack five hundred dollars for a new king-sized bed, but he slept in the bed, anyway. Carla Jo won one round. Jack had to bathe him once a week.

Leon had his own concerns about Bubba and didn't hesitate to share them with Jack. The dog was usually OK if Jack was around, but Leon didn't want to risk Bubba hurting his kids. Joseph was still a toddler and Amy was only six years old at the time. They both decided to be extra vigilant and when the kids were around, Jack put Bubba in the house. Only one day they discovered that their plan didn't work.

Leon stopped by one day to visit Jack and told Amy to stay in the truck. The two cousins disappeared into the garage. Bored, Amy decided she wanted to visit with Carla Jo, so she jumped out of the truck and ran to the front porch. Leon and Jack walked out of the garage in time to see Amy hit the bottom step. They both started to scream "NO!" but the word didn't come out fast enough. Bubba was lying on the porch and when he saw Amy he jumped up, growling. His teeth were showing and his hair was standing up on his back as he crept toward Amy. Amy stopped at the door, cocked her arm, punched him in the head with her fist, and yelled "HUSH, YA' OLE DOG!" Bubba stopped growling and they locked eyes. Bubba didn't know what to do, since everyone else ran from him. Not this one. Carla Jo opened the door and jerked Amy in the house like a rag doll.

Leon was still a little skittish about allowing Amy around Bubba, but eventually they were able to play in the yard under Jack's supervision. Bubba liked tug-o-war. He wouldn't fetch, but Jack liked to joke that the dog had taught Amy how to fetch. Every time Amy came to visit she would bring Bubba a little treat. It got to the point where Jack knew if Amy was with Leon because what was left of Bubba's tail would start to wag if she was in the truck. Bubba had a new friend but more importantly, so did Amy.

Chapter 15

When Carla Jo returned from Ed Gwinn's, she walked in the door and called out for Amy, assuming she had to be there by now. *Something's just not right*, Carla Jo thought. She picked up the phone and called Leon's house, then Granny Patches. No answer. She called Junior's and asked to talk to Jack.

"Jack, I can't find Amy," said Carla Jo, sounding a little more than concearned.

"What do ya' mean, you can't *find* Amy?" asked Jack.

"She was supposed to be here over hour ago. I called around, nothing," said Carla Jo.

"I'm done here so I'll see you in a bit. If you're that worried, drive up there and take a look. I can't imagine anythin' happenin' to her on that hill. I'm thinkin' she's wanderin' around the woods behind Granny Patches' place looking for deer and lost track of time", said Jack.

"I guess you're right. I'll run by the place and then see you when you get home. Love you," said Carla Jo.

"I love you, too. Bye," said Jack.

Carla Jo grabbed her keys, got in her car, and headed up the hill.

Amy opened her eyes. She could smell gas and oil on the dirt floor. She sat up and looked around. Everything was going in and out of focus. She rubbed her eyes and saw that she was in an old barn. Looking down, she was shocked to see that she was naked. She felt pain on her head and reached up to touch it. There was blood on her fingers. Off in the distance she heard voices.

"You handle it," a gruff voice said.

"We could bury her," said another voice.

"We should cut her up and burn her in the burn barrel. They can't find ashes," said yet another.

Regaining her senses, Amy remembered what had happened and realized they were talking about her. A feeling of terror shot through her body like a lightning bolt. She struggled to her feet and started to quietly walk toward the back of the barn, away from the voices. A white hot pain burned in her groin every time she stepped. While searching for a way out, she could see light coming in by one of the stalls in the corner. There was a small door there and she pushed on it, but it didn't move. She looked through the crack and saw that it was a latch door just like her barn at home. She stuck her fingers through the crack and opened it. Slowly sticking her head through the little door, she looked around and made sure that no one was there. Wincing in pain, she climbed through and stood up. From the top of the hill, way off in the distance, she could make out the roof of Uncle Jack's house. The little door slammed shut behind her.

"What was that?" asked a voice.

She heard the barn door open and then a shout, "She's gone!"

Amy took off running like a frightened rabbit toward her uncle Jack's. Tommy saw her as she made it to the fence line. "There she is!" yelled Tommy.

"GET HER!" shouted Ed.

Carla Jo checked Amy's house. It was locked. Then she stopped at Granny Patches' house. Granny was out weeding her garden and said Amy had left a couple hours ago. Carla Jo got a sick feeling in her stomach. She called Sheriff Carter.

With the adrenaline pumping through her veins, Amy knew she could outrun Timmy and Tommy, but not Ed. Once she cleared the fence she was on Mr. Gwinn's land. Having hunted it before, she knew where a deer trail was that cut through the woods. The trail ended on Indian River Road across from Uncle Jack's. She hit the deer trail at a full sprint. She always had on long sleeves and pants when going through the deer trails. She forgot about the briers and brambles.

The thorns ripped her skin and punctured her feet, but she kept her head down to protect her eyes and just kept running. After clearing the trail at Indian River Road, she looked to the left and saw that Ed was only about forty yards away. She took off across the road, but realized it was still almost a quarter mile to Uncle Jack's house. She could hear Ed breathing hard behind her. He reached for her and missed, and then he grabbed a handful of her hair. Just then Amy felt something brush by her leg. She heard a grunt and then a scream. Her head snapped forward as Ed let go. She didn't look back.

Amy made it to the house, burst through the door, and screamed over and over again for Carla Jo. She checked all of the rooms, but no one was there. Just then she heard Carla Jo's car. She ran out the front door and screamed, "THEY'RE COMING, THEY'RE

COMING!" Carla Jo stopped the car and got out. Her mind could not understand what she was looking at. Amy was standing at the bottom of the steps, naked and covered with blood. Carla Jo ran and grabbed Amy by the hand and took her in the house.

"LOCK THE DOOR, LOCK THE DOOR, THEY'RE COMING!" Amy screamed. Carla Jo locked the door, ran to the bedroom, and grabbed a shotgun. She went to the back door and locked it, and then looked out the windows. After a minute, Carla Jo went back into the living room and saw Amy standing with her arms in front of her and her fists balled up as she rocked back and forth. She was wailing hysterically. Carla Jo grabbed a blanket, wrapped Amy in it, and gently sat her on the couch. Through the front window she saw the police cruiser coming up the driveway.

Carla Jo sat down on the couch and hugged Amy. When she checked Amy for injuries, she found a pretty nasty head wound.

"Sheriff Carter is here, it's going to be OK," Carla Jo said in a whisper while stroking Amy's hair. Gene knocked on the door and Amy jumped. Carla Jo got up to unlock it and Sheriff Carter walked in. He saw Amy's bloodied and swollen face, and he immediately kneeled down in front of her and said, "Honey, it's me, Sheriff Teddy Bear. You have to tell me what happened."

Amy didn't answer. He reached out to touch her face and she recoiled and looked at him like she didn't even know him. *I've seen this before,* Sheriff Carter thought.

Amy doubled over in pain and began to moan.

"We gotta get her to the hospital, Carla Jo. We'll take my car," Gene said. They got up and were heading out the door when Jack pulled up.

"What happened?" Jack asked

"I don't know, but you need to find Leon right now. We are going to the hospital in Lewistown," said Carla Jo.

Jack went back to the house to lock it up when he saw Bubba sitting on the porch. *He looked like he was smiling,* Jack thought, but he was in a hurry and he didn't notice the blood spattered on

Bubba's face. It was a long, excruciatingly painful climb back up the hill for Ed.

Gene called ahead to the emergency room so they would be waiting for Amy. Carla Jo kept trying to get Amy to talk. "Who did this to you," she asked. "Please honey, you have to tell me. Who did this to you".

Amy said one word, "Hatfields."

By the time they got to the hospital, Amy had gone into shock. What Carla Jo didn't know was that she was bleeding internally. Amy would have to fight for her life twice in one day.

Chapter 16

$\mathcal{J}$ack and Leon pulled into the parking lot of the Lewistown Hospital just in time to see the helicopter lift off. Gene and the doctor were standing by the emergency room door. Leon jumped out of the truck and sprinted up to Gene with a look of terror on his face. "How is she, what happened?" Leon asked.

Gene looked at Leon and said, "She is stable and on her way to the children's hospital. This is her doctor."

"Doc, how is she? Is she gonna be OK?" Leon pleaded more than asked.

"She has sustained a concussion, numerous contusions, and lacerations, but what concerns us most is that we believe she is bleeding internally," the doctor explained. "We found numerous punctures in her uterus. A surgical staff is waiting for her at Children's. They are the best in the state. She's strong and in excellent physical condition, but you need to understand that her wounds are serious."

Gene put his arm around Leon and said, "Come on, I'll drive. We have to talk."

"Where's Carla Jo?" Jack asked.

"She's with Amy," Gene said. What he didn't say was that the flight crew told Carla Jo that they didn't take passengers. Gene told them they did.

The men climbed into Gene's squad car and headed toward the city.

"What happened to her, Gene?" Leon deadpanned.

"It was the Hatfields and a seventeen-year-old boy named Ed Henry who's stayin' with them. We think the old man was involved. They did some really nasty stuff to her, Leon. I've never seen anythin' like it. I sent Deputy Nolan to talk to them and told them that Amy had suffered a wild animal attack and probably wouldn't survive. Ed said he was attacked by the same animal; a big cat, he said it was. Near as I can figure, they intended on killin' her and she got away. I have deputies on each end of String Hill Road. They aren't goin' anywhere. I could arrest 'em all, but then Amy would have to relive the attack over and over again in court. What do you want to do, Leon?"

"I want to make sure Amy is OK, then I'll worry about it."

Leon looked over his shoulder at Jack, who was slowly nodding his head. Gene knew there wouldn't be any arrests.

The men made their way into the children's hospital and found the waiting room where Carla Jo was sitting. Her face was covered in anguish and streaked with tears. When Carla Jo saw Leon, she got up and hugged him.

"How is she?" Leon asked.

"She's in surgery. She lost a lot of blood. They said...," she paused, and then said, "Try to be prepared for anything."

An hour later Joseph and Granny Patches showed up. They all sat in a circle and prayed. Another four hours went by and the door to the waiting room opened. The surgeon, still in scrubs, called out "Leon Braxton." They all got up and surrounded the surgeon.

"That's one tough little girl you have, Mr. Braxton," said the surgeon. "She came through surgery flawlessly and her vital signs have returned strong. She will have a long recovery, but she should be fine. We are moving her into ICU for twenty-four hours where we can monitor her. There is one other thing. The damage to her uterus was pretty bad. It's possible she may never be able to have children."

Leon thanked the doctor through sobs. He was finally able to release his emotions. Leon sat down next to Granny Patches and she held him. Granny Patches whispered to Leon, "That thing about her not having children, that's not up to him. That's up to God. God will not deny her that."

Chapter 17

*L*eon stood by Amy's bed in ICU. The beep from the monitors seemed to be in cadence with her breathing. Her face was scratched, bruised, and swollen. Stitches poked out from under her lower lip where it had been split and her head was wrapped in bandages. He reached out and touched her cheek, and then brushed a stray hair away from her face. As damaged as she was, he couldn't help but think how beautiful she was. The nurse came in and announced that visiting time was over.

The family returned to the waiting room where Gene was standing, waiting for Leon.

"I stationed a Deputy outside of ICU just in case. You want a ride home, Leon?" Gene asked.

"Yep, thanks Gene," said Leon.

"I'll stay here tonight so someone is here when she wakes up," said Carla Jo.

"Thanks, Carla Jo. Joseph, Granny, let's go" said Leon.

"I ain't goin' nowhere," said Joseph.

"Me, neither," said Granny Patches.

Leon stared at them both and then Jack nudged him, leaned in, and whispered, "It might be a good idea if no one was up on that hill tonight."

Leon nodded, understanding exactly what Jack meant.

"Alright, Jack and I will see you all in the morning," said Leon.

There wasn't much to say on the way back to Lewistown. There was a quiet determination and no questioning of what needed to be done. The Old Testament was still alive and well in that part of the country. Exodus 21:23-25 was clear: *lex talionis*, the biblical law of retaliation or revenge.

Gene pulled into the parking lot at Lewistown Hospital next to Jack's truck, put the car in park, and said, "I ordered my men away from the hill. We have a traffic enforcement exercise on the other side of the county this evening. It will take us a while to get to Black Oak if something was to happen. I want you boys to be careful."

Leon looked at Gene and said, "Thank you for everything, Gene, I mean it. You're a good friend."

"Anytime. Later, Jack," said Gene.

"Later, Gene," said Jack.

Jack and Leon pulled up to the garage at Jack's house, parked, and got out.

"I'll be right back," said Jack.

Leon turned and looked at the top of the hill. He couldn't see much in the darkness. He thought about the horror of what his little girl went through. It didn't take him long to reach a murderous level of rage.

Jack came out the front door with Bubba in tow. He laid two pistols on the hood of the truck, reached into his pocket, and pulled out two silencers and screwed them on. He handed one pistol to Leon and tucked the other in his belt. He then went to the garage and got a can of gasoline and a mason jar. Jack screwed the lid off the mason jar, took a big swig, and handed it to Leon. Leon took a long pull and sat it on the hood of the truck.

"You ready, Cuz?" said Jack.

"Let's get it done," said Leon.

Amy awoke in the middle of the night.

"Hello, Miss Amy," said the ICU nurse.

"Where am I?" said Amy.

"The children's hospital's intensive care unit. You have had quite an ordeal," said the Nurse.

Amy began to remember why she was there. Her heart rate began to increase as a panic set in, but the nurse was ready with more sedative. As she injected it in her IV, Amy said, "They're dead, aren't they? All of them, they're dead. I'm thirsty."

Amy fell back asleep.

Carla Jo woke up in the waiting room and rubbed her stiff neck.She looked around the waiting room and saw Granny Patches sleeping in a chair in the corner and Joseph asleep on a couch. *Good Morning, Alabama* was on the television and there was something about Black Oak. Carla Jo grabbed the remote and turned up the volume.

Tragedy has struck the rural community of Black Oak as a trailer fire has claimed the lives of four people. The trailer, located on String Hill Road, was fully engulfed by the time firefighters arrived on the scene. The Sheriff of Jackson County will head the investigation into cause of the blaze. The identity of the victims is being withheld until family can be notified.

Carla Jo knew exactly what had happened. At first she was shocked and a bit horrified, and then slowly, a satisfied smile crept over her face.

Chapter 18

After seven days in the hospital, Amy was released to go home. Leon decided to let Amy stay with Carla Jo and Jack while she recovered. He knew someone would always be there for her. When Amy arrived at her uncle Jack's, she got out of the truck and looked up the hill.

"Where are they?" asked Amy.

"They're gone, Amy, Trailer fire," her daddy said without looking her in the eye.

Amy wasn't sure how she felt about that, so she just nodded her head. She gingerly walked up the porch steps where Bubba sat wagging his stubby tail. She knelt down slowly, hugged his neck, and kissed him on his head. Without looking at anyone she said, "When they chased me down the hill, I made it across the road. Ed had me, he grabbed me, and then Bubba attacked him. Bubba saved my life."

They all stood in stunned silence, looking at Bubba. Amy stood up and walked into the house with Bubba on her heels. Carla Jo gently grabbed Leon's arm and said, "This is how it's going to come out. This is how we will hear about it, in little bits and pieces. You are going to need more patience then you ever thought you had. Trust me, I know."

"OK," said Leon.

Days turned into weeks and Amy's physical wounds healed. The only sign that anything had happened was the end of a scar that went a half-inch below her hairline. Jack and Carla Jo made sure she was never alone. She didn't eat much and she didn't speak much. Her days were spent on the front porch reading. Occasionally she would set the book down and stare up the hill, trying to figure out why, reliving every moment she could recall. Blissfully she had faded in and out of conciousness during the attack. She played with Bubba, but that was the extent of her exercise. Leon and Joseph wanted her home, but she wouldn't go and they didn't push it.

Amy finished the last page and closed the cover on *Wuthering Heights*. Bubba was laying on the porch swing with her, his head in her lap. She hugged him and said, "Bubba, I think it's time to talk." Slowly, she walked into the garage and could see Jack's legs sticking out from under the car. Jack heard the stool by the bench squeak as Amy sat down.

"That you, Amy?"

"Yes, sir, I think I want to talk."

Jack knew this was coming and somehow he knew it would be him. Maybe it was their time in the barn caring for the animals after Kerry died. Maybe it was because he was wounded, too. Whatever the reason, he had thought about what he would say and how he would say it. He was honored to have the opportunity while at the same time fearing it. What if he screwed up? What if he made things worse? How would he live with that? He loved the little girl like she was his daughter.

"Uncle Jack, how did you deal with what happened to you in the war?"

Jack nodded his head and thought, *Here goes.*

"Oh honey, that's a big question," he said. "I can tell you it takes time and I can tell you I'm a better man because of it. Because of my wounds I have Carla Jo. I have a greater love and respect for people and for life. I didn't always feel this way but I had people around me like your momma and daddy, your granddaddy, Kerry, Carla Jo, and you; people that love me. When you see the love in their eyes it makes you want to be a better person."

"What about the people that did that to you, are you angry? Do you think about them? Dream about them?" Amy asked.

"Well, that's where what happened to you and what happened to me is different. I was in a war. It was not personal, it was just two soldiers doing their job. Hell, if I met the guy that did this to me I would probably take him to the VFW and buy him a drink. If I was angry at anyone, I was angry at myself. I made a mistake. I put myself in that position. No, I don't think about them at all."

"Why did they do that to me? Why, Uncle Jack? I was good to them boys. I talked to them when no one else did. I took them food. I, I...just, why?" Amy said, almost pleading.

And there was the tough question. It was the question with no good answer. Jack looked at the ground and then slowly lifted his head, looked her in the eye, and enunciated the two syllables, "E-vil, just pure e-vil. You saw it, you experienced it, and you survived it when some people don't. Amy, evil wants what it wants. It can't be bargained with or reasoned with. It is the scariest thing on earth. Those boys were infected with evil, that's why they did what they did."

Amy sat a minute and thought about what Jack had said. Then she blurted out quickly, "I'm afraid to go back up on that hill."

Jack leaned back with a half smile on his face and said, "Well hell, Amy, I would be, too. There would be somethin' wrong with you if you weren't. Honey, we all know that. Your dad, your brother, Granny Patches, Carla Jo; we get it and we all understand. The question is, what are you gonna to do about it?"

"I don't know. I have never been this afraid of anything before. I just don't know what to do. What would you do?"

"We are not talkin' about me, we are talkin' about you. This is personal. We each find our own way. The way I see it, you have a few choices. You can hide from evil, change your life, and allow your fear to decide your future. You can try to forget it and pretend it never happened—that's what most people do, but in the end it eats them up inside. Or you can confront it and prepare to deal with it the next time it shows up. I can help you with that. As horrible as what happened to you was, you were left with a gift. You see Amy, now you know what it is. You can see the evil. You can feel it. It can't sneak up on you again."

"Yeah, I suppose. But Uncle Jack, what would you do?" Amy asked again.

"I'd unscrew the top on a whiskey jar and hide in a hole 'til I died," Jack said with a straight face.

"No, you wouldn't. You would stand at the bottom of that hill and scream 'EVIL, HERE I COME!' Then you would march up there and...," Amy stopped talking.

"Are you talking about what you think I would do? Or maybe you are talking about what you know you need to do," Jack said with a serious face.

Just then Carla Jo's car pulled into the driveway. Amy got up, walked over to her uncle Jack, gave him a hug and a kiss, and said, "Thank you, Uncle Jack."

"Anytime," said Jack.

Amy got up early the next day. It was Saturday morning. She packed her suitcase and carried it to the front door. Jack and Carla Jo were sitting at the kitchen table drinking coffee.

Amy walked into the kitchen and said, "I think it's time for me to go home."

Jack and Carla Jo got up from the kitchen table and hugged Amy.

"I got used to having you around. I'm going to miss you," Said Carla Jo. "Do you want a ride home?"

"Nope, I'm gonna walk," Amy said.

"That suitcase is pretty heavy, why don't you let me take it to ya' later. I'm going up to visit your daddy, anyway," said Jack.

"OK, thanks, Uncle Jack. Thank you again. Thank you for everything. I love you both very much," Amy said, her eyes getting misty.

Amy turned and walked down the steps. As she walked away she heard a whimper and a whine. It was Bubba. Amy walked back to the porch and hugged him and kissed him on the head.

"Yeah, I love you, too, ya' ole dog," She said, then she turned and walked away.

Jack looked at Carla Jo and said, "What do you think? Is she alright now?"

"Its not that easy Jack, it's just not that easy," said Carla Jo, her voice wilting with sadness.

Chapter 19

Amy started down Indian River Road. She looked up the hill where she had come down four weeks earlier and thought about taking that path, but she was wearing shorts. She didn't forget about the briars and brambles. She reached String Hill Road and started up the hill. She always loved that road, the way the treetops came together and formed a tunnel. Today, however, it looked a little darker and kind of eerie, but still she kept going. About halfway to the top her thigh muscles began to burn. *I'm really out of shape,* she thought. It was warm out and she started to sweat. She reached the top and started around the bend, thinking that she should be able to see the rusted mailbox by now, but it was gone.

Amy arrived at the Hatfield's driveway. At first she couldn't bring herself to look. She stared at the ground as she walked off the road and up the driveway, but then she stopped and looked up. It was gone, all of it. The trailer, the barn, the old cars, and the junk were all gone. A flat, empty lot was all that remained. She walked to where the barn had been and looked out toward Uncle Jack's. It was a beautiful view.

"HERE I AM!" she yelled. "CAN YOU HEAR ME? HERE I AM! YOU TRIED TO KILL ME! YOU FAILED! MY NAME IS AMY

LYNN BRAXTON AND I WILL BE READY FOR YOU NEXT TIME. NEVER AGAIN!" Amy turned on her heels and with her head up and shoulders back, she walked off the property.

Walking down the road Amy felt free—at least, she felt more free than she had in a long time. She walked to the front door and could smell bacon cooking.

"I'm home," she hollered. As she walked into the living room she yelled, "Whose cooking in my kit...," she stopped. It was Ms. Francis.

"Hi Amy," said Ms. Francis. "Are you home now? For good?"

"Is that a problem?" asked Amy.

"No, oh no, Amy," Ms. Francis said as she wiped her hands with a towel and went to hug her. Amy put her hand up in front of her and stepped back.

"Where are Daddy and Joseph?" Amy demanded to know.

"They are at the barn getting the boat ready. We were going to the river. You can come with us," Ms. Francis said with a smile.

"You mean you can come with us, right Ms. Francis? That is what you mean, right? This is my house. You understand this is my house?" Amy said, sounding a little agitated.

"Of course dear, this will always be your house."

"Where is your car?"

"It's at my house. I stayed here last night."

"You did what? Where did you sleep?" Amy demanded.

"I'm not too comfortable talking to you about this," Ms. Francis said nervously.

Just then the back door opened and Amy's daddy walked in.

"Amy, you're home," he said as he walked over and hugged her. "We missed you so much."

"You saw me yesterday," Amy said in a terse voice.

"I mean here. Seeing you in the mornin', having dinner with us...the house is not the same without you," her daddy said, smiling.

"Why is she here?" Amy asked, motioning toward Ms. Francis.

Leon looked at Ms. Francis and began to notice the unease.

"Well, Amy, she's my girlfriend, we have been dating for a while now. Actually, we had been discussin' the idea of getting married. I wanted to wait 'til you came home to talk to you about it."

"You're not married yet. She said she spent the night here. Is that true, daddy? Did she sleep in my momma's bed in front of Joseph? Is that what happened, daddy? Is that true? IS THAT TRUE?" Amy's voice rose an octave as she grew more animated. Her big green eyes began to flash and her daddy knew her well enough to know what that meant.

Leon took a deep breath and said, "Amy, you need to calm down right now, we can discuss this like...."

Amy interrupted "Discuss? Discuss what? Discuss the fact that you have replaced me with a WHORE?"

Ms. Francis gasped and Leon yelled, "AMY!"

Then Amy lost it and started screaming, "YES, WHORE! WHORE, I SAID WHORE. GET OUT OF MY HOUSE, WHORE. GET OUT OR I WILL THROW YOU OUT. GET OUT, GET OUT!"

Then Amy tried to attack Ms. Francis, but Leon was able to grab her and put her in a bear hug. Amy fought and kept screaming, "WHORE, WHORE!"

"Carol, take my keys and go home, I'll call you later," Leon said while struggling to hold Amy. Ms. Francis ran out the door as Joseph was coming in.

"Amy?" Joseph looked at his daddy trying to hold Amy. "What's going on?" said Joseph.

"Jo, go unhook the boat from the truck for Ms. Francis, but first call Carla Jo. Tell her to get up here, NOW!"

Carla Jo and Jack were lying in bed. A fresh, glistening layer of sweat covered their bodies. Carla Jo had felt funny about fooling around while Amy was in the next room, so Jack had decided to make up for lost time. Then the phone rang.

"Don't answer that," said Jack.

"I have to, I'm on call for Doc Henderson. Let me up," she giggled, slapping his hands. "Hello? OK, be right there."

"What going on?" Jack asked.

"It's Amy," said Carla Jo

"Is she OK?" Jack asked.

Carla Jo threw on her clothes, grabbed the black bag from the top of the closet, and said, "To quote a line from one of my favorite movies, she's pretty fucking far from OK."

She grabbed her keys and out the door she went.

Carla Jo raced up the hill and saw Carol going the other way in Leon's truck. She pulled up in front of the house to find Amy having a full-blown meltdown in the front yard. Leon was just standing there, helpless, unable to calm her down. She opened the black bag and pulled out a hypodermic needle and a bottle of Pentobarbital. She loaded the syringe and got out of the car.

"Honey, it's OK, I'm here," Carla Jo said calmly as she approached Amy. She put her arm around her and with the other one injected her in the ass. Amy barley felt it. Within a few minutes Amy began to relax and then she sat on the ground. Carla Jo motioned to Leon to pick her up and put her to bed.

"Leon, we need to talk," said Carla Jo, then she hollered for Joseph.

"YES, MA'AM," Joseph yelled back as he came running through the yard.

"Keep an eye on your sister, we'll be back," she said.

"Yes, ma'am," Joseph replied.

"Let's take a walk Leon," said Carla Jo as she started down the sidewalk toward the road.

"Where we goin'?" Leon asked, even though he already knew.

"For a walk," said Carla Jo.

It was a hot day. They could feel the heat coming off the asphalt and see the shimmer on the road. They turned up the

Hatfield's driveway and stopped in the middle of the lot. Carla Jo looked down at the soft dirt and said, "Looks like a girl's tennis shoe prints." Then she turned to look at Leon. She knew what she wanted to say and she wanted to say it gently. In six words Leon threw the gentle thing out the window.

"What the hell's wrong with her?" he asked.

Carla Jo's mouth fell open and her eyes went wide. Her lips shaped the words but nothing came out. "W...W...W...What the hell is wrong with her?" She spoke under her breath. "No shit, Leon? Really? OK, you want to know? Then goddammit, I'll tell you."

Leon's feet shifted nervously. In all the years he had known her, he couldn't recall ever hearing Carla Jo swear.

Carla Jo calmed down a little and began to speak. "She was dead when the helicopter landed. She went into cardiac arrest during the flight. How they got her back I have no idea. When you came into the waiting room I almost told you she was gone. She's so tough Leon, so tough. Still, she is so much a teenage girl. See these footprints? They're Amy's. What kind of balls do you think it took to walk back up the hill by herself and come here? You and Jack scrubbed the hill clean of the vermin; nice touch. You think that's it? You think it's over?"

"Carla Jo, I...," Leon began, but Carla Jo interrupted.

"I'm not finished Leon, you asked a question. What the hell's wrong with her? I don't know Leon, let me think. Could it have something to do with her head being split open by a big rock? Maybe it was the piece of pipe they shoved in her vagina or the nipple that had to be sewn back on after one of those animals bit it most of the way off. Or could it be...," Carla Jo stopped as Leon interrupted.

OK, that's enough, I don't want to hear anymore," said Leon.

Something inside Carla Jo snapped. She suddenly went wild and started screaming, "You don't want to hear anymore? YOU DON'T WANT TO HEAR ANYMORE? THAT'S ENOUGH? REALLY, LEON? SHE WENT THROUGH IT, LEON! IT PLAYS

IN HER MIND LIKE A MOVIE, OVER AND OVER AGAIN AND YOU DON'T WANT TO HEAR ABOUT IT? WHAT THE HELL'S WRONG WITH HER, LEON? TELL ME LEON, WHAT THE HELL'S WRONG WITH HER? WHAT THE FUCK IS WRONG WITH YOU?"

"I DON'T KNOW WHAT TO DO! WHAT DO I DO? MY GOD, CARLA JO, SHE WENT CRAZY! SHE ATTACKED CAROL," Leon screamed back.

They both stopped talking and gathered their composure. After a few minutes Carla Jo said, "What was she doing?"

"Who?" Leon replied

"Carol, what was she doing?"

"What do you mean?"

"When Amy came in the house, what was she doing?" she asked again.

"Oh, cooking breakfast."

Carla Jo chuckled under her breath and said, "You got a lot to learn about women."

"What?"

"Women are territorial, just like a big buck in a herd. That's Amy's house, Amy's kitchen, and that's Amy's job. You and Joseph belong to Amy. When she walked in that house, she saw herself being replaced."

"Yeah, that's exactly what she said, that we were replacing her," admitted Leon.

"Under the best of circumstances, bringing Carol into that house would be difficult. Right now? I wouldn't do it, Leon. I'd cool things with Carol, at least until Amy gets better."

"I understand what you're sayin," Leon sighed. "I still don't know what to do for her. How do I help her?"

"Be there, Leon, just be there. Give her safety and security. Keep things as normal as you can. Right now every emotion she has is amplified and they're all sitting on the surface. Tell Joseph not to change, to treat her like he always has. Jack and I are going to help you, if it's all right. We have a plan. Jack has been through some major trauma. He knows what it takes to heal. Your not alone Leon, we will help you," said Carla Jo.

They started walking toward the road. Leon turned to Carla Jo and said, "I really love Carol. I haven't loved anyone like this since Katherine. If I lose her over this, so be it, but I sure don't want to. Women like her are hard to find."

Carla Jo put her arm around Leon's shoulder and said, "Women like her are a hell of a lot easier to find then men like you. She'll wait for you, Leon. She'll wait as long as it takes."

Joseph stayed with Amy as Carla Jo took Leon to Carol's to pick up his truck. As Carla Jo pulled into Carol's driveway, Leon grabbed the door handle and stopped. He turned to Carla Jo and said, "Thank you. I don't know how we would get through this without your help."

"You might be her daddy, but she belongs to all of us. She'll be OK. It'll take time, but she'll be OK."

"After all she has been through, how can you be so sure?"

"I know. Trust me, I know."

The Story of Carla Jo

Penelope Fairchild Herbst was the only daughter of one of the richest men in America, Carlton Herbst. Although her wealth and privilege gave her beyond a fairytale life, she spent most of her time holding it in contempt and trying to escape it. Her hero was Clara Barton, a nurse and founder of the American Red Cross, so she also became a nurse. She spent much of her time volunteering in orphanages and visiting skid rows throughout San Francisco. She gave away as much of her father's money as he would allow buying food, blankets, and medicine. She always did it anonymously, never in her own name.

When the Korean War broke out in 1950 she saw a steady stream of wounded returning from the war. She made her father furious by doing what Clara Barton would have done. She enlisted. She worked at the hospital in Seoul. She wanted to go to a mobile army surgical hospital (MASH unit), but her father, who financed the president's campaign, wasn't about to let her get that close to the front. A few months into her tour of duty she was making her rounds when she saw a gurney being pushed by an orderly. Under the sheet was a small body, a little boy no more that two years of age. He had Korean features with red hair. He looked malnourished and he was covered in bruises, sure signs of abuse. She found out that he had come from an Amerasian orphanage. She would find that orphanage.

They were known as dust children or "*bui do*" and were ostracized in their home country because of their mixed blood. Lt. Herbst found the orphanage and what she saw changed her life. Twenty-six children, and most were toddlers. They were filthy and malnourished. The army said there was nothing she could do, but she knew different. Penny called Daddy. She illegally bought the children from the orphanage by bribing government officials. In forty-eight hours they were at the hospital in Seoul. By the end of the week they were on a transport plane to America. The story made *LIFE* magazine and the children were put up for adoption. It didn't take long to find them homes. One of those children, a girl of African-Asian decent, ended up at the home of Walter and Nancy Watkins. They named her Annette.

Walter Watkins was a former Olympic track star. A kind, gentle, and honest man that worked his way out of poverty through athletics. He drove a city bus for a living and the passengers on his route loved the funny and helpful driver. Nancy Watkins was an only child that grew up in the black aristocracy of Philadelphia. When she was a child, her father was a prosperous businessman and she enjoyed the good life. A prim and proper woman, she knew how to speak and dress, and she knew which fork to use at dinner. It was Nancy's idea to adopt the child. It meant a sister for her pride and joy, her son Devin. There was also an ulterior motive.

Nancy liked the limelight. When she married Walter she believed that the notoriety he received by being an Olympian would continue. If not, at least he would parlay his experiences into something marketable. Nancy failed to realize that he had few marketable skills. He did not speak well and had little education. She felt shame when she was forced to take a job as an administrator in the Philadelphia school system to help make ends meet. The windfall she expected from her father also did not materialize. His businesses were treading water at best. Upon his death the bank seized his assets. There would be no inheritance. By adopting a child from the *LIFE* magazine story, she enjoyed being featured in a few more newspaper articles. That too, however, was short lived.

Nancy was never overtly mean to Annette. She was cold, stern, and demanding. Manners, etiquette, and proper behavior were expected at all times. Her warmest affections were reserved for her son. But what she failed to give Annette, Walter more than made up for. Annette was Daddy's girl. His pride and joy. She would curl up in his lap and he would read to her for hours. When she reached four years of age, she began to read to him. Devin also coveted his little sister. They played together and maintained a close relationship throughout their school years.

Annette excelled in elementary school. She skipped the first grade and was clearly intellectually superior to her older brother. This created some resentment; not from Devin, but from Nancy. Devin was grateful to have the help. Annette tutored him on different subjects and always encouraged him to chase his dream. Devin wanted to be a pilot. Occasionally, Walter would take Devin to the airport and for hours they would stand on the observation deck, watching the planes take off and land.

When Annette was twelve years old she received a letter from Penelope Herbst, inviting her and her family to a reunion at her estate in Santa Barbara. The Watkins were all very excited, especially Devin. In the early sixties, air travel was something reserved for white businessmen. Very few families flew and even fewer minority families.

The three days they spent in Santa Barbara were luxurious beyond imagination. Penelope had a horse farm and swimming pool, and she set up a small carnival for the kids. There were clowns, musicians, and top shelf entertainment. Penelope's friends from Hollywood also stopped by to visit, take pictures, and sign autographs. But Penelope's biggest gift would be reserved for the end of the reunion: full ride college scholarships for all of the orphans to any college they could get accepted to.

Annette graduated high school when she was sixteen. She applied to the most prestigious nursing schools in the country and she landed a spot at number one, Johns Hopkins. The letter of recommendation from one of their largest benefactors, Penelope Herbst, made it so.

Annette had struck a special relationship with a banking executive, a single white woman that lived down the street. It would be seven months before a slot opened up at Johns Hopkins so she took a part time job at her bank. Devin also took a major step in fulfilling his dreams. He was accepted to the army's warrant officer helicopter training program. Black pilots were a rarity and he endured a certain amount of abuse and heavy doses of racism, but Devin had his father's Olympian spirit and would not be denied.

Walter Watkins was diagnosed with cancer a few years later. He passed away but not before he saw Annette receive her diploma from Johns Hopkins and watched as a general pinned pilots' wings on his son. Walter was the heart and soul of the family and they suffered immense grief at his passing. They were comforted by Walter's words on his death bed. He smiled and said, "It's OK, I can go now. My children are successful, that's all I ever wanted."

Annette received several job offers and she threw them all away. The Viet Nam war was raging so she did what Penelope Herbst would have done; she joined the army. After officers training school she was assigned to the 71st evacuation hospital, one of the busiest, near the city of Pleiku. She never flaunted her Johns Hopkins degree but all of the doctors knew. She performed tasks far beyond her assigned duties, becoming an extra set of hands for the surgeons during the most difficult of operations.

Lt. Watkins had one major flaw, however; she took it all personally. Over time she learned to compartmentalize her emotions. Still, she would not allow any soldier to die alone. When possible she would sit and hold their hands, gently singing to them while they passed. What little down time she had she spent exchanging letters with her brother. She got to see him a few times as he was flying a helicopter ambulance. Devin was fearless behind the stick. He had been decorated several times for landing in hot LZs (Landing Zones) and rescuing soldiers. They had a nickname for him— Devin from Heaven.

Late in '71, after a long day of surgery, Annette went to the intensive care unit to visit with the soldiers. The head nurse knew why she was there and pointed to a young man off in the corner. He had suffered serious burns and was bandaged over most of his body. He was on a morphine drip and wouldn't last much longer. She sat down beside him to hold his hand, but they were bandaged. She rested her hand on his chest and, looking into the one eye that was exposed, began to sing. As the light extinguished in the young soldier's eye she got an uneasy feeling. She walked to the end of the bed and picked up the chart. She read the name: Chief Warrant Officer 3rd Class Devin Walter Watkins.

In those days they called it a nervous breakdown. The horrors of war combined with the death of Devin sent Annette into a spiral that she could not recover from. She began to drink to numb the pain. The army sent her back to the states and she worked an administrative job at Walter Reed until she was discharged. She wanted to move back in with her mom and try to get her life together. After making her way up the steps of the townhouse and knocking on the door, her Mom answered.

"Momma, I'm home," said Annette.

Her mom stared at her for a moment and said, "This is not your home."

"What?" said Annette in a shocked tone.

"My son is dead because of you. You put those crazy ideas of flying in his head. HE IS DEAD BECAUSE OF YOU," she screamed. "This is not your home and I am not your momma. Don't ever come back," Nancy said as she slammed the door.

Annette sat down on the steps and began to cry.

She found a small, furnished apartment and began to look for a job. Her degree from Johns Hopkins got her in the door of every major hospital in the area, but her alcoholism cost her the jobs within a few weeks. Her personal life was also a train wreck. She was still a beautiful and exotic-looking woman that men wanted to be with. The problem was, she wasn't black, she wasn't Asian, and she wasn't the type of woman that men wanted to take home to Momma. Almost out of money and most certainly out of hope, she was sitting at a bar drinking vodka on the rocks when he walked in.

His name was Maurice and he introduced himself as a local businessman. He was well dressed, tall, dark, and handsome. He sat down beside her and struck up a conversation. Within minutes Annette began to spill her guts about her situation. Maurice sat with her for almost an hour, listening intently. He invited her out to dinner and then later took her home. What ensued was a whirlwind romance. He paid her rent and bought her clothes and a few pieces of jewelry. She was sure she had finally found a good man. She could not have been more wrong.

After about a month, Maurice stopped by her apartment to pick her up. They were going to a party. They arrived at a hotel and walked into a room where another man was sitting on the bed. Maurice told Annette that she needed to be "nice" to the man. When Annette figured out what he meant, she refused. Maurice acted swiftly by slapping her to the floor. They held her down and Maurice pulled a black pouch from his pocket. It contained a syringe. He injected Annette with heroine and then the men spent the rest of the evening raping and beating her. When they were finished he took her back to his house where the abuse continued until he had her exactly how he wanted her, addicted and terrified. She thought about running away until the day that Maurice brought all of his girls into his garage. He had caught one girl that did run away, and he tortured and killed her in front of them to make a point.

Because of her long black hair he named her Raven. As prostitutes go, she was a big earner and before long Maurice gave her greater responsibilities. She started delivering drugs for him. Maurice had the local cops in his pocket but not the Feds. One day she unknowingly walked into the middle of a DEA sting and ended up doing two years in prison. While in prison she had two jobs: she worked in the prison hospital and she dealt drugs for Maurice. Thankfully, Maurice watched over her and she did not suffer the abuse that most women do in prison. When she got out, he was waiting for her.

Time, drugs, and alcohol took their toll on Raven. She was no longer one of his most requested girls so he put her out on the street. An especially sadistic police sergeant had a thing for her. He liked to tie her up and beat her before having sex. The shot of heroine coursed through her veins as the sergeant did his thing. Annette Wilamena Watkins decided she was done. If he didn't kill her this time, she would kill herself. Just then, the door crashed open.

Chapter 20

$\mathcal{A}$my woke up in her room still feeling a little groggy from the seditive. The clock read 6:30. She didn't know if it was morning or evening. The house was quiet so she went out on the front porch and found her daddy sitting in the big rocker. She sat down on his lap, buried her head in his chest, and whispered, "I'm sorry, Daddy, I'm so sorry."

Leon put his arms around her, hugged her tight, and said, "You got nothin' to be sorry about. I'm the one that should be apologizing to you."

"Ms. Francis didn't deserve that," whispered Amy.

"No, no she didn't, but I did. She won't be coming back for awhile," said Leon.

Amy lifted her head and said, "No, no, Daddy, I don't want that. I know you love her. I know you do. You need someone to love. I'm not going to ruin that for you. Invite her back, I'll apologize."

"Nah, she understands. We spent a couple hours talkin' today. Nothin' has changed with us. We both agreed you need your space and some time. Ms. Francis loves you too, more than you know," said Leon.

Amy saw the sun beginning to set in the west and knew it was evening. "Where's Joseph?" asked Amy.

"He's down with your uncle Jack foolin' with that old car, but he should be home directly. Speakin' of Jo, I owe him a fishin' trip. I was thinkin' that tomorrow we could take the boat down to the river, pack a lunch, and make a day out of it. What do ya' think?" asked Leon.

"Yes, sir, I'd like that. Did you and Joseph eat yet?" Amy asked.

"Nope, not yet," said Leon.

"OK, I'll fix dinner," Amy said as she jumped off his lap. She suddenly gasped and bent over. "Ow," she said under her breath.

Leon jumped up and said, "What's wrong, honey?"

"I'm OK, Daddy, just a little pain I get now and then. The doctor said it will take awhile for me to heal," said Amy.

"Why don't you relax and let me fix dinner?" said Leon.

"NO," Amy said just a little too loud. "I mean no, Daddy, please, let me do it."

"Alright, but do you mind if I keep you company?" Leon asked.

"No, sir, not at all," Amy said with a little smile.

They skipped church, which didn't happen often, and went to the river on Sunday morning. They fished a little and then Amy drove the boat while her brother and Daddy waterskied. They swam, ate too much, and got too much sun. All in all it was a great day.

When they got home, Amy took a shower and then went into her room to change. Her suitcase was still sitting in the corner and she had yet to unpack it. She unzipped it and put her clothes away. She loved the way her clothes smelled. She would have to ask Carla Jo what kind of fabric softener she used.

She saw her school clothes at the end of the closet and it occurred to her that she would be starting high school soon. A small wave of panic set in. Why did she feel that way? Where did it come from? She kept telling herself, *It's ok, it's ok, just relax.* She looked in the mirror and saw that her hair had not grown out enough where they shaved it to put the stitches in her head. Amy wasn't horribly vain, but she was a teenage girl and cared about how she looked. Maybe Carla Jo could take her to see Jean

Paul. If anyone could fix it, he could. Still, she couldn't shake the impending sense of doom, like something bad was going to happen. Then came a small knock at the door.

"Amy," Joseph said softly.

She opened the door.

"Hey, whatcha doin'?"asked Joseph.

"Oh, putting away clothes, thinking about school."

"I try not to think about that," said Joseph with a smile. "I was really scared when you were in the hospital." Then his face grew serious. "I thought you were gonna die. I thought me and Daddy would be alone. I sassed Daddy while we were in the hospital. I never did that before."

"You did?" said Amy with a chuckle.

"Yeah. The first night you were in the hospital he said I had to go home. I told him I ain't goin' nowhere. Granny Patches told him, too. Then they said I couldn't go see you. Sheriff Carter took me; folks don't say no to Sheriff Carter."

"No, no they don't," said Amy with a little grin. Then she asked, "Joseph, do you like Ms. Francis?"

"Yeah, I do. She's really good to me and Daddy."

"Is she a good cook?"

"Yeah she is."

"Better than me?" Amy asked.

"Your biscuits and corn bread are better. She puts sugar in her corn bread. She makes different things; things from other countries like Italy and China, places like that. Daddy says you cook like Momma."

"You don't remember Momma, do ya'?"

Joseph shook his head and said, "No, but Daddy said if I ever need to see Momma, all I have to do is look at you."

Amy started to cry. She reached out and hugged her brother. He was getting big. He had gotten taller and his shoulders were getting broad. She would be looking up at him soon. He was going to be a big man, like the Murphy side of the family, like Kerry and Uncle Jack.

"Why are you crying?" asked Joseph.

"Sometimes girls cry when they are happy," said Amy as she felt the love and concern of her little brother.

"Well, stop already," Joseph said as Amy's crushing hug was making it difficult to breath. "Ms. Francis made us an apple pie. It's pretty good. You want a piece?" asked Joseph.

"Sure, let's have pie," Amy said, putting her brother in a headlock and kissing his head. "Hey, Joseph," said Amy.

"What?" said Joseph with a smarty-pants tone.

"I wouldn't make a habit of sassing Daddy," she said with a smile.

"Don't worry, I won't," he grinned.

Chapter 21

$\mathcal{A}$my tossed and turned most of the night. She got up early and made her daddy's coffee and lunch. He left for work and about an hour later, Joseph's best friend and his mother came to pick him up to spend the day with them. Amy decided to go visit with Granny Patches to see if she needed help with anything.

"Hi Granny," Amy said as Granny Patches welcomed her into the house and ushered her into the kitchen.

"Hey baby. You don't look good, like you ain't slept in a month," said Granny Patches.

"Feels that way. Things swirl around in my head when I close my eyes," said Amy with a tired voice.

"You drink coffee yet? I got some of this fancy vanilla cream at the store, makes it taste pretty good," Granny Patches offered.

"Sure Granny, why not?"

Granny looked across the table at Amy for a few moments and said, "You know, honey, if you catch a woman being honest, she can tell you of at least one time when a man tried to force himself on her. It's an old story, old as the Bible. It happened to Granny, too."

Amy perked up and said, "What happened to you?"

Granny thought for a moment and said, "Well, I'll spare you the details, but let's just say I'm sixty-seven years old and ain't never forgot it"

"What did you do about it?"

"Nothin', I never told anyone. Back then there was a lot of shame involved. Seems folks would find a way to put some blame on the woman. B'sides, a ruined woman had a hard time finding a good man. Ain't that way no more," she said.

"How did you live with it, Granny? How did you get past it?"

Granny sat back in her chair, took a deep breath, and said, "To be honest, I don't reckon I ever did. But it was the reason I married Larry. Let me show you somethin'."

Granny walk into the living room, took out a small photo album, and took the Bible off the end table next to her television-watching chair. Granny opened the album and showed Amy a picture. "This was me when I was just a little older than you are now," she said.

"Whoa, Granny, you were beautiful," Amy said admiringly.

"Yeah baby, your granny had her pick of men. I picked Larry. He wasn't the purdiest or the richest, But that man that took advantage of me also took advantage of Larry's sister. Larry beat him half to death with an ax handle and ran him out of town. I knew then that he was the one. I was right. He was good to me and made me feel safe. Even when we found out I couldn't have babies I figured he would leave, but he stayed cause he loved me more. Let me show you something else."

Granny reached for the Bible, clicked open the hasp, and opened it up. Inside, the pages had been cut out and replaced with a two shot Derringer. Then Granny said, "Larry got me this when he started workin' nights at the mine and he taught me how to use it. This, along with the shotgun next to my bed and the pistol up in the top of that cupboard."

"Granny, I didn't know any of this."

"Weren't for you to know 'til now. Folks don't get old watchin' television. Everyone has a story."

Granny thought for a moment and said, "Another thing folks like to say is 'Jesus watches over me, Jesus will protect me,' and that's right, he will, but not in the way most folks think. Jesus gives us common sense, free will, and the ability to protect ourselves. It reminds me of a funny story that Miss Vickie told us at the beauty shop. This feller got caught in a flood and a man come by in a canoe and told him to get in. Feller said, 'I'm OK, Jesus will save me.' Another man come by in a boat and told him to get in, but the feller said, 'I'm OK, Jesus will save me.' Then a helicopter flew over and they waved for him to get in, but the feller kept sayin', 'Jesus will save me.' Then he drowned and went to heaven and he asked Jesus why he didn't save him. Jesus said, 'I sent you a canoe, a boat, and a helicopter.'"

Granny cackled and Amy laughed. Then Granny stopped and looked at Amy with a serious face and said, "Get in the boat Amy, get in the boat."

They sat quietly for a minute and then Amy said something Granny wasn't expecting. "Granny, I think my daddy killed the Hatfields."

"Hmm," Granny let out a little grunt as she reached for the Bible, closed it, and snapped the latch. She put both palms down on the table and her eyes grew cold. Amy had never seen Granny Patches face like that before. Then Granny said, "If he did, he was in his right. Amy, it's best you never know for sure. That way you never have to tell a lie. Just know this, them boys were dead anyway 'cause I'd a killed 'em myself."

Amy and Granny sat quiet for a while and then Granny pepped up and said, "I got a mess of okra to cut in the garden, you wanna help?"

"Yes, ma'am, I'll help ya."

They walked the rows in Granny Patches' garden, cutting okra. Amy thought about what Granny had said, "Get in the boat." *Yeah*, Amy thought. *I need to talk to Uncle Jack.*

They finished and Granny gave Amy a dollar like she always did. She hugged and kissed her Granny, and then walked back across the road to lock up the house. She grabbed another dollar and one of Carla Jo's books that she'd finished. She figured she'd go by Ed Gwinn's on the way to Uncle Jack's. *He should be up by now*, she thought.

Chapter 22

Amy tossed Bubba the last bite of her Moon Pie, gave him a hug, and then knocked on the door.

"UNCLE JACK," Amy yelled.

The door opened and a half asleep Jack looked her and said, "Amy, it's early."

"It's almost noon, time to get up." Amy said with a smile.

"OK, I need a shower, come on in," Jack moaned.

Jack got in the shower and Amy went into Carla Jo's library. She put the book she had with her back and started looking for something else. She saw a really thick book and took it off the shelf. The title read, *Gray's Anatomy*. She started flipping through it and became amazed by the pictures and descriptions of the human body. She got lost in it then Jack appeared at the door.

"Hey honey, watcha got?" Jack asked.

"A book about the human body. I've never seen anything like this," she said as she closed the book and followed Jack into the kitchen where he started making himself some coffee.

She sat down and said, "Remember when we were talking in the garage and you said you could show me how to confront evil?"

"Yep, I remember," said Jack.

"OK, show me," Amy said.

Jack thought for a minute then said, "Alright, but first I need to talk to your daddy. I got some things to tell you and show you that he may not agree with. I'll talk to him this afternoon."

This piqued Amy's interest but she decided not to ask any more questions.

"Sounds good," she replied.

"I was just fixin' to run into town to the auto parts store and then grab some breakfast at the Bluebird. You wanna come?"

"Sure, but it's lunch time."

"Dorothy the cook makes me breakfast if I talk sweet to her," said Jack with a smile.

Jack showed up at Amy's house after dinner. Her and Joseph were doing dishes when Jack asked Leon, "Hey Cuz, you got time to talk?"

"Yeah, what's goin' on?"

They sat down on the porch and Jack said, "While Amy stayed with us we had quite a few conversations, mostly about how I dealt with my injuries and such. Anyway, the subject went to why did they hurt her and I explained it was just evil."

"I agree with that," said Leon.

"Well, I sort of told her I could teach her to confront and defeat evil and, um, she sort of called my bluff."

"What exactly does that mean?" said Leon skeptically.

"I was thinkin' in terms of situational awareness, self-defense, and a little weapons training; enough to give her the confidence to handle herself if she ever got in trouble again like, well, the Hatfield thing. I also think it will help her to heal."

"If that's what she wants to do, I don't have a problem with it. But Jack, just remember that she's a teenage girl. That's a different animal," Leon said.

"Yep, that's what Carla Jo said. There is one more thing."

"What?" said Leon, waiting for the other shoe to drop.

"I'll have to tell her who I was and what I was to teach her what she needs to know."

"You mean who ya' are, don't ya'?"

"Yeah, and I don't want her to think less of me," said Jack.

Leon started laughing and Jack said, "What?"

"You could tell her your hobby is puppy strangling and she wouldn't think any less of you," Leon said, smiling.

"I was hoping you would tell her. That way I don't have to see her face if she is disappointed and it would give her time to think about it before we talk again," said Jack.

"How much do you want her to know?" Leon asked.

"I want her to know the truth."

"OK."

Jack went in the house, gave Amy a hug, and told her good night. Then he roughed up Joseph a little and left.

"Amy, come out here a minute," Leon said from the porch.

Amy came out and sat down next to her daddy.

"I guess you know what we were talking about," he said.

"Yes, sir."

"What do you know about your Uncle Jack?"

"What do you mean?" Amy said.

"Well, you asked him to show you things that would help you if you were ever in another bad situation. What do you think you will learn?"

"Whatever he thinks I need to know. Daddy, you know as well as I do that Uncle Jack was an assassin in the Vietnam war. If anyone knows how to handle bad people, he does."

Leon leaned back in his chair, chuckled under his breath, and said, "Who told you that?"

"Aunt Carla Jo. She gave me some books to read about what Uncle Jack did. One of them called him the Horror in the Jungle. A guy he was with in this place called the Rung Sat Special Zone wrote it. They called Uncle Jack 'Hatchet Jack' in the book. They didn't use his last name but I'm sure it was him."

"Does Jack know he's in a book?"

"I don't know. Aunt Carla Jo said he doesn't like to talk about the things he did," said Amy.

"OK, if your uncle Jack wants to show you some things, that's fine with me."

Leon looked at Amy. She was staring across the road at Granny Patches' house with a crooked smile on her face. Leon had never seen that look before. Amy was thinking to herself, *Time to get in the boat.*

Jack Brown's Last Mission

Jack opened the big green box and looked inside. He took out his equipment and laid it neatly on the bed. He pulled out his black tactical jumpsuit and put it on. It fit perfectly and looked good. He smiled in the mirror like a forty-year-old woman with three kids who just discovered that her wedding dress still fit. He disassembled and cleaned his weapons, sharpened his knife, and then pulled out the police reports that Miss Kitty gave him and started studying.

The Lewistown Library didn't have what he needed so he had to go into the city. He studied the areas around the precincts where Lt. Watkins was arrested to gather maps and put together a plan. With the maps laid out on his kitchen table he studied every street, ally, and dead end,as well as multiple ingress and egress points throughout the city. North Philadelphia would be as familiar to him as his hometown. Then he called Leon.

"Cuz, I need you to keep an eye on my place for a few days."

"Where ya' goin'?" asked Leon.

"Somthin' I gotta do. I'll be gone for a couple of days. If something happens and I don't come back, there's an envelope in my dresser. Do what it says for me."

"Jack, you're scaring me a little," said Leon in a concerned voice.

"I'm a big boy, Cuz, I can take care of myself," said Jack.

"Alright Jack, be safe," Leon said as he hung up the phone. Leon had no idea what Jack was up to, but he knew his voice and he heard the change in it. Leon had a strong suspicion that someone was fixin' to die.

Jack rolled into town and found a cheap hotel in the Tioga section of North Philly. He took a four hour nap, woke up, did some stretching, prepared his equipment, and then hit the street. He located a taxi driver that introduced him to a pimp. Jack coaxed him to a quiet spot off the street and showed him the picture.

"Yeah man, that's Raven. She don't be doin' freaks like you. Besides, dat's Maurice's bitch."

"Where can I find Maurice?" Jack asked.

"None of yo' mutha' fuckin' bidness. You want a bitch or not?" the pimp said, getting agitated.

Jack showed him a hundred dollar bill and said, "Where can I find Maurice?"

"Oh, a bidness man," said the pimp. "Maurice lives on forty-ninth off Washington. Brown house, look fo' da' red Lincoln out front."

"Thanks," Jack said. He looked around and added, "one more thing...."

He stunned the pimp with a quick punch, moved around behind him, and snapped his neck. He pulled the body into the weeds and headed for Maurice's house.

Jack found the house and drove by. There were two men on the front porch. He drove around to the ally in the back and saw one man by the back door. His senses were operating at full song, just like in the jungle. *Just like old times,* he thought. He parked his truck and went to work.

Jack neutralized the lookout by the back door and peeked in the windows. There was one man sitting in the kitchen, a shotgun on the table. Otherwise he could see nothing on the first floor, but he did see lights and could hear noise on the second floor. He moved quickly and silently up the side of the house and looked around the corner. There was only one man. *The other must be the man in the kitchen*, he thought. Jack made a little noise and the man on the porch decided to check it out. It would be his last decision. After he quickly hid the body beside some bushes, Jack went to the front door and unscrewed the bulb on the porch light. He slowly turned the knob and opened the door. Stepping inside, he looked down the hall, and could see the kitchen. He quickly pushed the door shut and stepped to the side, and then he crept down the hall until he saw the man at the table. The *click, click, click* of the razor blade chopping cocaine on the glass seemed to have him mesmerized. Jack snapped his neck then began to look for the stairs.

This is going too easy, Jack thought. On every mission there was always a wild card thrown in. Something unexpected. Jack found the stairwell and looked up and listened. Then the doorbell rang. *And there it is,* he thought. Jack walked to the door, cracked it, and stood to the side so he could not be seen.

"Yo," he said.

The man at the door said, "Maurice got the shit?"

"Later," Jack said and shut the door. Jack watched the man leave.

"Who the fuck was dat?" said a voice from upstairs.

Jack stayed quiet.

"Hey, I ain't talkin' to my fuckin' self," the man yelled as he walked down the stairs. *Perfect*, thought Jack, *one man comes down, one man goes up*. Stepping back around the corner he drew his old friend, his SEAL Team military issue KA-BAR knife. As the man cleared the bottom step Jack grabbed him from behind and shoved the blade in an upward motion into his back. Jack held tight until the man went limp. He set him gently on the floor then headed up the stairs.

Bright light beamed through the partially opened door as he peeked inside. He counted five men, but he couldn't see the back side of the door. Two men were standing and clearly armed. One large man with dreadlocks sat in a big chair and two sat on a couch. They were talking and laughing, clearly having a good time. That was about to end. Jack pulled the silenced pistol from the holster and pushed the door open gently a couple more inches. He fired two quick shots through the crack and the custom ammo did it's job. The heads of the armed men split like watermelons. Jack entered the room, glanced behind the door, and then turned his attention to the remaining three.

The two men on the couch were terrified, but the man in the chair was just a little too calm.

"Hands where I can see 'em," Jack said with a calm authority. Jack looked at the man in the chair and said in a friendly, conversational tone, "You must be Maurice."

"Yeah, I'm Maurice. Who the fuck are you?"

"Where is Raven?"

Maurice smiled and said, "Do you know who I...,"

The silenced pistol shooting the first man on the couch in the head interrupted him.

"Where is Raven?" Jack asked again.

"Mutha' fucka', you...,"

Maurice was interrupted again as the second man on the couch met the same fate.

"THE GREEN TOP HOTEL, SHE WORKS OUT OF THE GREEN TOP! DAMN MAN, WHAT THE FUCK!" screamed Maurice.

"Thank you," said Jack as he put the hammer down on his pistol and returned it to his holster.

He looked at Maurice and smiled. Maurice then did exactly what Jack thought he would do. He jumped out of the chair and came straight for him. He was faster than Jack thought he would be but not fast enough. Maurice never saw the KA-BAR that went in under his rib cage. Maurice fell to his knees and Jack grabbed him by his dreads. Four swipes of the knife and Jack was holding Maurice's severed head. Jack was disappointed. It used to only take him three. He wiped off the blade and returned it to it's sheath. He started to turn toward the door when he saw a stack of what looked like bricks of some sort of drug, and next to them a black leather case. He flipped the top up on the case and saw it was bundles of hundred dollar bills. He grabbed the case and went down the stairs.

Jack was behind schedule. His internal clock had put him past five minutes and that was a little too long. He reached the bottom of the stairs and listened; nothing. He went into the kitchen and put Maurice's head and the case on the table. He blew out the pilot light on the stove and turned on all of the jets. Then he grabbed the head and the case and headed for the front door. After slowly opening the door, he looked around and listened. All was quiet. Moving quickly, he walked down the sidewalk and on the way through the chain link gate he slammed the head down onto the fence post. He turned, took another step, and froze. There in front of him was a little old black woman. He looked at her and she gazed at him with a shocked look on her face. Her eyes kept going back and forth between the head on the post and the huge man standing in front of her.

"Pardon me, ma'am," Jack said as he walked by her and disappeared into the night.

Jack pulled into the Green Top Hotel and parked toward the back in the darkest area. He watched for a few minutes; he didn't want to go into the lobby if he could avoid it. He was spattered with blood, even though his black jumpsuit hid most of it. He took a towel and wiped his face. Then he saw a young, scantily dressed woman coming near his truck. He let her get close before he got out.

"Excuse me, miss," he said, not looking directly at her. He held out a hundred dollar bill and Raven's picture, then said, "I'm looking for this woman."

"Yeah, that's Raven," the young woman said while snatching the money. "She should be in room one-twenty." The woman started to walk away then said, "Be careful, she's with that cop. He's a son of a bitch."

"Thanks," Jack said as he watched her walk out of sight. He could see one-twenty from where he was standing. He didn't want to wait. As soon as they discovered the house or it blew up, the area would be crawling with cops. *Fuck it*, he thought. *I'm going in.* Casually he walked to the door, made sure the coast was clear, and then kicked it open.

The fat, naked cop stood over Annette holding a thick black leather belt. Annette was tied to the bed face down. Bleeding welts covered her body. Jack enjoyed killing this one. Afterward he cut the ropes and told her to get up. She curled up in the fetal position and wouldn't move so he grabbed the tote bag next to her clothes, shoved her clothes in it, wrapped her in a blanket, and carried her out the door. He put her in the front seat of the truck and covered her up with the blanket. Jack jumped in the drive'rs seat, fired up the truck, and drove toward the highway.

The house didn't blow up. The only witness was eighty-year-old Winifred Parker, a deacon in the Tioga First Methodist Church. The detectives questioned her, but all she would say was, "I swear on the name of Jesus Christ, It was a monster."

The entire evening was dismissed as a gang turf war. The chief of police had no interest in wasting the time or money to investigate. As the chief told the mayor behind closed doors, "Fuck it, they were all shit. Even the cop was dirty, good riddance."

The final count was one dead cop, one dead pimp, one dead gang leader, eight dead gang members and a missing hooker. All courtesy of Jack Brown, the Tioga Monster.

Chapter 23

Amy went to her uncle Jack's house the next day. They sat in the kitchen and Amy watched as he sipped coffee. He studied her for a moment and said,

"So, you want to learn the trade."

"Yes, sir," said Amy with a serious look on her face.

"You feel like talkin' about what happened on the hill?"

"Sure, what do you want to know?" said Amy.

"How did they get ya'? Did they grab you off the road? What happened?"

"Oh, yeah. Tommy told me he had a new hound dog puppy he wanted me to see."

"Uh huh, and what was the first thing you thought when he said that?" asked Jack.

"They couldn't feed themselves, how would they feed a dog?"

"So your mind told you it was a lie and you didn't listen. Why not?"

"I didn't want to hurt his feelings," Amy said.

"So he hurt yours instead," Jack said. He knew that comment stung a little.

"Amy thought for a minute and then said, "So it was my fault, wasn't it. I was stupid."

Carla Jo had told Jack she might blame herself, so he decided to try to put a stop to that right away. He put down his coffee cup, took Amy's hands, and said, "Not just no, hell no. Amy Lynn, you did nothin' wrong. You did as you were trained. You were taught to be kind, to think of others' feelings first, and to put them ahead of your own. Thoughts like that are just your mind tryin' to explain why it happened. It's not true. It's a lie. I don't ever want to hear that again, understand?"

Amy nodded.

"Remember when we were talkin' in the garage about evil and the gift you received?" Jack questioned.

"Yes, sir," said Amy.

"Part of that gift is the voice that told you the puppy story was a lie. That voice just got louder. Listen to it Amy, don't doubt it; use it. Your first lesson is over," said Jack with a smile.

"This isn't what I think it's going to be, is it?" said Amy.

"Nope, I'm hungry. Let's go get some lunch and we'll talk about it."

They got in the truck and Jack said, "Which coffee cup did I use?"

"What?" Amy said, confused.

"When we were talking in the kitchen, which coffee cup did I use? I held it up in front of my face and I looked over the rim while we were talkin'," said Jack.

"I don't remember," Amy said.

"That's the beginning of your next lesson. Most all movies and books about the military special forces, CIA assassins, and stuff like that are all fun to watch and fun to read. The big, strong, handsome man with the cold stares and fancy weapons—most all of it is a lie. I know many people that are good with guns, some are good with knives and others are good at fightin', but they are all easy to kill. They never see it comin'," said Jack as he glanced over at Amy. He could see the wheels turning. *Good,* he thought.

"In the world wars, Vietnam, and the Cold War, assassinations were common. The assassins were not; poor old men in cheap suits slowly walking down the street, a woman pushin' a baby carriage, a pretty girl drunk at the bar, someone walkin' a dog or an old woman with a cane. All of them were people that you would look past, people you didn't see. But if you looked closely, you would see that the poor old man had a manicure or a fifty dollar haircut. Did the woman pushin' the carriage look at her child, smile, and talk to it or was she movin' a bomb? Did the fat old politician really believe the pretty girl could be attracted to him? He usually did, and then he wound up dead."

"Wow, I never thought of any of this," said Amy in amazement.

"Let's practice. Look up ahead and tell me what you see," said Jack.

"There's a dirt road."

"Yep, and it's got tracks on it that weren't there yesterday. What else?" asked Jack.

"There's new spray paint on that bridge," Amy said as they passed under the railroad bridge.

"What did it say?"

"It said...somebody loves...,"

Jack interrupted Amy and said, "It says JP loves LS. What else?"

"There's a bumper sticking out of those bushes way up there," she said.

"WHOA," Jack exclaimed as he hit the breaks. "State trooper; good catch, Amy," Jack said with a laugh. "You just saved me a hundred bucks."

"You're welcome," said Amy with a smile.

They arrived at the Bluebird and sat down and ordered. Jack looked at Amy and said, "Where is the back exit?"

Amy started to look around and then Jack said, "It's six steps past the men's room on the right, around ten steps past the ladies room. Anytime you walk into any structure, find the exits and have a plan to get there. If there is a problem, people will jump up, run, scream, and trample each other and you will be long gone. What did you see when you walked in here?"

"I just followed the waitress to our booth," said Amy.

"Look around the room, see who's here. How are they behaving? How are they dressed? Look at their faces. Are they sad, angry, or nervous? Why does that guy in the first booth have a jacket on when it's ninety degrees?"

Amy turned around and looked at the man, and then said, "I don't know."

"Me neither, but it's different, it's just not right. It's something you might want to watch. I have an idea about it. I think he is going to try to skip out on the check."

"How do you know that?"

"He's nervous. He's watching the waitress when she goes into the kitchen, seeing how long she stays back there. SALLY," Jack said, waving at the waitress. She came over to the table. Jack motioned to the man at the booth and said, "Put that man's lunch on my tab and don't say anythin'."

The waitress gave Jack a funny look and said, "OK, Jack."

"The military has a new term for this, it's called an OODA loop: Observe-Orient-Decide-Act. I observed what was going on, now I have to determine the possible outcomes, how I can affect those outcomes, or how they will affect me." explained Jack. "Amy look," Jack said with urgency as he pointed at the front door. Amy turned in time to see the man quickly walk out.

"Somebody should stop him, he broke the law," said an excited Amy.

"Why? His check is paid," said Jack with a smile. "What do ya' say we go over my thinkin' about this situation."

"OK."

"I saw a man that I believe was poor and probably hungry. I know that hungry people are desperate and desperate people do crazy things. So, I think about what I could do and what could happen. I could have chased him out the front door and brought him back in. But I'm hungry, tired, and really don't feel like it. Besides, what if he had a knife or a gun? Do I want to face that? Nope, I sure don't. I could have told Sally, but then she would confront him and possibly put herself in danger. Did I want that? Nope. Or I spend five or six bucks, feed a hungry man, and watch what could have been a big problem walk out the front door. I made a decision, I acted, and paid the check. How did I do?" said Jack.

Amy smiled at Jack and said, "You did good."

"Just remember that things going on around you constantly change. That's why they call it a loop. Keep lookin' at what's going on around you, understand it, understand what you are doing. Decide if you need to do anythin' different, make a decision, and then act on it. Over time you will be able to predict what other people will do before they do it and that is the secret. That is what keeps you safe. That is also what makes you a very dangerous person. Food's here, let's eat." said Jack.

Amy sat quietly and took it all in. Jack said, "I know this is a lot of stuff. Do you have any questions?"

"I understand what you sayin'. It just that when you told me you could teach me to confront evil, this was not what I expected."

"What did you expect?" Jack asked.

"Self-defense, weapons...you know, stuff like that," she said.

"That's the other half of it, tthe half we work to avoid. TV or movies show people in big fights or gun battles. In real life, if that happens you have made a mistake. Unfortunately, we are all human and we make mistakes. The part that always made me laugh was all the talkin'. The long conversations about what the killer is gonna do or tellin' the other person why he's there and such. In real life you say as little as possible, get in, get it done, and get out. We'll get to the other half, just not yet. Trust me, give it time and the next individual that wants to harm you or yours will have a very bad day," said Jack.

Amy smiled a crooked smile and said, "OK, Uncle Jack."

Chapter 24

The week before school started, Carla Jo went with Amy to orientation. *It's a big school*, Amy thought as she walked in. The principal gave a speech and Amy realized that it was Mrs. Nolan. She had been promoted to high school principal. The previous principal had apparently been a drunk and, as the president of the school board put it, the clowns were running the circus. Beth Nolan would fix all of that. Amy was happy to see a familiar face. Then her class took a tour and she saw something she didn't expect: a big trophy case at the school's entrance and inside the case was a picture of Kerry and his MVP trophy.

Amy was still looking at it when Carla Jo said, "He was a great football player."

"Yeah, yeah he was," said Amy with sadness in her voice.

Picking up on the emotional change in Amy, she pressed a little, "That's nice isn't it?"

"Yeah, it's nice. I don't know how I feel about being reminded of his death everyday," Amy said.

There it is, Carla Jo thought. Then she said, "If it bothers you I can have Mrs. Nolan remove it."

"No, don't. He deserves being up there," said Amy as she turned and walked down the hall.

Carla Jo watched her carefully as she looked in the classrooms.

"So, what do you think?" asked Carla Jo.

"I think these classrooms only have one door. There's only one way in and one way out. The windows don't open. That could be a problem in an emergency," said Amy.

"What made you think of that?" Carla Jo asked.

"Just things that Uncle Jack and I talk about."

OK, Carla Jo thought to herself. Out loud she said, "Let's find your locker."

They found it and Amy tried her combination.

"Works just fine," said Amy.

Carla Jo thought that Amy looked down, almost depressed, but this time she didn't say anything. They started walking back toward the entrance when Carla Jo finally asked her, "OK honey, what's wrong? This is high school. It's a big deal. You should be at least a little excited."

Amy looked at her with a sad face and said, "I'm sorry, Aunt Carla Jo. I know I should be excited. I'm just not. It's school, whatever."

Just then a voice called out down the hall, "Mrs. Brown, Mrs. Brown!"

It was Principal Nolan. "There's some paperwork you need to sign, could you come in my office please?" she said.

"Yes, Principal Nolan, I'll be right there," Carla Jo replied. She looked at Amy and said, "I'll be right back."

"Hey, wait," said Amy, grabbing Carla Jo's arm. "She wants to talk about what happened this summer. I don't want anyone to know, do you understand? Anyone," Amy said with almost a panicked look.

"If that is what it's about, I promise I will demand that your privacy come first, OK?" said Carla Jo with an understanding smile.

"OK."

Carla Jo walked into the office and the principal asked her to close the door.

"Hi Carla Jo."

"Hi Beth," she said.

"Tim told me what happened to her on that hill this summer. My God," Beth said while shaking her head. "How is she?"

"Yeah, well, I'm not real sure yet. We are working with her and she seems to get a little better everyday. I think it's just going to take time."

"I can't imagine," said Beth. "Is there anything I can do for her?"

"I don't know yet. I do have one question, though. Who knows about what happened?" Carla Jo asked.

"In school it would just be me. Sheriff Carter locked it all down after the, well, mysterious trailer fire."

"She is terrified people will find out."

"If I wasn't married to Tim I wouldn't know. In my position I hear it all. I think her secret is safe," Principal Nolan replied.

"Good, thank you. She's pretty smart, Beth. She has a maturity I have never seen in a child her age. I don't know if that will work in her favor or not."

"Yep, I know. In all my years of being a teacher and an administrator I have been around some smart kids, but I don't recall any smarter than her. You know, when I was a girl, Mr. Braxton and my daddy were friends. Mr. and Mrs. Braxton, Leon, and the girls would come over for supper sometimes after church. Marcel Braxton was one of the kindest, sweetest men I ever met. He was quiet but there was a lot going on in his head. You could just tell. Amy reminds me of him so much."

Carla Jo nodded and said, "I've heard that before. I'm not sure she will be the same child you had last year. I don't know how different she will be or even what those differences are, but if you could look out for her, I'm sure her dad would appreciate it."

"She's a very special child, I'll watch over her like she is my own."

Carla Jo and Beth got up, gave each other a hug, and then Carla Jo met Amy in the hall.

"What did she say?"

"She knows what happened but only because she is Deputy Nolan's wife. No one else in the school knows or will ever know unless you tell them," said Carla Jo.

"Thank you, Aunt Carla Jo," said Amy with a sigh of relief.

"If you have any problems or need anything, just go see her. She's a good lady and she will help you." She paused, and then said with a smile, "Here's something that will make you happy. Saturday is Francois day."

"OK, that makes me happy. Maybe he can do something with my hair so I don't look like Frankenstein," said Amy.

"It's a tiny scar, but if somebody does asked about it, what are you going to say?"

"The truth. I got hit with a rock and I don't want to talk about it."

"That'll work," said Carla Jo.

"Thanks for coming with me," Amy said. "I appreciate it. I know I haven't been much fun to be around. It's like I'm in a fog except when I'm with Uncle Jack. Then it's like I'm working toward something even though I'm not sure what that something is."

Carla Jo hugged Amy and said, "It will go away, honey. I promise it will. It just takes time. And you are welcome."

Carla Jo drove them back to her house. Jack was up so Carla Jo left Amy there and went back to work. Jack was out in the garage so Amy went in, sat down at the bench, and said, "Hi, Uncle Jack."

"Good mornin', what did you think of your new school?"

"Well, it's big. One thing I noticed is that the classrooms are death traps."

"How's that?" Jack asked.

"One door, no other exit."

"You got a plan?"

"Yep, the desks are pretty heavy. I could probably throw one through a window and egress that way," she said.

Jack laughed to himself and thought, *Hey, I taught her the word egress.* Then he nodded his head in approval and said, "Sounds like a plan." Then Jack said, "How ya' feelin'? Your daddy said you were having some pain."

"I've had some, but it's less and less. I really haven't felt anything in over a week. I've been jogging up the hill when I leave here. If I'm gonna feel any pain, you know, down there, I would feel it when I'm running. Last time I saw the doctor he said I could to do whatever I want," said Amy.

"Good. I think it's time we get you into shape," said Jack as he handed Amy a key. "Follow me."

Jack walked to the back of the house and opened the door of his block building. They walked in and the first thing Amy saw spray-painted on the wall were the words, *THE ONLY EASY DAY WAS YESTERDAY.* Looking around the room she saw that it was filled with free weights and everything you could imagine for staying physically fit.

"What does that mean?" Amy said, pointing to the words on the wall.

"That's a reminder of what I need to do to keep myself physically where I want to be. Those were the words hanging at the place where I went through advanced military training."

"It's hot in here. You got a fan or something?" Amy asked.

"I like it that way. It's hot in the summer and cold in the winter. The weather does not change to suit your needs. Any opportunity to train in a bad environment is a good thing. It's another way to prepare," Jack explained.

"OK, when do we start?"

"Tomorrow. I've made lists of the things I would like you to do. I'll show you the proper way to do them and you can work on your own. I gave you a key so you can come in here anytime you want. Somthin' else I want to show you," He said as he walked to the back of his pickup and opened the tailgate. "Happy birthday!"

he said, smiling. Inside was a heavy bag like the one Jack had hanging next to his workout room.

Amy smiled and said, "Thank you, Uncle Jack. It's just like yours."

"We'll hang it up in your barn when we start trainin' on self-defense, but first I think we need to have a little talk. Sit up here a minute," said Jack as he sat on the tailgate of the truck. "I am very impressed with what you have learned over the past couple of weeks. We've covered a lot of stuff. School starts next week and we won't get to spend as much time together. That's OK, we will still work at it and move forward. What I want you to focus on, more than anything, is achievin' a balance in your life," said Jack.

"You sound like Aunt Carla Jo," Amy said, frowning.

Jack laughed and said, "Well, just imagine her sittin' here next to me because we had this conversation last night. I want you to give time to your daddy, your brother, Granny Patches, and your friends. I want you to dedicate time to your schoolwork. The mental part of what we do will be helped by exercisin' your mind in school. I would also like you to get your butt back to church. Your daddy said you haven't gone in awhile."

Amy looked at the ground and said, "There's that thing with Daddy's girlfriend."

Jack nodded his head and said, "Yeah, Miss Francis, I figured that's what it was. Go to her house and talk to her. She's a good woman. I have known her for years. Stand up and take responsibility, that's what Braxtons do. You will leave her house feelin' better than when you walked in, I promise. Don't leave bad feelin's hangin' out there, take care of it."

"Yes, sir, but with everything goin' on, how will I get down here to work out?"

"Maybe you won't, they have a pretty nice weight room at the schoolhouse. Maybe you can work out there," said Jack.

Amy thought for a minute and said, "You know, there was a weight training elective I could have taken on my school schedule."

"Now you're thinkin'. Find a way. Maybe if you talk sweet to your aunt she'll take you to the school tomorrow and you could try to change your schedule."

Amy smiled that crooked smile and said, "OK, Uncle Jack, I'll give it a try, but I have to go. Joseph will be home soon."

"You want a ride?" Jack asked.

"Nope, I'll run," said Amy. She stood up on the tailgate and gave Uncle Jack a big hug and a kiss and said, "Thank you, Uncle Jack, I love you."

"I love you, too," he replied.

Amy jumped down off the tailgate and started running across the yard.

"AMY," yelled Jack.

Amy stopped, turned around, and said, "Yes, sir?"

Jack said in a serious voice, "Take care of that thing with Ms. Francis."

"Yes, sir."

The next day Carla Jo took Amy back to school. Carla Jo waited outside in the car while Amy went to see her counselor. Amy knocked on the counselor's office door and said, "Mr. Brooks?"

"Come in. And you are?" replied Mr. Brooks as she walked into the room

"Amy Braxton, could I please speak with you?" said Amy.

"Well, you don't have an appointment. Is it important?" said Mr. Brooks.

"It's important to me," said Amy.

"Isn't it always," said Mr. Brooks under his breath. Then he said, "What can I do for you, young lady?"

Amy sat down and said, "I would like to change my elective from art to weight training"

Mr. Brooks smiled a condescending smile and said, "Miss Braxton, weight training was set up by Coach Ramsey for the football team. It's not available to girls."

Amy thought for a second and then said, "That doesn't seem right."

Mr. Brooks chuckled under his breath and said, "Well, Miss Braxton, what you think are right and wrong is of little consequence to me. Do you need anything else?"

"No, sir, thank you," said Amy.

She left his office and walked out feeling a little dejected. As she walked by Principal Nolan's office, however, she stopped. *What the heck*, she thought. Gently, she knocked on the door.

"Come in," said Principal Nolan.

"Hi, Principal Nolan," said Amy.

"Amy Braxton, come in here and sit down. What are you doing here today?" said Principal Nolan with a big smile.

Amy explained the situation to her and what she was trying to do.

Principal Nolan replied, "He said it's not available to girls? Really? He said that?"

"Yes, ma'am."

"Hmm. Amy, here's what I want you to do. Monday morning you come to the office and see Miss Sissy for your new schedule. If you need anything, if you want to talk or have any problems, you come see me."

"I'm not causing any problems, am I, Mrs. Nolan?" Amy asked.

"No, ma'am. I'm here for you. Anything you need, I'm here," she said reassuringly.

"Thank you, Mrs. Nolan."

Amy left and as Mrs. Nolan watched her leave the office she hit a button on her phone and said, "Miss Sissy?"

"Yes, ma'am?"

"Would you please tell Mr. Brooks to get his ass in here? Make sure he knows I'm not happy," she said.

"Yes, ma'am."

Chapter 25

On the first day of school, Joseph and Amy left the house together and as Amy locked it, she hugged her brother, smiled and asked, "Do you have everything you need?"

"Yes, Amy," said Joseph with a little bit of an attitude.

Amy put him in a headlock and kissed his head, and then said, "Have fun at school."

Amy walked toward the bus stop. *The first day of high school,* she thought. She looked down the road for Tommy and Timmy and then shook her head, not believing she did it. They had been at the bus stop with her every year since kindergarten. At least she would see Mary Beth. Mary Beth spent the summer with her mom's brother and his family, who lived in the Smoky Mountains. The bus came and Amy got on.

"AMY!" Mary Beth squealed. Amy sat down beside her and they hugged.

Amy looked at Mary Beth and said, "You look great, I love your hair."

"Thanks, I had the best summer of my life. I...," Mary Beth stopped talking, reached over to Amy and lifted her bangs, revealing the scar on her head. "What happened to you?" Mary Beth asked.

"I got hit with a rock," said Amy.

"It must have been a big rock, what happened?" asked Mary Beth.

"I really don't want to talk about it. Tell me about your summer," Amy said with a feigned smile.

Mary Beth went on and on about waterskiing, tubing, and a cute boy she met. As Mary Beth spoke Amy found herself unable to concentrate or listen. Mary Beth's voice kept getting farther and father away. Amy felt herself drifting, like she was in a cloud.

"Amy, Amy," Amy heard off in the distance. She snapped out of it and looked at Mary Beth. "Are you OK?" asked Mary Beth.

"Yeah, fine, it's just...I'm glad you had a great summer," said Amy.

Mary Beth looked at Amy. *Something isn't right*, she thought.

Amy thought about telling Mary Beth what happened but she couldn't. She just couldn't.

They arrived at school and Amy went to the office to get her new schedule. There it was, weight training, last period. Amy discovered she had a new name, too: Kerry's sister. As bad as it was not having her own identity in junior high, this was a hundred times worse. In junior high, Kerry was just a good kid that everyone liked. Here he was a football star that had been lost in the prime of his life.

She went to each of her classes and tried to listen to her teachers, but it was difficult. As last period came around she got her workout clothes on and went to weight training. Coach Ramsey saw her and she could tell he didn't want her there; that was, until he saw her last name. He pulled her to the side and said, "Kerry was the finest young man I have ever coached. I loved him like a son."

"Thanks, Coach," said Amy.

"Amy, each one of these young men has had workouts designed for them. If you want I can try to design something that fits your needs," he suggested.

Amy pulled out the workout her Uncle Jack made and said, "I have what I want to do written down. Would it be OK if I use this?"

He didn't even look at it. "Sure, that would be fine." Then the coach cleared his throat and barked across the room, "GENTLEMEN, WE HAVE A YOUNG LADY THAT WILL BE IN OUR CLASS THIS YEAR. YOU WILL SHOW HER RESPECT OR YOU WILL ANSWER TO ME. IS THAT UNDERSTOOD?" "YES, SIR," came a thundering reply. The coach smiled at Amy and returned to his office.

Weight training became her respite in an otherwise trudging slog through her freshman year in academia. She had a lot of anger and rage, and for that hour she could let it all go. The football players progressed from ignoring her to having a grudging respect for her and then full-blown admiration. By the end of the year, while the players cheered her on, she benched her own weight seventeen times. She had also physically changed. She had always been a little muscular with a layer of baby fat, but all that was all gone. Her body looked like the miniature version of an NFL wide receiver. She did not realize that through her example, she had pushed many of the football players to achieve new levels of strength. The coach noticed. Every coach of every girl's sport in the school all but begged her to try out for their sport, but she had no interest in their sports.

Report cards were not a highlight of her year. She got a couple of Cs, which had never happened before. Her daddy was not happy, but Carla Jo kept him from making a really big deal about it. She wasn't failing, but her daddy expected far more. The truth was, had Carla Jo not coaxed that out of her, she would have done worse. Concentrating was a problem she was struggling with and it wasn't getting any better. Carla Jo was her advocate and kept explaining to her daddy that it would take time.

Socially she still had Mary Beth. Mary Beth, however, had made some new friends. She kept Amy close but had a difficult time understanding Amy's standoffish behavior. Amy was one of the most beautiful girls in the school. The boys flocked around her, but she swatted them away. Any thoughts she had about sexuality had been badly distorted by what happen to her on that hill. The rumor in the school was that she was gay. She laughed when she heard it, but then she thought about it. She really didn't know what she was.

Outside of shool she kept up with her household chores. Joseph was old enough to help and he did. She kept her word to her uncle Jack and went to visit Ms. Francis. Uncle Jack was right. She was wonderful, kind, and forgiving. Amy taught her how to make corn bread like the boys liked it. Ms. Francis assured Amy that she had no intention of mothering her but would be there if she needed anything. Amy was sure to let her know that she was welcome in the Braxton home.

Amy also went hunting with Her daddy, Jack, and Gene, but it wasn't the same. She enjoyed her time in the woods but there was still a level of apathy she couldn't escape. Jack killed a deer but that was it.

During their last outing, Gene and Amy were attempting to drive the deer, leaving Jack and Leon alone. While they were waiting, Leon turned to Jack and said, "When do you think I'll get my little girl back?"

"Like she was?" said Jack. "Probably never. She will never be the same. But hopefully she'll be close. Trust Carla Jo. She knows what to do."

Jack kept working with Amy. By the end of the year she began to excel in self-defense. After dinner Amy would go down to the barn and practice on the heavy bag for about an hour. Leon would sneak down and watch her. Her rage and viciousness were only exceeded by her speed and skill. He was happy she was learning to defend herself, but at what point did it become something more?

When possible, she would visit Jack and they would spar. He was glad to have the workout but more than once he had to stop and let her calm down a little. It was the rage. After a particularly strenuous session, Amy gave her uncle Jack a hug and kiss like always and then ran home. Jack dragged his tired self into the house, looked at Carla Jo, and said, "She's as fast as I am. I'm bigger, stronger, and I know more so I can defend against her, but it won't be that way for long. She's dangerous, Carla Jo. She's dangerous right now."

Carla Jo had a concerned look on her face. She knew all about that rage. Love would eventually fix it, but until then she worried about what Jack and Amy were doing. Jack was clearly proud of her. This left Carla Jo walking a fine line between respecting what Jack was teaching her and expressing her concerns about it.

"Jack," Carla Jo said softly, "are your sure she has the temperament for these skills? She's not yet real stable. Aren't you afraid she may hurt someone?"

Jack stroked his chin and thought about it for a moment. "I see it when she throws the switch, the point where she doesn't see me anymore. She see's those boys. It takes me awhile to get her there. She's still the same, sweet kid she's always been. It would take a lot for her to hurt just anybody. No, I don't think she would hurt anyone. Then again, I wouldn't want to be the one to piss her off," Jack acknowledged.

Amy's fifteenth year of life was hard, confusing, frustrating, and lonely. If it could be described by a color it would be gray. The color of Amy's sixteenth year, however, would be tie-dye, definitely tie-dye.

Chapter 26

*A*my got out of bed and stretched. It was the first Saturday of summer vacation and for the first time in a long time, she felt pretty good. She dropped down on the floor next to her bed and did one hundred push-ups and three hundred ab crunches. After about five minutes of assorted stretches, she went into the kitchen and made her daddy some coffee. She pulled the curtain back on the kitchen window and watched the sun rise over the trees. It was going to be a beautiful day.

A car pulled up the driveway and soon afterward Amy heard a soft knock at the door. She opened it and there stood Ms. Carol Francis.

"Good morning," Amy said with a slight smile as she invited her in. It was still a little clumsy when they were around each other. Ms. Francis was a hugger, that's how she greeted people. Since the attack, however, Amy had a very short list of people she would let touch her and Ms. Francis was not on that list. They walked in the kitchen and Amy asked Ms. Francis if she wanted to help her fix breakfast.

"Sure honey, I'd love to," smiled Ms. Francis.

There wasn't much small talk between them, but there was kindness. Miss Francis had a heartfelt kindness. It was genuine. Amy's, on the other hand, was a little more manufactured.

Eventually Leon got up and walked into the kitchen. Carol was peeling potatoes and Amy was making biscuits. He smiled and poured himself a cup of coffee. Leon hugged Amy and kissed her, and then gave Carol a hug and kissed her. It wasn't lost on anyone that Amy came first, especially Amy.

Leon sat down at the kitchen table, took a deep breath, and said, "Amy, I have some good news. I've asked Carol to marry me and she said yes."

Amy didn't react. She stood at the counter mixing biscuit dough. After an uncomfortable silence, Amy turned to look at them and with a forced smile said, "Congratulations. When's the big day?"

"We were thinking before school starts. That would give everyone a chance to get used to Carol being here," Leon replied.

"OK, sure," said Amy.

Ms. Francis got up, took the peeled and sliced potatoes, and sat them on the stove. She turned toward Amy and said, "I was wondering if you would like to be my maid of honor?" Carol was sure this would be met with excitement. She wanted to do everything she could to include her step-daughter-to-be.

But Amy just stood there stoically, pinching off chunks of dough, patting them, and putting them in the pan. Without looking at anyone Amy said, "Don't you have friends for that?"

Amy didn't realize how hurtful that statement was. She thought she was just being honest. Her lack of empathy caught Leon and Carol both off guard.

"Amy, what Carol just offered you is an honor," Leon said with a hint of scorn.

"An honor for who, me?" Amy said, almost sounding confused.

She rinsed her hands off in the sink, turned to the stove, and poured bacon grease into the skillet before turning on the flame. She looked at her daddy and said in a calm, measured voice, "Daddy, I want you to be happy. If she makes you happy, then OK. You want to marry her and move her into our house, fine. I'll treat her with respect and I will try to be nice. Haven't I been nice to you, Ms. Francis?"

Carol nodded her head and said, "Yes."

"Amy, you know there's more to it than that," sighed Leon.

Amy put the potatoes in the skillet, salted them, and said quietly without looking up, "what's the more part, Daddy? Is that the part where I lie and say I want her in this house? I'm not gonna lie, I don't want her in this house. You both deserve better than a lie."

An uncomfortable silence fell over the kitchen and then Amy said, "Ms. Francis, would you please take the biscuits out of the oven in fifteen minutes? I think you know how to make potatoes. I need to go." Amy went to her bedroom, changed clothes, put her shoes on, and walked out the front door.

Carol looked at Leon and said sarcastically, "That went well."

Amy walked down the hill thinking about the events of the morning. Hearing her stomache growl, she stopped by Ed Gwinn's for a Moon Pie and a Dr. Pepper. While walking across the road and up the driveway, she thought about life with Carol in her house. Those were not happy thoughts. Arriving at her uncle Jack's front door, she knocked. Carla Jo answered, laughed, and said, "Well, that looks like a good breakfast."

"It's not bad," said Amy as she tossed her last bite of Moon Pie to Bubba.

"Jack's still in the bed. What brings you here so early?" asked Carla Jo.

They sat down at the kitchen table and Amy explained what had transpired earlier. With an understanding smile, Carla Jo said, "You had to know it was coming."

Amy nodded and said, "Yeah, but I don't have to like it."

Carla Jo sat for a moment, took a sip of her coffee, and put it down. She looked at Amy with a stern face and said, "Do you think your mother would have wanted Leon to be alone?"

Amy started to speak, "it's just that...,"

"No," Carla Jo interrupted, "I asked you a question."

"No," said Amy under her breath.

Carla Jo sat back in the chair and said, "Being a friend is a tough job. You have to look someone you love in the eye and tell them hard truths. Things they may not want to hear. You're my best friend and you need to hear the truth. Are you listening?"

Amy nodded.

Carla Jo got a little fired up and said, "It's time to put your big girl pants on. Yes, you DO have to like it. You DO have to go to that wedding, put on a dress, be the maid of honor, smile, and celebrate. If you don't, you will do far more damage to your daddy than any discomfort you may feel in the three short years you have left on that hill."

"You sound more like my momma then my friend," said Amy with a little edge to her voice.

Just then Jack walked in and poured himself a cup of coffee. "Good morning," Jack said, being just a little too happy.

Amy and Carla Jo's heads snapped around and looked at Jack. Jack saw the expression on their faces and said, "Whoa, OK then. I reckon I'll be on the porch with Bubba."

Carla Jo looked back at Amy and nodded with a half smile on her face and said, "Honey, I knew your momma very well and I doubt if she would have had this conversation with you. She would have gone out to one of those trees, cut her a switch, and whooped you ass for being so damn selfish."

"Oh, so now you think I'm being selfish?" said Amy with some surprise to her voice.

Carla Jo said, "No, Amy, I don't THINK you're being selfish, you ARE being selfish and you do not wear it well. It does not look good on you."

They sat quietly for a few minutes. Amy knew Carla Jo was right. She didn't like it and didn't want to admit it, but the more she thought about it the more Carla Jo made sense. This was her daddy's life she was disrupting. This was straight up childishness on her part. Amy let out a great big sigh and said, "OK, fine, now what do we do?"

Two weeks later Carla Jo and Amy were speeding down the interstate toward the city. This time they had a new destination and a new passenger. Amy was doing her duty and escorting Ms. Francis to buy a wedding dress.

"Amy, would you please stop calling me Ms. Francis. It makes me feel like an old nun, and trust me, your daddy is not marrying me to be an old nun," said Carol. Feeling comfortable around Amy was something she longed for. Finally it seemed to be happening.

Carla Jo giggled and it took Amy a second to get the reference. Then Amy recoiled in horror and in a panicked voice said, "OH MY GOD, OH MY GOD, I don't want to know," Carla Jo and Carol lost it and started laughing uncontrollably.

Over the course of the day, Amy started to realize that Carol wasn't who she thought she was. She was funny and could be just a little tawdry. She made Amy laugh out loud more than once. As Carla Jo and Amy stood outside the dressing room waiting for Carol to change into yet another dress, Amy said, "She's not who I thought she was."

"People never are until you get to know them. Even then they have secrets," Said Carla Jo.

Carol walk out of the dressing room and Amy looked at her and smiled. The look on Carol's face said it all; she had found the dress.

"Your turn, Amy," said Carla Jo. Amy sighed and went into the dressing room with the sales clerk. Carol came back out and stood next to Carla Jo.

"I think you're winning her over," Said Carla Jo.

"Good. I knew if we spent some time together it would work out. When she was helping me teach Sunday school we got along so well. I don't understand what changed," said Carol.

"Well, she's been taking care of those boys for a long time. That's her house and her men. If you think she's gonna step aside and hand them over to you, I'd think again."

"Yes, I suppose you are right. I'd be the same way. It'll just take time and some patience."

I know that sometimes things can get tense living under the same roof so I want to give you a little piece of advice," Carla Jo said.

"Sure," Carol replied, curious.

"Don't ever physically challenge her or put yourself in a position where she would want to challenge you."

Carol shook her head and said, "I have a pretty good handle on my temper. I don't think I would ever hurt her."

Carla Jo chuckled under her breath and said, "She's not the one I'm worried about."

Carol looked at Carla Jo with a little confusion on her face and said, "Well, I had older brothers, I can handle myself."

Carla Jo thought about what to say next and then said, "If you're gonna be in the family, I guess you need to know some things."

Just then Amy walked out of the dressing room and both women smiled.

"You are beautiful," said Carol. "Please try on the peach one."

"OK," said Amy as she walked back in the dressing room.

Carol looked at Carla Jo and said, "What things?"

Carla Jo walked her over to a little bench and they sat down.

"My husband, Jack, is not your typical Vietnam veteran. He was a Special Forces Navy SEAL. He killed a lot of people and he is very good at it. You know about what happened to Amy, right?" Carla Jo asked.

"Yeah, it was horrible. I really wanted to be there for her, but Leon thought it wasn't really my place. After all, she had you," said Carol.

Amy walked out of the dressing room again and both ladies looked at her, smiled, and nodded.

"Now the yellow one," Carol said.

Amy unconsciously rolled her eyes and walked back into the dressing room.

Carla Jo continued, "We thought it would be a good idea if Jack worked with her to teach her self-defense, to give her some confidence."

"That makes sense," said Carol.

"Yeah, we thought so, too. She has, however, become obsessed with it. There are those of us who believe that Jack has taken her a little too far. She has become a very dangerous young lady."

"What do you mean by dangerous?" asked Carol.

"She's a sweetheart, Carol, she's a really good kid. But somewhere inside her is a button. Whoever pushes that button might not survive it. Don't ever piss her off," said Carla Jo, looking deadly serious.

Amy walked out of the dressing room again in the yellow dress. Carla Jo said, "Carol, I think I like the peach."

Carol looked at Amy and with a nervous voice said, "Yeah, me too."

Chapter 27

THUMP, THUMP, THUMP. Jack awoke to the rhythmic punishment of the heavy bag.

"Is that my new alarm clock, you beating on that bag?" Jack yelled out the window of the kitchen.

Amy grinned and said, "Sorry, Uncle Jack."

"Get in here. At least let me drink some coffee."

Amy took off the padded gloves and wrist guards, leapt up the steps into the kitchen, and sat down at the table.

"What day do I have to wear a suit?" asked Jack.

"July seventeenth," said Amy.

"That's the third Sat...," Jack stopped mid-sentence.

"Amy looked at Jack, sighed, and then said, "Yep, one year to the day."

"Oh shit," Jack said under his breath. "Am I the only one that's caught that?"

"I guess so. I thought about sayin' something, but Carol's got family flying in and hotel reservations and all these plans. I've been a big enough pain in the butt. I'm not going to say anything. Maybe it's a good thing to turn it into a day to celebrate."

"Wow, honey, those are grown-up words that most grown-ups wouldn't say. I'm proud of ya'."

"OK, whatever," sighed Amy.

"No, not whatever. The biggest part of being an adult is doin' the right thing when it's hard. I can't imagine much harder. I'm proud of you."

"Thanks, Uncle Jack."

Jack smiled, and then said, "I need you to do somethin' for me."

"Sure, what do you need?"

"Sometime in your conversations with your dad and Aunt Carla Jo, tell them you're not gonna kill anybody," Jack asked.

"What?" said Amy, a bit surprised.

"Have you looked at yourself in the mirror lately? You look like a Viking warrior. Your daddy has followed you to the barn and watched you work out. Most daddies are just a little disturbed when they see their little girl committin' that much violence backed up by that much rage. Look, I know what you're doin' and why you are doin' it. I do the same thing for some of the same reasons."

"Uncle Jack, I would never hurt any one unless they tried to hurt me or someone I care about," Amy explained.

"I'm glad to hear you say that. I know that and you know that; please make sure they know that," said Jack.

"You know, I have pushed everyone but you away when it comes to this stuff. Maybe I'll invite my daddy down to the barn one evening and explain to him what I'm doing."

Jack smiled, nodded his head, and said, "Now you're thinkin'."

Jack took another sip of coffee and said, "I was thinkin' we could start talking about weapons today."

Amy smiled her crooked smile and said, "OK, I'd like that."

Jack explained the difference between lethal and non-lethal weapons. He talked about when to and when not to use a weapon. He explained when the OODA loop applied, which was always, and then he stressed his two most important rules.

"Amy, I want you to listen to these two rules and live by them. The first is NEVER, under any circumstances, surrender your weapon. If you do, you will be at the mercy of those that probably won't show any. It's much better to back out of a standoff and live to fight another day," said Jack.

"Never surrender my weapon, got it," said Amy.

"Good. Number two, if you are going to use a weapon, never let them see it until they've tasted it. This bullshit about waving around a knife or a gun will get you killed. The key to victory is surprise, keep it on your side."

"OK, got it."

"Another thing that goes along with that is assume everyone is armed. Watch for it," Jack said.

"Yes, sir," said Amy.

"Come on, let's go outside. I want to introduce you to your first weapon," Said Jack with a smile.

They walked out the back door and stood next to the blockhouse. Jack reached into a five-gallon bucket next to the building and showed it to Amy.

"Um, that's a stick," said Amy, a little skeptically.

"Very good."

"It's just a stick," she said, looking confused. "What do I do with a stick?"

Jack smiled and quickly poked Amy in the ribs with it.

"OW, THAT HURT!" exclaimed Amy, rubbing her side.

"No, it couldn't have, it's just a stick." said Jack with a smile. "Your good at math. Tell me, what's the area of the end of this stick?" Jack asked.

"Probably a half inch squared," said Amy, still rubbing her side.

"I just poked you with less than five pounds of force. How many pounds do you think you could generate? Fifty? A hundred? Imagine that in your ribs, kidney, eye socket, or temple. All of that force focused on the end of this stick. It's pretty devastating."

"I see what you mean," said Amy, beginning to understand.

"The best thing is, most people will look at it like you do, it's just a stick. You maintain the element of surprise. Now let's go to work," said Jack.

Amy smiled, nodded, and said, "OK."

Chapter 28

$\mathcal{A}$my, Carla Jo, and Carol's friend Debbie stood around the bride-to-be in a back room of the Black Oak Baptist Church. They fluffed her dress and touched up her hair and makeup 'til Carla Jo said, "That's it and you're beautiful."

A voice came through the door saying, "Five minutes."

"Thank you so much," Carol said while staring at herself in the mirror. "Do you think I could have a few minutes with Amy?"

"Sure," said Carla Jo.

Carla Jo and the other ladies left the room, and Carol looked at Amy and said, "I'm so sorry. I had no idea today was the same day."

Amy nodded and said, "I know." Then she took a deep breath and said, "Carol, there has not been a day in the past year when I haven't thought about what those boys did to me. I think I would like today to be a special day, a day where my daddy gets what he wants. More than anything, he wants you. He deserves you and Joseph deserves you. He loves you so much. I would never do anything to deny him that."

Carol reached over to hug Amy and this time Amy let her. It was time to let Carol in.

"Your Aunt Carla Jo is right," said Carol. "You're somthin' else."

Amy turned to walk toward the door and Carol said, "Amy?" Amy turned around and Carol said, "You know I love you."

Amy smiled and said, "Yeah, I know." Amy grabbed the door handle, stopped, and then turned around and said, "You know this family is pretty crazy. There's a door right behind ya'. You can still escape."

Carol laughed and said, "Thanks, I'll think about it."

"See you out there," said Amy.

The music started and Amy walked down the isle. The black Oak Baptist Church was one of the largest in the area and it was packed. Everyone was there: the Browns, the Murphys, the Gossetts, and Leon's friends from work. If you were going to rob a bank in Jackson County, today was the day. Most of the sheriff's department was there including Deputy Nolan and his wife, Amy's principal.

Amy was stunning as she walked down the isle with Leon's best man, Jack. Audible gasps were heard along with the occasional murmur of her mom's name. Amy saw her daddy standing at the altar but for the first time in her life, she saw him differently. There stood a man, not a daddy, and a handsome one at that. The groomsmen were Gene and Joseph, and the bridesmaids were Carla Jo and Carol's friend Debbie Donner. Brother Taylor officiated. A Taylor had married every Braxton as far back as anyone could remember. Amy hugged her daddy and her daddy said, "Thank you honey, thank you so much."

Amy smiled and said, "I love you, Daddy."

The wedding march was played as Carol walked down the isle. Amy thought to herself how she was glad she made the decision to accept Carol. Then Amy saw her daddy and how happy he looked. *It will work. I'll make it work*, she thought. Vows were exchanged and everyone adjourned to the Lewistown VFW. The party was on.

There was a live band and they were pretty good. Amy danced with Jack and then her daddy. It was fun and she was having a great time, but there was one small issue. Carol's seventeen-year-old nephew Paulie had decided to allow some of his post-pubescent angst spill over onto Amy. Amy sat down next to Carla Jo and said, "If he puts his hands on me one more time I'm gonna kill him, right here in front of God and everyone."

Carla Jo laughed and said, "It would be bad manners to kill someone at your daddy's wedding reception. Didn't Jack teach you anything non-lethal?"

Amy smiled a wicked little smile and said, "Yes, he did."

Amy walked to the bar to get a Dr. Pepper and just as she was stepping away, Paulie appeared and his hand immediately found her ass. Without taking the smile off her face, Amy reached down, slowly grabbed the middle finger of the hand on her ass and began to bend it toward the back of his wrist. With the other hand she grabbed a pressure point on his elbow, the ulnar nerve, and began to squeeze. The pain registered in his eyes almost immediately. Amy pulled him close, and then leaned in and whispered, "If you ever touch me again, I will kill you and I know how."

Carla Jo watched from a distance as Amy picked up her Dr. Pepper from the bar and walked away. Paulie was left standing there with a look on his face that fell somewhere between shock and terror. Amy sat down next to Carla Jo, who said, "Looks like you made your point. What did you say?"

"I told him the truth," said Amy with that same wicked smile.

Leon found Amy and told her they had a plane to catch. Jack and Carla Jo's wedding present was a honeymoon trip to the Grand Caymans. Leon wasn't too excited about it, but Carla Jo explained to him in no uncertain terms that the honeymoon wasn't about him.

The party was getting a little crazy as the mason jars came out and Carla Jo finally decided that she'd had enough. She told Jack it was time to go. Gene had taken Joseph and Granny home earlier. Joseph stayed with Granny and Amy was going to stay with Jack and Carla Jo. Carla Jo loaded Jack in the truck. He was pretty trashed. Amy laughed as he got in the truck singing an old

Alabama song. After helping Jack with his seat belt, he leaned back in the seat and within a few minutes he passed out.

"Uncle Jack is not going to feel real good tomorrow," said Amy.

"Nope, but he brought it on himself," Carl Jo said without sympathy.

"I don't think I have ever seen you drink."

"And you never will," said Carla Jo with finality.

"Why not?"

Carla Jo sighed a heavy sigh, smiled to herself, and said, "Oh honey, I've had enough substances for two lifetimes."

Jack and Carla Jo: Part 1

Jack saw the blanket move as Annette began to stir. She covered her eyes from the bright sun shining through the window of the truck.

"Where am I?" Asked Annette.

"Twenty miles outside of Blacksburg, Virginia. Good morning, Lt. Watkins," said a deep baritone voice.

Annette jumped. She looked at the man in the driver's seat. His scarred face had a slight smile. *Oh my God, a psycho killer*, she thought. Then something occurred to her. She said, "Wait a minute, Lt. Watkins? Do you know me?"

"Sort of. My name's Jack," he said.

She started to move the blanket and saw she was naked. The blood from her wounds had soaked into the blanket and stuck to her back. Sharp pain made her cringe as she moved in the seat. Then she began to remember what happened.

"Oh my God, you killed the Sergeant. Maurice is going to kill us, he's going to kill us both," Annette said in a panic.

"I spoke to Maurice. He will never bother you again, I promise."

Just then the stomach cramps began to hit Annette. She needed a fix. "I have to use the restroom," she said.

"I was thinking we could stop at a motel. You could take a shower, clean up a little. I bought you some clothes and some medicine for the cuts on your back," said Jack.

"Yeah, OK."

Jack got a room and Annette quickly grabbed her tote and went into the bathroom. She shut and locked the door, and then turned on the shower. Jack said through the door, "There's a restaurant next door, I'm gonna get us something to eat, do you want anything special?"

"No, anything is fine," she replied.

Jack left and came back twenty minutes later. The shower was still running. He ate his breakfast, and then he sat and looked at the door. He couldn't hear any movement. "Annette?" Jack called through the door. "Are you OK?" There was still no answer. Jack put his shoulder to the door and broke it open.

Annette was sitting on the toilet still wrapped in the blanket. She was leaning against the wall with a glazed look in her eyes, and then Jack saw the needle on the floor by her feet. "Oh shit," Jack said out loud. He had seen this in Vietnam. He gently peeled the blanket off of her and sat her in the tub. He bathed her, washed her hair, and then dried her off. He laid her across the bed and dressed her wounds. Then he put a pair of sweatpants and a sweatshirt on her and gathered her things. The last thing he did was throw her stash in the toilet on the way out the door. Jack thought to himself, *This is gonna be tough.*

Barley able to walk, Jack supported Annette as she staggered to the truck. Jack lifted her in and buckled her seatbelt, and their journey continued. Annette became lucid again a couple of hours later. Jack looked at her and said, "Heroine? Really, Annette? Heroine?"

She sat looking straight ahead and never answered. About two hours from Jack's house she said she had to go to the bathroom again. She picked up her tote and started looking through it.

"Where is it?" she asked. "Where the hell is it?" she asked again as a feeling of desperation began to take hold.

"I flushed it at the motel."

"You son of a bitch, YOU SON OF A BITCH!" she screamed and then attacked him. She grabbed the steering wheel causing the truck to go off the road. Jack regained control and brought the truck to a stop. She bit, scratched, kicked, punched, and screamed. She called Jack every vile name she could think of. She kicked the dashboard so hard she split it down the middle. For ten minutes she expended every once of energy she had until she collapsed, sobbing, against the door. Jack was hurt. He had a couple of pretty bad bite marks on his arm and a finger pointing the wrong way. He grabbed the finger, popped it back into its joint, and then started driving again. Annette leaned against the door and kept sobbing, saying, "I can't, I can't, you don't understand, I just can't."

By the time they arrived at Jack's house the heroine detox process had begun; intense cramps followed by bodily fluids spewing out of every hole in her body. Jack called Katherine for help. She washed clothes, kept the bed clean, and drove to Lewistown to get whatever Jack needed. After two days it still had not let up, so he called Doc Henderson for help. He did what he could and told Jack she should probably be in the hospital. Jack couldn't do that. He thought the law might be looking for her. After the third day she fell asleep. He watched over her as she slept for twenty hours. Annette woke up so sore she could barely move.

After awhile she slowly walked outside and sat on the porch swing next to Jack. She sat quietly for an hour or so, then said, "Now what?"

"Now we get you better."

"You kidnapped me," accused Annette.

Shrugging his shoulders and with a slight smile, Jack said, "Is that how you want to look at it?" Pointing across the front yard, Jack said, "The road is right there, you can go whenever you feel like it."

"Who the hell are you and how do you know me?" said Annette.

Jack sighed and said, "Yeah, you probably wouldn't remember but once upon a time there was a young sailor that was brought to the Seventy-First Evac. He was shot up and half dead. The doctors decided to let him die and a young nurse sat by his bed, singing to him. The young sailor woke up, saw her face, and heard her voice. The young sailor heard her when she fought with the doctors to get them to save the young sailor's life. He heard everything, every word. That young sailor was me, and that nurse was you. You gave me my life. Now I am giving you yours."

Annette shook her head and said, "It's not worth saving."

Jack laughed a compassionate, understanding laugh and said, "I know how you feel. When I came back here wounded, disfigured, and alone, I didn't want to stick around. But my family convinced me otherwise. You can stay here for awhile. Give it a chance. If you change your mind, if you think your life isn't worth living, I'll show you where the gun case is."

Annette looked at Jack and said, "I have nothing; no family, no friends, no money, nothing."

Jack reached out, held her hand, and said, "Not true, you got me."

Annette looked across the yard. She thought about how pretty it was, the grass, the trees, the little white house. It was nice, almost too nice. "I suppose you're gonna expect me to sleep with you," she said.

"No, you have your own room. All I want from you is to get well. Then I expect you to leave and start a new life. That's all I want from you."

Annette thought to herself, *Sure, whatever you say.*

"I have to work. Is there anything you like to do to pass the time?" asked Jack.

"I like to read," said Annette.

"OK, let's go to the library and get you some books," said Jack.

It took a few days for Annette to make herself at home, but soon she was doing a little cooking and some cleaning. Otherwise she sat on the front porch and read. Jack would come and go and talk to her in the evenings about a bunch of nothing. After a couple of weeks, Jack asked her if she was lonely. His cousin, he explained, lived up the hill and he was sure she would love the company. Annette balked and said she would think about it. Jack told her his cousin's name was Katherine and she was expecting her.

Annette stayed around the house for a few more days, but she was going crazy from boredom and decided to take a walk up the hill. It was a long climb. Tired and winded she finally made it to Katherine's front door. She knocked and was invited in. They sat at the kitchen table and talked, sort of. Annette didn't speak and Katherine prattled on and on about family and everything under the sun. Eventually Annette started talking about her family and after about a month, Annette had spilled everything. Katherine never judged her. All she would say was, "It's never too late to do the right thing."

Annette was looking better, feeling better, and the exercise going up and down the hill was doing her wonders, She had also put on some weight. With Katherine's cooking that wasn't hard to do. She would sit with Katherine and Granny Patches and listen to their stories while shelling peas or shucking corn. This was a life she never knew existed. It was slow and easygoing. She thought to herself, *I could live like this.*

Annette would watch Jack wash his truck or work in the yard. He was big and strong with a body like an athlete. More importantly, however, he didn't lie. He expected nothing from her and yet showed her a kindness that she had only experienced as a child. There was only one man in her life that ever treated her like that and that was her father. Exactly four months to the day of Annette's arrival, Jack invited her into the living room and told her they needed to talk.

Jack sat down on the chair and Annette on the couch. Jack said, "I made you a promise and I intend to keep it. It's time for you to go."

Annette knew this was coming but she didn't know when. Jack said, "I have a few things for you. First is a little gift from your old friend Maurice."

Jack sat the black case down in front of her. She opened the lid and saw the stacks and stacks of hundred dollar bills.

"Oh my God. There must be tens of thousands in here," she said, shocked.

"I never counted it, but I'm sure it's well north of a hundred thousand. It's enough to get you started in a new life," he said. Then he handed her the keys to a car. "I used some of the money to buy you a car. It's not new but it's nice and it runs good."

Annette looked at the keys and then Jack said, "there is one more thing." He handed her a piece of paper. "It's the birth certificate of my little sister, Carla Jo. She died when she was three. She would be about the same age as you. I have friends at the county and they modified the race to Asian so you should be able to get a driver's license with no problem. Your history in Philadelphia won't follow you anymore. You're free, good luck." Jack said while smiling at her.

Annette looked at the unbelievable gifts laid out in front of her. She looked up at Jack and said, "What if I don't want to go?"

"Well, I'm sure there are apartments and houses around here that you could rent or buy," said Jack, not quite grasping what she meant.

Annette got up and stood in front of him. "No, I mean here, with you. What if I don't want to leave?"

Jack shook his head, stood up, and started to walk away. She grabbed his shirt and pulled him back. Jack looked at her and said, "You don't know me. You don't know anythin' about me."

"Oh yes, I do. I know more than you think. Katherine told me quite a bit."

"Katherine doesn't know everythin' there is to know. But still...," Jack started to say something, but Annette put two fingers against his lips.

"Katherine loves you, and, um, well, I think I love you, too," Annette said. Jack was in shock. He never even considered this to be a possibility. She pulled her fingers away from his mouth and looked at him with those eyes; eyes that he had seen in his dreams for years. "Knowing all that you know about me, could you ever love me?" asked Annette.

Jack looked at her and said, "I don't know if I have ever been in love with anyone else. I fell in love with you while I was layin' on that gurney in Vietnam."

Annette smiled and said, "Well then, I guess that settles it. You like me and I like you." She cupped his face in her hands, pulled him close, and gently kissed him.

Chapter 29

*C*arol sold her house and she and Leon decided to use the money to put on an addition. Two women and one bathroom could make things a little testy. Other than that, Leon was pleased with the smooth transition of bringing Carol into the family. What he didn't see was that Amy and Carol spoke often. Each one worked to keep the peace for the sake of Leon. What truly made it better was a particularly enlightening conversation that Amy had with Carol when she moved in. Amy and Carol were sitting on the back porch when Carol asked, "Amy, what do you think are the duties of a wife in a family?"

Amy thought for a minute and said, "Well, I only know what my momma did. She took care of us. She cooked and cleaned and made sure we had everything we needed."

"Was she good at it?"

"Oh yeah, she worked so hard, loved on us, and did special things for Daddy. I would see her write little notes and put them in his lunch box. I never read 'em, but they always had little hearts."

"Do you think she was proud of her family and how she took care of your daddy, you, and your brothers?"

"Yes, yes she was," Amy said, looking off into the distance, her head clearly filled with memories."

"Do you think you could give me something to be proud of, too?" Carol asked.

Amy was still thinking about her momma when the question smacked her in the head. She turned to look at Carol. Amy saw her eyes and they were almost pleading. Then Amy heard Carla Jo's voice, telling her how selfish she had been. Amy looked at Carol and with an audible sense of sadness said, "Yeah, it's your house now. If I can help you, let me know." Carol began to cry and Amy reached over and hugged her.

Carol wiped her eyes and through the tears said, "I still need help. I don't know where anything is."

They both laughed a little at that one. As Amy began to let go she felt two things. The first was loss. Then there was the second she hadn't counted on, which was freedom. She worked hard and kept a tight schedule to take care of everything. Now she had something she never had before: free time.

Dark clouds were still almost visible above Amy's head. Her sixteenth birthday was just around the corner and Carol was determined to have a party. Amy finally agreed to a cookout on Indian River Beach. It was a popular place with the teenagers. Carla Jo and Carol took Amy swimsuit shopping at the mall. Carla Jo sat quietly while Carol did her first motherly thing; she gave Amy little hints about personal grooming.

Amy had to admit that the party was fun. All of her family and friends attended. They all enjoyed her favorite foods: venison steaks, potato salad, deviled eggs, and Dr. Pepper. Anchored about a hundred yards off-shore was a raft. The kids raced to it and nobody was faster than Amy. A man walked up to the family with a Lewistown High School tank top on and asked, "Is that your daughter?" He said, pointing to a crowd.

Leon said, "you mean in the middle of that pack of boys? Yeah," he laughed, "that's my daughter, Amy."

"My name is Carl Hixon. I'm the swimming coach at the high school. Could you tell me who trained her?"

"For what?" asked Leon, a little confused.

"Her swim coach. Who taught her how to swim so fast?" asked the coach.

"Oh yeah," said Jack. "That would be those copperheads that live in the swimmin' hole behind the house. I'm sure they sped her up a few times." Everyone started laughing at that one.

The coach smiled and said, "No, really. I'm serious."

Leon said, "Yeah, well, we are, too."

The coach just shook his head and said, "Then where did she get that body?" The coach suddenly froze and started apologizing profusely, "I'm sorry, I didn't mean it like that, I meant...,"

Jack interrupted him and said, "We know what you mean, coach. She looks like a Viking warrior. The truth is, she works out with me. I'm former military and that's how she spends quality time with her old uncle."

The Coach breathed a sigh of relief and then said, "That tall boy standing next to her is my son. He was regional champion last year and she just kicked his ass in a race out to that raft. Do you think she would want to be on the team?"

Leon shook his head and said, "Coach, she has never been interested in school sports. I think she's a little shy when it comes to the crowds. I wish she was interested in sports, though. Her brother was an outstandin' athlete but she never took to it. You can ask her. It's up to her."

"Who's your son?" asked the Coach.

"Kerry Braxton," said Leon.

"Oh God, I am so sorry. I loved that kid, we all did," said the coach.

"Thank you, Coach," said Leon.

"So that's Amy Braxton. I've heard some of the other coaches talk about her. That would certainly explain some of her natural talent. Thank you, Mr. Braxton," Said the coach.

"You can call me Leon and good luck," said Leon as Coach Hixon walked toward Amy and her group of friends.

Jack leaned over to Leon and said, "What do ya' think?"

"No way in hell," Leon said.

Leon was right. With a simple "No, thank you," she ripped the heart out of Coach Hixon just like she did every other coach at Lewistown High School.

Jack looked at Leon and said, "Hey, I got to ask you somethin'."

"Sure."

"Before Kerry died we were working on this old truck. It's still sitting in the garage with a tarp over it."

"I remember. Kerry bragged about it. You still got it?" asked Leon, a little bit surprised.

"Yeah, every time I look at it, it brings me a little sadness, but I could never bring myself to get rid of it. He put so much work into it.. I was wonderin' if I could give it to Amy and let her finish it. She'll be drivin' soon and there really isn't much left to do," said Jack.

Leon smiled at him and said, "You're showin' me up, Cuz. All we bought her was some new clothes." He thought for a moment, and then said, "Yeah, she'll be drivin' soon. If that's what you want to do, I'm good with it."

"I want you to be there. I know you gave Kerry money for parts. Maybe it could be from the both of us," said Jack.

"Yeah, I'd like that. Thanks, Cuz," said Leon.

Chapter 30

Amy's hand was cramping as she picked up the last knife. There were eight laid out on the bench in front of her. She had sharpened every one. Jack had started Amy on knives but he hadn't taught her how to use them; at least not yet. He taught her about them: different characteristics, shapes, sizes, metals, and even how they were manufactured. Finally, he taught her the proper way to sharpen them. Working with her uncle, she discovered that many of his lessons were tedious and mind-numbingly boring. In the end, however, there was always an important lesson to be learned.

Jack and Leon walked in the garage as she was finishing up. Amy was surprised to see her daddy.

"Daddy, what are you doin' here?" she asked.

Leon laughed and said, "Jack is my friend, too." Amy smiled and nodded. Then he said, "We want to show you something."

Amy followed them out of the garage and into the other garage where Carla Jo's car was kept. Behind her car was something covered with a tarp. Leon pulled off the tarp to reveal a 1960 canary yellow short bed Chevy truck. It had five spoke Crager wheels with T/A Radials. Jack lifted the hood and Leon's eyes went wide.

Jack had taken one of the engines he had used in his Chevelle and rebuilt it. It was a 454 C.I. bored .060 over.

"Wow, that's nice. Is that yours, Uncle Jack?" Said Amy.

"Nope, that was your brother Kerry's. He and I had been workin' on it for a few years before he died," said Jack.

"Me and your uncle Jack were talkin' and we know that you'll be getting your license soon. We wanted to know if you want it?" asked Leon.

"Kerry built this, wow," Amy said as she ran her hand over the fender. "It's beautiful."

"It's not finished," said Jack, "but I'll help you."

"Yes, I want it. I love it!" Amy exclaimed as she opened the door and climbed in.

Leon whispered to Jack, "How much horsepower does that engine have?"

"I detuned it. It's not like the one in the Chevelle. Around 450; more than she'll ever use," said Jack.

"You do remember who you're talkin' about, right?" said Leon.

"Oh yeah, hmm," said Jack.

Amy was no stranger to a steering wheel. She had driven the tractor on the farm and her daddy let her drive his old truck up and down the old road behind the house. But it was nothing like this. Jack and Leon gave her the standard responsibility lecture. Then Leon told her that she would need insurance and gas money, so she should plan on getting a job next summer. Amy barely heard any of it. She was floating.

Junior Gossett was part owner the local speedway. It was a half-mile asphalt track. Early one morning Junior opened the gates for Jack and allowed him to work with Amy. Jack put Amy in his Chevelle, strapped her in, stuck a helmet on her head, and let her turn a few laps. She would stop and they would talk about it and he would send her back out. By noon, she was running the old Chevelle around the track like a pro. She even spun it out one time and managed to keep it off the wall. Afterward she pulled up by Junior and Jack, laughed, and said, "I think I found the edge."

Junior looked at Jack and said, "What did she run before this?"

"Nothin' Junior, she has never done anything like this," said Jack, shaking his head.

"Bullshit," said Junior.

"No, it's not. The kid's amazin'. She learns things faster than anyone I have ever seen," said Jack.

"Damn, I'd put her in a car if she was interested," said Junior.

"She's not. Things are goin' on in her mind that we can't seem to get her past," said Jack.

"I heard a little somethin' about that. It's a shame. She'll find her way, we all do," said Junior.

Jack took Amy home. She had a blast and wouldn't stop talking about it. Then Jack told her about Junior's offer. She went quiet and said no.

When they got home, Amy went in the house to take a shower and clean up. "The track is a little grimy." Amy said. This was also a leftover from the attack. Amy didn't mind getting dirty, but she wouldn't stay that way for long. She showered at least three times a day.

Leon asked Jack, "How did she do?"

"Well, Junior offered her a race car," said Jack

Leon laughed out loud and Jack said, "I'm not laughin'. Junior offered up one of his sportsman cars to learn in. She's a natural. Hell, she's a natural at everythin' she does. She gets all of these amazin' opportunities and she just won't jump. She won't take the next step with anythin'. It's like she's in this mental prison. The only time I see her step outside herself is when she's learnin' how to hurt people; then she's damn near insane."

"Maybe if you stopped working with her she would move on to somethin' else," said Leon.

"She's your daughter, that's your decision. But do you want to take that away from her, too? You've seen her work out. It gets rid of her rage," said Jack.

"Yeah, I suppose you're right. Carla Jo says it takes time. It's only been a little over a year. I guess we just need to give it more time."

Meanwhile, Amy finished her shower, threw on one of her old sundresses, and went out on the porch. She sat down next to her daddy, gave him a kiss, and said, "Hi, Daddy."

"Hi, Miss Petty." Leon said, teasing Amy.

"That was fun, Daddy. You know the faster you go, the easier that car is to drive until you reach a certain point. Then the old Chevelle wanted to tear down the wall," Amy said, sounding like Dale Earnhardt talking to Richard Childress.

"Did you learn anything about driving a car with lots of power? That's why you were there," said Leon.

"Yes, sir, I learned they can get away from you, fast," said Amy.

Lesson learned, thought Leon.

Amy stuck her head in the house and said, "Carol, what time do you want me home for dinner?"

Carol yelled back, "Six o'clock."

"Yes, ma'am, I'll be here," Amy said, and then looked at her Daddy and added, "Spaghetti tonight, yum. I'm going to visit Carla Jo. Thanks, Uncle Jack, it was fun." She gave them both a kiss and headed down the hill.

Jack and Leon looked at each other a little puzzled as Amy jogged away.

"Did I just hear what I thought I heard?" said Leon.

"You mean the part where she treated Carol like a mom?"

"That was it."

Chapter 31

For the past three years, Carla Jo always took Amy on a little vacation before school started. This year would be no different. Amy walked into Carla Jo's house and found her in the kitchen with brochures spread across the table. Carla Jo had a big smile on her face and said, "Look at this; Ixtapa, Mexico. What do you think?

"It looks beautiful," said Amy.

"This is our hotel, ocean-front view," said Carla Jo.

"Does it have a weight room?" asked Amy.

Carla Jo sighed, shook her head, and said, "Yes, honey, it has a weight room. We leave on Thursday morning. Do you need any clothes?""Nope. Between Christmas and birthday presents, I have everything I need," said Amy.

"How about a new swimsuit? That river water has made yours a little dingy," said Carla Jo.

"It's not that bad," said Amy.

"Honey, when you go to a nice place, you play the part. This is a nice place," said Carla Jo

"OK, I just hate trying on swim suits. I got no boobs to hold anything up," Amy said with a sigh.

"That's because boobs are mostly fat. You have no fat on your body. Don't worry. The rest of your body more than makes up for it," said Carla Jo.

"You think?" asked Amy.

"Oh yeah, honey, oh yeah," said Carla Jo.

Seven days of being spoiled at the resort went by pretty quickly for Carla Jo and Amy. They arrived home and Amy passed out souvenirs that she bought for everyone. She showed all the pictures and even had a video of her and Carla Jo skydiving. Amy swore she would do that again someday. She looked tan and rested, but she never totally relaxed. In her mind and nagging at her soul were feelings she could not escape. Protecting herself preoccupied every thought.

Later that evening, Amy sat at the kitchen table. She was eating coconut cookies that she'd swiped off of the cooling rack. Carol always had some kind of treat for the family. Carol walked in the kitchen and Amy pretended to hide them. Carol chuckled and said, "Too late, caught ya'."

"These are so good. What's in them?" Amy asked.

Carol smiled and said, "Lotsa love."

"I was thinking; Carla Jo and I are having our monthly Francois visit tomorrow. You know, hair, nails, facial, stuff like that. Why don't you come along?" said Amy.

Carol laughed out loud and said, "Oh Amy, I would love to, but I can't go there. I can't afford anything like that."

"Well, it can't be that much. Aunt Carla Jo isn't rich," Said Amy.

Carol grabbed the milk jug out the refrigerator and topped off Amy's glass. Then she grabbed her a couple more cookies and said, "Amy, you are one of the smartest people I know, but I think something has completely escaped you." Carol pulled up a chair and sat down. "Honey, your aunt is a mystery. Nobody knows where she came from. She just showed up at your uncle's and never left. Some people believe that she is Asian royalty that your Uncle Jack rescued, but nobody knows for sure. One thing is for sure. She's a very special woman."

That made Amy think. She really knew nothing about Carla Jo's past.

"You just got back from a dream vacation most people will never experience," Carol continued.

"The plane was full," said Amy.

"Yep, I bet it was. Did you sit it the big seats in the front of the plane or the little seats in the back?"

"There's little seats in the back?" Amy said, shocked.

Carol laughed and said, "Yes, there is." Carol reached behind her and pickup a copy of *Vogue* magazine. "Do you see this? I sit and look through the pictures at all the beautiful clothes and accessories. Then I go to the discount department stores and try to find clothes that are close to the style or color. Plastic pearls, costume jewelry; I do all of that to try to stay current with fashion, look nice in public, and to look nice for your daddy. Let me show you something."

She walked into Amy's room and pulled a dress shipped in a fine garment bag out of her closet. "Do you mind if I unzip this?" asked Carol.

"No, go ahead. Aunt Carla Jo bought it for me to wear on the first day of school," Amy said.

Carol slid the magazine over to Amy and said, "Turn to page 167. Amy, this is that dress. This is a Dolce & Gabbana original. Two months ago this was on the back of an Italian super model in Milan, Italy. You could add up the value of everything in my closet and I couldn't buy the buttons on this dress. Yes, honey, your Aunt Carla Jo is a very wealthy woman."

"Nooo, she drives that old Buick everyday, she rarely drives her red car because she says she doesn't want to put the miles on it, she works every day and just look at that little house they live in," Amy said.

"She works because she loves her job," Carol explained. "She lives in that house because that's the way Jack wants it. If your uncle Jack said they were going to live in an outhouse, she'd start hangin' pictures. There is only one thing in this world that woman worships more than you and that's your uncle Jack."

Carol watched Amy as she thought about what she said. Then Amy said, "She doesn't act rich."

"I know, and that's part of what makes her wonderful. She is a cultured, classy woman. She's very well educated. She's the real thing, Amy. In the past four years, she has made you the real thing, too. You are the young lady version of Carla Jo. You walk like her, you talk like her, and you are well read like her. She has given you big thoughts. Black Oak won't be able to hold you. Alabama will not be able to hold you. You're going places, and because of Carla Jo, you will go there in style," said Carol.

Amy thought about it for a while and said, "You know, the first time she ever took me shopping she said she was doing what my mother would have done."

"Oh yeah, I believe that. Carla Jo was holding your mother's hand when she died. Carla Jo and your mom could not have been closer. It broke her heart so bad that she couldn't even come back to this house. It wasn't until your daddy thought you needed a woman in your life that she would come back up that hill. Then Carla Jo fell in love with you. Carla Jo is as much your mother as Katherine ever was," said Carol.

That last comment had Amy thinking about her and Carla Jo's relationship. Sometimes they were friends, sometimes Carla Jo was a close aunt and yes, sometimes she was very much a mother figure.

"How do you know all of this?" asked Amy.

"Your Daddy and I have been together a lot longer than anyone knows. When your mother died he needed a friend and I was there for him. We talked about you quite a bit."

"I'm sorry," said Amy. "I really wanted you to come."

"You have no idea how good that makes me feel. But, don't give it a second thought. Your time with Carla Jo is just that, your time. Besides, I have my own beauty shop I go to with my own friends. I'm not missing anything. I don't feel bad about not going, but I will tell you this; that woman loves you. Keep her close and listen to her."

As Amy and Carla Jo were headed to François that Saturday morning, Amy was a little too quiet. Carla Jo asked, "What's on your mind?"

"I invited Carol to come with us today and she said she couldn't afford it," said Amy.

"Oh, if she really wanted to come she would. Carol and I are different people. I enjoy a little extravagance now and then. Carol doesn't see a need for it. Besides, she has her own place she likes to go," said Carla Jo.

"Yeah, that's what she said. She said there is a rumor that you are Asian royalty and Uncle Jack rescued you. Is that true?" asked Amy.

Carla Jo started laughing and said, "Asian royalty? Wow. No, honey, that's not true." *Well, half true,* Carla Jo thought to herself.

"Where did you come from?" asked Amy.

Carla Jo sighed. She knew she would be answering this question one day so she had prepared a sanitized version. "I was abandoned when I was a baby and left at an orphanage in Korea. A very wealthy American woman found us and brought us all to America. I was adopted by a wonderful family. They made sure I got a very good education. The woman that rescued us followed us throughout our lives and made sure we went to the finest universities. I like to read, I like to learn things, and I like to treat myself to nice things. That's pretty much all there is to it," said Carla Jo.

Amy shook her head and said, "That's incredible. You should write a book."

"Maybe someday."

Amy thought for a moment and said, "Where's your family?"

"My adopted parents are dead, my brother died in Vietnam, and you are sitting right next to me along with Jack and everyone on that hill," she replied.

"You said that when you came to Alabama you had nothing. What happened?"

"That part of my life is very complicated and I will keep it to myself. Just like there are parts of your life you will keep to yourself, understand?" Carla Jo said.

Amy thought for a moment and said, "Yes, I do." She didn't know how to ask the next question so she just blurted out, "Are you rich?"

"You and Carol must have had one heck of a Carla Jo conversation," she said with a smirk.

"No, it wasn't like that. Carol was trying to make sure I understood all the things you did for me. To be honest, I really didn't. Then she pointed out a dress in *Vogue*, the one you bought me for the first day of school. Twelve hundred dollars? I almost fell off the chair. Then there are the vacations, the Francois visits, and I start adding all this up in my head and I wonder if I deserve this," said Amy.

Carla Jo nodded and said, "OK, let's start with your first question. Am I rich? Rich is one of those subjective words. Everyone has a different definition. Am I rich compared to Carol? Yes. Am I rich compared to the Gossetts? No. Early in my relationship with Jack I made some investments and they paid off big. I was half smart and half lucky. I work very hard for Doc Henderson and he pays me well. The biggest thing is I have no bills; none. My money is all fun money and yes, I spend what some would consider a large amount on you. But like I told you a long time ago, It's really not a lot of money to me. Understand?"

"Yeah, but twelve hundred dollars for a dress? I'm afraid to touch it," Amy said in disbelief.

Carla Jo got a guilty look on her face and said, "Well, there is something else. I have a confession to make."

"Go on," said Amy.

"When I was a little girl my adopted mom was a, well, severe woman. She wasn't much fun. I loved dolls and I loved playing dress up. My mom would have none of it, so I played with a neighbor girl. She was mean, but I didn't care as long as I got to play with her dolls. I'm older now, but I still like to play with dolls," said Carla Jo.

Amy laughed and said, "Let me guess, I'm the doll."

"Yep. You're not mad are you?"

Amy thought for a moment and with a half smile on her face said, "I'm not sure yet. So, if dressing me up did not bring you joy, I would still be wearing boots and bibs?"

Carla Jo laughed and said, "No. The first day you walked into my kitchen with those cow dung-covered boots and those old bibs, they were gone. You just didn't know it yet. You have a sense of style now: a little bit me, a little bit you. I am determined to make sure your style is developed and you understand the role fashion will play in your life. When you go out on your own, the first thing people notice is how you look. It's not neccesarily fair, but that's the way it is. The Dolce & Gabbana straight off of a runway in Milan, however? If I had the body for that it would not be in your closet. No, honey, that's all about me playing dress up with you."

Amy looked down at her violet Donna Karan sundress and matching open toed shoes and said, "OK, I guess I forgive you."

Carla Jo got a mischievous little grin and said "Hey look, a Budget Cuts. Maybe we should try that?"

Amy played along and said, "Do you think they have those silky little chocolates and the cherry fizzy drinks?"

"Oh, I'm sure of it," Carla Jo said sarcastically.

Amy put on a sad face and said, "But Aunt Carla Jo, we are far to compassionate to break Jean Paul's heart like that."

Carla Jo laughed, shook her head, and then said, "Yes, that's us; the empathy twins."

A little flash of shame crossed Amy's face and she said, "We are horrible. That's just mean, we shouldn't talk like that."

Carla Jo nodded her head in agreement and said, "You're right, but it's only horrible if you mean it and we both know better than that."

Chapter 32

Sunday after church, Jack and Amy pushed the truck out of Carla Jo's garage. Amy washed the dust off of it and lovingly dried it off. Jack made room for it next to his Chevelle. He hadn't started the engine in over a year so he pulled the distributor and the spark plugs. They changed the oil and filter, and then spun the oil pump with an electric drill. Jack used a big ratchet and rotated the motor by hand. Every step of the way he explained to Amy what he was doing and why. Then they drained the fuel and put in fresh gas.

"Premium only," Jack said to Amy.

They replaced the distributor and plugs, installed the battery, and Jack gave Amy a lesson on the proper way to start a high performance engine. Amy hit the switch for the electric fuel pump and watched the fuel pressure gauge climb to seven pounds. Jack had her turn the engine over with the ignition switch off until the oil pressure gauge began to climb. Jack smiled at her and said, "OK, pat the gas one time, hit the ignition switch, and let's see what happens."

Amy hit the switch, turned the key, and four hundred and sixty-eight fire-breathing cubic inches of big-block Chevy rumbled to life. You couldn't have wiped the smile off of Amy's face with a sledgehammer. Jack let it warm up, and then he used the carburetor linkage to crack the throttle, revving the engine to over five thousand RPMs. Amy felt the power of the big engine as the whole truck rocked to one side from the torque of the motor. Jack signaled to Amy to turn it off. Amy sat in the truck, shaking her head, and then said, "Wow, this is a bad girl."

Jack nodded his head and thought to himself, *I may have underestimated the horsepower*. Then he said to Amy, "Yep, it sure is. And just like most bad girls, they need attention. You can drive it everyday, but you'll be working on it every other day. I was thinking; you're sixteen, you're going to have a pretty full life. Are you sure you want to take this on? This is a hot rod and it's a time stealer. You see how much time I spend on the Chevelle. Are you sure you want this responsibility?"

Amy thought for a minute and said, "I don't have to drive it every day. There's plenty of other cars for me to drive if I need to go somewhere."

"Yeah, but don't you think you want your own car? Junior Gossett has been begging me for this truck since before I gave it to Kerry. I can trade this for a car like Carla Jo's, maybe even a used Corvette. You just put gas in it, change the oil and filters now and then, and drive."

Amy paused, and then said, "It wouldn't be a bad idea for me to learn a little about mechanics. Besides, how do I bring myself to get rid of Kerry's truck?"

Jack nodded his head. He knew that was why the truck was still there; he couldn't get rid of it, either.

"OK. It still needs some work. We need to finish the brakes, hang the bumpers, and replace the chrome trim," said Jack. Then he thought, *Maybe this will get her distracted from her obsession with self-defense.*

"Uncle Jack, do you think we can work on this later? I really wanted to work on knife skills this afternoon," said Amy.

Or maybe not, thought Jack.

Chapter 33

Carla Jo always took Amy to school on the first day. Amy walked out of the house and Carla Jo's eyes went wide. "Oh my, I knew it. That dress looks perfect on you. You are perfect."

Amy nodded her head, put her tote in the back seat, and climbed into the car. Carla Jo tilted her head a little, looked at her, and said jokingly, "You know, I always imagined my dolls being happier."

"Mary Beth called me last night. She's not coming back from Tennessee," said Amy.

Oh no, Carla Jo thought. Then she said, "Why not?"

"She didn't really give a reason, but she was so happy. I was crying, though. I have nobody at school now; no close friends," said Amy, shaking her head.

Carla Jo looked at her and said, "I'm sorry, but that has always been your choice. You have never really tried to make friends. I've talked to Mary Beth. She said you ignored her most of the time. To have a friend, you have to be a friend."

Amy looked a little guilty and said, "Yeah, but I always knew she was there."

Carla Jo nodded her head and said, "So you put nothing into your relationship with her and used her as a security blanket. Do you think that was fair?"

"No."

Carla Jo thought it might be time for some tough love. "Well, it's like this," she said. "We have all given you ideas to expand your social circle and you have ignored them. You are where you have put yourself."

Amy didn't like that. She snapped back, "I can't help it if I don't have anything in common with those people."

"Oh Jesus, Amy, do you hear yourself? Those people? Really? *Those* people? That sounds like something Candice Peterson would say. Your family are the only people in this world that care if you live or die. They will love you no matter what. *Those people* expect something in return," said an agitated Carla Jo.

Amy sat quietly looking out of the car window. Under her breath she said, "You just don't get it."

Carla Jo had a disapproving look on her face when she looked over at Amy and said, "Well, let's see if I get it. You have been twenty-five years old since you were seven. Every close friend you have ever had has either been an adult or someone you have known since kindergarten. You sit and listen to the conversations of other teenagers and shake your head at the stupidity, pettiness, and self-absorption. Those that share your love of hunting and fishing are boys and they listen to you passively with the hope that they can get in your pants. Oh, and your real obsession, what your uncle Jack teaches you, you can't share with anyone because it would scare the living hell out of any sane person. How am I doing?"

"OK, you get most of it," sighed Amy. "I still don't trust anyone, though. I just think of Tommy and Timmy, the last two people in the world I thought could ever hurt me, and I don't trust myself to judge who is good and who is evil. Every person I meet I have a plan to, well, neutralize. It's hard to make a friend when you're sizing them up to take them out," said Amy with a cold detachment.

Carla Jo knew Amy wasn't playing the helpless victim. She took a moment to reflect on her own life. Maybe she didn't get it. She decided to take her own advice and give it time. She nodded at Amy and said, "OK honey, if there is anything I can do, let me know. By the way, you look beautiful."

"Thanks," Amy said with a half smile.

Her second year in high school began like the first. She was sure to get weight training again, which was against the rules. Mr. Brooks made it clear to whoever would listen that the Braxton girl gets whatever she wants. She did her schoolwork but was still disinterested. It was difficult to concentrate. She still loved weight training, but there seemed to be a different air in the weight room. The little girl was leaving her body and the woman was taking over. This was not lost on any of the players, but they knew better than to act on any feelings they may have had for her because Coach Ramsey watched over her like a hawk.

Thanksgiving vacation arrived on String Hill Road and at 5 a.m. on Thanksgiving morning, Amy and the men went hunting. Leon got a six-pointer on the east end of Whiskey Creek. As they were coming back, Amy saw a rub on a tree. It was pretty high up. She started looking at the tracks and her eyes got big. "Daddy, Daddy, he was here! Ole Red was here. Look at these tracks," said an excited Amy.

Leon looked and there was no denying the size and depth of the tracks, or the scrape. This was an unusually large deer. "I'll be damned," he said. "There's a monster out here somewhere."

Amy scanned the woods and said, "He's watchin' us. He's watchin' us right now. I can feel it."

"Well, honey, everything he needs to be happy is right here. He's not going anywhere."

Thanksgiving dinner was a special event as it was Carol's first Thanksgiving with the family. Carol, Granny, Carla Jo, and Miss Kitty cooked a feast. But It was also special for another reason. It was the first Thanksgiving for Franklin Eugene Carter, Gene's newborn son. Amy carried him around most of the day. She couldn't get enough of him. As babies go, he was huge, but this was not unusual for the Carter clan. Miss Kitty didn't mind that Amy played with him all day. It was her first break since he was born. Amy sat back holding the baby while looking at her family. *This is the way Thanksgiving is supposed to be*, she thought.

What Amy didn't know was the day after Thanksgiving would be even bigger. It would be the day the dark clouds disappeared. It would be the day she got her life back.

Chapter 34

*I*t was 5 a.m. when Leon walked into the kitchen, following the smell of fresh coffee. Amy was sitting at the kitchen table dressed in her camos and sipping from a steaming cup. Her bolt was out of her rifle, which was on the table, and she had a small jewler's file next to it. Her daddy had to go to work for a half day to do some paperwork. He leaned over and kissed her on the cheek as he walked in, and then he asked, "When did you start drinkin' coffee?"

Amy shrugged and said, "It's mostly cream and sugar. Good morning, Daddy."

"What's wrong with the bolt?" asked Leon.

"It's just not smooth. There's a little catch in the action," replied Amy.

He picked up her rifle, took the little file, and pointed to a small groove on the right side of the receiver. "This is a post-1964. You got to clean that groove right there," said Leon.

"Oh, thanks Daddy," Amy said appreciatively.

Her daddy then asked, "You goin' after him?"

"I'm gonna take a look," said Amy.

"OK, just be careful. I don't know where you're gonna look, but don't go past Sibly Creek, understand?" Leon said in a serious tone.

"You tell me that all the time," said Amy. "What's the big deal about Sibly Creek?"

"It's not your land. Stay off of it," said Leon with an uncharacteristic forcefulness.

"Yes, sir," Amy said, rolling her eyes.

She got up, gave her daddy a kiss, and headed out the door. The wind was coming from the southwest so she headed east, parallel to Whiskey Creek. She walked for a good half mile and then she slowly made her way into the holler. About halfway down she stopped and took a look.

There he was, sipping water from the creek. He was at least three hundred yards away. She picked up he rifle to look through the scope and had a hard time controlling her breathing. He was huge; at least fourteen points. Then something spooked him and he turned and started up the north side of the holler. She quickly and quietly crept down the side of the holler and stopped by the creek. She remembered something Kerry had told her about him. He liked to loop around and he made a path in the shape of a candy cane. She knelt down by a stump and waited. Suddenly she caught some motion to the left at the top of the hill. He was taking a look. She moved nothing but her eyes. He turned and walked away. The chase was on.

For two hours they played a game. Amy didn't know if he knew she was there or not. It didn't matter, though, because she had him figured out. He crossed Sibly Creek and headed up the side of the hill. She thought about what her daddy said, but there was no way she was letting him go. She waited until he peeked down the hill and this time he circled to the right. Then she went up the hill after him. She broke through the tree line and found herself in some sort of farm: rows and rows of tall green plants on a small plot of land. She didn't recognize the plants at first and then it hit her: this was a Pot farm.

The shotgun slide got her attention and she turned to look. There was a young man about eighteen years old. He was wearing bibs and a dirty t- shirt. He had scraggly hair and bad teeth. He pointed the shotgun at her and said, "Who are you?"

Amy put the rifle in the crook of her arm. She figured if he wanted to talk, he didn't want to shoot. She decided to try to defuse the tension. Smiling her cutest smile she said, "My name's Amy. What's yours?"

He smiled back, lowered the shotgun, and said, "My name's Joe."

"Whatcha doin', Joe?" said Amy.

"Shootin' starlin's. What are you doin' here?" said Joe.

Suddenly a gruff, gravely voice to Amy's right said, "Yeah, what the hell you doing here?"

Amy smiled at the source of the other voice. He was rough looking with long hair, a long beard, bad teeth, and black, cold eyes. "I was chasing a deer. Ain't seen him, have ya'?" Amy asked.

The old man didn't feel threatened by the young girl so his features began to soften a little and he said, "Can't say that I have."

Joe spoke up, "She sure is purdy, Daddy. Can we keep her?"

"SHUT UP, BOY!" the old man growled.

Amy knew she was in a bad situation and the OODA loop started spinning. Amy thought to herself, *I'll play dumb and see what happens.*

"What's yo' name, little lady?" the old man asked.

"Amy Braxton," Amy said with sweetness to her voice.

The corner of the old man's mouth turned up into a wicked smile and he asked, "You wouldn't be kin to Marcel, wouldja?"

"Yes, sir. He was my Granddaddy,"

The old man spoke slowly, "That would make you...," the old man paused, "Leon's girl."

"Yes, sir."

"Well, hot damn; we got us a Braxton."

Just then another young man walked out of the field and stood next to the old man. Amy saw the evil in the old man's eyes. It was the real thing. The old man was thinking about all the fun he was going to have with this young girl before he skinned her and dumped her in her daddy's front yard.

Amy smiled at him and said, "Well, I need to be goin'."

The old man said, "You hold it right there. You're trespassing. Put that rifle down and we'll talk about it."

The old man watched as Amy's sweetness changes to something else and a crooked smile spread across her face. Her green eyes started to flash as her senses reached peak intensity.

"Sorry, mister. I. can't do that."

The old man became more animated and screamed, "YOU PUT THAT RIFLE DOWN NOW OR I WILL HAVE THAT BOY BLOW A HOLE IN YOU."

Amy responded by removing the safety with her thumb and leveling the rifle at his chest.

"He's got bird shot. It won't kill me, but I'll kill you. Please don't make me explain to Jesus why I had to kill you," Amy said calmly with unnervingly cold detachment.

The old man tried to stare her down, but the heat in her eyes started to melt the ice in his. He flinched and looked away. Then he laughed an evil laugh and said, "I reckon I can forgive you just this once. You go on back where you came from. Tell yo' daddy that Jeb McCutcheon said hey."

Amy never flinched. Her finger was on the trigger as she said, "I'll do that. Have good day, Mr. McCutcheon." Amy backed out, never taking her rifle off of the old man. When she got to the tree line she turned and ran down the side of the hill. She knew they were coming.

Jeb looked at his boys and said, "Git her."

Amy crossed the creek at a full sprint and headed up the deer trail. She was out of sight so she broke off the trail to the right, looped back, and stopped. She listened to them talking as they were coming down the side of the hill. She knew exactly where they were going. Joe ran past her on her left close enough that she could have poked him with her rifle. She never stopped looking around. She wondered if the old man would be walking up behind her. She sat for a couple more seconds, watching the top of the hill and waiting for the Old Man to come. He didn't.

If Amy could have seen herself in the mirror she would not have recognized what she saw. Her angelic face was dark and her own smile was twisted and evil. The hunters became the hunted. She would start with Joe. Everything Jack had preached to her began to take over. She didn't have to go far to get a good shot at Joe. She knelt down to maintain cover and unconsciously tried to hit the safety, but it was already off. She chastised herself momentarily for forgetting to put it back on. She lifted the rifle and put the crosshairs in the center of Joe's back. She put her finger on the trigger and began to squeeze. *How unfair,* she thought. *This is easier than deer hunting at a petting zoo. Uncle Jack was right. They never see it coming.* She stopped squeezing and said under her breath, "Bang, your dead."

Amy chuckled to herself and thought, *They're too stupid to kill.* She turned and went after the other boy. She cut diagonally across the hill as she knew right where he would be. She put the scope on him from about one hundred and fifty yards. As she put her finger on the trigger, she said to herself, *Bang, two down.* Then she turned and went after the old man. She kept stopping, looking and listening over her shoulder as she made her way over Sibly Creek and back up the hill. She followed the tree line at the top of the hill until she saw him. She turned to scan the holler behind her to make sure neither of the boys doubled back on her, and then she stepped out of the tree line and raised her rifle.

"Hey, Mr. McCutcheon," Amy said as the old man spun around and looked at her with a shocked expression. She smiled and said, "Bang, your dead. I could have killed all of you. Never forget that." She winked at him and then disappeared back into the tree line and headed for Sibly Road.

It was two miles east following Sibly Creek to get to Sibly Road and another ten miles to String Hill Road. She knew there were still two people out hunting her so she thought to herself, *I'm not out of the woods yet.* She chuckled to herself for the pun as she sat quietly in the tree line along the road. She knew that she would eventually see a car she recognized and get a ride. Ten minutes later an old, black Ford truck crested the hill coming right at her. It was Mr. Franks, the grandfather of Kerry's best friend, Rob.

She stepped out of the tree line and flagged him down. He didn't recognize her at first, but then she said, "Hi, Mr. Franks. It's me, Amy Braxton."

Mr. Franks smiled big and said,'"What the hell you doin' way out here, young lady? And when did you get so big?"

"I was chasin' a deer. I guess I just got carried away. You reckon I could hitch a ride home with you?" said Amy, already knowing the answer.

"Well, yes, get in. I ain't seen you in years. How's your daddy?" said Mr. Franks.

They continued to make small talk until he pulled up to the front of her house.

"Thank you Mr. Franks," Amy said, and then she leaned over and gave him a kiss on the cheek. For an old man, he was as cute as Rob was handsome.

Jack and Leon were sitting on the porch drinking sweet tea when Amy slowly walked up the steps. Her daddy smiled at her and said, "Where you been?"

Amy sighed and said, "Chasing Ole Red. Darn near had him, Daddy. He's smart. Oh yeah, and Jeb McCutcheon says hey."

Leon's eyes went wide as he dropped his tea glass, which shattered on the porch. "Where the hell did you see him?" Leon growled.

Amy told the story like she was talking about a trip to the mall. Jack looked at Leon and thought, *I can count the number of times I've seen him pissed on one hand. I'm about to see it again.* Jack was right.

"You crossed Sibly Creek. YOU CROSSED SIBLY CREEK!" Leon yelled. GOD DAMMIT, AMY, I TOLD YOU NOT TO DO THAT!" Panic covered Leon's face and he said, "Did he hurt you? Did he touch you?"

"No, Daddy, they didn't come close. I could have killed 'em all," Amy said like it was nothing.

"Amy....Dammit, Amy, THIS IS NOT A GAME, THIS IS A BLOOD FEUD. THEY WERE GOING TO KILL YOU. DAMMIT,

GOD DAMMIT. GET YOUR SHIT, JACK, I'M GONNA KILL THAT SON OF A BITCH MYSELF. IT ENDS TODAY."

Leon knows more about Marcel's history than he let on, Jack thought.

Carol suddenly stepped out on the porch and said, "Blood feud? WHAT BLOOD FEUD?

"This ain't nothin' to you," Leon said.

"BULLSHIT! Last time I checked my last name was Braxton," Carol said, none too happy.

Amy looked at Carol and said, "I warned you at the church, this family is crazy."

Here we go, thought Jack.

Leon turned his attention to Jack and said, "I BLAME YOU! NOW SHE THINKS SHE'S SOME KIND OF GODDAMNED ASSASSIN! SHE'S A LITTLE GIRL, JACK!"

Jack knew better than to say anything. Amy would handle that.

Amy just stood there, grinning like an idiot, and said, "Actually, Daddy, I'm not a little girl, I'm sixteen. I don't know why you're upset, nothing happened."

"THE BEST THING YOU CAN DO RIGHT NOW IS BE QUIET, YOUNG LADY. YOU HAVE NO IDEA HOW MUCH TROUBLE YOU'RE IN!" Leon yelled.

"WHAT BLOOD FEUD?" Carol demanded again with a little more volume.

Jack was watching Amy when something occurred to him. He looked at Leon and said, "Cuz, can I talk to you for a minute?"

"Oh, I don't think you have to worry about that, you're damn right we're gonna talk," Leon growled. He looked over at his wife and, trying not to yell, said, "Carol, we'll talk about it later."

Jack looked at Leon and said, "Please, Cuz, just a minute. I know you're pissed, you have every right to be, but please, just talk to me."

Jack and Leon walked out by the road, and then Leon looked at Jack and growled, "What?"

"Look at her, Leon, look at Amy. It's over."

Leon didn't understand what Jack was trying to say. "What's over?" he asked.

"Dammit, Leon, look at her. The weight she carried on her shoulders is gone. Look how light she is. Look at her smile, look at the way she's standin'. The attack, Leon, she's over it. You have your little girl back."

Leon watched Amy talking to Carol. Amy was getting her to laugh. His head tilted to the side as he stared in amazement, and then he said, "Oh my God, she's back."

Jack was mostly right. They got Amy back but with a little extra. It seemed she enjoyed turning the tables on the McCutcheons a little too much. She replayed the events for Jack in what the military would call a debrief. Jack was not happy with her major decisions and let her know about it.

After Amy broke down what happened in greater detail, Jack nodded his head and said, "So they ran by you, you had a clear escape, and you went after them. Why?"

"Because I was gonna kill 'em." Amy said seriously

"But you didn't. You made a decision and failed to act on it. That's a big mistake. Those boys were not as stupid as you thought. I would bet they know those woods better than you do. I taught you to escape and evade; live to fight another day when the odds are more in your favor. You chose not to. Looking back do you think you did the right thing?" asked Jack.

"No, probably not. I was just so angry. They were going to do to me what the Hatfields did. I could feel it. Just like you said, I could sense the evil," Amy said, beginning to sound a little deflated.

"That's where you screwed up. Anger, fear, or any negative emotions have no place in your head when you are operatin'. That's where the discipline comes in. You were fine right up to the moment when you decided to punish. Unless you or yours are in danger, you never punish. That is someone else's job. On top of that, you decided to play a game. That is the absolute worst decision you could have made. Those people were playing for keeps. You should have been, too. I am disappointed in you," Jack said in a stearn, slightly angry voice.

Amy was looking at the floor. She was sad she had let her uncle Jack down. Then she looked up and said, "But I won. Doesn't that count for anything?"

Jack shook his head and gave it some thought. She was hard to stay mad at. Then he said, "Be proud of what you did, alright? We both know that your hard work saved your life. But, honey, you were lucky; very, very lucky. We have more work to do when you get out of the doghouse. I've known your daddy since we were kids and I don't think I have ever seen him this angry. You disobeyed him. None of this would have happened if you had listened to him. I just hope he thinks you're too old for an ass whippin'."

Jack talked Leon out of killing Jeb and into calling Gene and telling him about the pot farm. Leon was also sure to tell Gene that they tried to kill Amy. Gene and the Sheriff of Sibly County mounted a joint operation against the McCutcheons. The McCutcheons didn't survive the raid. The feud was officially over.

Chapter 35

*I*t was all Jack could do to keep Leon from selling Amy's truck. Leon took away her rifle and grounded her for a month. And instead of selling the truck, he wouldn't allow Amy to get her driver's license until after the first of the year. Jack was right. Leon was pissed.

Amy took it all in stride. She felt bad about disappointing her daddy, so she didn't put up a fuss when it came to her punishment. She knew she screwed up and decided to focus on other things. She still got to go down to the barn and workout. Carol was easy to be around, which was good. Amy learned how to cook Italian food from her. While killing some time at home, she also got hooked on the television show *Dawson's Creek*, which was all the rage with the other girls at school.

Amy started to open up and talk to the group of girls that Mary Beth used to hang around with. They were not as shallow and dumb as she thought they would be. She should have known better. Mary Beth always had good taste in friends.

One day after weight lifting, Amy walked out to the pool, leaned up against the wall, and watched the beginning of swim practice. It looked like fun and for the first time she thought about participating in a sport. The next day she went to Coach Hixon's office and knocked on the door.

"Hi, Coach," said Amy

"Amy, hi. What can I do for you?" said a surprised Coach.

"When we were down at the river on my birthday, you said you would be interested in having me on the team. Were you serious?"

It was everything the coach could do to contain himself. He swallowed hard and said, "Well, the season has already started, but I think I could find a place for you."

"When's practice?"

"We start at six a.m. before school and practice a couple of hours or so after school, but we can be flexible."

"Hmm, let me talk to my daddy and I'll get back to you," she said.

"I can arrange transportation. I'll come get you myself and we can make this work," said the Coach with a hopeful look.

"I'll let you know tomorrow," she said. "Thanks, Coach."

Amy left and shut the door. The Coach got out of his chair and did a happy dance. *I'm gonna be in* Sports Illustrated, he thought.

Amy went home and talked to her daddy later that evening. Amy had never been involved in sports, so Leon talked about the commitment to the team and how it would take up much of her free time. In the end, he told her he would support whatever decision she made. Amy sought advice from several sources before she made a big decision. Uncle Jack would most certainly have an opinion.

"Oh, hell yes," said Jack. "As a SEAL we did ocean swims every day. It's some of the best exercise you can do. It will do nothing but help you."

"What about us? What about our work?" Amy asked.

"We will make time for that. You are so far past anything I thought I could teach you that everything else is just skills. Handguns and knives are critical. I want you to be proficient with a variety types and calibers, but we can make that happen. I'm not going to push you into anything, but I want you to know that competition is a big deal. It would be good for you," said Jack.

"OK, thanks, Uncle Jack."

The next day after weight training, Amy knocked on Coach Hixon's door.

The coach jumped out of his chair and said, "Amy, hi. Have you decided on anything?"

"Yes, sir, I have. If it's OK, I would like to be on the team."

Amy gave the coach a funny look when he let out a little squeal. Then he said, "OK, um, yes. When would you like to start?"

"Well, I don't have a swimsuit like the other girls, but I could start tomorrow morning."

"Everything you need will be here. And we will see you tomorrow morning," said the coach with a big smile.

"OK, thanks, Coach."

Amy shut the door and walked back to the locker room. She could have sworn she heard singing.

Coach Hixon could teach any kid to swim, but he couldn't teach fast and he couldn't teach the work ethic. He had to beg his kids to do weight training and Amy did it for fun, or so he thought. The coach cleaned up her freestyle stroke and taught her how to do kick turns. He was right about her because she was fast, approaching state record fast, according to his stopwatch.

For her first meet, the coach entered her in the 100 and 200-yard freestyle. She was slow off the blocks and her kick turns were sloppy, but she still won her races on pure athletisism. The speed was there. Coach Hixon could see it. But carreening left and right from one lane rope to the the other was also killing her speed. The shortest distance between two points is a straight line, he explained, but as soon as she got a little excited, she broke form. That too, however, would be fixed. She did not know the backstroke, breaststroke, or butterfly, but that was OK. The coach waited patiently for January 6th. That would be the arrival of NCAA champion, Olympic alternate and student teacher Summer Van Hollen. Coach Hixon would make her Amy's new personal coach. She would teach Amy all of the strokes and a little more.

Chapter 36

"HEY!" Amy yelled from under her truck.

"Don't get your face in front of the bleeder when you open it," said Jack.

Amy climbed out from under the truck grumbling. Her hair and face were soaked in brake fluid. Jack threw her a shop rag. "Thanks for the warning," Amy said sarcastically.

Jack laughed at her and said, "Back under the truck, Cinderella. Let me know when the air is out of the lines." He sat down in the truck and began pumping the brakes.

"How will I know that?" asked Amy.

"You'll be able to hear it. There should be no hissin' or spittin'. When you crack the bleeder, you should get a solid stream of brake fluid."

They finished bleeding the brakes and Jack showed her how to top off the brake fluid in the master cylinder. When they were done, Jack reach over, hugged her around the neck with one arm, and said, "How about a road test?"

Amy smiled and excitedly said, "OK, where we goin'?"

"I figured I'd take you by Junior's and buy you a Dr. Pepper. Go clean up." said Jack.

"Whoa, Daddy said I'm not to go to those places by the river," said Amy.

"Well, not by yourself. Anyway, I just figured you might want to show Junior your truck. He's a good guy to know in these parts," said Jack.

"He's an outlaw, Uncle Jack," said Amy

"So am I," said Jack.

"OK, but if I get in trouble...," Amy said, leaving the rest hanging.

"You didn't get in trouble when he opened his race track for ya'," said Jack.

I'll call Daddy anyway when I get in the house, Amy thought. "OK, I'll just be a minute. I'm goin' to take a shower and wash my hair."

Jack rolled his eyes. *She's so much like Carla Jo*, he thought.

Appreciative of the phone call, Leon told Amy he didn't much care where she went if she was with Jack. It was twenty-two miles of winding country roads to get to the river. Jack drove to make sure everything was working. He also pointed out all of the little crosses pounded into the ground or nailed on trees. Each cross has a story of a young person that didn't respect the old country roads. They got to the River Front Bar and Grill and walked in the door.

Jack ordered their drinks and asked for Junior.

"Where do you think Junior's at?" the bartender replied.

Jack tossed Amy the keys, popped the top on his Miller High Life, and together they got in the truck. Jack gave her directions and in less than ten minutes they pulled up to a big poll barn behind Junior's house. The big door was open so Amy and Jack walked in.

"Is that my truck I hear out there?" Junior yelled from across the garage.

Amy liked Junior. She didn't know why; she just couldn't help it. Harmless, jovial, and buffoonish would be how Amy might describe him, and that was exactly what Junior wanted her to see. He walked across the garage and gave Amy a hug.

"Hi, sugar! Junior exclaimed. "Well, let's take a look," he said with a bit of boyish anticipation.

Amy scanned the garage and saw two bright red racecars with "#4" on their sides. There was a young man under the hood of the first one. He glanced up and then took a double take. Amy was standing in front of the garage door, silhouetted by the sunlight. He could see the outline of Amy's body and suddenly he wanted to see the truck, too.

"This is my grandson, Earl," Junior said to Amy. Jack watched Amy as she tilted her head and smiled. He had never seen that look on her face before. It was an adoring look with an easy smile.

Jack could tell that Earl took after his momma. He was as handsome as his momma was beautiful, and he'd heard that Earl was at the top of his class at Rock Creek Prep School. By all accounts he was a kind and polite young man. He was Junior's pride and joy and at eighteen years of age, he was already one hell of a racecar driver.

Earl glanced over at the truck and took a double take on that, too. "Wow, that's nice. What's under the hood?" he asked Amy.

Amy opened the hood and Earl's eyes got big. "Big-block, very nice. What is it?" Earl asked.

"It's a 468, with 565/585 split pattern hydraulic cam, eleven to one compression, and old-style C port aluminum heads," said Amy.

Earl just looked at her with a stupid grin on his face.

"Uh oh," whispered Jack to Junior.

"Yep," said Junior.

Jack chuckled and said, "Imagine Hank and Marcel seein' this."

Junior shook his head and whispered, "No shit."

The smile left Jack's face as he looked at Junior out of the corner of his eye and said, "Talk to the boy."

"Yep," said Junior.

Before they left, Amy wrote her phone number down for Earl on the back of a Goodyear decal. *Maybe my first date?* She thought.

Earl watched her drive away. She spun the tires a little when she hit the asphalt just to prove she could. Junior put his arm around Earl's shoulders and said, "We need to talk."

Junior sat Earl down in front of the shop and said, "Boy, I want you to listen to me."

Earl's eyes were still a little glazed, so Junior gave him a playful smack to the back of the head. Then he said again with a little more volume, "I want you to listen to me."

"Sure Grandpap, go ahead," said Earl still grinning.

Junior looked at Earl with a stone face and said, "That little girl right there is not one of your racetrack bimbos that sucks dick behind the car hauler when you think nobody's lookin'. If you think you're gonna impress her with a plate of fried shrimp and a ride in your fancy car, you are sadly mistaken. Amy Braxton is somethin' you have yet to be exposed to. She's a good girl with a crazy-ass family. Do you really want to chase her? That staying out all night after the races and sleeping till noon on Sunday bullshit you do would be over. Eight thirty Sunday morning your ass will be in a suit and tie sitting in a church pew. Then you'll be passin' out cookies and pouring Kool-Aid for her Sunday school class. After that you'll be having dinner at her daddy's house. He'll be sitting next to you on the front porch, sipping sweet tea and looking at you while deciding whether or not he needs to kill you."

Earl stopped smiling.

"Oh, and let's not forget her uncle Jack. You know Jack, right, Earl? Or maybe you just think you do. I hired him to work for me after the war. I know things about him that most don't. Jack Brown has killed well over a hundred people, mostly with his bare hands. His specialty was cutting the heads off his enemies and putting them on a stick. The entire North Vietnamese army was scared shitless of him and he loves Amy like a Christian loves the Bible. Now I will ask you again Earl, are you sure you want to chase that?"

Chapter 37

"I don't understand why he hasn't called me," said a disappointed Amy.

"He's a hot shot racecar driver. He doesn't have a girlfriend. He has girlfriends. He's not a bad guy, he just is what he is," explained Carla Jo.

Carla Jo was taking Amy to school for early swim practice. After she dropped her off she had to drive into the city to do some business for the clinic.

"Coach say's he has someone he wants me to meet today. She's a student teacher and champion swimmer from California."

"Are you enjoying this as much as you thought you would?" Carla Jo asked.

"Yeah, it's harder than I thought it would be. It's a lot of little things that make you fast. Coach says I'm doin' fine."

Carla Jo pulled behind the school by the aquatic center and said, "Good, I'm glad you like it. Carol will pick you up this afternoon. I love you, honey."

"I love you too, Aunt Carla Jo," Amy said as she gave her a hug.

Coach Hixon and Summer Van Hollen were standing by the pool when Amy walked out of the locker room. Summer looked at Amy and knew right away who she was. "That has to be her," Summer said to Coach Hixon.

"Yep," said the Coach.

"Oh my God, what a body," said Summer in amazement.

"She works like no kid I have ever known," said the Coach.

"What drives her?"asked Summer.

"I have no Idea," said the Coach.

"That's important to know, don't you think?" asked Summer.

"Yes, I suppose it is. I can tell you all about the rest of these kids, but that one is a mystery. This is the first time in her life she has been involved in organized sports. Every coach in this school wanted her and I have her," said the coach with a self-satisfied smile.

"Is she smart?" asked Summer.

"Her grades are above average but her achievement tests are off the charts. Somewhere in the brilliant range," said the coach.

"What about her family?" Summer asked.

"Mother died when she was young, older brother died tragically a few years back. She comes from a good Southern Christian family. I met her Dad; good man. Her family has a good reputation and you will discover that's important around here."

"Hobbies?"

"She's a deer hunter and the boys tell me she's a pretty good one. She also has a custom hot rod truck that she fools with."

"Like, killing deer?" Summer asked with a little bit of disgust.

"Killing, gutting, skinning, and eating," said Coach Hixon.

"Wow, anything else you can think of?"

"Nope, other than that Principal Nolan treats her like the Christ child. No one knows why, but other than making sure she is in weight training for her elective, Amy doesn't use it to her advantage."

Hmm, and none of it explains how she got that body, Summer thought to herself.

Amy finished putting in her laps and the coach called her over, saying,"Amy, I'd like you to meet our new assistant coach, Miss Van Hollen. She's a student teacher from Pepperdine University."

Amy was awestruck by her beauty. It was as if they made a Malibu Gym Rat Barbie Doll and brought it to life. Amy smiled and said, "Nice to meet you, Miss Van Hollen."

"You can call me Summer," she replied.

"No, she can't," Interrupted the coach.

"Sorry, I forgot where I was. I look forward to working with you, Amy. We'll talk more at practice this afternoon."

"Yes, ma'am. see you then."

Summer shivered and thought, *Ma'am, ugh.*

During sixth period, Summer watched through the door while Amy was weight training. *Impressive,* she thought. Amy didn't stand around much. She worked out like an animal. *I can work with this,* she thought.

That afternoon, Amy finished swimming her laps and then she and Summer began practicing the strokes that Amy was unfamiliar with. Amy was clearly in great shape but because of the weight training, she lacked the flexibility she needed. It was clear to the rest of the team why Summer was there. She worked, more or less, exclusively with Amy. Some of the girls were a little jealous and made snide comments, but Amy ignored them. The time she and Summer spent together in the pool began to blossom into a friendship. Amy still didn't have a good friend other than Carla Jo and emotionally, Amy was still relatively closed off from the rest of the world. On those rare occassions that she did open up, Amy could come across as a little needy. Summer would use that to her avantage in more ways than one. After about a month, Summer knew what she needed to make Amy a better swimmer.

"Have you ever tried yoga?" Summer asked Amy.

"No," Amy answered.

Summer thought for a minute and said, "It's against the rules for me to invite you to my house, but if you were to show up I wouldn't turn you away. We really need to work on your flexibility. I can show you some things."

Amy thought for a minute and said, "I didn't drive today but I could tomorrow and stop over on the way home."

Summer plugged her ears and said, "La la la la la, I didn't hear that."

Amy giggled and said, "OK."

Chapter 38

That evening Amy stopped by her uncle Jack's. She checked the oil and transmission fluid in her truck, and then pulled the number one spark plug and check the color. It was a nice light brown. *Perfect,* she thought. She checked the air in the tires and told her uncle Jack she would be driving to school the next day. Amy's daddy didn't have a garage and Uncle Jack didn't care if she kept it there.

"Feel like doing a little work?" Jack asked.

"Probably Saturday, Uncle Jack. I have homework tonight and I'm going to visit a friend from the swim team tomorrow after school," said Amy.

Well, that's a good thing, thought Jack. *Amy needed to put her schoolwork first. And a friend? That's good, too.* "OK, I figured we would start working with handguns," Jack said.

"Can't wait, Uncle Jack, see you in the morning." Amy said as she hugged him and gave him a kiss.

"Don't bother waking me up. You got keys, just lock the garage," he said.

"Yes, sir."

The next afternoon, Amy followed Summer to her townhouse.

"I love your truck," said Summer.

"Thanks, I love your place," said Amy as she looked around.

"Everything is rented. My dad set me up with a place to live while I was here."

"Why did you come here?" asked Amy.

"Well, I'm not trying to insult you, but this is considered to be an underserved area. There's supposedly a lot of poverty. By volunteering to come here I get a grant and a stipend. My dad is all about me paying my own way through college and this will help," Summer explained.

"Yeah, there are a lot of poor people outside Lewistown. No offense taken."

"You seem to be doing OK," said Summer.

"My daddy works hard and my aunt and uncle kind of spoil me," said Amy.

Summer smiled and said, "Well, let's get started."

Summer worked with Amy teaching her yoga positions and stretches that Amy had never done. After about an hour, Summer said, "Are you hungry?"

"Sure, I could eat. I have to eat like a horse to keep weight on," said Amy.

"Oh, I miss those days. Do you like stir-fry?" asked Summer.

"I'm not picky," said Amy.

Summer picked up a bottle of wine and poured Amy a glass. She handed it to her and Amy said, "I don't drink."

"This isn't drinking, it's wine. Kids in Italy start drinking it when they're old enough to use a glass. Besides, there are things in wine that are good for you. I drank a couple of glasses with dinner all the time when I was training," said Summer.

"OK, but just one glass," said Amy.

Amy and Summer talked while Summer cooked. There was one word that kept coming into Amy's mind: cool. She is so cool. She was funny, interesting, educated, cared what Amy thought, and was interested in what she had to say. After dinner, Summer asked her if she wanted to watch the video from one of her swim meets.

"Sure, I would love to see it," said Amy in earnest. Summer put in the video and they sat down on the couch. It was a recording from ESPN; the Olympic trials.

"I missed being on the Olympic team by three one-hundredths of a second," said Summer.

"Wow, that must have been heartbreaking," Amy said as Summer filled Amy's wine glass.

"Yeah, it hurt, but I got over it. I was wondering, what drives you? I have never seen anyone work so hard."

"I have my reasons," Amy said guardedly.

"One of my majors is sports psychology. What drives people is one of those things I'm always curious about. Do you want to share?" asked Summer.

"No, no, I don't," Amy said with an air of finality.

Summer took a drink of wine and asked, "Do you have a boyfriend?"

"No, I gave a guy my number once, but he never called. I don't trust many people, especially boys," said Amy.

Summer put down her wine glass, turned sideways on the coach close enough for her leg to brush against Amy's, and said, "Do you trust me?"

Amy smiled and said, "Yes."

"Good, because I am going to kiss you," Summer said seductively. Summer leaned over and gently kissed Amy on the lips. The wine had made Amy feel warm and loose and she felt as though she was melting into the couch cushion. Overcome by some unexpected desire, she locked eyes with Summer. Totally enraptured by her beautiful face, she unconsciously licked her lips.

"Did you like that?" Summer cooed. Amy slowly nodded her head. Summer stroked her hair with one hand and leaned in to kiss her again. With her other hand she began to rub the inside of Amy's thigh. Amy's legs began to part as if by reflex. She couldn't stop it if she wanted to. As Summer's kisses became more passionate and aggressive, Summer slowly moved her hand up the inside of Amy's thigh. Amy didn't stop her.

Chapter 39

Amy's emotions were spinning in her head as she lay in bed that Saturday morning. Round and round they went like stock cars on a racetrack, each emotion determined to take the lead and sometimes crashing into each other. She felt shame and guilt, as though she had sinned a great big sin. But how could that be bad? Summer had taken her to a place she had never been before. Wave after wave of indescribable pleasure took over her body then and shook her to the core. She remembered that she had heard someone screaming and it was her. Memories of laying her head between Summer's breasts and Amy's arms and legs wrapped around Summer's body kept replaying in her head. She was trembling and whimpering while Summer gently kissed her and stroked her hair. Amy had never felt that physically close to anyone. *My God, how can that be wrong?* she thought.

Amy got up and took a shower, got dressed, and went into the kitchen. Her daddy was sitting at the table.

"Good morning," he said with a smile.

"Good morning, daddy," Amy said while pouring herself some coffee.

"A little late last night, weren't ya'?"

"You're in trouble," Joseph teased.

"Shut up," she said as she playfully reached over and smacked him in the head.

Turning her attention back to her daddy she said, "Yeah, sorry, Daddy. We got to talkin' and I lost track of time."

"I never thought about giving you a curfew and I really don't want to, but I think ten o'clock is reasonable. And if you are gonna be late, a phone call would be nice. Me and Carol don't like worrying about ya'," her Daddy said.

"Yes, sir, I'm sorry. It won't happen again," said a visibly distracted Amy.

"You OK, honey?"

"Yeah, just a little tired. I've been training really hard for sectionals."

"Well, I'm proud of you. I know how hard you work. I'm proud of your grades, too. You made the honor roll last semester. I'm very proud," said Leon.

"You can thank Aunt Carla Jo for that. I wouldn't have made it through Algebra Two without her."

"Just know that I see what you do and I am very proud," Leon said, smiling.

You don't see everything, Amy thought.

Later on, Amy went to Granny Patches to see if she needed anything. They sat and talked for a while and then Amy fired up her truck and headed down the hill. She had driven the truck to her house the previous night because she knew she was late. The garage was already open so she pulled in and parked. Then she heard her uncle Jack calling to her from behind the house.

"Good Morning, Uncle Jack. Whatcha doin'?"

"Setting up some targets. Handguns today," he said.

Amy was excited about that. *Good,* she thought, it would get her mind on something else.

They went into the garage where Jack instructed Amy to sit down at the bench. He pulled back a towel and there lay six handguns. There was a Colt M1911, a Glock 9mm, a Sig .380, a Colt .32 auto, a .357 Magnum revolver, and a .38 snubnose.

Before Amy could fire a shot she had to know how to take them apart, clean them, and put them back together; quickly. Jack was fanatical about a clean weapon.

The revolvers were not that difficult to master, but the automatics took a little more effort. After a couple of hours Jack was satisfied that Amy had learned what she needed to know. He put the weapons in an old tackle box and they went out back. Jack constantly gave Amy little bits of information that she soaked up. Mostly it was covert stuff, like wearing gloves to load the clips so as to not leave fingerprints on the shells. For the first day, Jack didn't get into anything tactical. He just wanted her to fire them all. She would get the feel of the weapons and understand their individual characteristics.

Jack was continually impressed with her natural abilities. It took a certain amount of strength to effectively fire a large-caliber handgun and she had it. When they finished he took her back into the garage where she cleaned them all, and then they called it a day.

"Where's Aunt Carla Jo?" Amy asked.

"She had to work today. I'm goin' to get something to eat, you want to come?"

"Sure, I could eat," she said.

"Good, you're drivin'," Jack said with a smile.

The following morning, she went to church. She felt like a fraud teaching her Sunday school class. Her big sin hung on her like a lead cloak, but her kids helped her to get over it. They were wonderful. They showered her with unconditional love and affection. After church, Jack told her to come by and wear her camos. They would be working on tactics.

Amy fired every weapon from every position imaginable. On her back, her side, her stomach, her knees, standing, sitting, and with both her left and right hands. She practiced speed loading and the whole time, Jack would bark different scenarios. Then he would watch her and just shake his head. She didn't miss the target often and by the time they were through, Amy was a puddle of sweat. She tried to put herself in those scenarios and with her past experiences, she was successful. At the end of the day she cleaned the weapons and placed them in the tackle box. Handing the tackle box to her uncle Jack, he said, "Good job today, honey. Damn good job." .

Amy smiled and said, "Thanks, Uncle Jack. It was a lot of fun."

Monday morning she rode with her daddy to school. He usually dropped her off on his way to work. She was nervous. She had not seen or spoken to Summer since they spent that evening together. Amy put on her swimsuit, quickly jumped in the pool, and did her laps. When she finished she climbed out and Summer was standing in front of her. Amy couldn't look her in the eye. Summer looked to see if anyone was close and then she took her finger and pulled up Amy's chin. She smiled an innocent smile and said, "I had a wonderful time on Friday. Anytime you want to visit, my door is open."

The only thing Amy could think to say was, "Yeah, me too."

Summer put a cartoonishly serious look on her face and said, "Now let's get to work."

Amy was smart enough to understand the fallout from her relationship with Summer if anyone found out. It would not only bring shame and humiliation to her, but also to her family. Was she falling in love? How could she know? It was something she had never felt. One thing she knew for sure, though, was that those feelings were addicting and intoxicating. She wanted more. She kept a normal schedule but still tried to get to Summer's house as much as she could. There was no pretense of a friendly visit. Amy fell into Summer's arms as soon as she shut the door.

Chapter 40

A small caravan of Amy's family left Black Oak for Lewistown. Sectionals were to be held on a Friday night at Lewistown High School. Amy walked out onto the pool deck with her team. The pep band was playing, banners were waving, and she could see her whole family sitting in the stands. *This must have been how Kerry felt before the football games*, she thought.

Her events would be the 200-yard medley relay where she would swim the final or anchor leg, the 50-yard freestyle, the 100-yard butterfly, the 100-yard freestyle, the 500-yard freestyle, the 50-yard breastroke, and the 400-yard freestyle relay. It was a lot of events, but she was in shape for it. Summer had made sure of that.

Amy performed well. Everything coach Hixon had planned was coming to fruition. Part of it was the coaching skills of Miss Van Hollen, but the other part, the part he didn't see, was Amy's near pathological desire to please Summer during her training. She lost only one race, the 50-yard breastroke. She beat the state record in the 500-yard freestyle by three-tenths of a second. In her last race of the day, the 400 by 100-yard freestyle relay, her team was behind by over half a lap when she hit the water. She touched the wall barely an arm's length in front of her nearest competitor and the crowd went wild.

Amy jumped out of the pool and as her team was celebrating, Carla Jo watched Amy run past them, past Coach Hixon, and into the arms of Miss Van Hollen. Carla Jo had to take a second look to see what she thought she saw. Amy tried to kiss Miss Van Hollen and at the last second, Miss Van Hollen turned her head. Amy mouthed the words, "Oh, sorry." Then Carla Jo watched their body language: how they looked at each other, how Miss Van Hollen touched her and brushed the hair away from her face. How intimate, Carla Jo thought. Red flags began to wave in Carla Jo's head. She would have to investigate this further.

Carla Jo invited Amy over for breakfast the next morning. She made Amy's favorite, cream cheese-filled crepes with strawberry topping and whipped cream. Amy was still floating a little bit from her performance at the meet. Carla Jo had to be careful, but she knew what she was going to say.

"Miss Van Hollen has helped you a lot, hasn't she?"

"Yeah, she's wonderful," Amy said.

Carla Jo nodded and said, "I had someone like that in my life when I was sixteen. She was a bank executive. It was a big deal for a woman to hold a position like that in the 60s. She was a beautiful woman and she gave me my first job at her bank. To be honest, we even had a bit of a sexual relationship," Carla Jo said, leaving the last comment hanging out there as she watched Amy's face.

Amy got real uncomfortable real quick. Carla Jo watched Amy's eyes dart back and forth as a blush appeared in her cheeks. *Well, I'll be damned,* Carla Jo thought.

Meanwhile, Amy was screaming inside her own head, OH MY GOD, DOES SHE KNOW? HOW COULD SHE KNOW? Carla Jo continued, "It was one of the best and worst experiences of my life. She was so good to me. She taught me how my body worked and believe me, she could make it work," Carla Jo said with a smile as she stared off into the distance. Amy didn't say a word.

Carla Jo looked at Amy and said, "I was ashamed of what I had done for a long time, but looking back on it, it wasn't all bad."

The smile left Carla Jo's face as she said, "But then there was the other half of it. When she was finished with me, she was finished with me. I liked her. Well, no, I probably loved her. When our relationship ended, I discovered something. She never really liked me for me. She made me feel like an adult so I would do adult things, but to her I was just an object that satisfied her needs. That part of it was soul-crushing. It was the first time I was used. After that I was more careful and discriminating about who I spent time with."

Amy swallowed hard, looked at Carla Jo, and asked, "Why are you telling me this?"

"I'm sorry Amy, maybe I shouldn't have. I have never spoken of that relationship out loud to anyone. I was sixteen. You're sixteen now. Maybe you can use my experience to help you see things clearly if you are ever in a similar situation."

"Thank you for trusting me with that. You know, you're my best friend," said Amy.

"'Til the day I die, honey, till the day I die," said Carla Jo, smiling.

That Sunday morning Carla Jo knew Amy would be in church so she decided to pay Miss Van Hollen a little visit. She picked up the phone and called Gene. "Hey handsome, whose on duty today?"

Gene laughed and said, "I thought you were married."

"Oh, you know how I feel about a man in uniform," said Carla Jo seductively.

"Well, believe it or not, I am. Tim and Beth have a wedding to go to."

"Are you busy?" she asked.

"Nah, not really, what do you need?" said Sheriff Carter.

"I have an issue to address and I would like a little back up."

"What's going on?" he asked, concerned.

"Well, it's kind of personal, but if I need you, I want you there," Carla Jo explained.

"Sure," said Gene.

"Meet me in the parking lot of the Food King in an hour," she said.

"Yes, ma'am. See you there."

When he arrived at the shopping center, Carla Jo got into Gene's car and they went to Miss Van Hollen's townhouse. They stopped on the street in front and Carla Jo said, "Stand outside the car."

"Yes, ma'am," he said.

Carla Jo knocked on the door and Summer answered. Carla Jo smiled and said, "Hi, Miss Van Hollen. Are you busy?"

"You're Amy's aunt, aren't you?"

"Yes, you can call me Carla Jo. I wondered if we could talk about Amy?"

"Sure, come in," said Summer.

Carla Jo followed her into the kitchen. Summer was wearing a tight-fitting pair of shorts and a tank top. Carla Jo thought to herself, *Amy certainly has good taste in women.* They sat down at the kitchen table and Carla Jo said, "You two have established a very close relationship."

"Yes, we have. She is amazing," Summer replied.

"Yes, we think so, too. You know, Miss Van Hollen...,"

Summer interrupted her and said, "Call me Summer."

"OK, Summer. In this state they have a name for the relationship you have with Amy. It's called statutory rape," Carla Jo said as she sat back and calmly watched Summer's reaction.

Summer leaned back in her chair, crossed her arms, rolled her eyes, put a smug look on her face, and said, "Did Amy tell you that?"

"No, honey, you just did. Here's what you are going to do. You are going to call Amy and say you have a sick relative and you need to go home. Then you will pack your things and be out of this state in twenty-four hours. You will never contact her again."

Summer laughed at her and said, "I don't think so. When I tell Amy what you have accused us of, I doubt if she will be real happy with you. I think this conversation is over. I would like you to leave now."

Carla Jo's face turned to stone and she said, "OK, have it your way. But before I leave you may want to look out the window."

Summer moved the curtain and saw Sheriff Carter standing by his car.

"That squad car is how I got here and that rather large man is Sheriff Carter, Amy's dad's best friend and Amy's hunting partner."

The smile left Summer's face. Carla Jo slammed her fist down on the table and growled, "Now you listen to me, you smug little cunt. You will do what I say or you will be arrested. In less than an hour you will be in a cell with a half dozen of the ugliest, meanest crack whores he can find. When they are done beating the shit out of you, I'm sure they will make good use of your oral skills. Twenty-four hours, do you understand me?"

Summer looked at Carla Jo and nodded. Carla Jo stood up quickly, slammed her fists on the table, and screamed, "SPEAK, BITCH!"

Summer jumped in the chair and said, "Yes, yes, I...I understand."

Carla Jo turned to leave, but then she stopped at the door, turned around, and in a calm voice said, "When you speak to Amy, you had better sell it. If I see one tear out of that child, it will be the worst fucking day of your life."

Carla Jo opened the door and left.

Chapter 41

Sunday night the phone rang. Amy took it out on the back porch. Ten minutes later, Amy hung up the phone and leaned against the door jam. Carol could see something was wrong by the look on Amy's face. Carol asked, "What's the matter, honey?"

Amy looked at Carol. Her eyes were misting as she said, "Summer is going back to California. Her brother is sick."

"Who?" Carol asked

"Miss Van Hollen," Amy replied.

"Oh, honey, I'm so sorry. I know you really liked her," said Carol.

"I'll be in my room. I have some homework to finish," said Amy. She walked in her room, locked the door, fell on her bed, and sobbed into her pillow. Amy had lost her first love and she was devastated, but the real pain didn't come until two days later when Amy took the phone number Summer gave her and tried to call. It was a wrong number. Carla Jo could not have described it any better. It was soul-crushing.

All teenagers struggle with the loss of their first love. With Amy it would be more difficult. When a girl loses her first boyfriend, friends and family comfort her. Amy's love was forbidden. She thought she would have to suffer alone.

Amy spent a lot of time with Carla Jo and went they went on their monthly trip to Francois the following Saturday, it became clear to Amy that Carla Jo knew about her relationship. She didn't know how she knew, but she did. Amy never spoke openly about it and Carla Jo skillfully danced around the edges of it, but Carla Jo was able to offer her comfort and help her through it.

It took about three weeks for Amy to come out of her funk, but then she started to get back in the swing of things. She was practicing hard for regionals and after swim practice, one of her teammates approached her. Her name was Kelly. She was not one of the best swimmers, but Amy noticed that she practiced hard.

"I really like your truck," said Kelly.

"Thanks," Amy said.

"You know, most kids with hot rods hang out at the A&W on Saturday night. It's lots of fun. Your truck would be a dude magnate," she said.

Amy smiled, nodded, and then turned to walk away. She took about three steps and stopped. *There it is*, she thought. *Someone stepped up to be nice to me and I'm blowing her off.* Amy turned around, looked at Kelly, and then said, "That sounds like fun. I'm not doing anything on Saturday night. Do you want to come with me?" asked Amy.

"I would love to," Kelly said, smiling.

Kelly was right. The two pretty girls in the yellow truck were bathed with attention. The goofy things the boys would do to impress her and Kelly entertained the heck out of Amy. They sat on the tailgate, drank Cherry Cokes and giggled the whole evening. At the end of the night, Amy pulled out onto the street in front of the A&W, nailed the gas, and did a smoky burnout. She could hear the boys hooting and hollering when she stopped at the next stoplight. When Deputy Nolan's squad car pulled up next to Amy, she could see he wasn't so impressed. He rolled down his window, looked at Amy, and said, "Nice burnout."

Amy looked at him, feigned embarrassment, and said, "Ooops, sorry, Deputy Nolan."

He smiled at her and shook his head, "Do it again and I'm telling your daddy."

"Yes, sir," said Amy. Deputy Nolan drove away and the girls started laughing.

Amy hadn't had a best friend since Mary Beth. The girls started hanging out together at school and spent several Saturday nights at the A&W. Amy wanted to help Kelly get in better shape for swimming so Amy asked her to transfer into the weight training class. Kelly tried, but they told her no, so Amy went to see Principal Nolan and as if by magic, Kelly's counselor changed his mind. But Kelly wasn't ready for the intense way Amy worked out. She thought she was going to die after the first day. Once the soreness was worked out of her muscles, however, Kelly could see it start to pay off, both on the stopwatch and in the mirror.

One evening, Amy invited Kelly to her house for dinner. The two were sitting on the front porch talking when Kelly looked at Amy and said, "You know, you're nothing like people think you are."

"How do people think I am?" Amy asked.

"Mean, stuck-up, and, well, gay."

Amy was aware of the rumors, but she didn't know how pervasive they were.

"Gay? Where did you hear that?" Amy heard herself say.

"People have thought that since junior high. You have never had a boyfriend, you're more muscular than most boys are, and that ass-kicking you gave Candice in junior high?, Well, you can see how one might think."

"I didn't kick her ass, I just kind of pushed her," said Amy.

"Oh no, I was there. You kicked her ass," Kelly said, shaking her head.

Amy took a deep breath and decided to open up a little. After giving it a little thought, she said, "My mom died when I was little and a couple years later, my big brother died. I had all of these family responsibilities,: cooking, cleaning, working on the farm, and taking care of my little brother. I put a lot of pressure on myself. I didn't know how much until my dad married Carol and she started doing the mom thing. I suppose I have always been a little too intense for my age. I'm trying to get over that. I guess I can see how people would think those things about me."

Just then Joseph walked up on the porch. He tried to smack Amy in the head and Amy playfully swatted it away, kicking him in the rear. Amy introduced him to Kelly and he smiled at her. Kelly was not hard to look at.

"You know, your little brother is cute," said Kelly after Joseph walked away.

"Kelly, he's twelve," said Amy.

"I'll wait," said Kelly.

"You're horrible," Amy said, shaking her head.

"I know," Kelly replied with a smile. Then said, "You know, I always defended you. I said anyone that dresses like that can't be gay, there's just no way."

"Thanks," said Amy.

"Speaking of clothes, I've always want to peek in your closet. That Dolce and Gabbana? I would love to try that on," Kelly said with a little excitement.

"Sure, why not? Let's take a look," said Amy. *So this is what teenage girls really do,* Amy thought. *It's not so bad.*

Kelly walked into Amy's bedroom and stood by the closet. As she put her hands on the double door handles, preparing to swing them open, she said, "Amy, if you are gay, I know a pom-pom squad, a cheerleading squad, and a bulimic debutant that would strip naked and jump in your bed just to have the chance to do what I'm doing right now."

Amy laughed and said, "You're a little dramatic and you're going to be disappointed."

Kelly pulled the doors open. Only one dress was visible. The rest of her school clothes were hung up and pushed neatly to one side. None of the clothes Kelly wanted to see were in there. "Where's the Dolce, the Donna Karan? My God, it looks like Bass Pro Shop in here," Kelly said with a panicked look on her face.

Amy shook her head and said, "Let me make a phone call, I'll introduce you to the rest of my family. That should answer your questions."

Amy called Carla Jo to see if she could bring her friend over and introduce her.

"Sure, I would love to meet her," said Carla Jo. After hanging up the phone, she looked at Jack and said, "You might want to put that thing back in your pants, we have company coming."

"Dammit," said Jack, tugging his underwear back on.

"We got all night, big boy," said Carla Jo as she nuzzled his neck.

Amy went into the kitchen, grabbed a pork chop off of the stove, and wrapped it in a paper towel. The girls headed down the hill to Carla Jo's and when they got to the front porch, Kelly jumped at the sight of Bubba.

"That's the ugliest dog I have ever seen," she said, startled.

Amy unwrapped the pork chop and gave it to Bubba, and then said, "Nooo, Bubba here is my hero. He's beautiful and besides, he likes you."

"How do you know that?"

"Because you're not bleeding," said Amy with a little grin.

Just then the door opened. A hulking man with a disfigured face looked down at Kelly. Kelly's eyes got big and her mouth fell open.

"Hi, honey, come on in. Who's your friend?" said Jack.

"This is Kelly, she's on the swim team. Kelly, this is my uncle Jack."

Jack shook her hand and welcomed her in.

Carla Jo appeared,introduced herself, and gave Kelly a hug. *Oh my God,* Kelly thought, *I've walked into an episode of the* Munsters.

The girls sat in the kitchen, talked, and drank sweet tea.

"Kelly's a big fan of your taste in clothes. Do you think she could see the closet?" asked Amy.

"Sure," said Carla Jo. They walked into the back bedroom that Carla Jo had converted into a huge walk-in closet. The walls were lined with designer clothes, and dozens of pairs of shoes sat on racks.

"Oh my," said Kelly as she looked with wonder.

"Do you see anything you like?" asked Carla Jo.

"I see everything I like," said Kelly.

"Would you like to try something on?" asked Carla Jo.

"YES!" said Kelly with a little squeal.

For the rest of that evening, Carla Jo would hand Kelly something and she would put it on. Kelly smiled like a beauty queen on a parade float. Amy just sat in a chair and laughed at the both of them.

"There she is, Aunt Carla Jo, the doll you always wanted," she said, smiling.

Kelly was in heaven and Carla Jo even let her take a couple of things home with her. By that time it was dark, so Carla Jo insisted on driving them both back up the hill. She dropped them off and Amy took Carol's car to drive Kelly home. When Amy got to Kelly's house, Kelly looked at her and said, "Amy, you've got the life."

Amy had never really seen her life through anyone else's eyes before. *Yeah*, she thought to herself, *I guess I do.*

Kelly and Amy were good for each other. Kelly fed off of Amy's uncompromising discipline and work ethic, which helped her with her schoolwork and her training. In return, Kelly gave Amy the permission to be a teenage girl.

Chapter 42

Coach Hixon watched his girls walk out onto the pool deck for regionals. He had never made it past sectionals before and he was nervous. He had noticed several of his girls getting leaner and physically bigger. The girls all knew Amy was a physical specimen and they had figured she was just a freak of nature, but when Kelly trimmed three seconds from her 400-yard freestyle relay leg, they took notice. Amy handed out her workout regimen to anyone that would take it and led the girls in the stretching exercises that Summer had taught her. The thick armor coat that Amy had worn to protect herself was slowly falling away. She was no longer the unapproachable loner. She was becoming a leader.

The girls won regionals, but not by much. Their combined improvement in the 400-yard relay put them over the top. They went to the state championships as a huge underdog and they turned a lot of heads. The rural school that no one gave a chance to had gotten past sectionals.

The coach gave the perfunctory "little engine that could" speech, but they were handily trounced. Amy finished second in her best event, the 500-yard freestyle. She lost her events to Karen Setzer, a senior that already had a scholarship to Arizona State. She was six feet tall and every bit the physical specimen

Amy was. After the meet, Amy sat in the locker room, feeling a little bit depressed. A few minutes later, Karen came over and sat down next to her on the bench.

"Hi," said Karen. Amy nodded at her and Karen said, "I wanted to come over and check you for gills. You are fast."

"Not fast enough," said a depressed Amy without looking up at her.

"You're just a sophomore, you have nothing to be sad about. Next year this will all be yours," said Karen.

"Thanks," said Amy.

"When you broke my record it got my attention and I turned up my training. I was getting lazy. Now I'm in the running to train at the Olympic training facility. I kind of owe you," she said.

"You're welcome," said Amy.

"You hate to lose. That's going to help you, too," said Karen as she leaned over and gave Amy a hug. Karen got up and started to walk away when she stopped, turned around, and said, "You know, in the swimming community you have a nickname now. The Lewistown Shark. I gave it to you."

Amy looked up at Karen, smiled, and shook her head. She was grateful for the way Karen treated her. She would have to remember that in the future.

The school threw a big pep rally for the swim team when they returned. Their pictures were in the local newspaper and their sectional and regional trophies went in the case with their team picture. The trophy case was rearranged a bit and Amy saw that her team's picture was kind of close to Kerry's. She liked that. Principal Nolan thought she would.

As the year wound down, finals came up and Amy and Kelly studied together even when Kelly didn't want to. Kelly talked Amy into taking a few more breaks than Amy would have liked, but in the end it evened out. Kelly made the honor roll for the first time and Kelly's parents were ecstatic. Amy made the honor roll too, but that was what her daddy demanded.

Then summer came and Leon sat Amy down and told her in no uncertain terms that she would need to get a job. That truck of hers was putting a dent in his wallet. He would keep her on his insurance, but gas and parts were all on her now. Amy agreed but wasn't quite sure where to begin her search. She went to see her aunt for advice.

"Daddy says I have to get a job," said Amy.

"Well, welcome to the real world, honey. What are you going to do?" said Carla Jo.

"I don't know. Uncle Jack has taught me a lot about guns and knives; maybe the sporting goods store? I've learned some things about cars. The auto parts store might need someone. And there's always the Food King," said Amy.

"Anything else interest you?" asked Carla Jo.

"Well, I have been reading that *Grey's Anatomy* book of yours. That's pretty interesting," Said Amy.

"Would you like to work with us?" said Carla Jo.

"Really? That would be great," said Amy.

"We work our asses off, honey. Some of it isn't very pleasant," Carla Jo warned.

"What exactly do you do?" asked Amy.

"Other than the doctors' offices we have in-home care for the disabled and elderly. We bathe them, make sure they have their medications, and when necessary, we educate their families on how to care for them. It's hard work. I have a little pull with the nursing supervisor, so I think I can put you with a nurse as an assistant. You would learn a lot," said Carla Jo.

Amy thought for a few minutes and then said, "You know, I think I would like that kind of work. That would be great. Ok, who do I see about getting started?"

Carla Jo smiled and said, "You're lookin' at her."

Jack and Carla Jo: Part 2

Annette lay on her pillow facing Jack and watched him sleep. He snored and drool ran out of the corner of his mouth. He was the most beautiful thing she thought she had ever seen. Then his eyes opened and he saw her watching him. She was smiling. "Good morning," said Jack.

"Good morning to you. How did you sleep?" she asked.

"Like the dead. You are pretty amazing. You wore me out," said Jack as he reached for her and pulled her close.

It was the first night they had spent together. Annette hugged him and stroked his hair. *He has beautiful hair*, she thought. Jack smiled at her and said, "You know, we are going to have to pick a day when we stop calling you Annette."

"Today is as good a day as any," she replied.

"OK, Carla Jo it is."

They lay in each other's arms for hours, both believing that they had found the one person that loved them no matter what may come. They were both right. They got up a little later and made breakfast together. Jack sat at the table and said, "Well, if we are goin' to do this, you need to know a few things. I don't care about money. I have no need to be wealthy. I'm never leaving this house or this land. I was born here and I will die here. There has never been anythin' fancy about me and there is never going to be."

"OK," said Carla Jo.

"That's it, just OK?" asked Jack.

"Yes, that's it. I lived the big city life. It didn't treat me very well. Just curious, what are you going to do with that?" Carla Jo asked, pointing to the black case on the floor.

"That's not mine, that's yours. Do whatever you want with it."

That could be a life changing amount, thought Carla Jo. While at Johns Hopkins University she had taken finance classes. She understood the stock market and how money worked. She also learned personal finance from her mom. Nancy was a very frugal woman even though she always made sure she had what she wanted.

Carla Jo had a lot of catching up to do when it came to the rest of the world. She went to the library and poured over the *Wall Street Journal, Barron's, Fortune,* and every other current financial periodical she could get her hands on. After a couple weeks of studying, her research pointed her in one direction, technology stocks. She counted out the money in the case, which came to $171,000. She knew she could never take it to a bank as there would be too many questions. Stockbrokers, on the other hand, were not so curious. She split it up among three different brokerage houses, invested it, and left it alone.

Carla Jo's addiction to drugs and alcohol nagged at her. Even though she was happy, the cravings wouldn't leave her alone, so she did the smart thing and confided in Jack and Katherine. She told them how she felt and what was happening inside of her. Jack liked to have a drink now and then, but Carla Jo was way more important to him. He removed all of the alcohol from his house and took her to AA meetings that were held at the VFW for veterans.

Katherine took another direction and through friendship, conversation, sweet tea, and cobbler, she kept Carla Jo's mind off of her cravings. After a while, Carla Jo began to live without the daily pangs of addiction. She was, however, getting chubby. Jack didn't care but Carla Jo did. As much as she adored Jack and her new-found lifestyle, she was getting bored. Wanting a life, a purpose, something that would get her out of bed in the morning, she talked to Jack about getting a job. She only knew how to do one thing, but under her new name, her nursing license was no good. Jack went to see Doc Henderson to see if he needed help.

Doc Henderson was a simple country doctor who had worked out of his home for almost thirty years. He was divorced because his wife thought she was marrying money. Doc didn't care about money. He would take a chicken and a couple dozen eggs, or handyman services as payment. He loved the people of Jackson County and they loved him. Jack asked him if he could use the help. He said he really couldn't pay very much, but he could always use a little help. He had an office assistant, Robin, but she was relatively useless. All she did was sit at a desk and answer the phone. Carla Jo didn't care about the money, she was happy to have something to do. Carla Jo cleaned his office, put away his supplies, and whatever else he needed. During Carla Jo's fourth day at work, that would change.

A woman ran in the office carrying a little boy of about five or six years of age. He had been playing with a gun and shot himself in the leg. Doc wasn't there so his office assistant called the ambulance. They were twenty minutes away. Carla Jo took one look and said, "He's bleeding out, the femoral artery must be damaged." She went into action, but Robin tried to stop her.

"You can't do that." She warned.

Carla Jo looked at his mother and said, "If I don't stop this bleeding, he's dead."

The little boy's mother said, "Do it, do whatever you have to do."

Carla Jo worked like a machine. She gave him a local, opened him up, found the artery, and clamped it off. She had Robin call Lewistown and tell them to get a vascular surgeon on standby. Just then, Doc Henderson walked in. He took one look at the boy's leg and stepped aside. Carla Jo put a temporary dressing on his leg just as the ambulance arrived and took him away.

"I told her not to do that," said Robin.

"Thanks. Robin. You can go now," said Doc Henderson.

Robin shot Carla Jo a dirty look and left. Doc Henderson looked at Carla Jo and said, "I think we need to talk."

Doc and Carla Jo sat down and he said, "I know three things about you. First, you're a heroine addict. I was there when you detoxed. Second, your name is not Carla Jo, I was holding Carla Jo when she died. Third, you just saved that little boy's life. So, Doctor, where did you go to school?"

Carla Jo took a deep breath. She wasn't sure what she should tell him, but he knew quite a bit already so she said, "I'm not a doctor. I was a surgical nurse in Vietnam. Sometimes we got busy and I did what I had to do to save lives."

Doc shook his head and said, "So where did you go to school?"

"Johns Hopkins."

"Well, I'll be damned. I got a Johns Hopkins-prepared surgical nurse with combat trauma experience sweeping my floors."

"I'm sorry, I'll go," she said.

"Go?" said Doc incredulously. "You're not going anywhere. I need help. I got elderly shut ins all over this county that won't leave their homes. I got little communities of poor children that have never even seen a doctor. They need check-ups and inoculations. I got so much to do I can't keep up. No, young lady, you're not going anywhere."

Carla Jo went home at the end of the day and told Jack what had happened.

"Who was the little boy?" Jack asked.

"I'm not sure. I was busy trying to save his life," said Carla Jo.

Two days later a big Chevy truck pulling a trailer parked in front of Jack's garage. On the trailer was a brand new red Z-28 Camaro. The driver of the truck unloaded the car and asked, "Is Carla Jo Brown here?"

"Nope," said Jack.

"This is hers. Please make sure she gets this envelope," said the man.

"OK."

Later that night, Carla Jo pulled into the driveway after a long day and saw the pretty red car sitting there. She got out of her car and walked around it, liking what she saw. Jack came out of the garage and said, "Nice car."

"Yes, it is. Whose is it?" asked Carla Jo.

"Yours," said Jack, handing her the envelope.

Carla Jo open the envelope and read the heartfelt thank you note.

"Who is Audra Spencer?" asked Carla Jo.

"Junior Gosset's daughter. Why?" said Jack.

"The little boy I had to cut on the other day, his name is Earl," said Carla Jo.

Jack laughed and said, "No shit, Earl Spencer. Well, honey, you'll never want for anything in this town."

As Carla Jo became more aquainted with the practice, Doc took her to the black communities because, well, she was sort of black. He introduced her to the families and community leaders. Carla Jo was not prepared for the poverty. There was poverty in the city, but there were also free clinics, welfare, food stamps, and other means of help. Out here there was nothing. Doc gave her very few rules and turned her loose.

Doc's financial situation was bleak. Every spare dollar that came into the clinic was used to buy medicine and supplies. They both lived lean and Carla Jo made about enough money to keep her old Buick in gas. The clinics in the city always had money; not a lot, but they had what they needed. Patience wasn't something Cala Jo had a lot of, however, and she was growing impatient with their inability to serve the community.

After a trip to the city and talking to some of the staff at the free clinics, it was clear what Carla Jo needed to do. She turned Doc Henderson's operation into a free clinic so they could be eligible for state and federal funds. She also went to night school and studied computerized medical billing systems. She Bought a computer with her own money, fired Robin, and hired Junie, a single mom that went to school with her.

After signing the indigent, elderly, and children up for Medicaid or Medicare, the dollars began to flow into the clinic. Expanding the reach of their services, she hired more nurses and home care specialists. They expanded into other communities with satellite offices and hired young doctors just out of school to staff them. Carla Jo made connections with all the local businesses including the mines. Within three years, medical services were available where none have ever been. Carla Jo found herself CEO of Henderson Medical.

Every morning before work, Carla Jo stopped by Katherine's and had coffee with her. Carla Jo offered her a job, but Katherine would hug Amy and say, "No, thanks, I have a job." Katherine had just had another baby and they named him Joseph. A year and a half later, Carla Jo and Katherine were having coffee when she began to cough. She pulled her hand away and it was spattered with blood.

The cancer hit Katherine hard and fast. Carla Jo took her to the city and the doctors threw everything they had at her trying to save her, but it was not to be. Katherine wanted to die at home so Carla Jo set up a virtual hospital room in her house. While sitting next to the bed talking to her best friend, Katherine took a deep breath and said, "Carla Jo, I know how this ends, I have seen it before. I don't want Leon and my children to see me like that. I need you to do something for me."

Carla Jo knew what was coming, she looked at Katherine and said, "Katherine, I don't know…,"

Katherine interrupted her and said, "Yes, you do. I have made my peace with Jesus. He's waiting for me. When it's time I want you to end it."

After all Katherine had done for her, Carla Jo didn't feel like she was in any position to tell her no. Carla Jo nodded and said, "OK."

One evening Katherine hugged and kissed Leon and her children and they went to Granny Patches for dinner. Carla Jo sat down beside her to enjoy a little conversation when Katherine smiled, looked up, and said, "It's time."

There was really no preparing for that moment. Tears rolled down Carla Jo's face as she took out the needle and injected it into the IV. As Katherine slipped away, Carla Jo felt a part of herself die. They held hands tightly as Katherine began a new journey.

Chapter 43

Amy had the best summer of her life. She and Kelly were attached like Siamese twins. Saturday nights at the A&W became a regular event along with trips to the beach on the river. Amy even allowed Kelly to set her up on a couple of double dates. The boys were nice enough, even though on one occasion she had to use a little non-lethal force to stop the advances of an overzealous young man. Amy gave her sexuality a lot of thought. She had the relationship with Summer and it was exciting. While alone in her room, however, as she enjoyed some, well, personal time, it was always a boy; a nameless, faceless boy. Her sexual urges didn't lead her around like they sometimes seemed to with Kelly, but they were certainly there.

She spent the summer working part time for Henderson Medical. Carla Jo placed her with one her best home health care nurses and paid her a decent wage, probably a little more than she should have. Carla Jo received regular reports about how she was doing. The nurse said Amy worked hard and learned fast. Amy began to think about a career as she realized that she really liked that kind of work, especially her work with children. When Amy started school she chose classes that would benefit a medical career.

Amy was tired of the football players looking at her ass while she worked out, so she talked to Principal Nolan to see if she could get a weight training elective for the girls. Principal Nolan told her that if she could get twenty students to sign up, she could have one fifth period. Amy signed up most of the swim team and a few softball players and got her elective. Amy ran the class like a general. There would be no slacking or girly banter. Coach Ramsey was present to teach, but mostly he just stayed out of Amy's way. The Lewistown Girls swim team would win state if it killed her.

There was also a new kid in school. His name was Andy Evans. He was in most of Amy's advanced placement classes. Amy would find herself looking at him out of the corner of her eye. Andy was really smart, smarter than Amy. He wasn't much to look at, a little taller than Amy and kind of thin with a mop of dishwater blonde hair and a nose a little too big for his face. His clothes weren't fancy, but they were neat and clean. But there was something else, something about the way he carried himself. It was like the pettiness of high school was beneath him. He was almost regal.

Amy sat at lunch looking across the cafeteria at Andy. He had his feet up reading a book. Kelly caught her looking at him and said, "You can't be serious."

"What?" asked Amy.

"Andy Evans? Really?" Kelly said accusingly.

"What?" said Amy with a half smile, knowing she had been caught.

"Oh my God, I know that look. I've just never seen it on you," said Kelly.

"I think I'm gonna go talk to him."

Without another thought she picked up her tray, walked over to his table, and sat down across from Andy.

"Hi," she said. "My name's Amy."

Andy looked up over the top of his book and said, "Yeah, I know who you are."

"Watcha readin'?"

"Asimov."

"Oh, is that one of the Foundation books?"

Andy tilted his head, looked at her, and said, "How do you know about that?"

"I like to read. I read *I, Robot*. Sci-Fi isn't my thing, but it was interesting."

Andy nodded and kept reading his book.

"Do you have a girlfriend?"

"You're kidding, right? Is this the part where you invite me to a party? All the pretty girls have a contest to see who can bring the biggest geek? This isn't the first time I've been the new kid in school," said Andy, trying to put an end to what he thought was a ridiculous conversation.

Amy reached across the table, pulled down his book, and said, "I would never do that. I would find that insulting if I didn't know how cruel kids could be."

"Tell me something I don't know," mused Andy.

"OK."

"That was rhetorical."

"Oh no, if I can tell you something you don't know you have to start having lunch with me and my friend," said Amy with a mischievous smile.

Andy shook his head and thought to himself, *This girl is beautiful, this can't be happening*. "OK," he said.

"Do you know why Fritz Freleng chose the coyote over every other animal as the foil for Roadrunner?"

Andy smiled. He had a beautiful smile with perfect teeth. Then he replied, "No, tell me."

"Because Mark Twain wrote in one of his books that the coyote is the perfect allegory of want. He needed an animal that wouldn't quit," said Amy with the cutest smile Andy had ever seen.

The bell rang and Amy said, "Come on, I'll let you walk me to my locker."

"Oh, that would be an honor, Princess Amy," said Andy sarcastically.

"So you're a smarty pants, I like that too," said Amy with a chuckle.

Andy never had a girlfriend before and Amy never had a boyfriend. Neither one really knew how to behave. It was an awkward dance. In Andy's wildest dreams he could have never imagined a girl so over-the-top smart and beautiful; probably one of, if not the most, beautiful girls in the school falling for him. He was afraid to even touch her. Amy didn't know what she would do if he did touch her. They spent weeks walking together, talking and laughing. Andy was witty. He had a sense of humor and used references that only the intelligent and well-read would understand. He was intellectually much older than his age. Amy understood him perfectly and she hung on his every word.

Andy could be brutally honest with his observations. That made most people uncomfortable, which was why Andy really had no friends. Amy liked it. She would debate him if she thought he was wrong and occasionally they could change each other's views. There was something else about him. It was something familiar that Amy would see when she looked in the mirror. She didn't know what it was, but it was there.

Kids like to talk and the rumor was that the whole relationship was a scam to hide Amy's homosexuality. Kelly told everyone that would listen that it was not the case. Over time, Kelly had been around Amy enough that she could see the difference in Amy whenever he was around. The way she walked, talked, and the expression on her face would change. Amy had always been stoic. Her smiles were never full, always controlled. She never walked in so much as marched in like a soldier. When he was around, she was a typical, wiggly-giggly teenage girl.

They held hands once by accident and neither wanted to let go. It was an innocent, sweet relationship that grew slowly. There was still another Amy, though, the Amy that Andy didn't know. There was the Amy that Jack Brown worked and drilled into a machine capable of violence on an unimaginable scale. On this day, Andy would get a glimpse of it. The whole school would see it. The button Carla Jo feared would be pushed got pushed and pushed hard.

Chapter 44

*B*ruce Clark was the school bully and as bullies went, he was particularly vicious. Even the football players steered clear of him. One day as Andy was leaving class, Bruce made a comment about Amy being gay. Andy shot back with a remark about Bruce's parentage. Amy and Kelly were walking to meet Andy at his locker and when they turned the corner Amy saw that Bruce had Andy by the throat. His feet were off the ground and his face was a bright red. Bruce was pounding him off the lockers. With cold calculation Amy dropped her bag and in the twenty steps it took her to reach them, she already knew what she was going to do.

Both of Bruce's legs were locked out straight. Amy took his knee out with a sidekick. The sickening pop could be heard all the way at the other end of the hall. Before he could even start to fall she transferred her weight to the ball of her left foot and put a powerful spin kick into his ribs. Another muffled pop was heard from a rib snapping. Bruce hit the floor and Amy landed on him like a cat. She hit him in the back of his head with a palm strike, driving his face into the tile. Shattered pieces of his teeth bounced across the floor. He tried to move and she hit him again and again until he didn't move. In less than thirty seconds it was over. She jumped up, grabbed Andy, and headed out the side door. You could have heard a pin drop in the hall until the pool of blood started to form around Bruce's head; then the girls started screaming.

Amy and Andy ran around the corner of the building and stopped. Andy, still not entirely sure of what just happened and in disbelief at what he thought he saw, said to Amy in a panicked voice, "What did you do? Oh my god, Amy. I think you killed him."

Amy was pacing like a tiger. Her adrenalin was still pumping. She said, "No one hurts the people I love, no one. Ever."

"What?" exclaimed Andy.

Amy grabbed him by the shirt, pushed him against the wall, and said, "I love you, Andy." Then she kissed him.

They could hear the sirens in the distance as Amy kissed him again. They held on to each other until a sheriff's deputy appeared around the corner. The Deputy knew to handle her carefully lest he earn the wrath of Sheriff Carter. He looked at her and said, "Amy, um, I think the principal wants to see you."

Amy walked into the principal's office and sat down. Deputy Nolan was already there. They both looked at Amy, each not knowing how to grasp the dichotomy of the horrific damage inflicted on Bruce and the pretty girl sitting in front of them. She didn't appear to have a scratch on her. Principal Nolan said, "Amy, honey, what happened?"

Amy told the story and the Nolans just looked at her. Finally Principal Nolan said, "I'm sorry, honey, but I have to suspend you until we sort this out."

Deputy Nolan was truly confused. He had no idea what to do. He threw up his hands and said, "To be honest I should probably arrest you, but Gene would lose his mind."

Phones started ringing all over Jackson County. Deputy Nolan decided to take Amy to the police station and let Gene handle it. By the time they got there it looked like a Braxton family reunion. Leon, Carol, Carla Jo, and Jack all stood in Gene's office. Amy sat in the chair in front of Gene as he began the conversation.

"So, honey, you want to tell me what happened?" he said.

Amy went through the story again and Gene said, "Did he hurt you? Did he do anything to you?"

"No, but he was hurting Andy."

"Who the hell is Andy to you?" said Leon.

Amy didn't say anything and Carla Jo spoke up, "Is he your boyfriend?"

Amy nodded yes and then Jack asked, "How come I didn't know you had a boyfriend?"

Carla Jo glared at Jack and said, "That's not really the issue here, Jack."

Gene brought the attention back to Amy and said, "I have arrested this boy several times. He is no stranger to the juvenile system. I also know he's a big, mean-ass kid. Who taught you to take him down like that?"

Every head in the room turned to look at Jack.

"Should have known," said Gene.

Amy was unusually quiet. When she finally spoke, she said, "Bruce has hurt so many kids, stolen their money, and terrorized 'em. The school did nothing, the adults did nothing, and Sheriff, you knew about him and did nothing. I'm not sorry, not even a little bit."

Gene looked at Amy and with all the sincerity he could muster said, "I know, honey. I deal with a lot worse than him. I have to let them go every day because that's the law. You are not the law."

Gene's secretary walked in with a sheet of paper and handed it to him. Gene sighed and said, "Well, he's not dead. Dislocated knee, broken rib, punctured lung, fractured skull, and other injuries too numerous to mention."

Damn girl, good job, Jack thought but dared not say.

Gene shook his head and said, "I'm sorry, Leon, but this isn't some Black Oak dust up. This is going to be on the news tonight. I can't bury this."

Carla Jo picked up the phone on Gene's desk and dialed a number. "Get Henry to the Lewistown Sheriff's office ASAP," she commanded. Then she looked at Amy and said, "You don't say another word."

"Yeah, that's a good idea," said Gene. "Amy Braxton, you have the right to remain silent...."

Chapter 45

Jack, Gene, Leon, and Henry Ballard, Attorney at Law, sat on the porch at Leon's house.

"I'm not comfortable with him here," said Henry, motioning toward Gene.

"The Carters and the Braxtons were friends long before we were born. That's not about to change," said Leon.

"Yes, but what happens when he takes the stand?" said Henry.

"He tells the truth," said Leon.

"He's right, Leon. This could be a problem. I love Amy to death and today damn near killed me. We need to listen to what the man says. Is there anything I can do to help?" asked Gene.

Henry smiled and said, "Nope, we could never ask you to leak the boy's juvenile record to the press. That would just be wrong."

"I understand," said Gene.

Leon walked Gene to his car. Gene turned to Leon nearly in tears and said, "I am so sorry."

"No, you have been a friend to this family. I will not hold you doin' your job against you. We were born friends, we will die friends," said Leon.

"Thank you, Leon," said Gene.

Leon walked back to the porch. Henry looked at him and said, "Having the sheriff in your pocket works for us."

Leon didn't care for that tone and replied, "He's not in my pocket, he's a family friend that is doing his job, come what may. You would be wise not to forget that."

"Well, I was just...,"

Leon interrupted Henry and said, "You would be wise to respect him and his office."

"My job is to protect your daughter. Are we on the same page or not?" asked Henry

"Yeah, we are," said Leon.

When Amy came home from Granny Patches' house, her daddy and Jack were still sitting on the porch. The jar had already been passed a few times. Amy sat down, looked at her daddy, and said, "Are you mad at me?"

Leon thought for a minute and said, "I was at first. Then I thought back to when your momma and I were datin'. I was sixteen, too. The only difference between me and you is I would have had help hidin' the body."

Amy sat down on her daddy's lap and said, "I'm a little scared. What are they goin' to do to me, Daddy?"

Leon hugged Amy and said, "What can they do to you? You took down a bad guy. You scared the hell out of 'em because you were a little too good at it. You have a whole bunch of good people on your side. Learn from it, but don't worry about it. If all else fails, you and your uncle Jack can overthrow the government."

Jack smiled, raised the jar, and slurred, "I'm good with that."

Carla Jo was on a mission. After she left Sheriff's Carter's office she made a few phone calls and drove to the city. When she arrived at Chez Geraud, she walked in the front door and saw her friend Sarah sitting at the bar, waiting for her.

"Sarah, it's so good to see you again," said Carla Jo as she walked up.

"You too, Carla Jo. This is long over due," said Sarah with a hug and a big smile.

Sarah and Carla Jo sat down at their table and ordered dinner.

"How's everything going?" asked Carla Jo.

"Everything is wonderful. I feel like I'm making a difference. Without you and Doctor Henderson's support, none of this would have been possible," said Sarah.

Carla Jo smiled and said, "I'm glad to hear that. The Doc and I know integrity when we see it."

"Thank you, Carla Jo, that's very kind," said Sarah.

"I know you would never violate ethics and I would certainly never ask you to, but if I could have a few minutes I would like to tell you a story about a girl named Amy."

"Sure, I'm all ears," said Sarah.

The bailiff stood up and announced, "All rise. The Superior Court of the State of Alabama, County of Jackson, Department Three, the Honorable Judge Sarah Crawford presiding, is now in session."

The judge spent most of the hearing trying not to laugh. The image in her head of the five foot nine, one hundred and thirty pound cute blonde sitting in front of her, in the most lovely violet Donna Karan dress, kicking the hell out of the six foot tall, two hundred pound juvenile delinquent was almost more than she could take.

The judge looked at the prosecuting attorney and said, "It says here you are designating Miss Braxton as a lethal weapon?"

"Yes, Your Honor. The physician caring for the victim has issued a statement that the damage inflicted clearly came from a highly trained professional in the area of the martial arts," stated the Prosecuting Attorney.

"Miss Braxton, have you ever received training from a *paid* martial arts or other self-defense professional?" The judge asked, putting the major emphasis on paid.

"No, ma'am," Amy answered.

"Miss Braxton, do you hold any ratings such as a black belt?" asked the judge.

"No, ma'am," Amy answered.

"Counselor, do you have any proof that Miss Braxton is not being forthright or is being dishonest in her answers to my questions?" asked the Judge.

"Well, Your Honor, all you have to do is look at him," said the prosecutor.

"It looks like he got hit by a bus, but that doesn't answer my question," said the judge as muffled laughter erupted in the courtroom.

"No, Your Honor," said the prosecuting attorney.

"I'll be back with my decision," said the judge.

Ten minutes later the judge returned to address the courtroom.

The judge looked out over the courtroom and said, "There is a law in this state called Depraved Indifference. When an individual comes upon a life or death situation and has the ability to render assistance and fails to do so, it is a violation of the law. Miss Braxton came upon such a situation. The victim in this courtroom was holding another student by the throat with his feet off of the ground. It is clear that any reasonable person would see this as a life or death situation. Miss Braxton provided assistance to stop this attack. If this court had any concern, it would be the level of zealousness that Miss Braxton used to render that assistance. Considering the size and strength difference between Miss Braxton and Mr. Clark, that too is understandable. It is this court's decision that Miss Braxton acted within the law and will face no further charges. Case dismissed."

BANG. The gavel slammed into the bench.

Amy and her family walked down the steps of the courthouse more relieved than happy. Carla Jo looked at Amy and said, "Did you learn anything?"

Amy nodded her head, smiled a wicked grin, and said, "Yep, next time get Uncle Jack to help me hide the body."

Carla Jo shook her head and said, "That's not the answer I was looking for."

Chapter 46

*J*udge Crawford called Principal Nolan and asked her to reinstate Amy into school with no penalties. Principal Nolan agreed and Amy returned to school. Andy had kept Amy up-to-date on all of her classes while she was out. Her teachers loved her and they too sent all of her assignments home and made sure she did not fall behind. Some of the parents, however, were not happy with Amy's return. The press reported the incident as an unprovoked attack on an innocent boy.

The students, on the other hand, treated Amy as a conquering hero. When she walked in to weight training, Kelly stood up and began to clap. The other girls all joined in with hugs all around. Amy was grateful for the reception. Then Amy said, "OK ladies, the party is over, the ice cream has melted. Back to work."

Groans were heard all over the weight room. The general was back. Many of the students asked Amy to teach them self-defense skills, but she refused everyone except Kelly.

The cat was out of the bag about Amy and Andy's relationship. They both figured it was time to meet the families. Amy went to meet Andy's mom first. They lived in an apartment in Lewistown. Andy's mom was a nurse who worked for Henderson Medical. Andy's dad had died many years ago. He was an engineer, a weapons designer for Raytheon. He died in a car crash on the way home from work. There were pictures of him in Andy's room. He looked like the adult version of Andy. He was a handsome man. Amy figured that when Andy filled out, he would be, too. Amy started to understand why she saw something familiar in Andy's face. The pain of losing a parent never goes away. But there was more. Much more.

Amy walked around Andy's room. Model rockets lined the walls and three guitars sat on stands.

"You play the guitar?" asked Amy.

"A little bit," said Andy, modestly. "My dad loved to play. He taught me some things and I just kept it up."

"What kind of music do you play?" asked Amy.

"Jonny Cash, a lot of the old country outlaws, and I really like the *Eagles*," said Andy.

"Play me something," asked Amy.

"Do you know 'Tennessee Flat Top Box?'" asked Andy.

"Know it? I love Rosanne Cash," said Amy with a smile.

Andy picked up his dad's old Gibson Dove and struck the first notes. Amy had been in church choir most of her life and she could carry a tune.

Andy played and Amy sang. In the next three minutes and eight seconds, the love they had for each other doubled. Neither could believe the other's talent. Andy's mom Rita watched through the door and started to cry. She had not seen him happy in a long time.

Amy invited Andy and his mom to her house for dinner. It was an event. The entire family showed up. Even Kelly, Gene, and Miss Kitty came. Andy was kind of quiet and Leon didn't know what to make of him. Rita knew who Carla Jo was, but Carla Jo didn't know her. Rita was a little intimidated, but after about two minutes with Carla Jo, Carol, Granny Patches, and Miss Kitty, it was like they were old family friends.

Amy made Andy bring his guitar and after dinner they sat on the front porch playing and singing. Little Franklin Carter would not leave Amy without crying, so he sat on Amy's lap and giggled. Then Andy played as Amy sang "Tennessee Flat Top Box." The family sat and listened, mesmerized. They were pretty good.

Joseph followed Kelly around like a puppy dog. Kelly led him on and Amy didn't care for that. Maybe she would tactfully ask Kelly to back off a bit. Then again, Joseph had his first crush. Hopefully he wouldn't get hurt, but it was all part of growing up. Knowing all of that, she would have to handle it carefully.

Leon studied Andy from across the porch. He was polite, he wasn't a delinquent, his mom was clearly a good woman, and Leon was impressed with his talent. Just the fact that Andy would come to the house and meet him was also a bonus. *OK,* Leon thought to himself, *I'll let this go on.* About that time Jack shouted across the porch, "Damn, Cuz, I reckon you won't have to kill this one."

They all laughed. Leon nodded his head slowly and said, "Yeah, I reckon you're right."

Amy leaned over to Andy and whispered, "They're serious."

Andy had received the blessing of the family. He had no idea what a big deal that was.

As the party wound down, Jack decided to share some concerns he had with Andy's mom. There was word in town about a possible retribution by Bruce's family against Amy. Jack went to see Old Man Clark and was assured that was certainly not the case, but Jack still got a funny vibe and was a little worried. Not for Amy but for Andy and Rita. As he, Leon, and Gene walked Rita to her car, he told her about his concerns. Rita opened her purse, pulled out her 9mm, and said, "It wouldn't be the first time."

They gave her Gene and Tim's direct line as well as every other number they could think of. They were sure Andy was OK as long as he was with Amy. Every sane person in the four-county area knew better than to screw with a Braxton, but they didn't want to take any chances.

Amy's antenna was also up. The following Monday, Bruce was making his way through the hall on crutches when Amy stopped him to ask how he was. He couldn't even look her in the eye. Amy got up on her tiptoes and whispered in his ear, "You or your family mess up one hair on Andy's head and I will bring hell to earth."

As pretty as she was, she could be scary. She had that look her momma had when she got angry. It was that I'm-ready-to-die-right-here-right-now-just-to-make-a-point look in her eyes. She made her point.

Chapter 47

The following Saturday was Francois day. Amy went on and on to Carla Jo about Andy and how smart and funny he was, how good he was to her, and so on. Carla Jo just sat and listened, smiling. She tried to remember the first time she was in love. It brought back some memories. Later, when they got back to Carla Jo's house, she sat Amy down in the kitchen.

"I have something for you," said Carla Jo.

"What?" asked Amy.

Carla Jo laid the little, round, plastic container in front of her.

"What's this?" asked Amy.

"Birth control pills," said Carla Jo.

"We're not having sex," said Amy.

"Good, that's the mature, responsible decision. Take them, anyway," said Carla Jo.

"But we are not havin' sex," said Amy again.

"OK. I heard you the first time. Thousands of well-meaning and responsible teenage girls get pregnant every year. It doesn't make them stupid or bad., but it does make them unprepared," said Carla Jo with a serious look.

"We haven't even talked about it," said Amy.

"And you won't. If you do have sex, most likely it will not be a planned decision. Nature has a way of taking common sense out of that decision. I don't ask you for much, honey, but I'm asking you to do this. If you get pregnant, your whole life will be turned upside down and so will Andy's. You have choices right now. A baby will take most of those away. Please, for me, do this," said Carla Jo.

"The doctors said I probably won't be able to have kids," said Amy with a little sadness.

"No, Amy, they said they didn't know. Please," said Carla Jo.

"OK, I'll do it for you," said Amy with a little smile.

"Thank you," said a relieved Carla Jo. She explained to Amy how they worked and what the different colors meant. Then she said, "Jack wants to see you. He's in the garage."

Amy walked out to the garage. "Hi, honey, you ready to do some work?" said Jack.

"Sure, whatcha got?" said Amy with a smile.

Amy followed Jack over to the bench. He smiled and said, "Long guns."

Laid out on the bench were an AK-47, an AR-15, an M-14, an HK33, an M40A1, a fully automatic specially modified Remington 870, and an Ithaca 37. "So I suppose I'll be cleaning all of these. I just got my nails done," said Amy with a sigh.

"Oh no, Cinderella, you just got your nails done?" Jack said, mocking her.

Amy rolled her eyes.

"We'll do this a little different than we did handguns. We'll just do one at a time. Then you can shoot on the same day. I want you to get the feel for these like we did with handguns, and then we will work on tactics." said Jack.

Amy looked at the bench and asked, "What's first?"

Jack said, "Pick one."

Amy looked at them again and said, "Which is your favorite?"

"It depends on where you're at and what you're doin'. But I guess if I had to choose a good all-around combat rifle, it would be this one," Jack said as he reached over and picked up the AK-47. "The Russians have made a lot of junk over the years, but this one was done right. Throw it in the mud, kick it down a dirt road, and you can still pick it up and start shootin'. I wouldn't want to use it as a sniper rifle, but anything inside two hundred yards in a hostile enviroment? It's hard to beat."

Amy picked it up, examined it a little, and said "OK, we'll start with that."

Over the next several months Amy would come by, pick a rifle, and familiarize herself with it. Jack set up targets out behind the house with different scenarios in mind and he always used them first to keep in practice. One Saturday afternoon Amy was out back practicing when she lost track of time. Andy's mom pulled up in the driveway and dropped him off. He could hear the gunfire coming from behind the house and he walked around to the back. He watched Amy perform a multiple target exercise with the AK-47. Awestruck, he just stood there and watched her operate. She was smooth, fast, and deadly accurate. On the run she reached into her web gear, grabbed a new clip, swapped them out, and kept firing; always moving, always attacking. She emptied the last clip and called, "I'M OUT."

Jack was impressed. All he could think to say was, "nice job, honey."

Amy stopped and turned around. "Hi, sweety," she said, smiling big. "What are you doing here?"

Holding up his watch, Andy pointed to it and said, "You said we were going out to eat at six. It's six."

She walked up to him, gave him a kiss, and said, "I'm so sorry. I got busy and lost track of time. Come on in the garage. I have to clean this and take a shower, and then we'll go."

Andy stood there amazed as he watched her fieldstrip and clean the AK, then she put it back together and took it in the house. She walked back out the front door and said, "I'm gonna take a shower here and steal some of my aunt's clothes. Keep him company, Uncle Jack."

"Ok, honey," Jack yelled back. "Hello, young man, how are you?"

"Right now, a little freaked out. She knows what she's doing," said Andy.

"Yeah, she's learnin'."

"Are you guys, like, militia or something?" asked Andy.

"No, I was in Special Forces in Vietnam. She and I have always been pretty close. Some people would take their niece fishing, I teach mine combat tactics. She enjoys it and I enjoy it. It's just what we do," Jack explained.

"Wow, I didn't know this about her."

"It's not a problem, is it?" Jack asked.

"Well, um...," Andy hesitated.

"Good, I have known her since she was a baby. I have never seen her in love with anyone like she is in love with you. She's a very special girl. You have done well."

"She can have anyone she wants," said Andy. "I still don't get why she likes me."

"Oh, I have a pretty good idea. You like her as a person and you respect her. Keep it up and you could grow old with her. Stop respecting her and you'll lose her. It's that simple."

Amy walked into the room just then and Andy looked at her.

"You are beautiful," said Andy, shaking his head with a small bit of sadness that Amy didn't pick up on.

"You make me that way," said Amy.

"Jesus, give it a rest," said Jack

Amy laughed, hugged her uncle Jack, gave him a kiss, and left.

As they took their seats at the restaurant,. Amy could see that there was clearly something bothering him.

"What's wrong?" she asked.

"I don't like guns," said Andy with a sad look on his face.

Amy shrugged her shoulders and said, "Well, I guess that means you won't be hunting with my family in the fall."

Andy looked at her and said, "It's more than that. I don't want you around them, either."

Amy shifted in her seat uncomfortably and said, "You knew I was a hunter when you met me."

"I know, but I never had to see it. After what I saw today, the violence, I can't take that," Andy said.

"So what are you sayin'?" said Amy, looking a little confused.

"I would never ask you to give up what you love. I love you too much for that, but I'm sorry, Amy. I can't be with you."

"What do you mean?" asked Amy, beginning to panic.

"I mean I'm sorry, it's over. I'll walk home," said Andy. He got up and left. Amy still wasn't sure what just happened, but it felt like someone punched her in the gut.

She drove back to her uncle Jack's playing over in her mind everything thing that had happened. She parked her truck, walked up to the front porch, and knocked on the door. Carla Jo opened it and she could see on her face that something was wrong.

"Honey, are you OK?" Carla Jo asked.

Amy walked in and sat down on the couch. She looked up at Carla Jo and with tears streaming down her face said," Andy broke up with me."

Jack jumped up and growled, "I'll go talk to him."

"You will not. SIT," barked Carla Jo, the only person in the world that could actually make Jack sit.

Chapter 48

K elly spent the entire Sunday with Amy bouncing around Black Oak between Amy's house, Carla Jo's, and Ed Gwinn's and later they took turns pounding the hell out of Amy's heavy bag in the barn. Jack pulled out his handguns and let Amy do some tactical work. Jack even worked with Kelly a little bit and let her get the feel for some weapons. As the day went on, Amy must have eaten a dozen Moon Pies, downed a six-pack of Dr. Pepper, and listened to "Tennessee Flat Top Box" more times than she could count. Amy ended the day tired and cried out with a bellyache. She felt a little better.

The next day, Kelly slid her books into the cubbyhole in her locker. She could hear Candice Peterson's voice and the irritating cackle of the little cheerleader cabal about twenty feet away.

"Well, of course he broke up with her, she's a queer," Candice said, laughing.

"SHUT UP, CANDICE!" Kelly shouted across the hall, "SHUT YOUR LYIN' MOUTH BEFORE I SHUT IT FOR YOU!"

A couple of the girls from the swim team wandered over to stand by Kelly.

Candice laughed and said, "Careful Kelly, your girlfriend isn't here to protect you."

"Why you little bitch," Kelly growled. "WELCOME TO THE KELLY COOK SCHOOL OF ASS KICKIN'. CLASS IS IN SESSION!'"

Kelly was headed for Candice when she suddenly felt someone grab her and turn her gently away. Amy whispered in her ear, "Shh, it's ok. Let it go. She's not worth it." Amy was having a difficult time holding Kelly. She was angry and a little stronger than she looked.

"Well, I guess your girlfriend is here to protect you," said Candice, who felt empowered to run her mouth around Amy. One of the conditions of Amy's reinstatement to school was that she could never strike another student. Candice knew that.

Amy looked over her shoulder at Candice and said, "You got five seconds to move your ass and then I'm letting her go. One Mississippi, two Mississippi, three Mississippi...,"

Candice was gone.

"Calm down," said Amy.

"GRRRR, I hate that bitch," Kelly said.

"I think she's figured that out."

Kelly took a couple of deep breaths, turned to look at Amy, and asked, "How are you?"

They started walking toward the lunchroom and Amy said, "I'm OK. It was hard being with him in class this morning. I fought off a few tears and didn't concentrate very well."

"I know how you feel, it sucks, but what about me, Amy? I had your wedding planned. I even had my maid of honor dress picked out. I had it planned all the way to the end of the night when I teach your little brother about the ways of a woman."

Amy shook her head and started to laugh. Kelly could always make her laugh. "Kelly, please take it easy around my brother. He hasn't woken up in a clean set of bed sheets since the night of that party. You got him playing with himself like a little monkey."

Kelly laughed and said, "Really?"

"Yeah," said Amy.

"EEEWW," said Kelly.

"I know," said Amy.

Amy kept a pretty busy schedule and didn't leave herself much time to think about him. Eventually they started to exchanged casual greetings in the hall. That moved on to a few conversations and eventually they were casual friends. Amy didn't know that Andy attended all of her swim meets, or that he kept a scrapbook with all of her newspaper clippings and even took the time to learn more of her favorite songs on his guitar. He would play "Tennessee Flat Top Box" and imagine her singing it. He even spent a lot of time talking to his therapist about his hatred of guns. Andy had a therapist. He needed one.

Carla Jo called Rita into her office. Rita was a little panicked. She sat down in front of Carla Jo and said, "Look, I'm sorry my son broke up with your niece, but I really need this job. No one else will hire an ex-con. Please, Mrs. Brown, don't fire me."

Carla Jo sat back in her chair, held up her hands, and said, "Whoa, take it easy, Rita. I'm not going to fire you. Kids are kids and my name is Carla Jo."

"Oh, thank God," said Rita under her breath. She was nearly in tears.

Carla Jo got up and walked around the desk to sit beside Rita. She put her hand on top of Rita's, gave it a small squeeze, and said, "Are you OK?"

"Better now. I just knew we would have to move again. It's been so hard on Andy. Then this thing with him and Amy...he's heartbroken. He plays that same song in his room over and over," said Rita.

"I can tell you what song it is. She walks around humming it or singing it under her breath. Amy is the same way. She puts on a good act, but she still thinks about him. Maybe someday they'll work it out," said Carla Jo.

Rita nodded. After a moment she said, "Carla Jo, why am I here?""Oh, sorry. My nursing supervisor is leaving. I made a list of five possible candidates based on performance and I had her choose her replacement. She chose you. Do you want it?"

"Really? Wow. What's the job? What would I do?" asked Rita.

"You watch over the nurses. You hire them, fire them, write their evaluations, and keep them on schedule. In-home care is most critical. There's some homework, you know, paperwork. Junie has agreed to stick around and train you until you are up to speed. Junie puts in twelve-hour days, but she is well compensated. She made over six figures last year with bonuses and profit sharing. You would be considered executive management with operational input, better benefits, and a company car. I want you to take a few days and think about it. I have very few rules and one of those is that I don't allow employees to go backward. If you can't handle it, I'll have to let you go," said Carla Jo.

"I'm honored, and I will think about it. Thank you," said Rita.

"You earned the opportunity. Did you eat lunch yet?" asked Carla Jo.

"No, but I bring my lunch," said Rita.

"This should have been a lunch meeting. Come on, let's go," said Carla Jo with a smile.

"I can't, I have a lot of work this afternoon. I'm sorry," said Rita.

Carla Jo picked up the phone and said, "Junie, I need coverage for Rita this afternoon." Carla Jo looked at Rita, smiled, and said, "you are suddenly free for lunch." Carla Jo was curious and when she was curious, she got answers.

They sat down at the restaurant and ordered. After a few minutes, Carla Jo decided to ask her a question. She wasn't sure how to approach it, however, so she just said, "What's with Andy's fear of guns?"

"He's not afraid of them, he hates them," said Rita.

"Do you mind if I ask why?" said Carla Jo.

"It's a long story," said Rita.

"We have all afternoon," said Carla Jo, resting her chin on her hand.

Rita hesitated, and then said, "I've never shared it with anyone around here. I need to ask you to keep it to yourself."

"I'm not a gossip, your secrets are safe."

OK, well, Andy's dad was a very smart and wonderful man. I am a nurse, he was an engineer, and we had this wonderful life. When he died, he left us very well off. I met another man a few years later who said the right things and did the right things and I married him. Not too long after that, I caught him draining our bank accounts. I confronted him and he got violent. I got my gun, but I wasn't ready to shoot him. We struggled, the gun went off, and I was shot. Andy found me on the floor. My new husband was a retired police officer so he had friends on the force. The police said it was an accident. They didn't even investigate. He emptied our bank accounts while I was in the hospital and one day I got a call from a neighbor saying he was packing all of our things into a moving van. He was stealing everything we owned. I capped my own IV, took a taxi home, and snuck in the back door. He saw me and threatened to hurt Andy. Long story short, I took a shotgun and killed him. Andy witnessed that, too. I got seven years for Manslaughter and served thirty months. When I got out, Andy was in foster care and he was not being treated very well. I had no money so I had to do some things I wasn't too proud of. I needed money for a lawyer to get him out of the system. Then I needed to get us out of there so I started searching for a job. I'm an ex-con, though, so I couldn't get hired at a pancake house. Henderson Medical was one of the last calls I made and Junie hired me. Then we moved here, end of story."

Carla Jo reached across the table, took her hand, and said, "YOU are a HELL of a woman and if you EVER need a friend, I am here."

Chapter 49

𝓘t was the first day of summer vacation and Amy didn't feel like getting up. The year had physically and emotionally worn her out. She turned on some music. As if she wasn't feeling melancholy enough, Rick Jackson's *Country Hall of Fame* radio show was featuring crying, loving, and leaving songs. She sang along with "Blue Moon With Heartache." She smiled to herself. Rosanne Cash always knew how she was feeling. She lay in her bed and thought about where she had been and where she was going.

Jack took the time to educate her on the McCutcheon Braxton feud. It kind of scared her a little when she figured out what kind of dangerous game she was playing with those people.

Karen Setzer, the girl who beat Amy in the regionals, was right. The state championship belonged to Amy. Unfortunately, her team did not fare as well. They finished third. Amy qualified for the AAU Nationals, won her heat race, and finished fourth in the final for the 500-yard freestyle. She finished third in the 200-yard freestyle and failed to qualify for the 100. Those darn starts were the bane of her sprints. Like her coach told her, those finishes in the AAU Nationals weren't bad for a swimmer with less than two years experience. College coaches from all over the nation began to call her and write letters. Amy had become a hot property to some of the best college swimming programs in the country. She was eyeing the ones with the best medical schools.

Amy didn't figure she would see Andy at all that summer. Andy was accepted to a twelve-week advanced math and physics camp at the University of Alabama. That was good. It had been getting easier to see him every day at school but it still wasn't fun. She absent-mindedly shook her head. It didn't matter. She saw him every night in her dreams. The nameless, faceless boy that held her so tight now had a name and a face. Kelly hinted at her about a couple of guys Amy might like. *Maybe*, she thought. She would wait and see.

Her summer job was a little different that year. Her new supervisor was Andy's mom. Carla Jo assured her that it would not be an issue. Amy didn't think it would be; she loved Andy's mom.

Rolling out of bed and dropping to the floor, Amy started to do push-ups. Suddenly she stopped and thought, *screw it, I'm gonna call Kelly and go to the river*. She packed a small cooler. Joseph asked her where she was going and she told him. He wasn't real interested until he found out Kelly was going, and Kelly in a bikini? Oh yeah, he wanted to go. Amy didn't really want to take him, but she rarely denied him anything.

After three days of being lazy and not working out, Amy couldn't stand it anymore. She went to her uncle Jack's little block house and did her thing. That was Amy's summer. Work, work out, hang out with Kelly, fishing with her daddy and Joseph, and of course, spending some quality time with Uncle Jack and Carla Jo.

Amy actually took two vacations that summer. The first vacation was with Carla Jo to New York City. They saw plays, concerts, visited fabulous restaurants, and enjoyed some of the best shopping in the world. The second unexpected one was with her uncle Jack. Jack showed up one day with his truck packed with camping gear, weapons, and enough supplies for seven days.

They crossed over the North Carolina state line and the last actual city she remembered seeing was Asheville. They stopped at a rural truck stop where Jack met a man in a camouflaged 4WD. They followed him into the Smoky Mountains for what seemed like hours until they crested a hill and looked out over a small valley. She could see a campsite in the distance. The curiosity got the best of her and she said, "What's this, Uncle Jack?"

"In southern slang, this is your cotillion," said Jack.

"What?" asked Amy, still puzzled.

It was another half hour to get down to the campsite. Jack explained that they were going to meet the Southern Patriots Militia group. It was made up of ex-military and former law enforcement officers dedicated to one thing: the preservation of the Constitution of the United States. He went on to talk about Waco and Ruby Ridge and the abuses of government power; how and why dozens of groups like this had sprang up all over the United States.

"So what do they do here?" asked Amy.

"Seven days of war games," aaid Jack.

"Cool," aaid Amy with a smile.

They stopped the truck. Jack looked at her and said, "I am not a member of this group, I am an instructor. Here, they call me Hatchet. I need you to call me that, too. We don't have names, only nicknames, and I'm sure they will give you one. One more thing and this is the most important thing: this place does not exist and you were never here, got it?"

"Yes, sir, Hatchet," said Amy.

Jack and Amy put up their tent and put their things away. Later that night a large group of men sat around a campfire telling stories of wars fought long ago. One man kept looking at Amy. It was making her uncomfortable. They called him Grits. Amy whispered to her uncle Jack how she was feeling and Jack got up to talk to him. Jack came back, sat down, and said, "He thinks he knows you from somewhere."

Suddenly Grits spoke up, "I know who you are, you're the Lewistown Shark. My daughter swims. I saw you at nationals."

Jack looked at him and said, "She can't confirm or deny that."

Grits smiled and said, "Boys, don't worry about her keeping up with us, worry about keeping up with her."

The man they called Skipper, who was the unit Commander, said, "Shark? I like that. Your name is Shark." Amy liked it, too.

Amy had a blast. Seven days of heavy and light weapons, tactics, classes on maps and navigation, guerilla warfare, blowing stuff up, booby traps, ambushing convoys, and all other applications of controlled violence. She impressed the hell out of them to the point that they invited her back the following year and gave her a unit patch. She would not be back. It would be Amy's last carefree summer as a young woman. The next time she played those games, it would be for real.

.

Chapter 50

$\mathcal{B}$asketball Coach Carl Traicoff taught Amy's favorite class. He called it Current Events and Life. Coach was a Macedonian immigrant who came to America with his wife and kids when he was twenty-eight. Occasionally, when he got excited or upset, he would lapse into his native language. The kids all thought it was funny, but they would have blushed if they knew what he was saying. He wasn't the best basketball coach in the state, but he regularly turned out fine, well-adjusted young men.

The first half hour of his class, the kids watched *Fox and Friends* on TV. They were required to take notes and then discuss whatever the issue of the day was. Amy was taking notes on an interview of the Spanish Harlem Mona Lisa. *How pretty*, she thought. The reporters came back on after a commercial and Steve Doocy sat with a couple of other reporters on a couch. Amy thought about how much he looked like Andy. Then she noticed that they all had a concerned look on their face. The date was September 11, 2001.

A look of horror spread across Amy's face as she saw the tower in which she and Carla Jo had lunch in just a few short months before. Smoke and flames leapt from the north tower right under the windows to the World restaurant. Coach never missed a teaching moment. He asked if anyone had actually been to the towers. Amy raised her hand and she was the only one.

"Give us your impressions on what you see," said the coach.

Amy started to speak. The class was mesmerized as Amy described the actual size and scope of what had just happened. Tens of thousands of people worked there. She described what was under the buildings, the mall as big as anything in the city, the train station beneath the building, and any other comparison she could think of to relate the actual size of what had happened. She started to say something else when the second plane hit. The coach started speaking in Macedonian and Amy said, "We are at war."

The class sat stunned as the buildings fell. Amy almost began to cry. Something stopped her. She was angry.

Over the next couple of months, Amy learned all she could about Muslim extremists. She wanted to know the why. As a Christian she couldn't imagine attacking another nation much less civilians in the name of her God unless it was in self-defense. She studied Afghanistan and became obsessed with Ahmad Shah Mas'ud, also known as the Lion of Panjshir.

She read everything she could get her hands on about Mas'ud and depending on the author, he was either an American-installed warlord or a heroic freedom fighter. The fact that the same people that attacked the United States murdered him two days before 9/11 gave Amy the answer she needed. She couldn't remember where she read it, but the phrase "A man is known by his enemies" was something that rang true to her.

Meanwhile, the world was busy laying itself at Amy's feet, but she was disinterested. The coach of the Stanford University swim team called Leon and told him there was a scholarship for her if she wanted it. The coach joked that as long as she didn't drown in the pool at nationals, it was hers. Leon was so proud. His daughter was going to be a doctor. Amy, however, had other ideas. Her future was decided on a cold, rainy day as she was standing along Main Street in Lewistown.

The family was somber as they climbed into Leon's truck. They drove to the Bluebird Café and parked next to Jack and Carla Jo. Then they all stood by the street as the parade went by. There were no floats, clowns, or bands, just one horse pulling a cart. On the cart was the flag-draped coffin of Sergeant Martin Colton. He was a former teammate of Kerry's. It was then that Amy realized that she had to help. She didn't know how, but she would help. She had to get in the war.

The following Monday at school, Amy went into Principal Nolan's office.

"Hi Amy, what can I do for you?" said Principal Nolan.

"What are the rules on graduating mid-term?" Amy asked.

"Well, I'm not a big supporter of it, but it's allowed for students that have enough credits and are starting class at a university in the spring or are joining the military. Why?" asked Principal Nolan.

"Just curious, thanks," said Amy.

That conversation made Principal Nolan very uncomfortable. She needed to call Leon.

Amy went that evening to talk to her uncle Jack.

"Uncle Jack, what is the military like?" Amy asked.

"Well, it usually just like any other job unless you're fighting a war, and then it's hell. It's not like what we do or, for that matter, even what we were doing in North Carolina with the Militia. That's Disneyland in comparison. What's goin' on now, this war they're fighting...soldiers without uniforms? That's a holy war, that's really some rough stuff," said Jack, shaking his head.

Amy nodded and just stared at him. It suddenly occurred to Jack where she was going with this. "NO, NO, NO, HELL, NO! Amy Lynn, don't even think about it. No, you are going to Stanford and you are going to be a doctor." Jack looked at her and she still didn't say anything. Jack walked to the door and yelled into the house, "CARLA JO, COME OUT HERE, PLEASE. WE HAVE A PROBLEM."

Carla Jo walked into the garage and Jack said, "Tell her, Carla Jo, tell her she's going to Stanford and she's not going to enlist in the military."

"Is this true? Are you thinking about enlisting?" Carla Jo asked.

"They attacked our country, I want to help," said Amy.

"You want to help, get your ass to Stanford and be a doctor. That's how you can help. Then go in the military if you want. But enlisting? Hell, no. Tell her, Carla Jo," demanded Jack.

"Honey," Carla Jo started, and then stopped and said, "You've already made up your mind, haven't you?"

Amy nodded.

"Oh shit," Jack said under his breath.

Carla Jo went into the house, dug through some files, and pulled out a bank statement. She would wait a couple of hours before seeing Leon. She knew there were going to be fireworks on the hill. After speaking with her aunt and uncle, Amy made her way back home and into the kitchen. Her daddy was sitting at the table, flipping through some papers.

"Hi, Daddy," Amy said, giving him a kiss.

"Hi, honey. I got a phone call today from Principal Nolan. She said you were asking her about graduating mid-term?" he asked, a little more than curious.

"Yeah," said Amy.

"Why?" asked Leon.

"I want to enlist in the military, help fight the war," said Amy.

Leon looked at her, trying to process what he had just heard. He was so shocked that he couldn't even yell.

"Have you lost your mind? Amy, it's war. Did you see the box with the flag on it? That's what war is. Oh sweet Jesus, honey, please, no," said Leon, pleading.

"I can go to college when I get out. It's just something I need to do."

"Amy, it's Stanford. Tens of thousands of dollars of free education and college-level sports. My God, Amy, you can't do this."

"I'm sorry Daddy," Amy said.

In the end, Leon did lose it and began to yell. The decision upset him so much that somewhere in the middle of his rant, he stopped making sense. Amy sat stoically and listened until he was done.

"Are you finished?" she asked, "because I have homework to do."

Shaking his head, Leon went into the kitchen and grabbed a full mason jar from the top shelf. Then he went and sat out on the front porch. Twenty minutes later Carla Jo pulled up in front of the house. Leon didn't even acknowledge her as she sat down next to him.

"I guess she told you?" said Carla Jo.

Leon kept looking off in the distance. Then she said, "Jack tried to talk her out of it. He is doing the same thing you're doing; sitting on the front porch and trying to figure out where he went wrong."

"He taught her all of that military bullshit, that's where he went wrong," said Leon angrily.

"No, I don't think so. She was on her way to college before the attack. We were there this summer. She was at the World Trade Center. We had lunch at the top of the north tower. She gets the magnitude of what happened. It's not just some TV show to her. She's a good person and a good American. She just wants to help. Besides, you made her that way," said Carla Jo.

"They're not going to hold a scholarship for her. What about college? What about her dream of being a doctor? It's all gone," Leon said, grumbling.

"Not necessarily," said Carla Jo, handing Leon the bank statement. "When Katherine died, I set up trust funds for the kids. Joseph has his own account with an identical amount. She can go anyplace she wants for anything she wants. That will not be an issue."

Leon unfolded the piece of paper and saw the number at the bottom of the page: $257,422.00.

"Shit," Leon said under his breath. "Still, all the money in the world won't stop a bullet. What if they kill her, Carla Jo? What if she doesn't come home? You got another piece of paper for that?"

"She's eighteen years old. She's going into the military and there's not a damn thing any of us can do about it. Right now I think she is wondering why her daddy can't support her. A little girl's daddy is everything to her. It's something to think about," Carla Jo said as she got up, gave Leon a hug, and left.

For two days Leon wouldn't speak to Amy. He wouldn't even look at her. Carol watched from a distance. Mothering Joseph was something nobody had a problem with, but when it came to Amy, she kept her opinions to herself. Finally, she had enough. While working on his boat down by the barn, Leon looked up and Carol was standing there. She wasn't happy.

"The silent treatment, Leon, really? What kind of bullshit is that?" she said.

"What are you talkin' abo...," Leon started to say, but Carol interrupted.

"I'm talking about Amy. I have sat back and watched that girl grow up. I have said nothing. YOU allowed Jack to teach her those things, YOU sat back and let Carla Jo teach her the Carla Jo version of what it means to be a woman. YOU did that. Now you want to act hurt because of the decisions she makes?"

Leon sat down on the fender of the boat trailer, looked up at Carol, and said, "This isn't really any of your business."

With her hands on her hips and with an angry tone to her voice, Carol shot back, "Well, I'm makin' it my business. You march your ass up to that house and you make things right, and I mean right now. I don't care how you do it, but you need to get it done."

Leon started to say something, but Carol was in no mood to hear it. "NOW, LEON," she demanded.

Turning to walk away, Carol stopped, thought for a second, and went back. "And another thing. If you ever again tell me that things that go on under my roof are none of my business, you can find yourself another wife."

That comment got his attention. He worked on the boat for another hour or so, thinking about what he was going to say.

After knocking gently on Amy's door, Leon walked in. She was lying on the floor of her room reading. When she saw him she got up and sat on the edge of her bed. Leon sat down next to her and said, "Take Uncle Jack to the recruiters with you to be sure you get what you want. Whatever you do, be careful and come back home. Honey, I can't lose another child. It would kill me."

Amy smiled and said, "Thank you, Daddy. I promise I'll be careful."

Chapter 51

Principal Nolan sat stunned as Amy informed her of her decision to leave school and enlist. As she went through the task of informing people, she began to understand how many people she would be affecting. Her family, friends, swim team, teachers, and coaches. The number of people that didn't support her also bothered Amy. Nobody stepped up and said, "I'm proud of you" or "Good luck," nothing. It was always, "You're throwing away Stanford?" or "Why would you do something foolish like that?" That was, everyone except for one person, Coach Traicoff.

She had just left an all but sobbing Coach Hixon when Coach Traicoff called her into his office.

"Sit, Amy, sit," the coach said as he motioned her to a chair and shut the door. "You join military, no?"

"Yes, sir," she replied.

"Good girl. I grow up behind Iron Curtain. No freedom, no choices; it even seemed there were no colors. Everything was gray. Here there is freedom, life, love, and happiness. You volunteer to protect it. Makes you very special."

"Thanks, Coach, I needed to hear that. Everyone else thinks I'm crazy," said Amy.

The coach got up, walked around his desk, sat in the chair across from her, and said, "You don't worry about them. They are sheep. You are sheep dog. The sheep never like the sheep dog until the wolf comes."

"Thanks, Coach."

"No, I thank you. When I was a boy, the Nazis on the Syrmian Front killed my papa. He died trying to free his nation. These Muslims are much like the Nazis. You study history?" he asked.

"Yes, sir. I have been reading about Afghanistan. Mostly books about the battles between the Taliban and the Northern Alliance. I'm learning about the Lion of Panjshir," she explained.

The coach smiled and said, "Yes, Ma'sud, a great freedom fighter. You are smart, Amy, you study the ways of your adversary."

Amy smiled and said, "Yes, sir. I thought it was a good idea."

"Not good Amy, great, great idea. I have experience with these Muslims. Not all bad people, just people from a very old culture. Many still live in the sixth century. Very different values than yours. Learn their laws and values. It will be disturbing to you, but it will help you survive," the coach said.

"Thanks, Coach, but they don't let women fight and I may not even go to Afghanistan," she said.

"Maybe, maybe not; just be ready. If you do go, understand that from the moment you step into that godforsaken country until you leave, you are at war. Treat it that way always. You go now, I will pray for you," Coach said as grabbed her face with his hands and kissed her on the forehead.

Wow, he's the only one in this school that seems to get it, Amy thought after walking out of his office. Coach Traicoff understood it better than anyone. A daring escape from behind the Iron Curtain and six years in the French Foreign Legion will do that for you.

That afternoon, Amy went to the recruiting office and took her ASVAB test. Her Armed Forces qualification test results put her in category 1 with a score of 93 out of a possible 99. When Amy and her uncle Jack went to visit the recruiters, the recruiters saw her test scores and nearly wet themselves. They offered her the world. In the end she chose the navy; not because her uncle Jack was in the navy, but because they offered her corpsman's "A" school and an advanced "C" school ("A" school is general training and "C" school is training in specific skills) as well as accelerated advancement.

It all happened so fast. She graduated unceremoniously with Mrs. Nolan's signature, filled out her paperwork, got her physical, and took her oath. There were sad visits with everyone she could think of and tearful goodbyes. The worst was Bubba. He was old and sick. She owed him her life and she knew she would never see him again. At 4 a.m. on January 3rd a black sedan with government plates stopped at her house. She got in and she was gone. A life force had left String Hill Road.

Chapter 52

$\mathcal{A}$my boarded the plane for the flight to Great Lakes Naval Training center. She discovered that there were indeed little seats in the back of the plane. Uncle Jack warned her that she would feel a little homesick and as the plane climbed to altitude, she had already begun to feel it. When the plane landed she found the meeting place for the new recruits. As they were herded toward the buses she stepped outside and felt the artic air. *OH MY GOD*, she thought. *This is cold.* She sat down on the bus next to another young woman.

"Hi, my name's Amy," she said, extending her hand. The other girl started to say something when the driver turned around and shouted, "DID ANYONE TELL YOU TO TALK? SHUT YOUR MOUTHS. WHEN WE WANT YOU TO TALK, WE WILL TELL YOU TO TALK."

Here we go, thought Amy.

Over the next nine weeks she learned all about the navy. She did as her uncle Jack instructed and kept a low profile, although her company commanders did spot her ASVAB score and made her company yeoman (administrative work). Amy was a natural leader through her deeds, not her words. She was clearly physically formidable. She had grown to five foot ten and wore a stoic iron facade, but she was kind to those that struggled.

A lot of her training was hurry up and wait: go here, stand in line and wait, go there, stand in line and wait. Then there was the fun stuff. She enjoyed damage control and shipboard firefighting school. They actually went in a burning mock-up of a ship and had to put out the fire. As the old chief put it, "If your ship catches on fire, you can't swim home."

Then there was the swim test. She swam the entire length of the pool and back underwater. The Petty Officer that ran the class was a SEAL. He smiled at Amy and asked, "State champ?"

Amy smiled back and said, "Nationals."

"Excellent," said the instructor.

There was lots of marching; hours and hours spent on the grinder, marching. She didn't understand the need for any of that, but she did it to the best of her ability.

She only brought attention to herself twice: once bad and once good. They had a firearms training class using what Amy thought were .45 Cal. 1911s, but they were copies that shot .22s. The recruits were all instructed to shoot body mass. Amy put one in the center of the chest and used the rest to draw a smiley face on the silhouette. The instructor came by and said, "Cute, Braxton. Enjoy your marching party for not following orders."

She enjoyed the marching party. It consisted of intense physical exercise run by company commanders who were clearly not happy to have that duty. It was used as punishment for assorted infractions of the rules. Most of the time she felt like a caged tiger. This wasn't near the physical regiment she put herself through for competitive swimming. She couldn't wait to get out of there and find a place to workout. She always got up a little early and did her push-ups and sit-ups, but she missed weight training.

The second time she brought attention to herself was during the final physical fitness test. Her bunkmate Dara was a little chubby and always finished last in PT training. In order to get out of boot camp there was a timed two-and-a-half mile run around a quarter-mile track. Amy blasted through it barely winded, but as she walked back she saw Dara struggling. Amy wasn't the only former high school athlete in her company. She rounded up a half dozen other girls and together they surrounded Dara. They were not allowed to touch her, but they cheered and called cadence. They did everything they could do to get her over the finish line. She made it but just barely. The company commanders beamed with pride because they had achieved their goal: they had built a team of good shipmates.

Her daddy, Carol, Jack, and Carla Jo all showed up for her graduation. The navy band, speeches, and pomp and circumstance made Leon feel proud and he began to doubt what his daughter had done a little less. When they were finally dismissed to greet their families there were hugs and kisses all around. Carla Jo looked at Amy and said, "Jean Paul would have a hissy fit if he saw your hair."

Amy's daddy hugged her and said, "I am very proud of you."

Jack gave Amy a big bear hug and said, "Welcome aboard, shipmate." Then he reached in his pocket and handed her something. He said, "I think he would have wanted you to have this."

It was Bubba's tag. It was bent a little and scratched up with his name, Bubba Brown, and address. Amy hugged her Uncle Jack and started to cry. Jack would have too, but he was already cried out. Amy had her first and only lucky charm.

New recruits were granted a week of leave after boot camp so she went back home. It felt strange to Amy. It was home but it wasn't; not anymore. At the end of the week she flew back to Great Lakes and got her room assignment and her school schedule. It didn't start for a few weeks, so she ended up answering phones and working the front desk at the BOQ, or Base Officers' Quarters. She had to learn to politely fend off the advances of the more flirtatious officers. It was like high school except that these men, and sometimes women, could be drunk and a little more aggressive. She would learn that sexual harassment was a daily event and the quicker she dealt with it effectively without starting trouble, the better off she would be. She called Carla Jo for advice and Carla Jo gave her some effective tools to use.

Her corpsman "A" school finally started and she did well. Working for Carla Jo had given her an advantage. Carla Jo always placed Amy with her most competent and educated nurses, and she quickly learned there were three ways to do things: the wrong way, the right way, and the navy way. They wanted everything done the navy way.

Amy hated the weather because it was so cold. Fortunately, most things were inside. They had an awesome gym and weight room. There were aerobics classes, a boxing gym with heavy bags, an Olympic-sized pool, clubs, and everything she needed to entertain herself. She didn't socialize much. Mostly she hung out at the gym or at the library, studying. Of course, they had church services every Sunday morning. It was non-denominational and not what she was used to, but she still got to sing and worship. Her goal was to finish close to or at the top of her class so she could get her choice of the next duty assignment. The navy guaranteed her a "C" school but not necessarily any one she wanted. She wanted the surgical technology "C" school. She finished second in her class and got it.

Amy packed her things and was off to Balboa Naval Hospital in San Diego. While walking through O'Hare International Airport in her dress blues, she stood tall and felt a sense of pride. It was three hours until her flight and she had some time to kill. Amy sat at a restaurant bar and ordered a bacon cheeseburger and a Dr. Pepper. Older men all wanted to shake her hand and talk about their past military service. It didn't hurt that she was drop dead gorgeous, but they weren't hitting on her, they were talking about their pride and past military experiences. They were always sure to thank her for her service. When the check came, it had already been paid. She never knew who paid it, but she understood that Americans loved their warriors and she was one of them.

Chapter 53

$\mathcal{A}$my checked in to her room at Balboa and met her roommate. Her name was Nicki Rossi. She was from Escondido, about twenty-five miles away. She was a local and had a car, so she took Amy out and showed her the city and, Amy's favorite place, the beach. They became fast friends. She also liked to workout, although not like Amy worked out. Nicki took her studies seriously, so Amy was glad to have a study partner. Nicki had a boyfriend, but he was a marine stationed in Afghanistan. They could not have been more different. Nicki came from a big, loud Italian family and Amy had her quiet, laid back Ssouthern way.

The following Monday they went to class orientation. There she met Senior Chief Birdsong. When she walked in, Amy didn't know if their instructor was a man or a woman. She was short, skinny, and had a graying, flat top haircut. The growl in her voice sounded like she smoked two packs of cigarettes and drank a half a quart of whiskey a day. That was because she did. Birdsong was clearly a tough old broad and she made it clear that she would not tolerate anything but their best.

Over time, Senior Chief Birdsong developed an affection for Amy. Amy worked hard, did well in class, and had a way of supporting and motivating the troops. That was important because they were getting more and more wounded returning from Afghanistan. Many were amputees that were far from home and in poor spirits. When the tall, statuesque strawberry blonde walked in the room with those big green eyes, a warm smile, and that slow southern drawl, they perked right up. Part of Amy's surgical tech training was to document post operation progress. Amy took the time to learn their names and where they were from. When the physical therapist came to get them, she was sure to give them little pep talks or at least a wink and a smile when they were going down the hall. Amy made a difference and Birdsong knew it.

It was the end of summer and Amy had a free weekend. She and Nicki had planned to spend it with Nicki's parents along with a little time at the beach. Amy loved Nicki's family. They must have been from the south of Italy because their hospitality was equal to her own family's. Then one day, Amy returned to her room after her workout and found Nicki on her bed, crying.

"Nicki, are you OK?" Amy asked, concerned.

"Yeah, yeah, I'm fine," Nicki replied through her sniffles.

"No, you're not. What's wrong?"

"Nothing," Nicki said.

Amy sat down on the bed next to her and said, "I have never seen you upset about anything. What's wrong, Nik?"

"Commander Grabowski cornered me in his office and felt me up," she finally said.

"Did you call the senior chief?"

"No, no Amy. I'm not going to do that. He can destroy my career," Nicki replied.

"No, you can't let him get away with that," said Amy. "Call the Senior Chief. She'll stand up for you."

No, Amy, I'm not and you don't tell anyone. I'll just stay away from him."

"Nicki, you can't...," Amy started to say but Nicki interrupted her.

"NO! Just leave it alone. I'm fine, OK?" she said.

"Yeah, OK," said Amy as she hugged Nicki.

Amy spent the weekend with Nicki and her family. She didn't bring up the incident, but she could tell Nicki was a little different. Amy was pissed. A fire had been lit within her that an intelligent person would never light in Amy Lynn Braxton.

The following Monday Amy went to see Senior Chief Birdsong and told her what happened.

"She needs to file a report," Said the senior chief.

"She's afraid it will ruin her career; she won't," said Amy.

"So what do you want me to do about it?" she replied.

"You said you would take care of us, protect us. You said that at our orientation."

"Well, if she doesn't file a report, there's not a hell of a lot I can do," Senior Chief Birdsong said.

"So he gets away with it?" Amy said.

"Braxton, Rossi is smarter than you think. I have been in this man's navy, and it is a man's navy, for twenty-seven years. She learned a lesson. Now let it go."

"NO," Amy yelled. "He grabbed her vagina without her permission. That's assault, that's wrong."

"I know that, but he is a surgeon and a commander, and she is an E-3. I don't know what kind of Pollyanna-fucking world you came from, but this is the military. If she does not defend herself, I cannot defend her. If you have nothing else, I suggest you get your ass back to work," the senior chief said.

"Yes, Senior Chief," Amy said angrily.

Amy went back to work not being able to understand how an organization that she held in such high esteem could let such things happen. What she didn't know was that Senior Chief Birdsong was asking herself the very same question.

A week later Senior Chief Birdsong saw Commander Grabowski looking through the window of a door into a operating room, which Amy was cleaning and prepping for surgery. Senior Chief nudged him and said, "Commander, that's a good Southern Christian girl. I would leave her the hell alone."

"What do you mean by that?" The commander said with a smarmy grin.

"You heard me," the senior chief replied.

"When I want your advice, I'll ask for it," said the commander.

"OK, you were warned," said the Senior Chief as she walked away.

Senior Chief knew Grabowski would make a move on Braxton. It wasn't an if, it was a when. Something told Birdsong that it wouldn't go as easy for him as it did with Rossi and the others. After some contemplation she decided to go to the mat for Braxton if necessary. Birdsong made the decision to defend Amy to the best of her ability. She had no idea that Braxton would defend herself.

Commander Grabowski, the Executive officer, or XO, of the surgical department, thought he had a good thing going. He smiled every six months when the six to twelve new, impressionable young girls came in the door. He had the power of rank and the respect of his colleagues because he was a fine surgeon, and he had an office and a reason to be alone with them. He interviewed the girls periodically to review their progress and they all needed his signature to graduate. If someone complained, he had his last line of defense: the commanding officer, Captain Martin, was a Naval Academy classmate of Commander Grabowski's. Whenever someone talked to an Academy graduate, he or she might have noticed the click of the graduate's class ring on the table or chair. That sound was a message, a signal that he or she has special stature and belonged to an exclusive club. The ring clickers always stuck together.

A few days later, Amy got a call to appear for her review. She dreaded it. As she left to go to the commander's office, the nurse she was working with stopped her. She looked at Amy and said, "Be careful, we don't call him Commander Grab Ass for nothing."

Amy nodded and went to his office.

When she got there, his yeoman was at the front desk. She wouldn't even look at Amy. She just said, "Go on in, he's waiting for you."

"Corpsman Braxton," he said with a big smile. "Come in and sit."

Amy sat down. She decided she would stay as professional as she could and get out as fast as possible.

"I have just finished reading your evaluations from Senior Chief Birdsong and the nurses you work with. Very impressive," said the Commander. Then Amy detected a change in his demeanor as he said, "You know, Amy...can I call you Amy?"

"No, sir," Said Amy. "I prefer Corpsman Braxton."

The commander chuckled under his breath and said, "Very well. You know, Corpsman Braxton, there is more to the navy than being a good sailor. Your success is based on how you treat people, especially your commanding officer. You know, you are very beautiful. Were you ever a model?"

"No, sir. If we are finished here, I need to go back to work," said Amy, becoming agitated.

The green in her eyes began to dance. He saw it but had no idea what it meant. His desk was positioned in the office so anyone in the room would have to walk past it to get to the door. Amy started to get up to leave, but he stood up and blocked the door. She could see that his pants were bulging and he clearly had an erection.

Amy stood up straight and said, "I need to leave."

The commander just looked at her with the same look that Ed and Jeb had on their faces only a few years before. She could feel the heat building in her chest. Then she said one last time, loud enough that the yeoman heard it outside his office, "I NEED TO LEAVE NOW."

The yeoman lifted her head. She heard every word and then jumped when she heard the sound of smashing furniture.

Chapter 54

*I*n each of us, the flight or flight response kicks in when we feel threatened or trapped. Amy felt trapped and threatened. The signal to her brain followed the path that progresses from thalamus to amygdala and then to hypothalamus. After that, it was over. Amy's brain took the information it had and in less than a second it observed, oriented, decided, and acted. Her first kick struck the commander's weight-bearing leg in the patella, hyperextending the knee. As the commander began to fall forward, Amy drove her palm into the tip of his nose. As the nasal bone snapped with a loud popping noise, his head flew back and bounced off the door. The pain from his knee caused him to let out a scream as he fell forward toward her. Stepping to the side, she grabbed the back of his collar as he was falling and dragged him into the center of the office to the open part of the floor. After dropping him to the floor she kicked him in the back of the head and drove his face into the carpet. He curled up in the fetal position trying to protect himself, but she wasn't done. She kicked him in the ribs while talking to him. "This" KICK "is" KICK "for" KICK "Nicki" KICK.

By the time the Shore Patrol arrived, Amy was standing over the commander's broken, sobbing body. She wasn't saying a word. She just looked at him with that crooked smile. Shore Patrol took her into custody and off to NCIS. She told the story of what happened and of course her version was different from his. They took her to the brig and sat her in a cell by herself. She was charged with assaulting an officer. She was in a lot of trouble.

Senior Chief Birdsong arrived in the ER after she heard what had happened. She could hear Grabowski screaming in pain as the nurses worked on him. They weren't exactly gentle. None of them were fans. Birdsong had a smile on her face that she couldn't wipe off. The ER doctor asked her what the hell happened. Senior Chief looked at him with a little smirk, shook her head, and said, "He fucked with the wrong little hillbilly girl."

Senior Chief went back to her office and went to work. If she was going to get Braxton out of this mess, she would have to pull out all the stops. Birdsong dialed an overseas line, hung up, and waited. The phone rang. She picked it up and said, "T, how the fuck are ya'?"

"Good, Kate, how are you?" said T.

"It's been a holy fuck of a day. I think I got one for ya'. She reminds me of you. Really smart and a bad mother fucker," said Birdsong, smiling.

"Really? Tell me about her," said T.

Amy sat in her cell, looking at the wall. She knew she was in trouble. They said if she would plead guilty she would do a year and get a bad conduct discharge. She wouldn't do it. Amy could have called home, but what would she say? She was ashamed. She could have just as easily moved him and escaped, but something inside her snapped. There would be no calls to Sheriff Teddy Bear, her daddy, Carla Jo, or Jack. She was on her own. At least, she thought she was. Amy was exhausted by the adrenalin rush so she stretched out on the little bunk and fell asleep. There was no sleep for Senior Chief Birdsong. She had work to do.

The next morning Senior Chief walked into Captain Martin's office.

"Good morning, Skipper," Birdsong chirped.

"What's so good about it? Braxton won't plead guilty. I will need you to type some stuff up. She's unstable, et cetera," said the captain.

"Skipper, I have a better idea. Request permission to speak freely."

"Granted."

"Here is what we are going to do," said Birdsong. "We are going to charge Grabowski with attempted rape, we are going to dismiss the charges against Braxton, you are going to sign her meritorious advancement to E-4, and then we are going to ship her ass out of here."

Captain Martin laughed a nervous laugh. He knew Birdsong was a cagey operator and had established connections over her career.

"Have you lost you mind, Birdsong?" he said.

"Probably," said Birdsong. "But I have a file with three dozen complaints of everything from sexual harassment to sexual assault, all against Grabowski, all seen and signed by you. Are any of them in his service file?"

Captain Martin stared at her with his mouth open. Birdsong continued, "Oh, and here is the statement from Grabowski's yeoman stating that Braxton was trying to leave before she defended herself. Last but not least, the dozen or so nurses and corpsman that were waiting for me at my office this morning to give statements and testify for Braxton."

"THIS IS BLACKMAIL," yelled the Captain.

"Oh no, sir. The blackmail part is where you're sitting in the cell next to Grabowski. I have all of this information copied and in a manila envelope addressed to the Judge Advocate General. We both know what a fucking bitch she can be," said Birdsong with a little grin.

Captain Martin turned his chair and looked out the window.

"Sign it, Skipper. Make this shit storm go away. I'm going to get my girl out of the brig," said Birdsong as she got up and walked out the door.

Amy sat in her cell thinking about everything. Jail gives you that uninterrupted chance for self-examination. Then she heard a voice off in the distance that sounded amazingly like the Senior Chief.

"Jesus fucking Christ, I have the paper work right here. Let her the fuck out," said the voice. Amy stood up and looked out of the cell to see Senior Chief Birdsong coming down the hall with two marines.

"Come on, Braxton, let's go," said the senior chief while handing her some civilian clothes.

"Where are we going?" asked Amy.

"We're going to go get drunk," said Birdsong.

"I don't drink," Amy said.

"Well, I do and you're buying," said the Senior Chief with a smile.

Amy and the Senior Chief sat down at the bar. Amy ordered a Dr. Pepper and the Senior Chief ordered a Jim Beam on the rocks. Senior Chief took a sip, looked at Amy, and said, "I talked to Rossi when I picked up your clothes. I apologized to her for not stepping in. She's a good girl and a good sailor."

"Thanks, Senior Chief."

"You call me Kate, you earned it," said Birdsong.

"Now what?" Amy asked.

"There is going to be a trial and it's gonna suck. I'll help you get ready for that. You and I also have to do a little career planning. You're not going back to Balboa."

"Why not? I love my job. I have to lose my job over this? That's not right," Amy said, concerned.

"I know, but some people are going to jail over this. You're not real popular with the command. We need to get you the fuck out of there. I do have good news, though, Petty Officer Braxton," said Kate, referring to her promotion.

Amy looked at Kate and said, "This was all you, wasn't it? You saved me, why?" asked Amy.

"Well, there are two things an old bull dyke senior chief knows when she see's it: another lesbian and a good sailor. You're not a lesbian, but you are a damn good sailor. I've sat back too many times and watched things happen to my girls that were questionable at best. Fuck them, I'm never gonna make Master Chief anyway," said Kate. Then she chugged down her drink and ordered another.

"Thank you, Kate," said Amy.

"Oh, honey, it's not over. I'm like the Godfather. Someday I'll come to you and you cannot refuse," Said Kate with a smile. Then she said, "I have an offer for you, Braxton. Seems some split-tail senator has decided that girls are just as good as boys. She opened up some non-traditional billets. How would you like to train to be a Fleet Marine Force Combat corpsman?" Kate asked.

"Really?" said Amy. "Train with the marines? Running, shooting, and breaking things? Oh yeah, I would love that."

"It's a mother fucker, Braxton. It's Marine Corps boot camp with an ass-full of emergency medicine thrown in. They will bust your ass, they will call you names, they will make things unfair, and it will be because you are a girl. They will not want you there. You'll have to be better than them. I'll give you time to think about it. You have until I finish this drink."

"I'm in," said Amy.

"I would like to know one thing, first," said Kate. "Where the fuck did you learn to fight like that?"

"Oh, my uncle Jack showed me a few things," said Amy.

"Bullshit, Braxton. You took down a big man and stopped just short of killing him. If you owe me anything, you owe me the truth. Now what the fuck."

"All right, I've never told anyone outside of my family...,"

Amy told Kate the Hatfield story and when she was finished, Kate needed another drink.

"So, your uncle Jack. Where did he learn his skills?"

"SEAL Team, Vietnam," Amy replied.

Kate's eyes went a little wide and she said, "No shit. What's his last name?"

"Brown," said Amy.

"Jack Brown," Kate mumbled under her breath. "Hatchet Jack Brown?"

"Yep."

Kate was stunned. She looked at Amy wide-eyed and asked, "What else did he teach you?"

"I don't talk about that. That's between me and him," said Amy.

"Yeah, I bet. I would like to meet him sometime," Kate said.

"Not a problem. Just let me know."

"OK, Braxton. Let's go back to the base, say your good-byes, pack your shit, and get you the fuck out of there," said Kate.

"Wait a minute. Petty Officer Braxton?" Said a surprised Amy. The change in her title had just sunk in.

Grabowski cut a plea deal so Amy did not have to testify. They gave Amy a week's liberty before school started so Kate put her on a plane back to Alabama. Then Kate made another overseas call.

"T, she bit. She's on her way to FMSS and infantry school. She practically begged me for it."

"Thanks, Kate. I opened a file on her. We'll watch her and see how she does with the marines. If she can hold her own, we'll go from there," said T.

"One more thing, T. You'll never guess who has been training her...."

Chapter 55

Amy walked through the terminal and as she past security, she saw Carla Jo and Kelly waiting for her. She hugged them both. There were some tears. She missed her family and her friend.

They drove home and everyone was curious about what happened. Jack noticed the brand new crow (the eagle above the stripe signifying petty officer rank) sewn on her uniform and that made him even more curious. Carol cooked a feast and her family sat on the porch at the end of the evening. Amy told the truth: exactly what happened, how it happened, and where she was going next. The only one that understood the gravity of her next assignment was Jack. He got real quiet and waited until they could be alone to talk.

"So your going to train to be a doc," he said.

"A doc?" Amy asked.

"Yep, that's what they will be screamin' when they are layin' on the ground, shot, in the middle of a fire fight. You will be expected to run out into a hail of bullets to go get 'em and patch 'em up. That's the job," Jack explained.

"Yeah, I read a little about it. I'm going to the school, but they made it clear that I would not go into combat. I'll end up at some evac hospital," she said.

"Are you sure about that?" asked Jack.

"Yeah, I'm sure. I won't be deployed in an infantry battalion, just training with one," said Amy.

"OK, well, I feel a little better," said Jack. "You know, the marines are a slightly different animal than what you are used to."

"I worked with them at Balboa, I get the esprit de corps. I understand what I'm walking into," said Amy.

"It's a tough school, really tough. They will push you," said Jack with a serious look on his face.

Amy smiled at him and said, "Yeah, well, I'm a tough girl."

"That you are, honey, that you are," said Jack, smiling.

The week flew by. The only person Amy didn't visit with was Andy. It bothered her that he had never written her a letter. She wasn't about to go see him. After all, he broke up with her. Still, though, his memory nagged at her. She was hoping she would meet someone else. Trust issues, and the fact that every man that had shown interest in her seemed to only want one thing, made that improbable. On the outside she was confident and just by her physical presence she could seem larger than life. At night, though, when the lights went out and she lay in bed alone, there was an infinite sadness. She was a woman like every other, longing to be held and touched. She was blatantly offered opportunities to establish relationships with other women and more than once she gave that serious consideration. Amy, however, was not one to accept temporary solutions for long-term problems. As powerful as those feelings were, she would wait. The person that lay with her would be the one, period.

Amy packed her things and said her good-byes. Each time she said good-bye, it got a little easier. She sat down next to the window in the plane, rested her head on a small pillow, and began to nod off. In six hours she would be in Camp Pendleton and her new adventure would begin.

Colonel Harland Knox sifted through the paperwork on his desk. He knew that being the commanding officer of Fleet Marine Force training was a very important job, but he missed the field. Knox was a hardened warrior, an old school marine. He never married. He felt that if the corps wanted him to have a wife, he would have been issued one. The phone rang on his desk and he picked it up.

"Please hold for Senator Dahl," said the person on the other end. *Shit, shit, shit, shit; now what the fuck did I do?* Knox thought.

Senator Martha Dahl was the chairman of the Armed Services Committee. She seemed to take perverse joy in belittling military officers. She was a liberal that took every opportunity to turn the military into something that more resembled a Girl Scout troop. Her constant pressure to push for gays and women in non-traditional roles was especially troubling to Colonel Knox.

"Colonel Knox, how are you?" said the senator as she launched into a prattling, predictable bullshit line about how proud she was and what a great job they were doing, blah, lah, blah. Colonel Knox thought to himself, *oh yeah? Well how about some more money for training, you stupid bitch?*

"Yes, ma'am, it's a pleasure to speak to you. What can I do for you?" he said out loud.

"You have a trainee on the way, Petty Officer Third Class Braxton. Amy Lynn Braxton. She will be placed in combat corpsman's school. She is very special and is being watched by some very important people," said Senator Dahl.

Colonel Knox shook his head and thought knew what was coming next. He was wrong.

"I know what you are thinking," said the senator. "Be sure she doesn't fail or something like that, right?"

"I don't think, ma'am. I wait for orders," said the colonel.

"Bullshit, Colonel. I know I'm not real popular with the brass. I know you may not trust me," said the senator.

She's a master of the understatement, thought the colonel.

"You're orders are this: I want her to go through everything everyone else goes through. She will be participating in FMSS and infantry training. If she fails, she fails on her own. All I'm asking you to do is keep it fair," said the Senator.

Dahl was well aware that the entire military saw her as having blood on her hands after she pushed through a female F-14 pilot that crashed and died during a carrier landing. The senator had pushed her through training even after being warned that she was not talented enough to succeed. The senator meant what she said, although Knox could never be sure when trying to decipher the politician's code.

"Yes, ma'am. I give you my word that she will endure no less and no more than any other trainee," said the Colonel.

"Thank you, Colonel. If you need anything, do not hesitate to call," said the senator.

"Yes, ma'am," said the Colonel.

He hung up and put his head in his hands with his elbows on his desk. "Oh fuck, why me?" he mumbled to himself. Colonel Knox picked up the phone and said, "Sergeant, I need to put together an all-hands staff meeting, ASAP."

"Yes, sir," Said the sergeant.

Chapter 56

*M*uch to the relief of Colonel Knox, Petty Officer Braxton was a non-issue. As soon as Amy checked in and went through orientation, she started to smile and didn't stop for seven weeks. The first thing they did was swap her navy uniform for marine corps camouflage. She loved camo. Her instructors were marines and they reminded her of Uncle Jack when they trained together. Training in the marine way of operating and thinking felt comfortable to her. It was like a little taste of home. They got up every morning at 4 a.m., exercised, and went on a six mile forced march. Intense compressed classes in emergency medicine, combat tactics, firearms training, and something that Coach Traicoff had mentioned to her: they studied the religion and culture of the Middle East. They took exams at the end of every week and Amy did very well, acing most of them.

Gunny Sergeant Makowski, or Gunny Mak as the students called him, was the leading non-commissioned officer of Amy's class. He was a former Recon Ranger and a Gulf War veteran. Colonel Knox called him into his office for a scheduled update on the current class. After a perfunctory report, Knox asked Makowski how Braxton was doing. Gunny Mak shook his head and said, "Yes, sir, I wanted to talk to you about that."

Knox sat up in his chair and asked, "Is there a problem?"

Gunny Mak leaned back in his chair and said, "No, not really. I am curious, though. Where the hell did she come from?"

Knox thought for a second and said, "Alright, but what I'm telling you is confidential. A commander at Balboa tried to rape her and she sent him to the emergency room. Someone very high up decided she would be a better fit here. After this she is going to infantry training. They won't deploy her, but they do want to see how she does. So spill it, Gunny, what do you see?"

Gunny leaned forward in his chair and said, "Well, sir, let's start with academics. She has aced most of her tests. She has had previous medical training and I'm talking about before she enlisted. During our simulated casualty training, she's unshakable. She is very familiar with the M-4 and the M9, to the point that she was teaching the other three women in her class. She acts like she has fieldstripped and cleaned those weapons a thousand times. On the range, she is just as good as or better than her instructors. During free fire with the M9 she put a smiley face on the target at ten meters. When we were teaching hand-to-hand combat she just played with people. She did just well enough to keep it at a draw. One sailor got frustrated, though, and took a cheap shot at her and she dropped him like a sack of shit. The biggest giveaway was when we were in the field teaching combat tactics. We teach rudimentary tactics and she has her unit doing Spec Ops shit. I have never seen anyone like her. She's as strong as a bull, runs like a deer, and moves like a cat. I would take her into combat with me right now, anytime, anyplace."

Knox leaned back in his chair and said, "Do you think she's a plant? Someone command sent to evaluate our training?"

Gunny shook his head and said, "I thought that, too, but she's just twenty years old. To learn what she knows she would have had to start training as a kid. No, sir, someone who is very good trained this girl. I'm talking RECON, Green Beret, or SEAL Team caliber. Maybe even a foreign entity."

Knox laughed and said, "A foreign entity? Really? KGB? Mossad? You're kidding, right?"

Gunny shook his head and said, "No, no, I'm not."

Knox shrugged his shoulders and said, "OK, I have to send a report on her progress. Write it up for me."

"Yes, sir," said the gunny sergeant.

Somewhere in an undisclosed building, in a country receptive to rendition, the phone rang. T picked it up.

"T, it's Adele. Did you learn anything?"

"Enough; the report is on the way," said T.

"I got that report on Petty Officer Braxton from FMSS. Seems you were right about her," said Adele.

"What's her status?" said T.

"She's on her way to infantry training. We'll keep an eye on her," said Adele.

"Has she been vetted?" asked T.

"Four generations. She's as pure as they come," said Adele.

"I can't wait to meet her," said T.

"I didn't think you liked to recruit," said Adele.

"I don't, but something about this one has piqued my interest," said T.

"I already have assets fighting over her," said Adele.

"Yes, but I know you love me best," said T.

Adele laughed, "Yes, I do. Be safe honey, I love ya'."

"Love you too, Adele. Bye," said T.

Chapter 57

Amy got her orders to an east coast Expeditionary Strike Group. She reported in and was placed in a rifle platoon. A rifle platoon was made up of thirty-six marines and was divided into three squads with each squad made up of three fire teams. They already had a corpsman, although he wasn't exactly popular in the platoon. They referred to him as Corpsman Shitbird. He spent more time in sickbay than in training. His specialty was getting out of PT, or physical training.

Petty Officer Braxton was introduced to the platoon and audible moans and groans were heard along with a few catcalls. She had learned to ignore such things and began to do as she was taught. She pulled the medical records of everyone in her platoon and began to study. She learned all she could about each of them. As she talked to them one on one and concerned herself with their well-being, the skepticism about her position in the platoon began to slowly change.

They played the occasional prank on her. While in the field she climbed into her sleeping bag only to feel something wiggle against her leg. She reached down to find a snake, and a rather large one. If it hadn't bitten her already she knew it wasn't poisonous. The guys in her squad waited for a scream that never came. She figured the snake just wanted to be warm so she let it sleep with her. The next morning she draped it around her neck and showed up at breakfast. The Marines just laughed and shook their heads.

They were all relatively young and full of testosterone. Most of them, whether overtly or covertly, suggested that they would like to enjoy Amy's company privately. She lied and said she had a boyfriend back home. She didn't like to lie, but it was the quickest and easiest way to slow those activities. She blew off their lewd behavior and dirty jokes. She also had to get used to the non-stop swearing. They could use "fuck" as a noun, verb, pronoun, and adjective.

PT was Amy's proof that she was the real thing. She ran several of them into the ground, but when she kicked everyone's ass on the rifle range that sealed the deal. They began to come to her with aches and pains and she treated each one like she would have treated her own brother. She noticed something else, too. They were all becoming extremely protective of her. Whether in the field, on base, or in town, it was like she had thirty-six mean-ass big brothers. Then it happened; the thing that every navy combat corpsman wanted to hear. The ultimate form of respect, Gunny Sullivan called her doc while they were in formation. Amy knew the gravity of that one word. She almost cried.

Orders came down from command and they were going to Afghanistan. First they went through training in both desert warfare and something called TRUEX: training in an urban environment exercise. Amy thought she knew a lot about combat, but they taught her much more. Training was hard and realistic. Several of her boys got banged up so she received some pretty good practice in dealing with injuries. Their trust in her abilities and affection for her personally continued to grow.

After five months of non-stop training and preparation, they boarded the USS Kearsarge for the trip to the Middle East. Amy wanted to stay with her boys but they insisted that she report to the female's berthing area, or sleeping quarters. She felt a little guilty because it was much nicer than theirs. She still ate with them though, did PT with them, and went to daily classes.

One day one of her marines got a Dear John letter. They found a quiet place together and she held him as he cried. You couldn't do that with just any doc. She spent her down time trying to horn her way into the weight room, studying the latest combat trauma techniques, and writing letters to her friends and family.

Mail call was as big a deal to Amy as it was to every sailor and marine. Time did not stand still in Black Oak, Alabama. Joseph was making his dreams a reality. Junior sold him one of Earl's old racecars. He and Jack put it together and were running in the sportsman division at Junior's track. He had yet to win a race, but Jack said he was getting more competitive every week. Carla Jo and Doc Henderson got an offer from a major healthcare provider to buy out their interest in Henderson Medical. Carla Jo said it was an insane amount of money. She knew, however, what would happen to her employees. They were more family to her than anything else, which was probably why she was so successful. She and Doc passed on the offer. They agreed that they were doing fine.

Kelly went to work part time for Carla Jo and enrolled in the local college to get a nursing degree. Henderson Medical paid her tuition. Kelly was also Carla Jo's new best friend. She just slipped right into Amy's old spot. Amy was a little jealous at first, but after giving it some thought she was glad Carla Jo had her. Then there was the biggest news of all. Carol was pregnant. She didn't know if it was a boy or a girl yet, but she didn't care. The Braxton family was getting a little bigger. There was another letter, too. It was the one Amy carried around in her pocket and wouldn't open. It was from Andy.

The ship made port and they disembarked. There was a lot of work going on to stage the equipment and figure out where everyone was going; more hurry up and wait. Amy worked to keep up the morale of her boys. It was 107 degrees in the shade, so she stayed on them about keeping hydrated. On her way to get the mail, she sweet talked a supply chief out of extra Gatorade powder and then went to stand in line. She was reading a letter from Kelly when Gunny sat down beside her and said, "How ya' doin, doc?"

"Good, Gunny, thanks for asking."

"I can't help but notice you busting you ass to take care of these boys. I was just wondering, who's taking care of you?" he asked.

"I'm fine, Gunny. As long as I stay busy the time goes by and we'll be out of here shortly," she said.

"Yeah, well, that's what I need to talk to you about. I have our orders and you're not coming with us."

"Yeah, I know that," said Amy.

"You know, I know, and the lieutenant knows. The boys don't. To them you are 'Doc,' and that's that. When I tell them, I'm gonna have a god damned mutiny on my hands," said Gunny.

"Do you want me to tell 'em?"

"Nah, that's the lieutenant's job. I just hope he remembers that their clips are full," said the Gunny, laughing. Then he said, "Hey, Doc, what's with that envelope you carry around that you won't open?"

"How did you know about that?" said Amy, surprised.

"Gunny sees all, Gunny knows all. That's my job. You want to talk about it?"

"Not much to talk about really," replied Amy. Then she began to talk about it.

Amy's rifle platoon boarded personnel carriers for the two-hour ride to the airbase. They unloaded their equipment on the tarmac and stood in formation behind two V-22 Ospreys waiting to board.

"DOC, FRONT AND CENTER," barked the Lieutenant.

Amy fell out of formation and saluted. The Lieutenant handed her a manila envelope with her orders to the evac hospital and pointed her to the CH-53 helicopter that would take her. A chorus of "Wait a minute," "Bullshit," and "What the fuck?" echoed across the flight line. Corporal Jimenez finally spoke up and said, "That's our Doc, she goes with us," followed by a chorus of "Fuckin' A."

Amy was facing the Lieutenant and the gunny, and without a warning she turned around and in a commanding voice said, "HEY! I GOT BOOBS AND A VAGINA. I CANNOT GO INTO COMBAT. TIME TO PUT YOUR BIG BOY PANTS ON AND GET YOUR BUTTS TO WORK. YOUR NEW DOC IS WAITING FOR YOU AT THE FORWARD OPERATING BASE. I HAVE TO GO TO THE EVAC HOSPITAL AND I LOOK FORWARD TO SEEING NONE OF YOU BECAUSE THAT WOULD MEAN YOU GOT HURT. REMEMBER TO STAY HYDRATED. WASH YOUR BUTTS AND YOUR LITTLE PECKERS. GOOD HYGIENE IS EVERYTHING. ONE MORE THING, I LOVE YOU GUYS! OORAH!"

"OORAH!" came blasting back at her. Amy stood at the bottom of the Osprey's ramps and gave each one a hug as they boarded. Finally it was the gunny's turn to board. He smiled at her and said, "Thanks, Doc. Good job." Then he asked her, "Did you open that letter yet?"

"Soon, Gunny, soon," She said as she hugged him and said good-bye.

Amy grabbed her stuff and walked over to the CH-53. A Corporal was standing at the ramp and with a snarky attitude said, "Anytime you're ready, Petty Officer Braxton."

"That's Doc to you, Marine," said Amy.

He saw the Fleet Marine Force insignia on her uniform and said, "Oh, sorry, Doc. Welcome aboard."

"How long 'til we get to the evac hospital?" asked Amy.

"About an hour," said the Corporal.

Well, why not, Amy thought. She reached into her pocket and pulled out the worn envelope. She opened it and began to read.

My Dearest Amy,

I'm sorry I have not written you until now. To be honest, I didn't know what to write. It's been a couple of years since we broke up but I want you to know something. I never, ever stopped loving you. I think of you every day. I wonder where you are and how you are doing. I pray that you are well and are happy.

I went to your house on the day that you left. Your dad said you were already gone and that you had left that morning. I expected him to be upset with me, but he wasn't. I think he was trying to deal with the fact that you were gone.

I'm sorry I waited so long. I'm sorry I didn't have the guts to come see you and say these things to your face. Just know I still love you, and I guess I always will.

Amy folded up the letter, leaned back against the bulkhead, and closed her eyes. Whenever she told the guys that she had a boyfriend, she always pictured Andy. She had told the lie so much that she had begun to believe it. Then there it was, reality. She wasn't really sure if she even loved him anymore. Maybe the idea of having a love was easier than actually having one. Gunny told her something while they were sitting on the dock. He said, "You know, I have always found that it's a hell of a lot harder to let go of something than it is to hang on to it." *He was right*, thought Amy. Her feelings had to be let go and the sooner the better. She dug around in her bag and pulled out a thin plastic box that contained her stationary. She addressed an envelope, put a stamp on it, pulled out the pad of paper, and began to write.

Andy,

I carried this letter around for two months before I decided to open it. I guess it was fear. I would either have to read that you don't love me any more or that I would have to write back saying I don't love you.

I waited a long time for a visit, a call, or something. I was done waiting long ago. I have no idea what's going to happen in the future, but I do know that I have to let you go. You were my first love and there will always be a place in my heart for you, but you need to move on. I know I have.

You are a very special man and you will do very special things. Good luck, Andy.

Amy

Chapter 58

$\mathcal{A}$my looked out the door of the CH-53 as it made a lazy turn before touchdown at the base. There was already activity at the heliport. Several wounded soldiers were being rushed from a Blackhawk Medevac. She grabbed her stuff and the corporal gave her directions to where she would check in. Her senses were immediately assaulted by the smell of diesel fumes and raw sewage. She looked around and thought, *Coach Traicoff was right, this is a godforsaken place.*

Amy checked in with the Officer of the Day and got her tent assignment. She dropped the letter to Andy in the mailbox. She found the tent and saw a sea bag next to the door. She reached for the door and it opened. A woman who had clearly been crying rushed passed her, grabbed the sea bag, and quickly walked away. Amy gently knocked on the door and a woman answered.

"Hi, you must be my new roommate. My name is Katherine Rodriguez," said the woman. She had a First Class Petty Officer insignia on her uniform. She was also a corpsman.

"Hi," said Amy. "What's wrong with her?"

"Oh, I guess the job can be a little stressful," said Katherine.

"My boys call me Doc," Amy said with a smile while sticking out her hand. She liked being called Doc.

"Well, I'm not your boys. What's your name?"

"Amy, Amy Braxton, nice to meet you. Katherine is my mother's name," Amy said as she put out her hand again.

Katherine shook her hand and said, "Well then, it should be easy to remember. First time in Afghanistan?"

"Yep," said Amy.

"Why don't you put your stuff away and I'll show you around," said Katherine.

"I'd like that. Thanks, Katherine."

Amy looked at Katherine and thought how pretty she was. For some reason the mental image of Felina, the mexican maiden from the Marty Robbins song "El Paso" popped into her mind. Amy put her things away and they toured the base. Amy was amazed at the bits of home they managed to drag into a foreign country. They had a workout tent with free weights and Amy was sure she would spend some time in there. The USO had also set up a pretty nice tent with televisions, games, and computers to e-mail family and friends.

"Are you hungry?" Katherine asked.

"Yes, I am," replied Amy.

"Well then, let's go have some lunch," said Katherine

They sat, ate, and talked. Katherine said she was from Maryland. Her dad was a marine corps master sergeant. She had traveled the world as a military brat. Amy then shared a few things about herself. They finished lunch and returned to the tent. Thankfully it had air conditioning. Amy found a envelope stuck into the door with her name on it. She opened it to find that she had her assignment.

"Pediatrics?" said Amy.

"Oh yeah, we get lots of kids through here. War seems to hit them the hardest; war and that blood cult they call a religion. You got both the best and the worst job on the base," said Katherine.

"I love working with kids, this will be great," said Amy with a smile.

Katherine's face went solemn. She looked at Amy and asked, "Do you know how to hate?"

"What?" said Amy, looking confused.

"Just what I said. Do you know how to hate?" asked Katherine again.

"No, I don't hate. Jesus teaches us that is wrong," Amy said.

"You will learn, Amy. I promise you, you will learn."

Amy didn't know what to make of that. Then her face brightened up and she said, "So, what do you do here?"

"I work with the captured and injured enemy, Taliban and Al Qaeda. I write reports on their health and wefare and go to Central Command and present my reports to the Red Crescent, their version of the Red Cross," said Katherine.

"That must be tough," said Amy.

"It's fun watching them die," Katherine said under her breath.

"What?"

"Oh, nothing. Do you speak any of the language?" asked Katherine.

"I've picked up a little; very little," said Amy.

"I have a computer program on my laptop that teaches Dari Persian. About half the country speaks it. The rest speak a combination of languages. The enemy and those to the north mostly speak Pashto. Most of the kids around here speak Dari. Would you like to learn a little?" she asked.

"Sure, that would be helpful," said Amy.

"Good, that will give us something to do in the evenings."

Amy looked at Katherine and noticed that throughout the day, she had seemed hard and cold. Katherine really had to try to be warm. She was personally neat and clean. She kept the tent immaculate. Amy figured she could have done worse for a roommate.

The next day Amy reported to the pediatric ward. The first thing she noticed was that kids are kids no matter where they are from. Some of the boys were running around and the girls stood in little groups, talking. Some of the children were on cots with IV's in their little arms. The nurse in charge, Nurse Collins, said, "So you're a doc? Awesome. OK, Braxton, they'll start coming in with their parents and we need to triage them. You'll start to see what we do here and just join in. Any questions?"

"No, ma'am."

"Good, here we go," said the Nurse as she opened the door and the families began to come in.

Their injuries were varied; anywhere from snakebites to broken bones, gun shot wounds and the worst sexual abuse Amy could imagine. The latter hit her hard. The little boys had torn sphincters and gonorrhea. Little girls had massive infections from botched circumcisions and vaginal mutilation. She soaked the scabs off there little vaginas and clipped the stiches where their vaginal lips were amateurishly sewn together. She watched a little girl of no more than six years of age die when they couldn't control the infection caused by genital mutilation. That was the first day. Katherine was right. Amy was learning to hate.

For three days Amy hardly left the hospital. She had all but forgotten to eat, sleep, or shower. She poured her heart and soul into those children. Finally, Nurse Collins pulled her outside and said, "Sit down, we need to talk."

Amy looked bad. Nurse Collins put her arm around Amy's shoulders and said, "Honey, this job will eat you up. You have a year here. You cannot keep this up. It's impossible. You will spend at most twelve hours a day at work. I would prefer ten but no more than twelve hours. You will also take off one day a week. That's an order, do you understand?"

"Yes, ma'am," said Amy, feeling relieved.

"Good. Go take a shower, eat, and get some rest. Hell, go to the USO tent and find a young marine to play touch and tickle with, I don't care. We will see you tomorrow morning. You are doing a great job. Those kids are lucky to have you, but you have to take care of yourself. If you don't you will be no good to them and no good to us. You are dismissed," said Nurse Collins.

"Yes, ma'am. Thank you," Amy said.

With her head down she walked back to her room. She was exhausted. As she walked in the tent, Katherine looked up and said, "Hey, I do have a roommate." Katherine sniffed the air and said, "Oh my God, do you stink. Go take a shower."

Amy took a long, hot shower. She collapsed into her bunk and fell asleep so fast she didn't remember her head touching the pillow.

Amy awoke to the sound of Katherine pecking away on the computer.

"What time is it?" Amy said sleepily.

"Eight a.m.," said Katherine.

"NO! I'm late," Amy exclaimed as she jumped up and started running around trying to get ready.

Katherine laughed at her and said, "Collins stopped by earlier. She said take the day off. Relax, OK? I was thinking we could go into town and go shopping, maybe get a little exercise, and then we could go kill some paper evildoers at the rifle range. What do you think?"

"OK, but how about some breakfast? I'm starving," said Amy, rubbing her belly.

They got to the chow hall and walked down the line. Amy picked up a biscuit and took a quick bite. Then she yelled back into the kitchen in a thicker-than-usual Southern accent, "Am I gonna have to come back there and teach y'all how to make a decent biscuit?"

A big black sergeant stuck his head around the corner and shouted back, "I know how to make a damn biscuit, but if you know something I don't then get your skinny ass back here and have at it. Just remember you need to make five hundred of 'em."

"Five hundred?" yelled Amy. "Well then, I guess this is a pretty good biscuit."

"You damn right it is," said the sergeant, walking around the end of the table. He picked up Amy in a bear hug and said, "How ya' doin', Doc?"

"I'm good, Chef. I'm working in pediatrics. How are my boys?" asked Amy.

"They're good. They miss you, but the new Doc is a great guy. He fit right in," said Chef.

"Good, I'm glad to hear it," said Amy. "I'll see you later, Chef."

"Nice to see you, Doc," said Chef.

"So you know him?" said Katherine.

"Yeah, he got banged up in a training accident and I took care of him," said Amy.

Katherine thought to herself, *this girl has a way with people. They adore her and that could come in handy.*

Chapter 59

$\mathcal{J}$ack hit the gas as he came down the hill by Copperhead Creek Road. The 512 cubic-inch aluminum engine pushed him back in the seat. He could see the dark SUV with all the antennas in the rearview mirror getting smaller. *Not today, boys,* he thought.

Jack realized something was wrong with the car when the oil pressure light came on above the gauge. The pick-up tube in the oil pump stuck down into the bottom of the oil pan, sucking up oil to be distributed throughout the engine. The tube was press-fit into the oil pump and Jack had always put a small tack weld on it to keep it from vibrating out. He didn't tack this one. The gauge read 0. *Maybe the gauge is bad,* he thought, but the increasingly loud knock coming from the engine as the main and rod bearings began to deteriorate told him otherwise. Then the engine locked up. He pulled to the side of the road and watched as the SUV pulled up behind him. The federal officers got out, guns drawn. One tapped the barrel of his glock on the driver's side window. This game had been going on for years.

The agent smiled big and said, "Mr. Brown, good to see you. Step out of the car."

Carla Jo called the lawyers, paid his bail, and got him out of jail. As they walked down the steps of the federal building, Carla

Jo looked at him and said, "What do you think? Are you ready to grow up now?"

Jack just shook his head and mumbled, "Sorry."

"Sorry?" replied an exasperated Carla Jo. "You're sorry? I'm the one that has to sit home alone while you're in prison. You are in big trouble. Do you understand that?"

Jack nodded. He never thought about the consequences of getting caught. He was thinking about it now.

Amy sat looking at the computer screen as she checked her e-mail at the USO tent. She put her hands on her face and mumbled, "Oh no, God bless it."

"What's wrong?" asked Katherine.

Amy wasn't sure what to say, but what the heck, it was all public knowledge. She looked at Katherine and said, "My uncle Jack got busted hauling moonshine."

"Moonshine?" said a surprised Katherine. "You really are from way back in the sticks, aren't you?"

"Yep, it's a family tradition. The thing is, my aunt is worth millions. He doesn't have to do it, it's just how he has fun."

"Did you ever do any of that?" asked Katherine.

"No, my daddy kind of broke the mold. He believes in making a legal living. He wouldn't tolerate me doing any of that," said Amy. She shook her head and then said, "Come on, lets go to the range. I need to shoot something."

They stopped by the armory and checked out an M4 and a M40. They got to the range and Amy put on her hearing attenuators and lit it up.

"Damn girl, you can shoot," said Katherine. "Can you do that every time?"

"Yeah, there's nothing hard about this," said Amy.

"Katherine saw a group of marines standing to her right and said, "I need you to miss."

"What?" said a confused Amy.

"Miss; you know, shoot badly," said Katherine.

Amy knew she was up to something, but she wasn't sure what. "OK," Amy said.

Amy loaded a clip and looked to her left. She saw a group of men with slightly different uniforms. They all had longer hair and beards. One kept his eyes on her. *Oh my God, is he handsome,* Amy thought. She could see his bright blue eyes from thirty yards away. He had blonde hair and a reddish beard. She kept looking over her shoulder and smiling.

"Hi," said Katherine, walking up to the group of marines. "I got a sailor over there that's looking for a little competition. Any of you boys want to get your ass kicked by a girl?"

The marines laughed.

"That's not gonna happen," said one of them.

"I got twenty bucks that says it will."

Katherine ran the hustle like a pro. An hour later the marines were all broke and disgusted. As they walked away, Amy motioned her head toward the table where blue eyes was sitting and said, "Who are they?"

"SEAL Team," said Katherine.

"Really? I think I need to introduce myself," said Amy as she walked over to the table. Amy thickened up her Southern accent a little and said, "How y'all doin'?"

Blue Eyes nodded and said, "Pretty good. That was quite a show you put on over there. What's your name?"

"Amy, what's yours?"

"Badger," He said, smiling.

"What? Badger? Your momma didn't like you?"

They all laughed and then he said, "Matt."

"Whatcha got there, Matt?" asked Amy, looking at the large rifle on the table.

"That's a Barret .50 Cal sniper rifle. You want to try it?"

"Dammit, Badger, I just cleaned that," said one of the other SEALS.

"Sure," said Amy with excitement in her voice.

He picked up the rifle and they walked to the firing line. Matt gave her a quick lesson on it and told her she should probably shoot it in the prone position. Amy laid down and flipped the covers open on the scope. She found a target at one thousand meters, opened the bolt, put one in the chamber, and started to squeeze the trigger. The rifle made a huge *BOOM* when it fired. The recoil stung Amy's shoulder a bit, but she wasn't about to show it. It was a tracer round and she watched it fly toward the target.

"That's a hit," Matt said with a smile. "You're a talented woman, Miss Amy," he said with a hint of southern twang. "How about dinner tomorrow night?"

"OK," said Amy, "but it'll be a little late. I work in pediatrics and I tuck my kids in for the evening. Would 9:30 be OK?"

"Oh yeah," said Matt.

Amy walked away with a little more wiggle in her hips than usual.

"Damn Badger, she's beautiful," said one of the other SEALS, "but you're cleaning that fucking rifle."

Amy and Katherine walked back to the Armory and turned in their weapons. Katherine turned to Amy and said, "You've had a good morning. You got a date and here's your cut," said Katherine as she handed her a wad of money.

"What's this?" asked Amy.

"We took those marines for four hundred bucks," said a grinning Katherine.

"You were gambling?" Amy said, surprised.

"Oh, you are so cute," said Katherine as she put her arm around Amy's shoulders.

As they were walking across the base, Katherine stopped said, "I need to stop in and see the XO. You want to meet him?"

"Sure," said Amy.

They walked into his office and the XO's admin assistant rolled her eyes. She told Katherine to go on in. Katherine introduced him to Amy. Amy could tell there was some kind of relationship between her and the XO. Katherine got on his computer and showed him something, and then they hugged for just a little too long.

When they left his office, Amy looked at her and said, "Are you having a relationship with him?"

"I cannot confirm or deny that," said Katherine with a little smile.

"He's an officer, be careful," warned Amy.

Katherine nodded and shrugged her shoulders. They walked out the front gate to the bazaar that the locals had set up. Amy really like the handmade items. She shopped for her family and let Katherine haggle with the locals over the price. Katherine lapsed into the native tongue easily more than once.

"I didn't know you spoke the language so well," said Amy.

"That was Pashto. We are learning Dari. I've picked up a lot from the Taliban soldiers," said Katherine.

They finished shopping and walked back to the base. Outside the gate Amy saw a little dog; a girl dog. She looked injured and starved. Amy stopped and Katherine said, "No, no, no, keep walking; don't, Amy."

But it was too late.

"But she's hurt," said Amy. "I am a doc, you know."

"Amy, they won't let it on the base," said Katherine.

Amy held out her hand to the small, frightened dog. It began to sniff her and then licked her hand. Suddenly Amy had an Idea.

"I think I need a therapy dog for my kids," she said with a smile.

"There is no way in hell, Amy. They will never let it on the base."

"But if I got it on the base, you could talk to the XO. After all, you seem to know him very well," said Amy with a sly smile.

"Amy...dammit, fine. If you can get it on the base, I'll see what I can do," said Katherine.

Amy didn't believe in using her sexuality to get her way, but sometimes a woman's got to do what a woman's got to do. She walked up to the gate guard and showed her ID. He waved her through and she stopped, cocked her hips, tilted her head, and in a slow Southern drawl said, "Hi, what's your name?"

The guard froze for a second and said, "Corporal, um...,"

"Hi, Corporal Um," said Amy.

"No, Corporal, um, Rogers," said the corporal.

"You sure are handsome, Corporal um Rogers. My name is Amy. Do you think you would like to buy me a Dr. Pepper at the USO this evening?" Amy said with every drop of seduction she could muster.

He couldn't even speak. He just nodded his head.

"Good," said Amy. "I need you to do something for me."

"Sure," said Corporal um Rogers.

"I need you to go into that guard shack and focus real hard on that log book for about twenty seconds, and then I will see you this evening for a Dr. Pepper," Amy said while batting her eyes and pursing her lips.

He nodded his head and as soon as he turned, Amy picked up the dog, stuck her in the shopping bag, and walked through the gate.

"I'll be damned," said Katherine after they were past the guard shack.

"I did my part. Now me and Patsy Cline here will wait for you to do yours," said Amy with a wink.

"You named it already? How in the hell did you name it already?" asked Katherine.

Amy kept her word and met Corporal Rogers for a Dr. Pepper. He was a really sweet guy. She gave him an hour of her undivided attention and then a kiss on the cheek, a thank you for a wonderful time, and a good night. When she got back to her tent, Patsy Cline was sitting on her bunk waiting for her. Katherine had to go to Centcom, but before she went she left something on the table next to Amy's bunk. It was a dog tag with a sheet of paper that read, "Second Class Petty Officer Patsy Cline, K-9 therapy animal, USN."

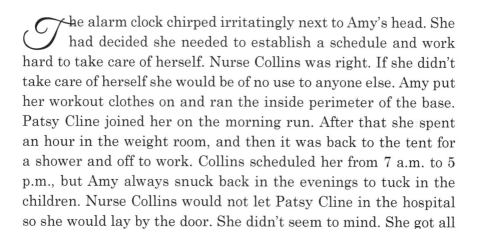

Chapter 60

The alarm clock chirped irritatingly next to Amy's head. She had decided she needed to establish a schedule and work hard to take care of herself. Nurse Collins was right. If she didn't take care of herself she would be of no use to anyone else. Amy put her workout clothes on and ran the inside perimeter of the base. Patsy Cline joined her on the morning run. After that she spent an hour in the weight room, and then it was back to the tent for a shower and off to work. Collins scheduled her from 7 a.m. to 5 p.m., but Amy always snuck back in the evenings to tuck in the children. Nurse Collins would not let Patsy Cline in the hospital so she would lay by the door. She didn't seem to mind. She got all the attention she wanted from passersby.

Matt met her at the USO later in the evening. His arm was bandaged and Amy asked, "What happened to you?"

"The bad guys get lucky now and then."

They talked for hours. Matt Oliver was from outside of West Memphis, Arkansas. His life growing up was much like Amy's. They had so much in common: hunting, fishing, and Matt even had a hot rod '71 Camaro that he coveted. She knew what he was and what he did, but still there was a boyish innocence about him coupled with a mischievous glint in his eye. He seemed so familiar to Amy, but she just couldn't place him. *This one would be easy to love*, thought Amy. Matt was thinking the same thing.

At the end of the night he walked her back to her tent. They stopped at the door and Amy said, "I had a nice time."

"Maybe we could do this again?" asked Matt.

"What about your other girlfriends?" asked Amy with a little grin.

"I don't have other girlfriends," said Matt. "And if I did, I don't have them anymore."

"We'll see," said Amy.

She had turned to walk into the tent when Matt said, "Hey, how about a kiss?"

"OK, but just one," said Amy and, oh my goodness, it was a good one.

Amy loved her job. She had decided that when her time with the military was over she would go into pediatrics. Katherine was right about one thing: the more she saw, the more she began to hate. How people could treat children like that, she had no idea. It was difficult, but she stayed focused on her job and did all she could do to help. The boxes began to show up after Amy put out a call for dolls, stuffed animals, and soccer balls. Henderson Medical, the Black Oak Baptist Church, and Junior Gossett's companies were very generous. Every child got something. Amy made sure of it.

Matt's visits were sporadic. It was the nature of his job. When they were together, it was electric. They were falling in love.

One evening a country singer came to entertain in the USO. It was just him and his guitar. Amy didn't care much for the newer country songs, but she went with Matt, anyway. The singer was really talented. He asked for a request and Amy said, "How about 'Coat of Many Colors'?"

"I love that song," he said. "OK, but only if you'll sing it with me."

Amy had painted herself into a corner on that one. Matt gave her a little shove toward the stage and all of the marines, soldiers and sailors cheered her on. She sat down next to him and he began to play. After the first line, he stopped singing lead and switched to back up. Amy wasn't Dolly, but she wasn't bad. Matt watched and imagined her singing to his children. Right then and there he decided that Amy was the woman he would marry. When she was finished, the crowd went wild.

Matt returned late one evening from a mission and walked to Amy's tent and knocked. Katherine answered the door.

"Hi, is Amy here?" asked Matt.

"No, she has duty and she's staying the night with the kids," said Katherine with a little edge to her voice.

"Can we talk?" asked Matt.

"Sure, come on in," said Katherine with a sigh.

Matt sat down on Amy's bed and said, "Does she know who you are?"

"No," said Katherine.

Matt looked at the floor and quietly whispered, "Are you recruiting her?"

"That's classified," Said T.

"Dammit," Matt said under his breath.

"You love her, don't you?" said T.

"Yes, yes I do," said Matt.

"Do you think you want to marry her?" said T.

Matt looked at her, drew a deep breath, and said, "Yes, T, I want to marry her."

"Well, we both know you don't marry spooks. Isn't that right?" said T angrily.

Matt nodded his head and said, "Look, I am really sorry, T. But the idea of my wife jetting all over the world assassinating people isn't exactly something I imagine when I think about raising a family."

"What exactly do you do for a living, Matt?" snapped T.

"I'm not going to do this forever," said Matt.

T laughed and said, "Yeah, that's what we all say."

Matt stood up and stepped toward her. His eyes were almost begging when he said, "Please T, let this one go."

"It's not up to me, she's already in the system. It's up to her," said T.

Matt looked at her and said, "I need to go. Good-bye, T."

Matt was walking to the door when T said, "Hey, Matt, we were good together, weren't we?"

Matt smiled and said, "Yeah, we were good together."

He started to walk out and T said, "You know, she has all of the skills, but I don't think she'll sign up. She'll make you a good wife someday."

Matt stopped, smiled at her, and said, "Thanks, T." Then he left.

Amy sat at the desk updating files. The room was dark with the exception of the task lighting on her desk and the glow of the monitors attached to some of the children. She sensed the air pressure change in the room as someone tried to silently open the door. She reached down to her thigh holster and drew her M9. She heard the light sound of sand scratching the floor as someone crept in. Then she smelled him.

"I hope you are better in the field than you are right now," she said quietly without turning around.

"Don't worry, I am," said Matt as he put his arms around her neck and kissed her.

A little girl in one of the beds started to giggle.

"Go to sleep," said Amy softly in Dari. Then she said to Matt, "You have to go, I'm at work."

"I know, I just wanted to say I love you," whispered Matt.

"Oh yeah? We shall see. Now go," whispered Amy. She gave him a long, soft kiss and sent him on his way.

The Story of Tatiana Aziz (T)

Tatiana Chamoun was born on Christmas Day 1973 in Lebanon, two years before the start of the Lebanese civil war. She was the middle child of seven. Her father was a captain in the Maronite Christian-controlled army. Her mother was a beautiful, hard working woman that doted over her children. Tatiana was a handful. She constantly sought attention by any means possible. Her father would never admit to having favorites, but the truth was she was it.

Tatiana's father was right in the middle of the first event that sparked the Lebanese civil war. In Sidon, February 1975, three Lebanese fishermen's unions jointly protested the establishment of the Protein Company, a modern, high technology, monopolistic fishing company owned in large part by former president Camille Chamoun, a Maronite Christian, and her father's cousin. During the protest, the army unit led by her father began firing upon protesters, mortally wounding Ma'ruf Saad, the Sunni Muslim leader of the Popular Nasserite Organization of Sidon. Following Sidon's events, street demonstrations erupted in virtually all of Lebanon's major cities and intense fighting occurred between Christian troops and gunmen aided by Palestinian commandos. Her father was marked for death.

Her family lived in a walled compound that was guarded and relatively safe from the violence going on in the cities. She loved all things western. Her little neighbor friend went to America with her family to see relatives and she would always bring back things and share them with Tatiana. One day her friend slipped her a cassette tape by an American singer named Madonna. She went to her secret hiding place, a little cave where the dirt had been wash out from under a concrete wall, put the tape in her Christmas/birthday present, a Walkman, and then turned it up all the way. She didn't understand a word the singer said but the music was wonderful. Then, off in the distance, she heard some loud popping noises.

She pulled off the headphones and heard screams and gunfire; the compound was under attack by Palestinian commandos. Her father had always taught her to hide if something like this were to happen and she was already hiding. The assault seemed to go on forever. In reality it was about fifteen minutes.

Suddenly it became quiet. She peeked out from under the wall and saw nothing, so she snuck to her back door and peeked in through the glass. Her mother was lying on the floor in a puddle of blood. She wanted to run, but something drew her into the house. Her entire family had been butchered. She saw something she could not understand strewn across the floor of her living room. It was her baby brother, beheaded and disemboweled.

Slowly the front door began to open and a man with a machine gun walked in followed by a man in a suit. His name was Tony Aziz, CIA officer. He picked up the little girl, took her out to a car, and sat her next to a blonde woman. The woman put a blanket around her, held her close, and said in Lebanese, "My name is Adele. We are your friends, we will help you. It will be OK."

Aziz smuggled her out of the country. He became attached to the pretty little girl. A couple of forged documents later and she was his daughter, Tatiana Adeline Aziz. Aziz already had a wife, infant daughter, and a two-year-old son. The kids never knew Tatiana as anything but their sister. Her new father was honest with her. He retrieved a large family photo out of Tatiana's house before he left and made sure she kept it so that she would always know who she was and where she was from. That was important to him. He was the son of Lebanese immigrants and he still held a special place in his heart for his parent's birthplace.

Tatiana loved her brother and sister and was very protective of them, but she was a dark, angry child. Her father knew why, though, so he channeled her anger into martial arts. It worked to a degree. She excelled at many different forms of martial arts and had a room full of trophies to prove it. The darkness, however, remained. She was smart and did extremely well in school. When she graduated she went to Georgetown to study pre-law. By the time she got her bachelor's degree, however, she was bored with school and took a job as a translator with the State Department. She eventually became bored with that, too, and was particularly disturbed whenever she had to come into contact with them: Muslims. She hated them all with the heat of a thousand suns.

While walking through the State Department offices, she saw an advertisement for CIA Foreign Service Officers. If it was good enough for her father, she thought, it was good enough for her. She applied and was accepted. She trained at Langley and her instructors saw something very special. Occasionally an older woman would come by and inquire about her. The woman looked very familiar to Tatiana, although she couldn't figure out where she had seen her before. Her name was Adele Harris. Upon graduation she was asked to volunteer for "advanced" training. She gleefully accepted. She ended up at the farm: the CIA training facility for covert operatives.

On her first mission she took a Concorde airliner to France and boarded a train for Berlin, Germany. There she met Adele, who was sitting at a table in front of a coffee shop.

"Do you remember me?" asked Adele.

"Yes, but I could never remember from where," said Tatiana.

"When you were a little girl, officer Aziz brought you out of your parents home and put you in a car. I wrapped a blanket around you and brought you to America," said Adele, smiling.

"Yes, now I remember," said Tatiana with her own smile.

"This is your destiny. This is who you are. It is time to avenge your family. Shall we go?" asked Adele

Tatiana's eyes grew dark as she said, "Yes."

Tatiana's first target was an Egyptian banker that financed the Palestinian Liberation Organization. He had a penchant for fine champagne and even finer young women. Tatiana sat at the Moet & Chandon Ice Imperial Bar at the Hotel Adlon. She dripped sex like honey off a comb. He spotted her almost immediately. She played a little hard-to-get, but one thing led to another and they went to his room. Outside the room his bodyguards stopped her and roughly searched her. She fully expected it.

The door shut behind her and she unzipped her dress, letting it fall to the floor. A thousand dollars worth of red French silk stockings, garters, bra, and panties turned him into a babbling child. She slowly undressed him and pushed him onto the bed. She stood in front of him and licked her lips while playfully rubbing her hand on her crotch. She used her middle finger to push the tube holding the straight razor farther up her vagina, and then she slowly removed her panties. She crawled onto the bed like a big cat, a slow, sensual, mesmerizing motion that hypnotized. She crawled on top and straddled him, and then leaned close to him and rubbed her breasts against his chest while gently kissing his neck. With her left hand she stroked his hair while whispering to him all of the nasty things they were going to do. While whispering she took her right hand, slid the tube from her vagina, popped the top off of it and slid the straight razor into her hand. Just like she and Adele had practiced.

She slowly sat up and smiled at him like a long lost lover, and then she grabbed a handful of his hair with her left hand and jerked his head back. With her right she cut his throat to the bone. Quickly, she grabbed a pillow, put it over his face, and leapt up so she could hold the pillow down with her knees. She grabbed the headboard and pushed down as hard as she could until he stopped moving.

Throat cutting was a messy business and she was spattered with blood. With a damp washcloth she gingery wiped off the blood, touched up her makeup, and got dressed. Then she turned on the TV and watched the news for a half hour. She walked out of the hotel room and told his bodyguards that he said he didn't want to be disturbed. She flipped her purse over her shoulder, flirtatiously winked at the bodyguards, and sashayed down the hall. She confidently walked out the front door of the hotel and into an awaiting car driven by Adele.

"How did it go?" Adele asked.

She smiled and said, "Perfect, it was wonderful."

It was her first kill, the first of many.

Chapter 61

Matt received an invitation to the Marine Corps Ball at Centcom. It was a yearly birthday celebration of the establishment of the marine corps. Spoiling Amy was something Matt was longing to do. Growing up a Southern gentleman, he wanted to show her that part of himself. Matt was scheduled to go home on leave, but he put it off for a couple of days to escort her.

Carla Jo sent Amy a dress and of course it was in true Carla Jo fashion. It was a red Donna Karan with matching heels and ruby-accented jewelry. Katherine did Amy's hair and Amy actually let Katherine apply a little makeup and a lipstick color that matched her dress. When Matt got to Amy's tent to pick her up they were both pleasantly surprised. When Amy opened the door, Matt was clean-shaven with a fresh haircut. He had on his dress blue uniform with his medals and SEAL Team trident insignia. They were both very pleased with what they saw.

Matt arranged to have a Little Bird Special Operations helicopter fly them to Centcom. It was a wonderful night of music, dancing, and good food. It was clear to anyone that bothered to look that Matt and Amy were deeply in love. When the night was over, they flew back to the hospital and Matt walked her to her door. They kissed passionately for a very long time. Matt let his hands wander over her body and then he touched something that Amy was not used to anyone touching. She stopped and pulled her face away from his. Amy looked at him with a half smile and said with a purr, "Do you want that, Matt?"

Matt nodded his head and said, "Yes."

"Good," Amy said as her big green eyes smoldered, "Because I really want you to have it. Do you want to know how to get it?" She said in a more conversational tone.

"OK," Matt said, beginning to sound a bit unsure.

Amy smiled and said, "You need to go to the Black Oak Baptist Church and stand at the altar in front of my God, my pastor, my daddy, my family, and my friends. Then you need to promise to love me and only me for the rest of your life. You do that and I will give you as much as you want, however you want it, whenever you want it. But until then, keep your hands off of it. I love you, Matt. More than I have ever loved any man."

She gave him one last long, soft kiss, said good night, and walked into the tent. Matt walked away shaking his head, thinking he would never tolerate that kind of rejection from any woman except her. He would be taking a cold shower that evening.

When Amy opened the door, Katherine nearly fell on her butt. She had been kneeling by the door listening. "Oh my God, oh my God, oh my God; you are brilliant," said Katherine, sounding just like a teenage girl.

"What do you mean?" asked Amy

"Oh, the church thing with your daddy, all of it. He is talking to himself all the way back to the barracks," Katherine said, grinning. Katherine took perverse pleasure in watching Matt crawl.

"I'm still not sure what you mean," said Amy, sounding a bit confused.

Katherine looked at her and said, "Well, you know, the whole thing about...," Then she stopped. "Amy, you were serious? You meant that? You really did. You meant that."

Amy stood by her bunk folding the dress that she knew cost more than she made in two months. She carefully placed it in a box to ship it back to Carla Jo. Amy looked at Katherine and said, "Yes, I meant it. I meant every word. My daddy told me when I was a little girl that things you get for free mean nothing to you. Those things are easy to throw away. But now, those things you work for, those things you have to bleed to get, they matter. Those are the things you protect. Those are the things that you keep close and are hard to throw away. I am not free and I certainly am not easy."

Katherine shook her head. *Amy has a point*, she thought. She had slept with Matt an hour after they met. Katherine wasn't much for relationships or maybe it was that they weren't much for her. She had always been a loner. It was her nature and the nature of her job. Amy was so honest with no pretense. She caught herself beginning to care deeply about this seemingly simple but intrinsically wise beyond her age young woman. T wanted her as a friend, a real best friend, but there she was living a lie, using Amy's dead mother's name as her own to bring her close.

The next morning Amy was in the courtyard next to the hospital. Patsy Cline was playing with a little boy that had an injured leg because he needed to exercise. Then suddenly Matt appeared, looking a little harried.

"Hey, beautiful," Matt said, looking a bit down.

"Well, hello to you, handsome. I thought you were on a plane heading home," said Amy.

"No, they cancelled my leave. We have a critical mission, or so they tell me," said Matt.

Amy told the little boy in Dari that she would be right back. She took Matt by the hand and led him to the side of the building. She gently pushed him against the wall and with a wicked little grin said, "I'd like to say I'm disappointed, but I'm not. Let me kiss that frown 'til it's upside down."

She did and in less than five seconds, it was.

Matt smiled at her and said, "I really have to go. Maybe I'll see you tomorrow?"

"OK, I love you, Matt Oliver," said Amy.

"I love you, too, Amy Braxton," said Matt. Then they kissed one last time. Neither could know that it really was their last kiss.

"BRAXTON," yelled Nurse Collins.

"Yes, ma'am," said Amy.

"The CO wants to see you in his office ASAP."

"For what?"

"I don't know, he hasn't reported in to me yet today," Nurse Collins said sarcastically, rolling her eyes.

Amy laughed and said, "OK, on my way."

The CO's name was Colonel Charles "Crush" Lubash, former Commanding Officer of Third Recon, Marine Corps Special Operations. He was a man that understood combat and had the scars to prove it. He sat in his office with the XO and a man in civilian clothing: Jon Smith, CIA. The CO looked at Jon and said, "Isn't that whole area under the control of the Taliban?"

Jon chose his words carefully and said, "Not really control; more of an influence. The Taliban know better than to screw with a tribe because the other tribes would turn on them. It's a lawless region. The tribes are the only real form of law and order. To win the heart of a major tribe like that would be a big victory for us. The best part of it is, we won't have to fire a shot."

"Why don't you send a doctor?" asked the CO.

"It's not a place for glorified civilians. It's still a tough neighborhood and we need someone that can function in a hostile environment," said Jon.

"Hmm," The CO grunted. "Why this kid?"

"We had an hour to find a woman who is experienced with children, that speaks the language, and can survive a fire fight. She's it." said Jon.

"Alright, but if you take one of my kids out to that shithole and get them killed, you'll be dealing with me. Do you understand that, Mr. Smith?"

Jon nodded his head.

The CO's admin stuck her head in the door and said, "Petty Officer Braxton is here."

"Send her in," said the CO.

Amy walked in and stood at attention.

"At ease, Doc. We need your help. We have a sick twelve-year-old girl in the Panjshir Valley. Her father is a Tribal Chief and he has asked for our help. This is a 'winning hearts and minds' mission. It is in a tough neighborhood, however, and you must volunteer. We cannot order you to go."

"Panjshir Valley? Like the Lion of Panjshir? That valley?" asked Amy.

"Yep, one and the same. This is a big deal, Doc. Assuring peaceful transit through that portion of the valley could save many American lives. But I have to warn you, it is dangerous," said the CO.

"I would be proud to go, sir," said Amy, beaming with pride.

"OK, go get your gear and then go see Nurse Collins for your med kit. You have an hour to report to the heliport," said the CO.

After Amy left, the CO looked at Jon and said, "I meant what I said. Don't get her killed."

Amy jogged back to her tent. Katherine was sitting and typing when Amy came through the door.

"What are you doing here?" Katherine asked, but she already knew.

"I have a mission," said Amy excitedly.

"Outside the wire?"

"Way outside the wire."

"Have you ever been out there?" Katherine asked, already knowing the answer to that, too.

"Nope."

"Would you mind if I helped you get ready?"

"No, I don't. That would be great. I haven't been in the field in a while," said Amy.

Katherine got up and slid a box out from under her bunk. She opened it to reveal fully prepped field gear. It was very different from military issue: smaller, lighter, and better fitting.

"Where did you get this stuff?" asked Amy.

"It's good to have Spec Ops friends at Centcom," said Katherine with a little smile.

Katherine spent time showing Amy what was in all of the little pockets. She gave Amy a hijab, the traditional headscarf worn by women of the Muslim religion.

"Save yourself some time and wear this under your helmet," said Katherine.

To finish the ensemble, Katherine took out her custom Glock .40 with a thigh holster and handed it to Amy. "There is nothing wrong with the M9. I just like this better," said Katherine.

"Oh yeah, me too," said Amy with an appreciative smile.

Katherine also added four extra clips along with the two in the pockets on the holster. Amy looked at the round in the clip and said, "What kind of ammo is this?"

"The good kind," said Katherine with a sly grin.

Amy and Katherine jogged across the base with Patsy Cline close behind. They stopped to pick up the specially packed medical kit from Nurse Collins. Collins slipped it on Amy's back and said, "Everything from antibiotics to anti-venom. Keep your head down, honey." Then she gave her a hug.

They walked to the gate by the heliport. Katherine and Patsy Cline stopped at the gate. Amy turned to Katherine and gave her a hug. Katherine usually didn't like people touching her, but Amy's honest warmth felt good.

"Thanks for everything, Katherine. I'll be back," said Amy with a smile. She bent down, hugged Patsy Cline, and started walking.

Katherine debated on one last thing. "AMY, WAIT," she called out.

Amy came back and Katherine slipped a small metal box into a little pocket on her shoulder. She grabbed Amy's collar with a force that surprised Amy. Then she said, "In that box is a little blue capsule. If you get captured, bite down on it. I promise you, there are things worse than death. Now go."

Amy looked hard at Katherine and thought, *what the heck is she talking about?* Amy smiled a nervous smile and said, "Thanks." Then she turned and walked toward the flight line. She suddenly felt unsure about what she was doing. The little voice that Uncle Jack told her to listen began babbling, but she didn't quite understand what it was saying.

Amy turned the corner past the hanger and saw the XO and a man wearing a plain tan flight suit. "Doc, this is your pilot, Rocky," said the XO. Rocky shook her hand and said, "Can I call you Doc?"

"Sure, as long as I can call you Rocky," said Amy with that cute smile.

Amy looked at the AH-6 Little Bird gunship. It didn't look like any Little Bird military helicopter she had ever seen. It was black and armed to the teeth. Rocky invited Amy aboard and strapped her in. He put on her headset and showed her how to use it, and then he climbed in, put on his seat belt and headset, and cranked the Little Bird up. Amy hit the ICS, or Interior Communication System, button and said, "So, Rocky, what branch of the service are you in?"

Rocky smiled back at her and said, "I'm not."

The little voice in Amy's head began to scream.

Chapter 62

The Little Bird zoomed above the barren landscape at a cruising speed of one hundred and fifty knots. Amy keyed the ICS and said, "So, Rocky, what's the plan?"

"I thought you had the plan. You forgot the plan?" said Rocky with a serious face. Then he started to laugh. "You virgins are a hoot," he said..

"What did you call me?" said Amy, losing her sense of humor.

"This is your first mission outside the wire, right?" he replied.

"Oh, yeah," said Amy, feeling a little silly for taking it personally. *I really need to relax,* she thought to herself.

"OK," said Rocky. "Here's what's going to happen. In about thirty minutes we are going to land and top off our fuel tanks. We will then proceed to FOB Apache where I will drop you off and you will be picked up by your bodyguards in a big fancy Blackhawk."

"Wait, FOB Apache? That's my rifle platoon. I get to see my boys," said Amy excitedly. Then she stopped and said, "What do you mean by bodyguards?"

Rocky looked at her with a serious face and said, "Well, Doc, if you're gonna visit hell, you're going to want some bodyguards."

Amy looked out of the windscreen at the hostile landscape and thought, *what have I gotten myself into?*

A little over an hour later later, Rocky called in to the FOB. "FOB Apache, this is Little Bird inbound, over."

Lieutenant Simpson replied, "Negative, Little Bird, we are currently engaged with enemy forces, over."

Little Bird replied, "Roger that, Apache. You want some air cover, over?"

Apache replied, "Roger that, Little Bird. Mortar positions five hundred meters to the north. Bad guys two hundred meters to the north and east, over."

Little Bird replied, "Roger that, requesting permission to engage, over."

"Little Bird, you are clear to engage, over," Apache responded.

"Well, Doc, I have some of that fancy pilot shit to do, so hang on."

"Roger that," said Amy.

Rocky banked hard to the left and came around behind the mortar positions. Amy watched the exhaust of the FFAR rockets after they left the tubes. Rocky banked hard again after Amy saw the explosions.

"Direct hit, Little Bird," called Apache.

The Little Bird came back around in a hard banking move that had Amy unconsciously talking to herself.

"WHOA," exclaimed Amy.

"Fun stuff, hey, Doc?"

Rocky fired more rockets at another mortar position and then banked hard again. He made a strafing run to the east. Amy could feel the Little Bird vibrate and could see the tracers from the 7.62 miniguns. Rocky banked hard again behind the FOB and then came out on the north side for another strafing run. He made two more passes and the called in to Apache, "I need to drop my passenger. Stand by for reception, over."

"Make it quick, Little Bird. We are still taking fire, over," replied Apache.

"Roger that, here we come," replied Little Bird

Rocky dove hard for a power insertion. Amy swore they were going to crash, but he sat it down as soft as a mother's touch.

"They're shooting at me, Doc. Get out and good luck," Rocky said with a wink and a smile.

Amy grabbed her stuff and ran like the wind to take cover behind a wall where she almost tripped over Gunny Sullivan.

"Hi, Gunny," Amy said with a big smile.

"Doc? What the fuck are you doing here?" said the Gunny.

"Just figured I'd stop for a visit," said Amy, still smiling.

Gunny grabbed her by the arm and sat her down between some sandbags and said, "I have no idea what the fuck you are doing here, but there are about two hundred Taliban out there trying kill us. You don't fucking move, that's an order."

It wasn't the welcome she thought she would get. Gunny screamed across the FOB, "SIMPSON, WHERE THE FUCK IS MY AIR COVER?"

"SANDSTORMS TO THE SOUTH, NO CHOPPERS," yelled the lieutenant. "WE GOT HAWGS INBOUND FROM THE EAST. SHOULD BE HERE IN TWENTY."

"Shit," said Gunny under his breath.

"PATROL INBOUND," yelled one of the marines.

The gunny watched as the Humvee came up over a rise at full speed.

"GIVE 'EM COVER, LIGHT 'EM UP," screamed Gunny as the marines fired every weapon they had at the enemy. Gunny was talking to himself under his breath, "Come on, come on, almost there." Just then the white smoke of the rocket propelled grenade, or RPG, made a path to the front of the Humvee. The explosion hit the front wheel, causing it to go out of control and flip over. It teetered on it's side, the bottom facing the enemy, and it came to rest about one hundred meters to the west of the FOB and about fifty meters to the north.

"DOC, SPEEDY, DONUT, GO GET 'EM," shouted the Gunny, looking for the doc who had replaced Amy at Apache.

Speedy and Donut came running up and Gunny yelled, "DOC, DOC! GET YOUR ASS OVER HERE, DOC!" Then Gunny looked over the edge of a stack of sandbags and saw that half of the doc's head was gone.

"SHIT," screamed Gunny.

Amy jumped up and took off her backpack. She ran low behind the Gunny and picked up the other doc's medical kit. She took her gloved hand and wiped away the hair, skull fragments, and chunks of gray matter stuck to the kit and threw it on her back, and then she ran back by the Gunny and said, "OK, let's go."

Gunny's eyes got big and he yelled, "I TOLD YOU TO SIT, NOW SIT YOUR ASS DOWN."

Amy's eyes started to flash as she growled back, "You can shoot me, or they can shoot me, but I'm goin' to get my boys."

The gunfire increased from the enemy as the wrecked Humvee came under attack. Gunny knew she was well trained and she was really all he had. He shook his head and under his breath he said, "Fuck." Then he said, "OK, when I tell you to go I want you to sprint along the front of this wall. Thirty meters to the west there is a drainage ditch. Get in it. Crawl until you are parallel with the Humvee. Signal me and we will cover you on the sprint to the Humvee. Get them out and stabilized and we will cover you back to the ditch. Get ready."

Amy gave the Gunny a little grin and said, "Did you know I had a full ride scholarship to Stanford?"

Gunny shook his head and said, "You are not as bright as I thought you were."

Amy shared a few words with Jesus, rubbed Bubba's dog tag, and then she was ready.

"LIGHT 'EM UP," shouted the gunny. Then he looked at Amy, Speedy, and Donut and said, "GO."

Chapter 63

Two Blackhawks flew in formation about a hundred miles to the west of FOB Apache. The first one was a UH-60L. Inside was a six man squad of SEALs. The second was a MH-60L DAP, or Direct Action Penetrator, gunship with a crew of four. Both were outfitted with external fuel tanks for long-range operations.

Lieutenant Commander Bernard "Buck" Casey commanded the SEAL Team. Army Major Alfred "Buzzard" Church was the pilot and squadron commander.

"Buck, you got a copy, over?" called Buzzard.

"Go, Buzzard," said Buck.

"We have turbine problems on the gunship. They have to head home. Call Centcom and see if they want to scrub the mission," said Buzzard.

"Roger that," said Buck.

All of the SEALs were wearing headsets and could follow the conversation.

"Centcom, Angel Flight, over," called Buck.

"Go, Angel Flight," called Centcom.

"We lost our gunship to mechanical failure. Permission to scrub, over," said Buck.

The radio was silent. There was clearly a conversation taking place.

"Angel Flight this is Centcom. Negative. Continue the mission with new parameters. Proceed to FOB Apache, make the pick-up, and continue to the target. Land, retrieve the target, and evacuate, over," said Centcom.

"Roger that, Centcom," said Buck. Buck looked around at the faces in the helicopter. None of them were smiling.

The Blackhawk touched down at a remote fueling base to top off the tanks. The men got out to stretch and started checking their gear. Buzzard was hooking up the fuel hose when he saw a Spec Ops Little Bird. Rocky came out of the building and said, "Buzzard, how ya' doin', man? Nice to see you."

"Rocky, what the fuck are you doing out here?" said Buzzard.

"Taxi service. Had to make a delivery to Apache. This woman was a doll. Close to six feet tall, blonde hair, and these beautiful green eyes. It had to be a spook."

Badger looked up and said, "Hey, are you sure it was a spook?"

Rocky said, "No, I'm not sure, but she was dressed like a spook. She had on all the high tech body armor and was carrying a Glock."

Matt walked over to him and said, "Did she have a little scar above her left eye?"

"Yeah, even that was sexy," said Rocky.

"GOD DAMMIT!" Badger growled. "WHO THE FUCK SENT HER OUT HERE?"

Buck walked over by Badger as Rocky held up his hands and said, "Hey, man, I just brought her out here. I have no idea."

"Easy, Badger," said Buck.

Badger looked at Buck and said, "She's the doc. She's the one we're taking to Panjshir."

"OK, so, we have a mission. We will stay professional. Do not let your personal bullshit get in the way. If you don't think you can do this, I will leave you right the fuck here. Are we clear?" said Buck.

Badger nodded and said, "When I find out who sent her out here, they're fucked." He turned and walked away.

Buck shook his head. He knew Badger didn't make threats and there wasn't a hell of a lot he could do to stop him.

Chapter 64

Amy sprinted along the wall as the deafening roar of cover fire blazing over her head. Chips of concrete peppered her face as the enemy's bullets bounced off the wall. She dove into the ditch followed by Speedy and Donut. It didn't take her long to get in the war. Twenty meters ahead of them, two Taliban soldiers were crawling toward her. She drew the Glock and double tapped the first one in the top of the head. The roar of Speedy's M4 in her left ear sent the second soldier to meet his virgins. They continued to crawl, however, eventually having to crawl over the bodies of the men that had just been killed. Amy always wondered what it would be like and now she knew. Her uncle Jack was right; it ain't like the movies.

They made it to the position parallel with the Humvee and Donut waved his arm. Cover fire erupted again. They made a sprint to the Humvee. Donut and Speedy set up at the front and rear of the Humvee to guard their flanks, and then Amy climbed through the hatch.

"I Need A situation report," Amy shouted.

"DOC! WHAT THE FUCK!" shouted Nick.

"Give me a situation report now," commanded Amy.

"Ricki's dead, I got a through and through on my arm, and Jerry is stuck in his seat belt," said Nick.

"I think my leg is broke, Doc," said Jerry.

"OK, Nick, hold him up. I'll cut his seatbelt," said Amy as she drew her uncle Jack's old KA-BAR. Amy cut the belt and let him down slow. It was a compound fracture.

"OK, Jerry, this is gonna hurt, but I have to splint it," said Amy.

She pulled out the SAM splint and began to wrap it up. Jerry screamed and Amy said, "That's what you get for putting a snake in my sleeping bag."

Jerry stopped screaming and said, "How did you know it was me?"

Amy kept wrapping his leg and without looking up she said, "I didn't, until now." Then she looked up and winked at him. "Now let's get out of here."

Amy had blocked out the battle going on around her. As they climbed out the hatch she started hearing the rounds bouncing off the bottom of the Humvee. Off to her right she saw a trail of white smoke as an RPG went wildly past.

Nick and Amy supported Jerry under his arms and Speedy signaled the FOB for cover. The FOB erupted as they made a sprint to the ditch. They dove into the ditch as Jerry screamed again from the pain. Amy turned to look back toward the Humvee and saw Donut lying ten meters away in the open screaming, "DOC! DOC!"

Amy didn't even think about it. She came up out of the ditch, grabbed Donut by his web gear, and dragged him back into the ditch. She could here the bullets whizzing over the top of them as she opened her kit, got the scissors, and began to cut Donut's pants to find his wound.

Then suddenly, Speedy yelled, "GET LOW!"

Amy dove on top of Donut as the heat and concussion of the blasts passed over their heads followed by the whine of the Warthog's engines. The Cavalry had arrived. They stayed put as the Warthogs delivered devastating firepower and rained holy hell on the enemy. After the forth pass of the Hogs, the Taliban had enough.

"THEY'RE BUGGING OUT!" Came a shout from the FOB. "STAY PUT, WE'LL COME GET YOU."

Amy continued to work on Donut. There was a bullet wound by his spine. He was paralyzed. There wasn't a lot she could do so she put his head in her lap and gently stroked his cheek. "You'll live," said Amy with a smile.

"I can't feel my legs," said a panicked Donut.

"Most of the time it's just temporary," Amy lied. Then she asked, "Hey, Frankie, why does Gunny call you Donut?"

"Because I ate three donuts," said Frankie.

"That's it?" asked Amy.

"They were Gunny's donuts," said Frankie.

"Oh," said Amy with a smile.

Gunny brought a couple of Humvees around and parked the vehicles between them and the enemy's position. The Taliban occasionally left a couple snipers to get in some last kills if someone got careless. Amy climbed out of the ditch and Gunny hugged her and put his head on her shoulder.

"Do you hug all of your docs after a fire fight?" asked Amy.

"No, dumbass, just you," said a relieved Gunny.

They were getting the wounded back inside the FOB when, off in the distance, Amy heard a chopper. She was hoping for a Medivac, but it wasn't. It was her ride. When it landed, Buck jumped out of the Blackhawk and said, "Come on, Doc, let's go."

"I'm busy, be with you in a moment," said Amy as she worked on Jerry.

"No, Doc, right the fuck now. We are on a timeline," said Buck.

Just then Amy saw a Medivac coming over the horizon and she yelled, "OK, GOTTA GO. I LOVE YOU GUYS, OORAH!"

"OORAH!" her boys shouted back.

"Amy grabbed her medical back pack and jogged toward the Blackhawk. She was covered in dirt and smeared with blood. She climbed aboard, sat down next to Matt, and said with a grin, "Hi, Badger." She wanted to kiss him, but it was not the time or place. Matt looked at her and just shook his head.

Chapter 65

Badger slipped a headset on Amy so she could hear what was going on. The Blackhawk lifted off and headed north.

"What the hell were you doing down there?" said Badger.

"My job," said Amy.

"You are not supposed to engage in combat," said Badger with an edge of anger to his voice.

"The other doc is dead. My boys were hurt and I went to get 'em. If you don't like that, well that's just too bad," said Amy, sounding irritated.

"Who sent you out here?" asked Badger.

"I volunteered," said Amy.

"Are you out of your mind? Do you have any idea where we are going?" asked Badger.

"Panjshir Valley; next question?" said Amy, sounding even more irritated.

"Excuse me, I hate to interrupt this episode of the *Jerry Springer Show*, but maybe you two could focus on the mission," Said Buck.

The other SEALs started to laugh.

One of the other SEALs, who's call sign was Fish, said, "Hey, Doc, is this your first combat experience?"

"Yep," said Amy.

"Well then, tell us a war story," said Fish.

She gave Matt a little half smile and said, "OK, well, it all started with a Little Bird ride into the FOB...,"

While telling the story, the others had comments and suggestions. They gave her constant reinforcement that she did a good job and that they were glad she was OK.

Badger knew what Fish was doing. The technical name for it was a critical incident debrief. Amy went through the trauma of combat. She had taken another human's life. Very few people go through that without some strong residual emotions. By sharing her story with the group, she multiplied her victory and success while dividing her pain and regret. There was a possibility that she would be heading right back into combat. They wanted her head on straight.

Amy reached over, patted Matt's knee, and smiled. Badger shook his head. He didn't know what to think, so he just smiled back at her. *How do you stay mad at her?* he thought. As the helicopter dove into Panjshir Valley, Amy keyed her mic and said, "You know, my uncle Jack was a SEAL," said Amy.

The other SEALs shook their heads and rolled their eyes. Everyone a SEAL meets has an uncle or cousin that said they were on the teams.

Matt thought Amy didn't really know how to lie, so he said, "You never told me that.".

"It never came up. Where do you think I learned how to shoot?" said Amy.

"Was he in Vietnam?" asked Matt.

"Yep," replied Amy.

"What was his last name?" asked Matt.

"Brown," said Amy. "Jack Brown."

Every head in the helicopter snapped around and looked at her.

"Hatchet Jack Brown?" asked Buck.

"Yes, sir, that's what they called him," said Amy.

"That explains everything," said Buck.

"This was his KA-BAR. He gave it to me for good luck."

She handed it to Buck. He looked at it like a Christian looks at the Holy Grail. He also noticed something that Amy hadn't: small knurls carefully carved out of the handle. Well over a hundred of them. Somebody was keeping count, Buck thought. Each SEAL held it and then passed it to the next.

Matt began to point out the window and share with Amy the roads and trails that ran through the valley. While he was talking to her, it suddenly occurred to Amy why she fell in love so hard and so quickly with this man; the reason he was so familiar and so comfortable. He was a younger version of her uncle Jack.

Buzzard keyed his mic and said, "Buck, village dead ahead."

Buck looked out the door and saw the compound. It was tucked into a small valley and made up of several huts partially surrounded by a wall. They had studied satellite photos of the area and he felt fairly comfortable with the extraction. Still, something just didn't feel right.

"Buzzard," called Buck.

"Go," replied Buzzard.

"Take a three-sixty around the compound. I want to take a look," said Buck.

"Roger that," said Buzzard.

There's no welcoming committee, just a few people waving at the helicopter. Where are the children and the women? Thought Buck. Buck looked around and saw a small bluff above the village.

"Buzzard," called Buck.

"Go," replied Buzzard.

"Do you think you can drop us on that bluff at three o'clock?" asked Buck. Then he said, "We'll call you down when the area is secure. Stay close and cover us."

"Roger that," said Buzzard.

The Blackhawk wasn't a gunship, but it still had an impressive array of weaponry.

"Doc, get your stuff together and get ready to jump out," said Buck.

"Roger that," said Amy.

The SEALs began to move around and grab their things while Amy stood by the door. Badger slid it open as Buzzard touched one wheel on the edge of the bluff. Buzzard didn't even have time to get an "Oh, shit" out of his mouth. He keyed the mic and screamed, "RPGs!"

A volley of a half dozen RPGs came screaming toward the Blackhawk. Three things happened simultaneously. The first rocket slammed into the external fuel tank causing a massive explosion. Buzzard jerked the stick trying to get away and that act threw the SEALs back into the helicopter. Then Matt Oliver did the last conscious thing of his life. He shoved Amy out of the door.

The blast sent Amy skipping across the bluff and she came to rest in a small crevice at the back of the bluff. The Blackhawk made a quick pivot and dove nose first into the side of the hill where it began to tumble down. More explosions happened as rockets smashed into the mortally wounded bird.

Amy was lying in the crevice, stunned, and trying to figure out what had just happened. She had the wind knocked out of her and was trying to catch her breath. Whatever happened, she thought, it wasn't good.

Chapter 66

Aziz jumped out of the Little Bird at Centcom and made her way through the phalanx of security checkpoints until she got inside the war room. There was a strange pall over the room. Usually it was a very active place. Several large screens adorned the walls with the largest in the center. She saw Danny Kerr sitting at a large control panel. He ran communications for the center.

"Danny," T called out. "How goes Angel Flight?"

"It's over, T," said Danny.

"Are they on their way back?" asked T.

"No, T, it's over. ERIC," Danny called out across the room, "roll the video from 4:50."

T watched the recording from the satellite video, which showed the Blackhawk approaching the bluff and then exploding. She felt her heart sink as it tumbled down the side of the hill.

"What happened?" asked T. "WHAT THE FUCK HAPPENED?" she said so loud that everyone in the room stopped what they were doing.

"It was all a set up, T. There was no sick child. It was an ambush," said Danny.

T spun around and looked at the general in charge sitting at a table surrounded by other officers and said, "How did you let this happen? What the fuck were you people thinking?"

The general stood up and with a stern expression on his face said, "Now you hold on a second, young lady. This had nothing to do with us. This was a CIA op. I just lost half a squad of SEALs, a corpsman and a Special Ops Blackhawk. I'm going to be in search of a few answers myself. You got a problem, take it somewhere else."

T knew he was right. She walked back over by Danny and said, "When do the Search and Rescue teams take off?"

"Not right now, we got sandstorms in the area. It will be awhile. As hostile as that area is, they will need escorts. It will probably be a long while," said Danny.

T put her head down and felt grief, an emotion she hadn't experienced in a long time.

"T, it was an op and ops go bad. It's the nature of the business," said Danny.

"Yeah, well, that corpsman was my best friend," said T.

Danny turned back to the screen, shook his head, and said, "I didn't know spooks had friends."

As soon as he said it he wished he could have taken it back. He felt the heat of T's stare on the back of his neck. Then he said, "I'm sorry, T. I'm really sorry. I didn't mean that. Please, T, I'm really sorry."

He was as afraid of her as everyone else. He turned to look over his shoulder at her and she was gone.

T walked out to the Little Bird and headed back to the evac hospital. She tried to block out her feelings about Amy and tried to figure out what went wrong. She would be visiting Mr. Smith and it wouldn't be congenial. *One wrong answer and I will take him the fuck out*, she thought.

The Little Bird sat down at the evac hospital. She got out and walked to the gate. T hadn't cried since she was nine years old; then she saw Patsy Cline at the gate, waiting for Amy. T stopped, sat down, and hugged the dog. A little moan snuck out of her mouth and then tears started to fall.

Chapter 67

*A*my finally got her breath back and began to check herself over for injuries. Her knee throbbed a little and there was a sharp pain in her side. *Must be a cracked rib*, she thought. She wasn't exactly sure what to do next. She was hidden, but did anyone see her get out of the helicopter? Did anyone need help? She jumped as a secondary explosion rocked the Blackhawk. Matt knew where she was. He would come get her. She pulled her Glock and put herself in a position to shoot anyone that tried to capture her. If they stuck their head over the crevice, they were done.

She kept waiting for the sound of the Squad Automatic Weapon, SAW, or the HKs carried by the SEALs. There was nothing. Then she heard cheers and the warbling battle cries of the Taliban soldiers as they fired their AK-47's. *Is Matt gone? Are they all dead? Why are they cheering? We were here to help them,* she thought. Was this an ambush? She decided that she needed to follow her training. She would wait for dark or help, whichever came first.

Amy played the conversation over and over in her head with Matt about the roads and trails. She wished she had been paying more attention, but she was distracted by her thoughts on their relationship. *Should have known better than that,* she thought.

The voices below her on the side of the hill became louder. She understood a little of what they were saying. Something about, "When they come, we will get them again." It was an ambush, Amy thought. It had to be. And now they were setting up for another one.

Amy kept hidden for another hour and then it began to get dark. *It's too early for it to get dark,* she thought. Then she heard the wind kick up. It was a sandstorm. *Choppers don't fly in sandstorms*, she thought. *They're not coming, at least not right away, but the enemy might. Escape and evade,* she heard her uncle Jack say, *escape and evade.* She reached into her kit and pulled out an N95 medical mask. She also had clear goggles. She took a big drink from her CamelBak. *That wasn't smart,* she thought. She would need to conserve all she could. She wrapped the hijab snug around her face and crawled from the crevice.

Visibility was low and the wind was blowing hard. *Good,* she thought. *They won't be able to see me from the valley.* As she took her first step, her knee felt tight, but not too bad. Her side, on the other hand, ached with every breath. She decided to try to make it to the top of the hill and down the other side before daylight. As they were making the three-sixty, she thought she remembered a trail. Travelling directly on a trail was not too smart, but as long as she kept it in sight she knew she was going in the right direction. She needed to go southwest; that was where a road was located that was used by the good guys and the bad guys. It was going to be tricky. As she took her second step up, her knee throbbed and her side ached. Then she thought to herself, *I should have gone to Stanford.* She laughed at herself. It was grim humor, but she would need all she could get.

It was a heck of a lot further than it looked to the top. Slowly the sandstorm started to let up and it became brighter out as the winds died down. Being exposed on the side of the hill would surely get her caught, so she picked up the pace. Thankfully, it would be dark before the windstorm completely died down. When it finally did stop, the sky cleared and a half moon appeared. She would need that light. She had a flashlight, but there was no way she would use white light for anything. You could see that for miles. There were cliffs, drops, crevices, and loose rocks everywhere. It was treacherous.

Four hours later, she made it to the top of the hill. *Hill*, she thought to herself. *These aren't hills, these are mountains.* Sitting down between two rocks, she took a drink and looked around. She could see the outline of the village in the moonlight way off in the distance and the smoke as it continued to rise from the Blackhawk. She checked her watch; it was 2 a.m. She had about three hours to find the trail before the sun came up.

After the blast, Amy went more or less on autopilot. As the shock of what happened continued to wear off, she thought about Matt. She felt the blast and had to accept the fact that he was dead. Grief began to creep in. She had to stop thinking about that. There would be time to grieve later. She started down the other side of the hill and her knee felt even worse. Going down was harder that climbing up. She would take two steps down, three over, two up, four down, and on and on. It seemed endless. Two hours later she stepped from behind a boulder and there was the trail. She stopped and listened for anything; any sound, a step, a voice, a deep breath, anything. She heard nothing. She broke her rule and began to slowly walk the trail. She doubted she would be seen because she was not silhouetted in the open. Still, she went slow and was careful.

A glow slowly came up in the east and she realized that she needed to find a place to sleep. She walked off the trail and found a well-hidden area between a couple of rocks. It looked like it would offer her some shade, at least until the afternoon. The sun began to rise and she got comfortable, or at least as comfortable as one could get resting against a rock. She thought about tending her wounds, but she was exhausted. Her dreams came quickly. They were all about Matt. Three hours later a Taliban soldier poking her in the chest with his AK-47 rudely awakened her.

Chapter 68

*J*oseph sat on the front porch opening his birthday presents. He pulled a brand new fire suit out of the box. It had his name stitched on the chest and it was amazingly similar to Dale Earnhardt's. He loved it, but he didn't get what he really wanted. There was no bow on Kelly. Leon brought out a package that had been shipped from Afghanistan. Joseph opened it to find a handmade oil lamp with a letter. Joseph opened it and read,

Hi Jo,
Rub it all you want, but I don't think you'll get a genie. I miss you. I'm doing fine and should be home in a few months. You'll have to let me take some laps in your car when I get home. Give everyone my love and I love you,
Amy.

P.S. Kelly likes you, too, more than you think. Just give it a few more years. She'll be there.

Joseph smiled and said, "I really miss her."
The whole family was sitting on the porch eating fried chicken when Carla Jo looked out to the driveway and saw the dark sedan with government plates stop in front of the house. She made an

involuntary noise and drew a deep breath. Jack saw her and looked. They both knew exactly what it was. The commander in his dress uniform and the chaplain got out of the car and walked to the front porch. It didn't occur to anyone else what they were looking at.

"Leon Braxton?" The commander inquired.

Leon said, "Yeah, what can I do for you?"

"Is there a place we can talk?" Said the commander.

By the look on his face, Leon began to understand that something just wasn't right. He stood up and said, "We're all family here, go ahead."

The commander did not mince words. He pulled out a letter and began to read, "Mr. Braxton, the Department of Defense regrets to inform you that your daughter, Petty Officer Amy Lynn Braxton, is missing in action. The helicopter she was riding in was shot down in the Panjshir Valley. Recovery efforts are under way and we will keep you informed about any further developments. I'm sorry, Mr. Braxton."

Silence fell over the porch. The chaplain stepped forward and said, "I would like to pray with you if that is OK."

"Wait a minute," said Jack, "MIA? You don't have a body?"

"No, sir," said the commander. "Recovery efforts are underway."

"Leon, don't go there yet. The military makes mistakes all the time. Don't give up."

"Is that true, commander?" asked Leon.

"Yes, it is. Now would be a good time to pray," said the commander, not believing what he was saying.

They prayed and prayed hard. The officers left and hugs and tears were shared on the porch. Kelly reached over and hugged Joseph. They both began to weep.

Jack and Carla Jo went home and Jack pulled a box out from under his bed. He searched through it and found a card, and then he sat down by the phone and dialed a number. The voice on the other end said, "Central Intelligence Agency, how can I help you?"

"John Masters," said Jack.

"Hold, please," said the operator.

The phone rang and Masters' admin picked up immediately.

"Office of John Masters, how can I help you?"

"I need to speak to John," said Jack.

"I'm sorry, but Mr. Masters is not accepting any calls right now. Would you like to leave a message?" said the admin.

"No, ma'am. Tell him this is Hatchet, code 6," said Jack.

"Please hold," said the admin.

John Masters, or as they called him in the Teams, Johnnyreb, was Jack's SEAL Team swim buddy. They went out on many missions together and Jack had saved his ass more than once.

"JACK! WHAT THE FUCK! IT'S BEEN YEARS! Hold on a minute," said Johnnyreb.

Jack could hear him clearing people from his office. It got quiet and Johnnyreb said, "Damn, Jack, it's good to hear from you. How ya' doin'?"

"Not good, Johnnyreb. I need to call in a favor." said Jack.

"Anything for you, buddy, you know that. What's goin' on?" said Johnnyreb.

"I have a niece, Petty Officer Amy Braxton. Got a visit from the grim reapers today telling us she's MIA. Supposedly her helicopter was shot down in the Panjshir Valley. Tell me what you know."

"Heard about it Jack, let me do some digging and find out. You gonna be at this number?"

"Yep," said Jack.

"OK, I'll call you back," said Johnnyreb.

Jack sat and watched the phone. Two hours later it rang.

"Jack?" said Johnnyreb.

"Go," said Jack.

"Wow, quite a niece you have there. She was being recruited."

"By who?"

"By us," said Johnnyreb.

"You're shittin' me," Jack replied.

"Nope. Her recruiter was an officer they call T. She doesn't usually recruit. Her specialty is, well, um, off-site interrogation.

She's the meanest bitch on two legs. She scares the fuck out of me. I'm reading these reports and she writes about Braxton as if she's a cross between Mother Teresa and, well, you. You taught her the trade, didn't you?"

"I showed her some things," said Jack.

"Yeah, OK. I watched the satellite video of the attack. I'm not saying she didn't get out, I'm just saying I don't know how she could have. Get her family ready for the worst. If I hear anything else, you'll be the first to know. I'm sorry, Jack," said Johnnyreb with sadness and sincerity.

Jack's chin fell to his chest and the hope he was holding onto drained away to be replaced by the hot pain of grief. Jack took a deep breath and said, "Thank you, Johnnyreb. I appreciate it."

"Anytime Jack, don't be a stranger."

Chapter 69

"GET UP! GET UP!," the soldier yelled in Pashto.

Good guy or bad guy? she wondered. Amy got up slowly and said in Pashto, "American friend." That was the wrong thing to say. The butt of the AK-47 whipped around toward her head. She ducked just enough so that it clipped her helmet and knock it off. She fell backward and landed on her ass.

"GET UP, GET UP!" The soldier yelled again. They walked around to the trail and Amy had her hands raised. He stuck the barrel of the AK into her back and pushed her up against a rock. Quickly she made the decision that she would not be captured. She had practiced things such as this with her uncle Jack. She knew exactly what she was going to do.

He took her Glock out of the holster and stuck it in his belt.

"HANDS DOWN," he barked. She saw the twine as he pulled it out of his pack to tie her hands. *So far so good*, Amy thought. He kept the AK pressed into the center of her back. She presented her left wrist to be tied. When he took it, she had him.

She quickly spun to her left, grabbing his wrist and jerking it across the front of his body. The move forced him to spin and the AK to be pointed away from her. At the same time she drew the KA-BAR with her right hand and with it in her fist, blade pointing out, she lunged at his throat. She felt no resistance and thought she missed so she swept the knife back the other way and buried it in the front of his shoulder. He dropped the AK and opened his mouth to scream, but nothing came out. Then a gusher of frothy blood spewed from the huge gash in his throat. She got him.

Amy watched him writhe on the ground until he stopped moving. She began to tremble. *Snap out of it*, she kept saying to herself, but her body wouldn't listen. It took her a few minutes to calm down, and then she started evaluating her situation.

The first thing she thought was that where there was one, there were more. Grabbing him by his feet, she dragged him behind the rocks. Then she started to go through his pack. Three canteens of water, four full clips for the AK, and a pair of binoculars. This one was the Taliban equivalent of a forward spotter. Then she found the radio. Did he call in that he had found her? She didn't know. But right then she knew she had to go. Then she thought, *how did he find me?* She looked up the trail and immediately saw her footprints leading behind the rocks. *That was stupid*, she thought.

It was still daylight so she looked around for the best cover to operate in. Unfortunately, it would mean going back up. Her knee was really hurting and her side wasn't much better. She would have to find a secure place and take care of herself.

She slowly worked her way across the mountainside above the trail. Every once in a while she stopped and used the binoculars to look around for any sign of the enemy. She saw nothing. It took awhile to find a place where she couldn't be seen from any angle, but she found one. Her kit was stocked with everything but not very much of anything. The swelling in her knee was causing her pain so she figured she would drain it. She found a needle that was long enough, sterilized a spot and stuck the needle in. Oh my God, did it hurt. Suddenly she felt bad for making fun of her boys when they whined as she worked on them in the field. As she drained it, the pressure was relieved and it felt better.

Reaching back to her side by her ribs where she felt the pain, she pulled her hand away and saw blood. She opened an alcohol wipe and started to clean the wound. The wipe caught on something. It felt like a small, jagged piece of metal. *Shrapnel?* she thought. She started to tug on it and excruciating pain shot through her side. She wasn't sure how big it was, but it was lodged in the cartilage between her ribs. *Might as well leave it,* she thought. More damage would be done trying to remove it.

Exhaustion began to take hold of her again and she really wanted to rest. Safety was never guaranteed, but she couldn't imagine anyone seeing her where she was. The radio was off so she clicked it on, put it up to her ear, and listened. She could not understand every word, but she understood some and a few phrases. She went across the pre-programmed channels, listening, and heard very little. Nobody was talking about or looking for her. Finally, she decided to rest.

Chapter 70

The Humvee pulled up next to the hanger and T jumped out with four big uglies she called the "Quiet Ones." Making her way to the Cessna Citation jet, she noticed Jon Smith standing by the door. He had a bandage across his nose, two black eyes, and his arm was in a sling from a dislocated shoulder. T laughed to herself and said, "I guess Crush Lubash found you?"

Jon didn't say a word. As T walked by she said, "You're damn lucky I didn't get to you first."

They all boarded the plane and it quickly reached altitude for the three hour flight. Staring out the window, T thought about her friend and how much she missed seeing her every day. That eventually turned to thoughts of vengence. *I'll hunt those son of bitches to the ends of the earth*, T thought to herself.

Three hours later, T felt herself being nearly thrown from the seat as the Cessna Citation came under hard breaking to stop at the little airfield. She grabbed her big black gym bag, jumped out and together they boarded a Blackhawk for the short ride to a little outpost thirty miles north of Tashkent, Uzbekistan. The jet immediately taxied away and took off. Looking around the inside of the Blackhawk, T was thinking, *this is what Amy must have seen as she died.* T had never even entertained such crazy, emotional thoughts, but there they were, running around in her head. *Good,* she thought. *I will use them to my advantage.*

After the Blackhawk set down, T walked into a house where Uzbek secret service personnel greeted her. They directed her to a table where three files were laid out. She sat and studied each one, learning and remembering as much as she could. Three captured Taliban soldiers, all of whom took part in the ambush. Army Rangers captured them on a trail to the north of Panjshir. T picked up her bag and walked toward the basement door. She saw herself in a mirror and stopped. She was looking older. Small crow's feet had appeared in the corners of her eyes. Maybe Matt was right. Maybe she wouldn't do this forever. Then again, she loved it. Oh God, how she loved it so.

T opened the door and walked into the room, locking it behind her. She turned and smiled at the three naked men bound tightly to big wooden chairs. When they saw who it was, one soldier involuntarily began to urinate. None of them knew her, but every one of them knew of her. She had let a few go, as disfigured as they were, to tell the tale of T.

"Hello," She said in Pashto. "My name is T and it is very nice to meet all of you. I will be asking a few questions and I expect answers. Do you understand?" She said while screwing a self-igniting torch tip onto a small bottle of propane. The men immediately began to whimper and weep.

"My first question. Who led the ambush?"

She had already decided who she would make an example of. The man in the middle was seemingly the strongest and least likely to know anything.

"Very well," she said. The button on the igniter clicked and a three-inch blue flame appeared at the end of the torch. She thought for a second and turned it off, setting it down on the end of the table. Her fingers reached into her top pocket and pulled out a picture. While holding it up in front of each of their faces, she said in Pashto, "This is me. That woman next to me is my best friend, Amy. She died in that helicopter you shot down. MY BEST

FRIEND, AMY," she screamed. T needed them to know it was personal. Then she lit the torch and went to work on the middle soldier's face.

T knew how to boil the flesh on his face without killing him; or at least without killing him too quickly. Sometime during her work, over the screams of the middle soldier, she heard another soldier shouting, AMIR, AMIR, AMIR!"

T stopped and turned off the torch. The smell of burnt hair and flesh permeated the room.

"What was that?" she said.

"General Amir, he planned it," said the soldier on the right.

"Pakistani General Amir?" asked T.

"YES, YES, YES, he is Taliban."

The soldier on the left said, "Quiet."

T picked up the torch, hit the button, and went to work on the soldier on the left's face. Occasionally she looked at the soldier who spoke about Amir and said, "I don't think you want to be quiet. Do you? Do you want to be quiet?"

"NO, NO, Amir planned it. Achmed led it."

T stopped and turned off the torch. She stepped out in the hall and cornered Jon.

"Jon, where did you get the intel for that mission?" T asked.

"I told you, T, the Pakistanis," said Jon.

"WHO?" screamed T and Jon jumped.

"General Amir," said Jon.

T walked back into the room, looked at the soldier on the right, and said, "Thank you. You have been helpful. I only have one more question. Where is Achmed?"

"I do not know," said the Soldier with his head down.

"That is too bad. I was hoping you and I could be friends, but it's not working out that way," said T while picking up the torch.

"He went north to sell the tribal chief's daughters, and then he was supposed to meet Amir in Pakistan. That's all I know, I swear, that is all I know," said the begging soldier.

T hit the igniter on the torch and the flame shot out of the tip. Then she asked, "How does he travel?"

"He rides in a small caravan with three trucks and eight bodyguards. He disguises himself as a merchant. He takes the Khyber Pass. Please, it's all I know," said the soldier, in tears.

T brushed the torch across his face enough to singe his beard and said, "OK, then; I will go see if you have told the truth. If you have not, I will be back and there will be no talking."

T turned off the torch, unscrewed the top, put it in her bag, and walked out. *What is wrong with me,* she wondered. *I was entirely too good to those people.*

T had two missions and the first was Amir. He would be easy to find, but hard to kill. *Fucking politics,* she thought. Achmed would be hard to find and easy to kill. She would go after him first.

Chapter 71

Staff Sergeant Zachary Bain walked down the tailgate of the C-130 for the jump into the night sky. He wasn't a SEAL, although he went to most, if not all, of the same schools. They never made movies about his job. Maybe if they had a cooler name or something? He didn't really care. He didn't have a team and didn't want one. He operated alone. He was one of only three hundred in the world with his particular skill set. A truly talented, brave, deadly, and elite soldier if ever there was one. Staff Sergeant Zach Bain was an air force combat controller.

Zach and another combat controller were hand-picked by T for this particular mission. T knew Zach didn't screw things up. It didn't hurt that she also appreciated that he was good in bed. Zach would make a HAHO, or high altitude high opening, jump into the Khawak Pass. There he would camouflage himself high on the hillside, sit, watch, and wait. He was looking for three trucks with specific writing on the side transporting possibly nine men. If he saw them, he would contact Centcom and direct an airstrike against the convoy.

Amy looked through her binoculars up the side of the mountain and could see headlights off in the distance. She had found the road. Her knee was screaming with pain so she decided to take the cortisone she had and shoot it up. *Four hours until daylight,* Amy thought to herself. If she could find a secure area along the road, she would wait for friendlies. The cortisone took effect immediately. Her knee felt brand new, although she knew it wouldn't stay that way. She took a big drink from her Camelbak. It tasted like bad pool water. Combining the Taliban soldier's water with her own meant she had to use the purification tablets that Katherine sent with her. It was nice to have them. The dressing on her side was soaked through so she cleaned her wound and changed the dressing. The last shot of antibiotics was loaded into the needle and she injected it. In forty-eight hours she figured her wounds would really started making her life miserable.The ground was relatively flat where she was so she slung the AK onto her back and started to jog.

Danny looked over at T who was nodding off in a chair and said, "Coyote is in place at the Anjuman Pass and Fox is moving into position at the Khawak Pass."

"Thanks, Danny," said T.

"Hey, T, you know I am sorry about that comment I made, you know, about your friend," said Danny.

"Well, you didn't lie. I guess I'm not supposed to have any friends," said T.

Major Brad "Cowboy" Snyder climbed into the cockpit of his A-10 and strapped in. He looked over at his youngest and newest pilot strapping into the plane next to him and thought, *what a great kid. I hope he doesn't fuck up.* Major had no clue where they were going, but he did know they were loaded to do some heavy damage. Along with the 30mm cannon mounted on the nose, they were loaded with Rockeye cluster bombs and Maverick AGM-65 air-to-surface missiles. Somebody was going to have a bad day.

Achmed was having a few challenges of his own. A warlord and his men surrounded his convoy. They controlled the Khawak Pass and tense negotiations were underway. In the end it would cost $500 American to ensure safe passage.

Amy had to slow down as she started up the side of the mountain between the valley and the road. Time once again had slipped away and she saw the color of the sky changing in the east. The sun would be up soon. Looking up with her binoculars she found the place she would wait. A large berm of rocks created by rockslides that followed the road would offer her perfect cover and allow her to maintain a visual on the road.

"Centcom, Fox in position, over," said Fox.

"Loud and clear, Fox," called Danny.

"Now we wait," said T.

Chapter 72

*A*my found a shaded place below the rocks next to the road. She drifted in and out of sleep until she heard what sounded like an engine in the distance. She found a place between the rocks that would give her a good view of the road. A convoy of three trucks appeared. This particular place on the road had a widening and the squeal of brakes let her know that they were stopping.

Two thousand yards away, Staff Sergeant Bain called Centcom. "Centcom, this is Fox, over."

"Go, Fox," said Danny.

"It's them, they're here," said Fox.

T jumped up and told Danny, "Scramble the Hogs. Tell them that their forward controller is call sign 'Fox.'"

The White House

President Elizabeth North was the quintessential conservative that arrived just in time to give a fast living, big spending country some tough love. Liz, as her friends called her, was a woman of the great outdoors. Hunting and fishing filled her family's freezer for the long northern winters. A mother of five with a thundering velvet hand, she came from a working class family. She understood middle America and they adored her. The elites on the coasts despised her. They called her a hick and a simpleton. Those closest to her, revered her as honest, pragmatic, and determined.

Liz also had a dark side, if you could call it that. It was a desire to protect the country against all enemies and she didn't much care how it got done. An hour after she was sworn in she fired the directors of the FBI, the CIA, the NSA and several other less-discussed departments tasked with the defense of the country. She replaced them all with battle-hardened warriors more concerned with the eradication of America's threats than with the bureaucracy and the law as written. She filled their coffers, gave them a handful of presidential pardons, and turned them loose. There would be no 9/11s on her watch.

"Madam President, Director Dotson of the CIA is on line one," said Steven Collier, the president's chief of staff.

"Yeah, Tim," the president said into the phone.

"We have Taliban's number two on the screen in the Sit Room," said Director Dotson.

"Be right down," said the President. "Spock, let's go to the Sit Room."

The president's chief of security, Conrad "Mr. Spock" Mason, was hand-picked by Director Dotson from the Secret Service's best and brightest. The president called him Mr. Spock because he had never shown any emotion on the job. Of course, that was Liz teasing him. She had seen him with his kids. Spock lifted his wrist to his face and said, "Polar Bear moving."

Khawak Pass

"Centcom, this is Fox, over," called Fox.

"Go, Fox," called Centcom.

"The convoy has stopped. The targets are leaving their vehicles. They seem to be gathering at the last vehicle in line," said Fox.

"Roger that, Fox. We have the position on satellite," said Centcom.

The big screen in Centcom and the Sit Room lit up with a fairly clear satellite picture of the activities on the Khawak Pass.

"Fox, this is Cowboy, over," Said Major "Cowboy" Snyder, commander of the A-10 squardron.

"Go, Cowboy," said Fox.

"We are nine minutes out," said Cowboy.

"Roger that. Target is currently static; will keep you posted," said Fox.

Amy checked the AK, put her stuff down, and worked her way to where the men had gathered at the rear of the truck. She could hear them laughing and underneath that, a muffled cry that sounded like a child or a puppy. She still had no idea if they were friendly or not. From the way they were dressed and the weapons they carried, she doubted they were friendly.

Achmed dragged the daughter of the tribal chieftain out of the back of the truck. He demanded that she marry him. She spat on him. He had murdered her father and her family before the attack on the Blackhawk. She screamed that she would rather die and that was just fine with Achmed.

The Sit Room

"Madam President, we can black this out if you would like," said Director Dotson.

"No, Tim, I need to see it. So this is a stoning," Liz said aloud. "Live for us to see. How brutal, how horribly brutal; where are the A-10s?"

"Eight minutes out, ma'am," said Secretary of Defense Grant Engel.

Liz put her head in her hands and said, "Animals; that's somebody's little girl. How those assholes excuse this, I have no Idea."

Khawak Pass

Amy lifted her head up just in time to see a rock strike what appeared to be a teenage girl on the side of the head. It made a sickening thud and blood sprayed from the wound. *Oh my God, they are killing a child*, thought Amy. She sat down, terrified. It brought back memories of her own attack. She looked back through the gap in the rocks just in time to see a man in the red scarf carry a rock the size of a bowling ball toward the girl. The rock went up and then the rock came down. The sickening sound of skull crunching made Amy nauseous. She slid back behind the rock, struggling to breathe. Panic was setting in and then, just as suddenly, something replaced the panic. It was an eerie calm. Everything she was as a human being, the core of her soul, was out where she could look at it. God had put her here. He had prepared her for this one moment. Her own brutal attack suddenly had a reason. Everything she knew about right and wrong would be proven with her combat skills. She was a soldier of the Lord. If she should die, then it was God's will. *They want a war?* Amy thought to herself. *I'll give them one.* She rubbed Bubba's dog tag as she bowed her head and prayed, *Yea, though I walk through the valley of the shadow of death, I will fear no evil. For thou art with me....*

"Fox, this is Cowboy; six minutes out," called Cowboy.
"Roger that, Cowboy," said Fox.

The Sit Room

"Six minutes out, huh, Tim?" said the president.
"Yes, ma'am. They won't miss."

Khawak Pass

The OODA loop was working in Amy's head. She had a plan. They had practiced this scenario behind Uncle Jack's house: multiple targets at close range. There were nine of them against her. Amy had surprise and cover. They were in the open, so she figured the odds were just about even. Moving to the right, she found a position that would allow her to drive them where she wanted them to go. She raised the rifle and took aim.

Centcom

"CENTCOM, THIS IS FOX. THE TARGET IS UNDER ATTACK; TWO DOWN, THREE DOWN, WHOA, HEADSHOT, FOUR DOWN," Fox shouted.

"What the fuck?" T said. "Danny, pan out, pan out with the camera."

"I'm trying, T," said Danny.

The Sit Room

The president leaned forward in the chair and said, "Tim? Grant? What the hell is going on?"

They looked at each other, both surprised by the activities.

"No idea, Madam President. We have no assets in the area," said Grant.

Centcom

"DANNY! RIGHT THERE, BEHIND THE BERM," said T.

"I don't know who he is, but they're running right at him," said Danny

Khawak Pass

Amy fired quickly from behind the berm and began to run low and to the left, racing them to the front truck. Amy heard them return fire. They fired at her previous position. *Crappy Russian ammo,* she thought. It sure made a lot of smoke when it was fired. She waited until she heard footsteps close by and then raised up her rifle and fired.

"FIVE DOWN, SIX DOWN," yelled Fox.

"Fox, this is Cowboy, three minutes out over," said Cowboy.

"Roger that, Cowboy," said Fox.

The Sit Room

"Could someone please tell me what the hell is going on?" said the president.

Tim leaned over, hit a button, and said, "Fox, this is the Sit Room. What do you see, over?"

The Sit Room? Oh shit, Fox thought. "Sir, I'm sorry, I see nothing."

"Sit Room, this is Centcom. They are being attacked by a lone assailant. Check your screen along the bottom center. You should be able to make out a figure," said Centcom.

"Roger that, Centcom," said Tim.

Khawak Pass

Amy ran back to her right. She figured they would try to escape in the lead truck. She aimed her rifle through the window where the door handle would be and started talking softly to herself, "Grab it, grab the handle, grab it; there, good boy."

"DAMN, ANOTHER HEAD SHOT, SEVEN DOWN," said Fox.

"Fox, this is Cowboy, two minutes out, over," called Cowboy.

"Roger that, Cowboy," said Fox.

Amy felt no need to maintain cover. She could take whoever was left in a straight-up gun battle. She knew they were hiding behind the truck, so she got low looking for feet. She saw one, hit her belly in the prone position, and blew the foot most of the way off. The body it was attached to fell to the ground where she put two more rounds in it. Only the man in the red scarf remained.

"Centcom, this is Fox. I have a spotter's scope on her and I mean her. It's a woman; apparently an American by the uniform," said Fox.

"Fox, this is Cowboy on final approach. Request permission to engage, over," said Cowboy.

Centcom

"Centcom, Cowboy is requesting permission to engage, over," said Fox.

T stared at the screen. "It can't be, it just can't be," said T to herself. "Give me a close up on her, Danny. NOW, DANNY, NOW!" yelled T.

The camera zoomed in.

Khawak Pass

Amy figured out where the man in the red scarf would be. She ran back to the last truck and went around behind it. She wanted some distance in case he decided to take a shot. Slowly she crept around the corner. There he was, huddled by the front tire of the first truck. *Coward, child killing coward,* she thought. Then she heard Uncle Jack's voice again saying, "Assume everyone is armed."

The Sit Room

"Tim, are you going to vaporize this woman or are we going to find out who she is?" said the president.

Centcom

"ABORT!" screamed T at Danny, "ABORT! OH MY GOD, IT'S HER!"

"I can't do that, T. I communicate, I don't give orders," said Danny.

"YOU TELL COWBOY TO ABORT OR I WILL SHOOT YOU IN THE FUCKING HEAD," Said T, pulling her pistol.

"Cowboy, this is Centcom. Abort, I repeat, abort. Go to the S/W and circle at fifteen thousand," said Danny.

"Roger that, Centcom. You copy, Fox?" said Cowboy, not sure about where the order was coming from. He was supposed to follow the directives of the combat controller.

"Cowboy, this is Fox. Circle and await orders," said Fox.

"Roger that, Fox," said Cowboy.

The Sit Room

"Well, Madam President, someone read your mind," said Tim.

"About time," said the president. "Oh look, I don't think she's finished yet."

Khawak Pass

"GET UP," Shouted Amy in Pashto at Achmed while leveling the AK at him.

"I speak English," said Achmed.

"GOOD, WALK," commanded Amy.

Achmed started to walk. Amy pulled her Glock with the other hand and shot the other soldiers as she walked by their bodies. She didn't want any surprises. Achmed jumped every time the gun went off. She stopped him by the body of the little girl and screamed, "LOOK! WHY? WHY KILL A CHILD? WHAT IS WRONG WITH YOU?"

Achmed smiled and said, "She was mine to kill."

Amy had fire shooting out of her eyes. She raised the AK and Achmed said, "No, no, no, remember? The Geneva Convention?"

Amy stopped, smiled a crooked, cold smile, and threw the AK behind her. Then she drew the Glock and threw that behind her. Then she said, "You want to kill a girl? Kill me. Here I am." She walked toward him.

Centcom

"I think she just challenged him to a fight," said Danny.
"Nah, she's just setting him up to kill him. It's personal to her. Besides, she wouldn't shoot an unarmed man," said T.

The Sit Room

"What is she doing?" asked the President.
"No idea," said Tim.

Khawak Pass

"Go ahead," Amy said while still walking up to Achmed. "Pull your knife, I know you have one. Let's see it. Come on, you're tough, LET'S SEE IT," Amy growled.

Achmed let out a yell, pulled his knife, and charged her. He missed; she didn't. He swung the knife at her face. She ducked it and buried the KA-BAR under his sternum. Amy jerked it hard to the right and then to the left, puncturing the lower lobes of both lungs. Violently, she began pumping and twisting the knife as hard as she could. He fell to his knees and she slapped his headscarf from his head and grabbed a handful of his hair. Then she had a little flashback.

Amy was sixteen. She and Jack were sitting in the garage sharpening knives after a day of lessons when Amy asked, "Is it true you cut the heads off of your enemies?"

"Yes," said Jack.

"That doesn't seem like you. I mean, you know, you're a nice man," said Amy.

Jack nodded his head a little and said, "Thanks, honey, but that's not what it was about. War is psychological. Remember when we talked about keeping yourself in emotional check when you operate?"

"Yes, sir," said Amy.

"Well, when the enemy saw their friend's head on a stick, it scared the hell out of 'em. As we both know, a warrior that operates in fear isn't at his best. You read the Bible. I know in Sunday school they don't teach the kids about David's last act after slaying Goliath. He took Goliath's sword and chopped off his head. Then he held it up for the Philistines to see and they all ran like hell. It's not pretty, but it works," said Jack, unashamedly.

Amy looked down at Achmed. Rage accumulated over a lifetime blew like a volcano and with four powerful swipes of her knife, she removed his head. She held it up and let out a guttural scream that bounced off of the mountainside.

"Centcom, um, whoa, holy shit," said Fox.

Centcom

"Damn, T, I didn't know you had a sister," said Danny with a shocked look.

"Danny, call Fox and tell him to go get her," said T.

"Fox, this is Centcom. Go make contact with...hold. What's her name, T?" asked Danny.

"Get the hell out of the way," said T, pushing Danny over. "Fox, this is T. Her name is Petty Officer Braxton. Call her Doc; that should calm her down. Now get your fucking ass down there and get her," said T.

"T, the president is listening, what the fuck?" said Danny.

"Roger that, T," said Fox.

The Sit Room

The president stared at the screen as the young woman, fresh from beheading Taliban's number two, gently washed the blood from the face of the young girl that was stoned to death. The Sit Room was stunned.

"Tim?" said the President.

"Yes, ma'am, I'll have a report for you within the hour," said Tim.

The president got up, shaking her head, and said, "I thought I had seen it all. Come on, Spock."

Spock spoke into his wrist, "Polar Bear moving."

Khawak Pass

"DOC, DOC!" Bain hollered from behind a rock. "I am Staff Sergeant Bain, United States Air Force. I'm here to take you home."

Amy nodded her head as she heard the Blackhawk coming over the mountain. Amy picked up the little girl and began to walk toward the landing zone.

"Doc, you need to leave her here," said Bain.

Amy looked at him with hollow eyes and in a very low voice said, "She's coming with us."

"OK, that's fine, Doc, OK," said Bain.

Chapter 73

Director Dotson walked into the Oval Office. The president looked up and said, "So, what do you know?"

Director Dotson went through the entire story as relayed to him by Adele and assets on the ground. He started with Amy's time at Balboa and finished with the battle at Khawak Pass.

"Jesus Christ," said the President in disbelief. "When's she coming back?"

"Ma'am, she is injured. We are taking her to Germany for treatment. We are keeping her isolated until we can debrief her. She should be stateside in three or four days, depending on her injuries. We will take her to Langley for the final debrief," said the director.

"Do her parents know she's alive?" said the president.

"Not yet, ma'am."

"STEVIE," yelled the president.

"Yes, ma'am?"

"Get me Braxton's parents on the phone," said the president.

"Yes, ma'am," said Stevie.

"OK, keep me posted." she said.

"Ma'am, we have one more problem. We have a mess with no good explanation at Khawak Pass. It is my suggestion that we sanitize it," said the director.

"Yep, good thinking," said the president.

The director turned to leave and the president said, "Hey, Tim."

"Yes, ma'am?" said the director.

"Send Adele to watch over her," said the president.

The director checked his watch and said, "Adele went wheels up thirty minutes ago."

The president smiled and said, "I love ya' Tim. Give Joy and Whitney my love."

"Yes, ma'am," said the director with a smile.

Carol was standing at the sink washing dishes when the phone rang. Carol picked it up and said, "Hello?"

"Please hold for the president of the United States," said the voice.

"Hi, this is President North. Who am I speaking to?"

Carol stammered a little bit as she said, "Carol Braxton."

"Amy's mom?" said the President.

"Stepmom," said Carol.

"Is Leon available?" said the president.

"No, ma'am. He is at his cousin Jack Brown's house. What's this about?" asked Carol.

"Good news; we have found Amy alive and in pretty good shape. We should have her home to you within a week," said the president.

Carol felt her legs go weak as her seven-month pregnant body slid down the front of the cabinets. She sat on the floor and began to weep. "Thank you, thank you so much," she said, not being able to say much more.

"You say Leon is at Jack Brown's house?" asked the president.

Carol said yes through her sobs.

"OK, I'll call him there. Thank you, Mrs. Braxton," the president said as she hung up.

Carla Jo was sitting in her kitchen when the phone rang. "Hello?"

"Please hold for the president of the United States," said the voice on the other end.

"Hi, this is President North. I would like to speak to Leon Braxton," said the president.

Carla Jo recognized her voice immediately.

"Yes, ma'am," she said as she started shaking. She stuck her head next to the kitchen window and yelled, "LEON, PICK UP THE PHONE." Carla Jo didn't hang up.

Leon picked up the phone and said, "Hello?"

"Mr. Braxton, this is President North. I have good news; we have found your daughter and she is alive," said the president. She quickly pulled the phone away from her ear when Carla Jo let out a joyous scream. It took about five minutes for the joyful noises to stop on the other end. Then President North said, "Mr. Braxton?"

"Yes, ma'am?" said Leon through his tears.

"You will never know everything your daughter has done or what she went through, but know this: she is an American hero. She is the real thing. My administration cannot be more proud of her and you should be, too. We would like to fly you out here in a few days to meet her if that would be OK."

"Yes, ma'am, thank you, thank you very much," said Leon through tears of joy.

The president hung up and thought, *boy, do I love this part of my job*. Then she saw the list with the names of six SEALs and two Blackhawk pilots. Her phone calls would continue without the celebrations.

Moments later the phone rang again. It was John Masters.

"Jack, you will not believe this. They have found her," said John.

Jack was still in a little shock from the president's call. He was also getting very emotional and through tears he said, "Yeah, Johnnyreb, I know. The president just called."

Khawak Pass

The bodies of the Taliban soldiers were loaded into the trucks that brought them to the pass as the American personnel evacuated the area. Staff Sergeant Bain called in Cowboy and his young number two. They released their ordinance and wiped away all physical evidence of the battle at Khawak Pass.

Chapter 74

The helicopter touched down at the airbase. Amy climbed out carrying the child and an imam met her on the tarmac. "Thank you, we will care for her now," said the imam.

Amy kissed the girl's cheek and handed her over. Then two large men in civilian clothes directed her to a C-9 Nightingale air ambulance. She climbed aboard and an entire staff of doctors and nurses converged on her. She was the only one on the flight. They were all there for her.

Eighteen hours later, Amy awoke in a private hospital room in the Landsthul Medical Center in Ramstein, Germany. She was thirsty. She looked around the room and said, "Hello, anybody here?"

Suddenly the door opened and an older woman that looked like a cross between Aunt Bea and Richard Simmons walked in. In a thick Texas accent she said, "Hello, my name is Adele Harris and I am your new best friend."

Adele Harris was a veteran of the cold war. A CIA assassin by trade, she left bodies scattered around eastern Europe like fast food wrappers in an inner city neighborhood. She was one of the most dangerous senior citizens on the planet. Her title was assistant director of personnel.

"Well, OK," said Amy with a little suspicion. "I am really thirsty."

Adele reached down to a little refrigerator next to the bed and pulled out a Dr. Pepper and a straw.

"Here ya' go, honey," said Adele.

"How did you know I like Dr. Pepper?" said Amy.

Adele smiled and said, "Believe me when I tell you that I am your new best friend. I know everything about you. I even know how you got that little scar on your head."

"Really?" said Amy skeptically.

"Yep, you were hit with a rock when you were fourteen," she said. Then Adele paused and, deciding that she needed to get Amy's full attention, she added, "While you were being raped."

Amy's eyes flashed and she stared at Adele as she said, "How do you know that?"

"I told you, honey, I'm your new best friend. I know everything about you. My only job right now is to watch over you, protect you, and make sure you get everything you need," said Adele with a sweet, understanding smile.

Amy hit the button on the side of the hospital bed so she could sit up. She winced a little at the pain in her side.

"Now what?" asked Amy.

"Well, that little battle you participated in was seen by a few people on satellite. Some very important people saw that and I'm sure they will want to talk to you about it. Would you like to talk to me about it?" said Adele.

Amy looked at Adele and asked, "Are you navy?"

"No, honey, I'm CIA," said Adele.

Amy looked up at the ceiling, shook her head, and said, "What have I gotten myself into?"

Adele reached out, held Amy's hand, and said, "Listen to me. You have nothing to worry about. I am here for you and I will be here for you until this entire situation is put to bed."

"Does my family know I'm OK?" Amy asked.

"Yes, they do, and they are very happy. They thought you were dead. The whole world thought you were dead. Then you show up in the middle of nowhere plinking Taliban like you're at some arcade," Adele said with a little chuckle. "Ole Hatchet Jack taught you well."

Amy smiled, nodded, and said, "I guess you do know everything."

"No, Amy, not everything. You see, your Angel flight mission was on satellite, too. We didn't see you get out of the Blackhawk. Maybe we can start there. How did you get out of the Blackhawk?" asked Adele.

Just then the phone rang by Amy's bed. Adele answered it and said, "Yes, sir, she's right here." Adele put her hand over the phone and said, "We'll talk later. I think you'll want to take this. Amy, everything you have done is classified. Do not discuss it with anyone but me, understand?"

"Yes, ma'am," said Amy.

"Here ya' go," said Adele, smiling.

"Hello?" said Amy.

"HONEY!," Leon exclaimed over the phone.

"DADDY? DADDY? IT'S ME, AMY, I LOVE YOU...,"

The next day Amy, Adele, and four "Quiet Ones" got out of an armored SUV and walked around the corner of a hanger. Amy saw the troops boarding the Kalitta Flying Service 747 and started toward it. Adele stopped her and said, "No, honey, this is our plane."

Amy turned to look in the hanger at the shiny blue and white Gulfsream 5 with "United States of America" written on the top. A very pleasant man invited them in to take a seat.

"Hey, Adele, this looks like a miniature version of the president's plane," said Amy.

"Honey, this is one of the president's planes. I told you, very important people are watching over you," said Adele.

"Oh," said Amy with a shocked expression.

Amy took a seat and buckled in. The pleasant man approached Amy and said, "Dr. Pepper?"

Amy smiled, looked at Adele, and shook her head. Then she said, "Yes, please." *This is unbelievable,* Amy thought.

The White House

"Madam President, Director Dotson on line one," said Stevie.

The President picked up the phone and said, "Yeah, Tim,"

"Petty Officer Braxton is scheduled to touchdown at Langley tonight. She will have a medical checkup, one more debrief with Adele, and then her final debrief at eleven a.m. with JAG, NCIS, and DOJ," said Tim.

"Do you foresee any problems?" asked the president.

"I hope not, but bureaucrats like making names for themselves. The beheading thing was a borderline atrocity," said Tim.

"I didn't see it that way, I just thought she was pissed. Kill my child and find out what happens," said the president.

"Yes, ma'am, I'm just letting you know," said Tim.

"Thanks, Tim," said the president.

"STEVIE," called the president after she hung up with the director.

"Yes, ma'am?" said Stevie.

"I would like to workout at eleven a.m. in the Langley gym. Then I would like to have a luncheon for three at noon," she said.

"Yes, ma'am," said Stevie.

"Schedule the ceremony for five p.m., followed by dinner in the Residence for everyone," said the president.

"Ma'am, you have a dinner scheduled with the leaders of Congress," said Stevie.

"I thought I had a vice president," said the president.

"Yes, ma'am," said Stevie.

Chapter 75

Three lawyers finished interviewing T concerning Petty Office Braxton. She had been dismissed, but when she got to the door, she stopped.

"Sir, I know her better than anyone. Perhaps I can stay and listen to your interview with her. I can tell you if she is lying and maybe help you get where you want to go with this," said T.

The lawyers looked at each other and agreed. They directed her to sit at the end of the table. Keeping a blank expression on her face, T thought to herself, *I know what you're going to do and I hate you fucking bureaucratic pieces of shit.*

Amy walked into the interrogation/conference room and the door closed behind her. In the hall opposite of the one she had traversed, another door opened. Two men walked into the viewing room and watched through the one-way glass. Amy stood at attention facing forward and said, "Petty Office Braxton reporting as ordered."

Amy looked straight ahead without making eye contact with anyone in the room.

"At ease, Petty officer Braxton," said the first man at the table. "Take a seat and let me introduce everyone."

Amy looked around the table and suddenly saw Katherine sitting at the end.

"KATHERINE!" Amy exclaimed and smiled. T looked away. She was discovering another emotion she had very little experience with; shame.

"Who?" said the first man.

"I'm sorry," said Amy, "I meant Petty Officer Rodriguez."

"That is CIA Officer Aziz," said the man. "Now, if I can continue," he said brusquely. "This is Kurt Mitchell, judge advocate general, and next to him is Angela Bolin, lead prosecutor for NCIS. I am Abraham Stein, director of legal at the Department of Justice. We would like to discuss the event that took place at the Khawak Pass."

"Yes, sir, what can I help you with? I've gone on record with the entire story," said Amy, sounding a little hurt. She was still stinging from Katherine's blatant disregard.

"Let's look at the video," said Stein, picking up the remote and clicking on the television.

Amy watched as she threw down her weapons, attacked Achmed, and then, after some contemplation, cut off his head.

"Would you like to explain that, Petty Officer Braxton?" asked Stein.

Amy looked at them and said, "Yes, sir. Well, I guess I was a little upset," said Amy.

The men behind the glass laughed out loud. T chuckled and Stein shot T a hard look before saying, "You find something funny, Officer Aziz?"

Then Stein gave Amy an angry look and said, "Upset? Really? Upset? Petty Officer Braxton, we have a name for that. It's called an atrocity."

Amy sat up straight in her chair and said, "Did you see what they did to that little girl?"

"I'm not talking about them, I am talking about you. I'M TALKING ABOUT AN AMERICAN SERVICE MEMBER COMMITING WAR CRIMES," shouted Stein.

Amy began to realize what was happening and anger started to seep in. Then she said, "War crimes? If you want to see war crimes, I'll take you to the evac hospital where I worked and show you some children that know all about war crimes."

Stein slapped his hands on the table and said, "Are you that stupid? Apparently you are. I am charging you with war crimes. I am going to put you on trial and send you to jail. Do you understand that?"

The men behind the glass looked at each other. The first man shook his head and said, "The president isn't gonna like this. Get her on the phone."

Amy started to panic, she said, "I want to see Adele Harris. I want to see her now."

"SHE CAN'T HELP YOU," shouted Stein while reaching for a sheet of paper. He slid it over in front of her and said, "Sign this, it's your confession. Sign it and you won't get life in prison."

Amy looked at the piece of paper and then looked over at T. T gently shook her head no. Amy looked back at Stein and said, "I'm not signing anything until I see Adele."

Stein started to speak when the door opened. In walked Tim Dotson and Grant Engel, followed by two marine MPs. Amy recognized Engel immediately. She saw his picture every day at the evac hospital. Amy stood up quickly and yelled, "ATTENTION ON DECK."

Secretary Engel smiled and said, "At ease, sailor."

"Petty Officer Braxton, can I call you Doc?" asked Secretary Engel.

"Yes, sir," said Amy, somewhat in shock.

"It's very nice to finally meet you," he said, reaching to shake her hand. "This is Director Dotson of the CIA."

"It's nice to meet you, Petty Officer Braxton," said Director Dotson, shaking her hand.

Amy's guts were twisted in knots and she felt like she may become sick. Amy looked at the secretary of defense and in a weak voice asked, "What's going on here?"

Secretary Engel gave her a warm smile and said, "A great big misunderstanding. Amy, would you please follow these men out to the office area? we need to have a private conversation."

"Yes, sir," Amy replied.

The MPs escorted Amy out to a chair in the office area and she took a seat. It was a large room full of cubicles. She had come in a different way earlier and the CIA officers on duty did not know she was there. They had all seen the video from Khawak Pass. It quickly went viral among those with the proper security clearance.

"It's her, It's her," came a murmur across the room.

Slowly, one at a time they began to stand up and look at her. She couldn't figure out what they were looking at. Then suddenly they began clapping and cheering. Amy blushed, put a slight smile on her face, and meekly waved.

A man came out of an office. He was short but built like a tree trunk. He was wearing a short sleeve shirt with a tie and on the inside of his forearm was tattooed a little red seal.

"Petty Officer Braxton, I presume?" asked John Masters with a great big smile.

"Yes, sir," said Amy, still a little overwhelmed by the ruckus.

"I'm John Masters, an old friend of your uncle Jack's. Job well done, young lady. Job well done," John said, shaking her hand.

Chapter 76

When Amy left the room, Stein looked at Dotson and with an edge to his voice said, "How can I help you, director?"

"I am here under the order of the president. This investigation is over. The incident at Khawak Pass has been deemed a matter of national security and is now classified," said Dotson.

Stein was visibly upset. He said, "So now this administration covers up war crimes?"

Dotson looked over in the corner where T was standing and said, "How are you, T?"

"Good, sir, thank you for asking," said T.

Stein sunk back in his seat. He knew of T, but he did not know that Aziz was her. He thought she was a fictional legend, someone that didn't exist; and he had belittled her. He suddenly felt very uncomfortable. Bolin and Mitchell sat quietly. They both knew they were in way over their heads. Stein still wouldn't let it go, though.

"I am in disagreement with this. Who do you people think you are?" said Stein.

"Maybe I'll have T explain it to you," said Dotson.

T looked at Stein with a smile that she usually reserved for the most hardcore of terrorists.

"Are you threatening me?" said Stein.

Secretary Engel hadn't said much until now. He believed that you should listen to twenty words for every one you speak. It had always served him well. He finally said, "Son, the director of the CIA doesn't make threats. Time to move on. The penalty for discussing this incident is a charge of treason. The president thanks you for your service. You are all dismissed."

T started to leave, but Dotson stopped her as the attorneys cleared out.

"What do you think, T?" said the Director.

"I sometimes think we're killing the wrong side," said T.

"Yeah, the politics get to me, too. We are very lucky to have President North. She flies good air cover," said Dotson.

"So what happens to Braxton?" said T.

"Nothing…whatever she wants. She's got the president in her pocket and she doesn't even know it. She will know, soon enough," said Dotson.

"OK, well, I need to head back to the sand box," said T.

"Nope, I have something for you. Something I want you to lead. We'll talk about it later. Right now I want you to escort Braxton to my suite. There is a lunch planned for her. You and Adele will attend with a special guest," said Dotson.

"Who?" asked T.

"Classified," said the director as he checked his watch. "You have forty minutes to get there," said Dotson.

"Thank you, director," said T.

T walked out of the interrogation room, down the hall, and into the office area. Amy was swamped with well-wishers and people wanting to shake her hand. T smiled to herself, walked up to Amy, and said, "Hi, Director Dotson has asked me to escort you to lunch. We have to go."

Amy looked at T out of the corner of her eye and then said, "You know what truly aggravates me? Being lied to."

T's head went down and she said, "I can understand that. I just want you to know that it's my job. It's what I do."

"So, is our friendship a lie, too?" asked Amy.

"No, at least I hope not," said T. They started to walk to the director's suite when T said, "I would really like you to know who I am and what I do. Maybe then you will understand."

Amy laughed and said, "Oh, why not. So far today I have been called a war criminal and have been told I was going to prison. Then I was cheered by a bunch of strangers. Confusion is my middle name. Go ahead Katherine, or Officer Aziz; whatever your name is."

"OK, my name is Tatiana Aziz. I am a CIA covert operative. My job was to work with captured terrorists and figure out who would be worth interrogating and then interrogate them. The XO of the base was not my boyfriend. He is also CIA. He is my handler. My identity had to remain a secret, but my affections are not. You are the only true friend I have ever had. My job is a lonely one and you have made my life better. I love you very much, Amy," said T.

Amy was quiet for a few minutes and then said, "We had a lot fun, didn't we?"

"Yes, yes we did. And the best could be yet to come. By the way, I would like you to call me what my father called me, Tatiana. That is my name."

Amy smiled and put her arm around T's shoulders, saying, "OK, Tatiana it is."

"There is something else. When you had that incident at Balboa, Kate called me. She thought you might be a good fit with us, so we started watching you," said T.

"What do mean, watching me?" asked Amy.

"Everything you did, every place you went, and everything you said has been studied and documented. We want you on our team."

"CIA? You want me to join the CIA?" said Amy in disbelief.

"You are very special. I don't think you understand how special you are," T explained.

"How do you know Kate?" Amy asked.

"I was in Bosnia and let's just say I got into a bad situation and Kate bailed me out," said T.

"She's good at that, isn't she?" said Amy.

"Yes, yes she is. Did Kate give you the *Godfather* speech?"

"Yep, she sure did," said Amy with a little smile.

"Well, she means it."

They continued slowly across the courtyard when suddenly Amy remembered her little friend and asked, "How's Patsy Cline?"

"I wondered when you were gonna ask about her," Tatiana chuckled. Then she explained," She is so spoiled. Nurse Collins took her in. She misses you. She sat at the gate for a long time and watched the choppers unload, waiting for you."

Amy stopped and looked at the ground, took a deep breath, and said, "Did they find Matt?"

Amy looked up and saw the sorrow in T's eyes. She didn't need to answer. Tatiana gently nodded.

Amy started to cry so they sat at a small bench. Tatiana held her while she let it all go.

Twenty minutes later they walked into the director's suite where Adele was waiting.

"Where were you today? I could have used a little help," said Amy.

"What, the secretary of defense wasn't good enough for you?" said Adele.

"Oh, OK, I guess I can let that go."

Amy saw the door to the suite open and a large man walked in followed by a little woman in a t-shirt, sweat pants, and tennis shoes. Amy thought, *she had on those glasses, just like the Pres... Oh my God...*

"ATTENTION ON DECK," Amy yelled as they all quickly stood.

"At ease," the president said. "It's just us girls." She walked over to Amy and said, "Petty Officer Braxton, it is a pleasure to meet you." Then she gave Amy a warm hug that only a mother would know how to give.

The president looked around the table and acknowledged Adele with a "Nice to see you again." Then she looked over at T.

"Well, well, well, the infamous T. Why do I feel like I should have a Secret Service agent between you and me? Then again, I don't suppose it would do any good, would it?" said the President with a knowing smile.

"Probably not, ma'am," said T, smiling back.

Amy was still stiff as a board at attention.

"Relax honey, can I call you Amy?" asked the president.

"Yes, ma'am."

The president sat down and waiters appeared with trays and drinks. The president had two hot dogs and a bag of chips. Amy had no clue what to say so she tilted her head curiously and said, "I could never imagine the president eating hot dogs."

"It's good, it's cheap, and it's not my money. I try to live like it was my money. The tax payers deserve that," said the president as she took a bite of the hot dog. "So, how are you?" asked the president.

Amy looked across the table at Adele and gave her a combination what-do-I-say/deer-in-the-headlights kind of look. Adele caught it and shrugged her shoulders. Amy rolled her eyes as if to say, "Thanks a lot."

"Well, ma'am, I'm not very good at telling stories so I'll tell you the truth." Then Amy talked straight like her daddy taught her, "I'm honored that you would spend this time with me, though I'm still not sure why. I'm devistated after losing the man I loved when the Blackhawk we were in was blown out from under us. Finally, I'm pretty sure a department of justice lawyer just told me I'm goin' to jail. Other than that, I reckon I'm fine as a frog's hair."

The President caught the last comment in mid-drink and soda bubbled out of her nose as she laughed. Once she composed herself, she said, "Honey, I wish more people around me were as honest as you are. No, you're not going to jail. STEVIE," the president called. "You got that envelope?"

Stevie handed the president an envelope and she handed it to Amy.

"What's this?" said Amy.

"A blanket pardon. They couldn't touch you if they wanted to, but I really don't think they want to," said the president.

Just then Amy's food arrived and she looked down at her plate. "Bacon cheeseburger; how did you know?"

Adele started to speak and Amy said, "Never mind, you know everything about me." Amy was hungry so she took a bite of her burger.

The president licked her thumb and reached over to wipe BBQ sauce from Amy's face and said, "Right about now your family is arriving at Reagan International Airport. We will bring them to the White House where they will take a tour. Then you will put on a dress uniform and I'm going to pin some medals on you in the Oval Office: a Purple Heart for the metal they dug out of your side and a Silver Star for heroism at FOB Apache. Then we will all adjourn to the Residence for dinner."

Amy tilted her head and said, "FOB Apache? I just did my job."

The president smiled and said, "Not according to the men you saved."

Then the first thing the president said sunk in. "My family is here?" said Amy excitedly.

The President took another drink and said, "Yep." Then she called out, "STEVIE, WHO'S COMING TO DINNER?"

Stevie walked in and said, "Mr. and Mrs. Braxton, Joseph Braxton, Mr. and Mrs. Brown, and Deloris Tilley," said Stevie.

Amy shook her head and said, "Wow, thank you so much."

"It's the least I can do, which leads me to the real reason for this lunch. We need to come to a little understanding. That little war you waged in Khawak Pass never happened because if it did, you would have to use that pardon. I don't want that. Do you understand?" said the president.

"Yes, ma'am," said Amy.

"Amy, I was watching that on satellite as it went down. You left the most powerful people in the world speechless. I would give you the Congressional Medal of Honor if I could, but it never happened, so I can't," said the president.

"I understand," said Amy. "But what about my job? Where will I go now?"

"Well, I think Adele and T have a job offer for you. The country really needs your special skills right now. Maybe you want to go to college? Pediatrics is your specialty, right? I'll write you a letter of recommendation. I can promise you a slot anywhere you want to go. The door is open, whatever you want," she said.

"I have a lot to think about," said Amy, feeling a little overwhelmed.

"Yes you do, honey. You know, this being the most powerful person in the free world thing has its privileges. Is there anything I can do for you?" said the president.

Amy thought for a moment and said, "Yes, yes there is. Do you think you could put in a good word for my uncle Jack Brown? He got arrested, but he's really a good man."

President North laughed and said, "The legendary navy SEAL turned moonshiner. I didn't even know they did that anymore. That's already been taken care of. It's hard to get people in the White House with pending felonies. Anything else?"

"Yes, ma'am, just one more thing. I rescued a dog outside of the evac hospital. Her name is…,"

The president interrupted and said, "Patsy Cline. Sweetest thing I have ever heard. STEVIE," yelled the president.

"Yes, ma'am?"

"Make sure she gets her dog."

"Yes, ma'am."

Chapter 77

The Braxton family and their bags were loaded into a government SUV and they were taken to the Hilton Garden Inn. As they went to check in, Jack spotted a familiar face in the distance. John Masters walked toward Jack and neither said a word. They just hugged. Jack introduced John to his family and they all were taken up to their rooms. John looked at Carla Jo and said, "Jack, you didn't tell me she was pretty."

Carla Jo rolled her eyes. Then John looked a Carla Jo and said, "Do you think it would be OK for me to take this old sea dog for a drink?"

The family's escort, a very attentive and friendly woman, said, "We will be departing for the White house in two hours."

"Hurry back, Jack," said Carla Jo.

John drove Jack to a small bar nearby and ordered some drinks. They sat down in a booth at the back of the bar. He pulled a laptop from a pouch, opened it, hit a few keys, and turned the screen toward Jack.

John said, "You never saw this 'cause this never happened."

Jack's mouth fell open as he watched the battle of Khawak Pass.

"Taught her a few things, huh, Jack?" said John with a little smirk.

Jack was speechless as John told him the whole story from beginning to end.

"We want her, Jack, we want her with us," said John with a serious look on his face.

Jack's eyes narrowed a bit and he said, "Yeah, well, I think she's done enough. I don't want her in that shit. I want her to go to school, be a doctor, get married, and raise a family. That's what I want for her. I want you people to leave her the fuck alone."

"Don't you think that's up to her?" said John.

"John, leave...her.... the fuck...alone," Jack said with a tone that bordered on menacing.

"OK, Jack, I'll do all I can. But she is in the system and they will be contacting her. I can't do anything about that."

Jack nodded and said, "Thanks, John."

The Family was awed by the tour of the White House. It was a history lesson that couldn't have been found in any book. At the end of the tour they were brought into the Oval Office where Amy was sitting, drinking a Dr. Pepper. As they walked in, she got up and immediately hugged her daddy. There were hugs and kisses all around until the president entered with the secretary of defense. The family sat as Amy stood in front of the president while she read Amy's commendations, and then the president pinned her medals on her uniform.

Afterward, they adjourned to the Residence where they enjoyed a wonderful dinner. The president's husband Mike and Leon hit it off immediately, talking about hunting and fishing. Jack seemed a little quiet and distant; Carla Jo asked if he was OK more than once. Granny Patches had the president laughing with tales of the family, even though the president left and returned to the gathering more than once. Her job never stopped. Carol and the president talked about babies and Carla Jo even got to ask a few questions on health care. Joseph was making his own memories with the president's oldest daughter, Cali. Joseph told her stories about driving stock cars until Cali asked him if he knew Jeff Gordon. Joseph didn't, but Cali did. Even so, there was a little bit of chemistry between the two.

The evening seemed to go a little too fast. There were pictures with the president then it was time to leave. The family walked out to the SUV for the ride back to the hotel, but before they left, the president asked Amy to stay behind for a moment. The president hugged Amy and thanked her once again for her service to the country. Amy thanked the president for the wonderful time they showed her family. Then the president pulled out a little card, handed it to Amy, and said, "If you need anything, call."

"Thank you, ma'am," said Amy.

Their flight was leaving the next day, so Amy joined them at the hotel. The suites that were booked for them were very large and luxurious. They sat, talked, and laughed. They all caught Amy up on the going's on in Black Oak. Jack was still very quiet. Amy caught it, but didn't say anything. They would have plenty of time to talk at home. Amy had two weeks to decide her future, but in reality, it would only take three days.

The Final Chapter

*A*my couldn't sleep that night. She walked down to the hotel pool at 2 a.m.and swam some laps. There was a lot on her mind. She swam lap after lap until she was exhausted. Grabbing the side of the pool she hoisted herself out of the water, and sitting in the chair in the corner was her uncle Jack.

"I figured I might find you down here," said Jack.

Amy heard his baritone voice and said, "Hi, Uncle Jack."

"Can't sleep?" said Jack.

"No," said Amy.

"That's what all that killin' does for ya' honey. Trust me, I know," said Jack.

"What do you mean, all the killin'?" said Amy curiously.

"I saw it Amy, I saw it all. John Masters showed me the video of what you did. I was very proud, but at the same time I was horrified. I taught you those things and you executed them flawlessly," said Jack.

"Horrified? They killed a little girl; they got what they deserved," said Amy.

"I didn't say you did anything wrong. You did your job. But, honey, the lives you take never leave you. They take little chunks out of your soul. It doesn't matter if they deserved it or not. I need you to understand that," said Jack with a seriousness that Amy had never seen coming from him.

"Well, that's not why I can't sleep," said Amy.

"Are you sure?" asked Jack.

Amy dried off, put on a pair of shorts and a t-shirt, and said, "I'm hungry, wanna grab a bite?"

"Sure, but I bet it ain't the Bluebird," said Jack.

"Yeah, I know, but what is?" said Amy with a smile.

They sat down at the twenty-four hour café just up the street and ordered. Amy saw the apple pie and ordered some with a scoop of ice cream. Her uncle Jack reached across the table and held her hand, smiled, and said, "I thought I would never see you again. I'm not big on prayer, but I prayed so hard for a miracle and here you are. I can't tell you what to do, but if I had my choice, you would go back to school, be a doctor, get married, have some kids, and live a normal life. It's not so bad, really. It's not."

The waitress brought Amy's pie and she took a bite. "It's not as good as Carol's," she said with a little smile. Then Amy looked at Jack and said, "When the helicopter went down, I lost the man I loved. His name was Matt. He was a SEAL, like you, and he was a lot like you. That's probably why I fell in love with him. I wanted to marry him, have his babies, and be his lover and his best friend; just like you and Aunt Carla Jo. But he is gone and I am lost. I am so lost."

"I'm sorry, honey, I didn't know any of that. Carla Jo told me you were seeing someone, but I had no idea," Jack said at he sat and struggled for something to say.

"I'd like to live a 'normal life,' but when have I ever been normal? Have I ever been normal? Do you know I have never had sex with a boy? They either dump me or die and I refuse to be a whore, going from man to man, hoping they think I'm good enough. I watch women belittle and embarrass themselves, and I refuse to be like that."

"Are you sure you wouldn't rather have that conversation with your aunt? I'm not real good at the relationship thing," said Jack uncomfortably.

"I'm sorry. Wandering around in the desert gives you too much time to think. Do you know what I remember about what went on out there?" asked Amy as Jack sat quietly and listened. "Nothing; well, hardly anything at all. I watched the video and I couldn't believe it was me. I remember being scared to death when they killed that girl. I remember praying and rubbing Bubba's dog tag. Then I left, I wasn't me. Do you understand what I'm saying?"

"Yes, honey, I do," said Jack.

"Something took over. I remember little snapshots, like looking through a photo album, but that's it. Next thing I know I'm in a Blackhawk carrying a dead girl with a crushed skull in my lap. I'm crying and sobbing thinking, 'Oh my God, why am I here, why am I here?'"

"Yeah, I know how you felt," said Jack.

"Do you, do you really? And now, apparently, the CIA wants me? For what? I'm not that, I'm not some sneaky, cold-hearted assassin. I'm not one of them. I'm a good corpsman, that's it, or at least I think I am. I don't even have a degree. But a spy or spook or whatever, that's not me. I'm a fraud, Uncle Jack. If they knew who I really was they would laugh at me," said Amy, bowing her head.

They sat quietly for a few minutes. Amy pushed the half-eaten pie to the side of the table. She wasn't hungry anymore. Jack smiled at her and said, "Do you know what happened to me the first time I was in combat? I froze and then pissed my pants. Bullets were flying all around. I looked to my right and saw my swim buddy, the man I was responsible for, dead on the ground. Then my training and instinct took over. That's what it was; that's what you experienced. Trust me, they know exactly who and what you are. They like what they see. To be honest, I can't blame them. Come home, honey, build a nice house next to your daddy's, be a doctor, go to work with you aunt, and just live your life."

"I don't know if I could learn to live like that anymore. I don't know who I am. I not even sure what I am or," she paused for a moment, "Where I belong." Said Amy sadly.

As Amy and her family boarded the plane to Alabama the following morning, T walked into the CIA director's suite. Conrad Murray, the director of the FBI, sat in a chair at the side of the room.

"T, do you know Director Murray?" asked Director Dotson.

"No, sir, I don't think we have ever met," T said, shaking his hand.

"Have a seat T," said Dotson.

Director Murray began to speak, "Over the past two years we have noticed a sharp rise is child abduction and patterns are starting to form. All girls, blonde or with light-colored hair, five to ten years old are vanishing; twenty-two in all with no evidence, not even a trace. Two weeks ago, this man," the director put a picture up on the television, "Otto Von Bruno, a German politician, was found dead of a heart attack. He was discovered sitting in a chair, naked, in front of his television. His wife found this DVD in the machine."

Director Murray pushed a button and a little girl in a fancy dress appeared on the screen. She looked to be glassy-eyed and drugged. She was wearing a pretty pink dress and the room she was in seemed to be an idyllic little girl's room. Then a man appeared wearing leather bondage gear. He stripped and raped the little girl on the bed, then he took out a large knife. What T saw next shook her to the core. He slowly and methodically butchered the child.

Director Murray turned it off and said, "The German police found ten of these in his home and all were identified as some the missing American children."

T was stunned.

"We believe the children are being kidnapped and taken to eastern Europe. The German government has been kind enough to set up a command post for us in a secret facility maintained by the German Special Forces, Kammando Spezialkrafte. Put together a team; you have unlimited international resources. Find out who is making these, find who is selling these, and find who is kidnapping these children and then kill them, every goddamned one of them. Those are not my words, T, those are the president's."

T nodded and walked over to the director's desk. She wrote down a half dozen names and handed them to the director. Then she said, "Can I have that DVD?" Director Murray took it out of the machine and handed it to her.

"I need a plane," she said.

"OK, T, whatever you want. Where are you going?"

"Alabama," said T.

The End

21667265R00249

Made in the USA
Lexington, KY
22 March 2013